AF065736

THE SHADOWS OF AVALON
PAUL CORNELL

Published by BBC Worldwide Ltd,
Woodlands, 80 Wood Lane
London W12 0TT

First published 2000
Copyright © Paul Cornell 2000
The moral right of the author has been asserted

Original series broadcast on the BBC
Format © BBC 1963
Doctor Who and TARDIS are trademarks of the BBC
ISBN 978-1-84990-648-7
Imaging by Black Sheep, copyright © BBC 2000

With thanks to:

Eddie Robson - who came up with the title.
Jac Rayner - editorial and inspiration.
Clayton Hickman, Matt Jones, Nick Setchfield, Jim Smith - good ideas.
Alan Barnes - an offer not taken up.
Lawrence Miles - his arc plot and his designs at the end.
Shaun Lyon and the Gallifrey crew - hands across the water.

And to all my friends, for their love and patience.
And thanks to Mum and Dad, for Bread and Butter and Honey.

For Stephen and Viv (especially), Nick, Annabel, Guy, Dave, Mandy, Mark, Tom, Clayton, Felicity and Anthony. Happy times and places.

Prologue One

July 2012.

The ground and sky rotated around the cabin as Flight Lieutenant Matthew Bedser rolled the Tornado to the right. His assignment this evening was to take his flight of three aircraft on an Armed Target Run to an area on Salisbury Plain. His voice fuzzed over the com to his navigator. 'Are we under the radar?'

'Affirmative, Flight. They'll be writing to their MP down there.'

'Just obeying orders, Steven.' Bedser flicked down his HUD and watched the annotated countryside flash by across a red neon grid. 'Six minutes to target. Arming weapon.' He flicked open a series of toggles on his right-hand board and clicked along the buttons.

'Weapon armed,' the navigator confirmed. 'We know a song about this, don't we, children?'

The Tornadoes were supposed to be planting three parachute-launched nuclear weapons into a ten-by-ten-kilometre triangle, near an army installation on Salisbury Plain. The three devices would, if genuinely fired, open up a crater that was twenty klicks across and flatten the imaginary large city that stood there. The weapons were to be armed, the moment of firing registered. But the Tornadoes would then go ballistic to get clear of an imaginary mushroom cloud as the weapons traced a computer-simulated course and stayed on their wings.

Ahead in the red was the sudden swelling of the Wiltshire Downs. A tiny copse of trees swept from right to left across Matthew Bedser's visored eyes.

And stopped.

The green lozenge that was Bedser's aircraft vanished.

Jack Dobson, piloting the second Tornado, jerked his helmeted head around the sky. 'Tango One? T One, respond.' He could hear his navigator suddenly start to yell at Lyneham tower. 'Flight, come in.'

An urgent query from the third Tornado came crackling into

Dobson's earpiece. 'Confirm T One is not on our target radar. Mark the last twenty seconds. Ground radar?' He looked back over his shoulder to his navigator, who held up his hand saying wait. Then he cut his throat with his glove and swore quickly and vehemently. He switched channels on his left board. 'Lyneham tower, we have a bird down, we have a bird down. T One is down.' There was a crackle of response. 'Negative, negative, we don't have visual.'

There was a sudden joyous shout from his earpiece. 'Scratch that. What?' He stared at his HUD in astonishment. 'Erm, Lyneham tower, T One is back on display.' He clumsily slapped channels. 'Flight, do you copy?'

Matthew Bedser watched as the triangle of his target swept by underneath his aircraft.

'Ah... copy.' A long pause. He could feel the silence from his navigator also. 'Have we... aborted the target run?'

'Affirmative, Flight. That happened while you were away.'

Bedser numbly lowered his left hand and automatically found the bomb-arming controls. 'Steven, what do you –' His hand had closed on the control. His question to his navigator was silenced by the red light that had appeared as soon as his finger pressed the button. Bedser took in a huge snort of oxygen through his mask. 'Lyneham tower...' he began, with all the care he could muster. 'Lyneham tower, be advised: we appear to be missing a nuclear warhead.'

Prologue Two

He knew he was dreaming, and that it was one of the two recurring dreams. Not the terrible one. The other one.

He was about six or seven years old. This was a real incident, he knew as he dreamed. This had really happened. He was on holiday with his mother and father, living on a caravan site in Sussex. One day, they attended an air show. It was all very exciting, and his father had bought him a red balloon, the kind that was filled with helium. His parents weren't getting on very well at that point. They had their moments, though they lived happily together all their lives. They kept snapping at each other as the family made their way through to the front of the crowd.

But he was more interested in the aircraft, the new monoplanes and the seaplanes that were competing for the Schneider Trophy. He could name every type at a hundred paces. He was just looking around the airfield in front of them, behind the white rope that held back the crowd, noting all the makes on the ground, when, suddenly, a Supermarine racing aircraft roared over the crowd from behind. An old flyer's trick. Most of the sound trails the plane, so they can surprise a crowd. He loved the plane, he loved the bright blue wings, but its sudden appearance must have shocked him. He burst into tears.

The next moment in the dream, his parents were bundling him back into their little car. He was protesting, because he wanted to stay, but he thought Father must have used this as an excuse to get back to the caravan, because neither of them listened to him. He was still crying, but was trying to stop, to show them that he'd actually enjoyed himself. They paid no attention. They were too busy fighting. They got back to the caravan site, and he was still squalling, and his mother took his hand and led him back towards the caravan, Father promising him ice cream when all he really wanted to do was go back and see the planes. He was nearly at the door of the caravan, when his other hand slipped on the string of the balloon, which he'd been grimly holding on to all the way. It leapt up out of his grasp, and flew swiftly up into the air, away from him, away from everything. 'Off to balloonland,' Mother said. And he looked after it, watching it go, and it was the most terrible memory of his life, the balloon soaring away, for ever lost to him now.

The Brigadier woke gently, with a horrible emotional ache from that image still behind his eyes. He kept them closed.

'Terrible dream,' he said. 'That balloon thing, again. Not as bad as the other one, though.' He automatically stretched his arm across to the other side of the bed. 'The one where –'

He stopped, frowning as his hand encountered nobody where there should have been somebody.

He opened his eyes, and looked. The sight of the empty bed reminded him of the truth, and the realisation of it again made his mouth slowly form into a tight line.

He made himself finish the sentence. 'The one where you died.'

Part One
The Road to Avalon

Chapter One
Compassion Fatigue

'So, tell me about the dream.'

Lethbridge-Stewart sighed, not bothering to hide it from Cronin. They were sitting on opposite sides of the desk in the lieutenant's oak-panelled study. The Brigadier, who was actually a general now, of course, though nobody called him that, had become irritated as soon as he'd sat down. It had taken him a few minutes to work out why. He had been used, for a very long time now, to being the one sitting behind the desk. Being the subject rather than the object. To be placed on the other side, away from the palmtop and the pencils and all the other paraphernalia of control, was subtly, but at the same time powerfully, limiting him.

He realised that Cronin was looking at him in that damned interrogative manner of his, and decided to pad the question away. 'What, the balloon again?'

'The other one, the one I haven't heard.'

'Doesn't seem worth it, really. All rather obvious if you ask me.'

Cronin leaned back in his chair and spread his arms wide. 'It's up to you, sir.'

'If it were up to me, Lieutenant, I wouldn't waste these two hours. I'm only here because I was ordered to give you a try.'

'Why do you think it's a waste?'

'Why do I –' Lethbridge-Stewart found that he was on his feet. About to let rip at this impertinent youth and stalk out of the room. But the Chief of Operations in Geneva had personally, and strongly, recommended the British Army doctor. Cronin had some of the right clearances, should anything sensitive be uncovered: he'd written a much-read and utterly suppressed paper about how alien invasions were the expression of unconscious human desire.

Nonsense, obviously. But it had impressed the top brass.

The next step, if the powers that be felt that it was justified, would be to suspend the Brigadier from duty on 'compassionate leave'. That would be sheer hell. He'd agonised over the leave they'd made him take immediately after her death. He just wanted to get on, to get things done. At least they'd finally given in to his request to return to duty.

But then, almost a year after she'd died, had come the incident with Franks. A tiny thing, but people had noticed. These days, it seemed it wasn't done to respond to a rookie private breaking from the line during an exercise and running away by slapping him about the face.

Lower ranks had pulled him off the man.

It had been Franks's own posture that had earned him the broken jaw. There had been talk of his suing until his own CO had persuaded him that that might not be in his best interests.

People had noticed that incident, it seemed, and so the Brigadier had chosen to follow his commander's suggestion and come here. Now, he paced jauntily towards the big picture window, his hands curling behind his back. 'Always asking "why?", aren't you, you trick cyclists?'

'I haven't heard my profession called that in years, sir.'

The grounds of the hospital were parched in the light of summer, the brightness blinding Lethbridge-Stewart for a moment as he approached the window. He wanted to be out there in the fresh air. Better for him. Better than this. He wondered for a moment why Cronin kept his rooms so dark. 'Well, you ought to expect things like that. I should be well past retirement, yet here I am, walking around in the body of a man in his late thirties.' He found himself watching two of the nurses playing tennis in the bright sunlight outside the hospital, the echo of their shots arriving a moment after their actions. 'It must be exciting for you, having a unique case on your hands. Get some sort of award out of it, I shouldn't wonder.' Lethbridge-Stewart glanced back over his shoulder at the boy behind the desk.

'Why...?' Cronin visibly stopped himself. Then he slapped his palms down on to his desk, meeting Lethbridge-Stewart's gaze. 'OK, let me make a few statements instead of asking questions.

You're not unique as regards the nature of your problem, sir. The onset of moments of uncontrollable rage is a very common difficulty among soldiers. And, this isn't an interrogation. And if you'd prefer this to be handled by a superior officer, we could probably find one somewhere, but –'

Lethbridge-Stewart clicked his tongue against his palate impatiently. 'You can stop calling me "sir" if that makes this easier for you. To answer your question, I think it's a waste because I doubt that I will ever feel "all right" again. I doubt that I will ever fully recover from the death of my wife. But that's not so terrible, is it? Lot of people out there have such difficulties. A lot of people have lost someone. One is a soldier; that implies a duty; one will simply live through this until one stops.'

Cronin shook his mop of sandy hair as if fending off blasphemy that would shake his faith. 'You're wounded.'

'I am not wounded. I am fit for duty.'

'You wouldn't be talking like this if the wound were physical.'

'I've had a few of those, too, Lieutenant, and carried on through some of them as well.' Lethbridge-Stewart took a deep breath, and squared his shoulders, focusing on the distant hills beyond the grounds of the hospital. 'For a while after I returned to active duty, my superiors treated me with kid gloves, as if I was still my original age. It took combat to prove myself once more.'

'The circumstances of your becoming young again. They –'

'Are classified beyond your clearance, as far as I'm aware. But it all happened in a small village called Cheldon Bonniface, a couple of years ago. I was attending a wedding, as a matter of fact. Wedding of a friend of mine, a Professor Bernice Summerfield.' A small smile curled his lip as he remembered. Then the smile faded.

How sunny things had been then, and how dark they were now.

He turned back towards Cronin, and rather self-consciously made himself go back to sit opposite him once more. 'Having heard the balloon dream, I hope you're not going to tell me I was abused as a child, because I most certainly was not.'

'Nothing suggests that.'

'Good.' There was a long pause. The Brigadier looked around the room, and then said, hesitantly, 'You know, I have, on occasion, thought it might be a luxury to have someone... well, someone just to talk to. To recall the details of the night I... I... lost her. Never mind the dratted balloon, or drawing any of the vast conclusions that you chaps seem to draw from such tiny evidence. If it were possible for me just to talk...'

Cronin put down his pad, smiling. 'Fine by me.'

There was a knock on the door. Cronin turned to look at it, incredulous, and yelled, 'I said we weren't to be disturbed!'

But the door opened and a man in UNIT courier uniform entered, carrying a motorcycle helmet under his arm, and saluted. The Brigadier acknowledged the salute, feeling his heartbeat accelerate. Cronin was getting to his feet, starting to blurt out that the man had no right, but Lethbridge-Stewart held up a hand to stop him, and told the courier to come in.

He handed a red envelope to him. 'Absolute priority, sir. From Trap Zero.'

'Thank you, Corporal.' He tore open the envelope and scanned the enclosed document. The message put fear in his stomach, but with the fear there came relief. He was being called upon to do something. He handed it back to the courier. 'Tell them I'll be there by thirteen hundred hours.' The man slammed to salute once more and marched out. Lethbridge-Stewart swung back to Cronin. 'I'm afraid duty calls.'

The man looked defeated, bitter almost. 'And I suppose I can't ask what that duty is?'

'Oh, just the usual, Lieutenant.'

'In your case, that really scares me. But I'm looking forward to hearing all that you have to tell me. So if you manage to save the world within the next couple of weeks...'

'I'll see what I can do.' Lethbridge-Stewart went to the sideboard and picked up his cap and gloves. 'But it may not be possible.' He headed for the door.

Cronin swung in his chair to call after him. 'You are not to deliberately get yourself killed. That's an order, General.'

Lethbridge-Stewart raised an ironic eyebrow. 'That depends on whether my duty demands it – sir.'

Compassion woke on the floor. She'd been sleeping on the carpet, without any sort of blanket, fully clothed. She sat up, and immediately felt the swell of last night's red wine in her forehead. She put down an arm to support herself. She'd woken, she supposed, because of the shaft of summer sunlight that had slid across the room and touched her eyelids. It was right on her now, battering her head, but the breath of cool air that came with it through the open window was good. The room otherwise stank of cigarette smoke and open cans of beer.

She blinked hard and looked around. There were five or six people still asleep, draped over the ends of furniture or curled in chairs. Marcus, the one with the beard, was twitching as he slept. Last night, he'd run from corner to corner of the room, shouting out at the top of his voice a new synonym for the male genitalia every time he hit one. George, who for some reason referred to her as 'TV's Compassion Tobin', was snoring like a baby. Allan, who was in love with her, lay nearby, a hand unconsciously reaching out in her direction. At some point last night she remembered running into the bathroom with him, shoving the door closed, and kissing him at length. He'd grinned for the rest of the night. Patrick, who was flat against the far wall, snoring throatily, had talked to her about the end of the universe and how we were all going to be saved by a cosmic intelligence that would, naturally, be benevolent. She had indulged him at length also.

She had known these people and inhabited this city for exactly six weeks. These were her friends.

She stood up, like a puppet being jerked to its feet, at the sensation in the base of her skull.

The call. This was the call.

The Ship was talking to her, from long ago and far away, saying that it was working its way through time and space towards her. She caught sight of it for a moment, in the absolute black shadow cast by the sofa: a blue box, spinning through the butterfly vortex that lay underneath all reality. The light on its apex was flashing faster and faster as it approached her, and it would be here –

It told her when and where.

Time to go.

Compassion smoothed down her gingham skirt in one movement, then bent to pull her sandal tight. She stepped softly over Allan, careful not to let her hem brush his face, because then he might wake and ask her questions.

That would slow her down.

She stepped out into the hallway of the little flat, and paused by the door to Joe and Catherine's bedroom, listening. She couldn't hear anything.

Last night, in the King's Head, while Joe had been laughing at something, Catherine had leaned close to her and said, 'They really like you. You ought to ask Patrick about a regular job with his lot, and then you won't have to be a temp any more and you can get a better flat, and let me tell you all the prints you ought to get for the walls.'

'Good.'

'Allan's all quivery about you.'

'Good.'

She'd beamed with happiness. 'D'you really think it's good? I'll bring him over, and I'll leave you two alone, and then you can tell him that and take him back to your place to make sweet love like a man and a woman should.'

'Not tonight.'

'Oh, is it a bad time?'

'Soon.'

'OK.' A whisper. 'You just let me know when, so we can all whisper.' She'd caught a secret smile from Lovely Judy the secretary at that point as well, and had realised that she had become part of a female group, too, inside her complex of friends in general.

Catherine had grabbed the bottle and filled Compassion's glass.

Now, the cat she'd named Cheese brushed up against her legs and mewed silently, wanting to be let out along with her. She'd brought it along as a guest last night, knowing that the call would come sometime in this twenty-four hours, not wanting it to be left locked in her flat. She picked it up, placed it inside the lounge, and quietly closed the door on it, so it couldn't follow her.

She went into the bathroom and picked up her toothbrush and a bottle of CK1. These went into her bag. Everything else from her barren flat was in the van.

She went to the door, and gently eased the latch open.

Which was when Joe came out of the bedroom, his hair in a messy sort of knot. 'Oh, are you off?'

'Yes.'

'Well, cheers, then. Wahey about Allan. Are you going down the King's Head tonight?'

'Yes.'

'Great! See you there.'

'Yes.'

Without a backward glance, she stepped out on to the brilliantly illuminated landing, and clicked the door closed behind her.

She walked slowly down the steps, aware that she needed water. She'd buy some at the first petrol station.

Six weeks ago, the Doctor had given her a list of eight things to do. She counted each one off on her fingers as she made her way down the steps.

She stopped when she reached the dark mass of the front door. Only seven.

She'd write the poem on the way to the rendezvous.

She swung the heavy door open, and stepped out on to the streets of Bristol. The brilliant morning of Clifton blinded her for a moment, and she put a hand up to shade her eyes. The van sat anonymously on the road a way down the pavement.

'They can teach you, human beings,' he'd said to her. 'They taught me everything I ever needed to know.'

She reached into her bag and pulled out the keys to the van. 'No,' she said, to no one. Then she threw her bag over her shoulder and set off towards her vehicle, her steps getting faster and faster.

* * *

And among the spires of distant Gallifrey, in a white tower that was one of three hundred and sixty-three set around the Presidential Wheel, its number selected to be as incurious and dull as possible, a meeting was about to take place.

Cavisadoratrelundar loved the classical Time Lord robes that Interventionists were allowed to wear if they really wanted to appear godlike. They set off her messy blonde hair and her pencilled eyebrows and her biceps. Gandarotethetledrax, her partner in all ways – they'd decided to become a romantic couple when they were last on Earth, and Cavis hated the fact that they had to hide it from their masters – wouldn't be seen dead in them. He preferred his plain black jacket and gloves, and his groovy little beard. The white collar set off the darkness of his skin and hair and eyes. And he had about him the exciting scent of flesh that the overworked Looms had been writing into Gallifreyan warriors for the last few decades.

Right now the two of them were standing as much to attention as they could manage. They had just heard the clarion of the approach of the President, and the Chancellery Guard that stood with them had snapped to attention also. The white column that contained the backstairs Presidential elevator to the Tower was humming as that vehicle approached.

Cavis began to giggle. She couldn't help it. She always did it when things started to get extremely serious and she was meant to be sombre or attentive or compassionate or whatever. Gandar was the only one who was close enough to her to understand that it wasn't a sign of weakness. The opposite, if anything. She was unregenerated after thirty field missions, Cavis the one-hearted who had kicked Sontaran arse.

She nudged Gandar, and he quickly returned their private little salute to each other, a smack of palms in midair that curved into a snake lock of their arms.

He always looked so brave in that moment when their stares met. He would die for me, Cavis thought. He really would. 'This is a dangerous one, I can feel it,' she whispered.

'Could this be a case for Gandar and Cavis?' he whispered back.

They quickly separated as the hum stopped, and two more guards emerged from a door that had suddenly appeared in the column. Behind them came the Lady President, the War Queen, Mistress of the Nine Gallifreys. She was dressed, utterly typically, in scarlet chinoise pyjamas with a high square collar. The usual lengths of pearls were the only accessory, save for the bangles at her left wrist. She wore, Cavis noted, oriental clogs, and her toenails were painted in the swirling colours of the vortex. She'd had a tiny Prydonian Seal tattooed on her left ankle, or perhaps it had appeared there when she'd regenerated.

She regarded the two agents with her usual mixture of humour and impatience, those green eyes flashing out at them from underneath her coal-black flapper fringe. 'It's really too, too bad. Do I actually have to be so boring as to ask you to do the thing with the palms?'

Cavis and Gandar snapped their palms upright and blurted at once, 'We have no rank and no college, but we will serve you unto our last death, Lady President Romana.'

'Fabulous.' She wandered to the Time/Space Visualiser that formed the majority of one wall of the room. 'To dispense with the formalities: you are, of course, not here, and we are not speaking. Betray us, and your existences and histories will be forfeit.'

The two agents bowed. 'We understand, Lady,' said Gandar.

'Then let's say no more about it.' Romana flashed them a dazzling smile, and tapped a fingernail against a tab on the wall. The TSV came to life, its blue screen filling with the silver lines of a universe graph, a topographic picture of space-time with Gallifrey's Now at the centre. The standard symbol of Gallifreyan power. The cone of light that was designed to minimise her shadow snapped down around her. 'Concentrate, here comes the science part.' She tapped the tab once more, and the image was replaced by that of a number of ancient, bearded, Patrexian elders, bent over screens in a dark and cobwebbed room. 'We're here today because of an unusual future development in Time

Lord technology. Those dignified Time Lords who scan the future, as far as they are allowed to scan, discovered this development. The first new thing they've come up with in three centuries. The shock was so great that a few of them regenerated on the spot. Stand by for a narrow-band telepathic briefing.'

Cavis and Gandar closed their eyes and clenched their teeth as information blasted into their heads.

Then they opened their eyes again and looked at each other in astonishment.

'Yes,' Romana nodded. 'That's what's on the way. You don't need telling that such a development would be a vital advantage in our continuing dispute with the People. And in the future, during our first contact with the Enemy. The creation and first manifestation of this development are the events that you are to go and... observe.'

Cavis couldn't resist it. She made a mock gesture of innocence, tapping her chin with her finger. 'But, gosh, what if those events fail to happen? Do we just return and report?'

Romana met her gaze levelly. 'If I were you, Cavis, I really wouldn't bother.'

'We understand, ma'am,' Gandar said quickly.

Romana produced a pad from her pocket and tapped out a few instructions. 'Requisition a time capsule with a clean memory from stock. Settings have been prepared that will take you into the unusual domain where this game will be played. File no flight plan.' She handed the pad to Gandar, then headed for the door once more, her retinue clicking their heels and swinging to follow. She stopped on the threshold of the elevator. 'We need this, Cavis. Gallifrey needs this. Don't let anyone get in your way.' A little pause. 'Not even him.'

And then she was gone, the hum of the elevator speeding her away to a more public place, where she would continue to be innocent.

'Well,' said Gandar. 'That told us.'

Cavis made the Horns of Rassilon in the direction of the elevator. 'Him, indeed. Othering Other, Gandar, I've been wanting to take him on for millennia.'

Gandar pointed to his suit. 'Me, too. Why do you think I dress like this?'

Cavis took his arm and they headed for their own traveltube. 'You know, sweetheart, in case we do meet him, I think we'd better get hold of some disguises.'

And in a distant, silver castle, in the land of dreams, a young woman of royal blood and her best friend were playing Nine Men's Morris.

They sat in a plush chamber of velvet and polished wood, and the curtains billowed with the gentle winds of the dreamlands. She was hearty and buxom, with a flower behind her ear, a permanent smile on her face. He was older and hawklike, with deeply furrowed brows and a passive expression that made his every deeply wise move on the board look like an accident.

'Fey, Margwyn!' she threw back her hands. 'I keep walking into your traps.'

'That's why you keep me at your Court, Queen Regent. So I can see those traps for you in the world. I have set another here for you, by the way.' His finger sliced a piece across the board.

'I keep you here because who else is there for me to talk to? I'm too young for this. Mother should have hung on a while. I felt happy for her when we lit her pyre. To be free of all this. I want to go and dance.'

'When?'

'In general. Always.' She glanced at a servant boy who was gathering plates and goblets from the floor. 'Leave them, I'll do that.'

Margwyn inclined his head to a point a few inches from hers. 'You should let him. You are the leader. They will become nervous if you act as if you do not wish to lead.'

'Dung to that. They'll think me a great and noble leader who takes heads and likes her ale. That's what they like.' Her brow furrowed into a frown. 'Brigida's blood. You've got me again.'

Margwyn inclined his head. 'This is what occurs when you ignore my advice.'

* * *

The Brigadier's BMW shot along the M4, heading east. He could feel it now, as the grey of the motorway strobed over his window, and Radio 4 chuckled away in the background, that sense of despair folding over him. That dreamlike disconnection from all the awful little things that marred a day. Little phrases that played endlessly in his mind.

Choppy day out there. Just once round the lighthouse.

Never coming back.

'I hope you're not blaming this problem of yours on me,' she said to him, from the passenger seat. As usual, she had a map on her lap, and a box of mints resting on the surface by the gear stick. She was wearing a summer dress, and he could see a tiny scar on her calf where she'd cut herself shaving.

Her hair smelled of her, and of her herbal-mixture shampoo, and of the old deckchairs they always used to take out on the lawn on summer afternoons.

'Of course not,' he told her.

'Because of course it's not me who's doing it. It's you.'

'I'm well aware of that, dear.'

'I miss you. Are you coming to see me?'

'Soon. I shall be with you soon.'

The radio said something about a bomb, and the Brigadier reached to turn the volume up. It turned out to be a drama set in Ulster in the 1970s. As his thoughts had turned to it, Doris had gone back to the depths of his grief where she came from.

'Wounded?' the Brigadier whispered, unaware that he was letting his lips make the words. 'Yes. Yes, I dare say I am.'

Chapter Two
Get Through It

October 1967. Rex sat on the park bench, looking into space, daydreaming. Sometimes it felt as if he'd been dreaming all his life. He didn't know for certain how old he was. The cold and the damp and the cheap wine had robbed him of his memories. He wore ancient boots that had been bound together with duct tape, and had once been repaired at a hostel. His old coat, the most comforting thing of his life, smelled of him. He'd fought a man who tried to take this off him, once. Down where he was, nobody had time to be civilised. Anyone would hurt you. Rockers would kick you in the street. All he had was himself, and he hated it, and it hurt. And he wished someone would just reach down, one of those passing folk with money and lives, and help him out of it. Any way they liked.

He blinked as two people walked into his view, which had previously been of the gasometer and the leafless trees and a row of iron railings. The one who'd walked in from the left was a blonde, a looker in a white minidress and boots and one of those beehives. The one on the right was a darkie, with a huge mop of hair and sunglasses, though the day was too dark already.

They looked at him, then they looked at each other, then they nodded, and started walking towards him.

'Hoi!' he called. 'Get out of it! Whatever it is, I don't want it!'

The girl put a hand on one of his shoulders. The man put a hand on the other.

'Oh yes you do,' she said sweetly. 'My friend here has something to say to you.'

The man cleared his throat, and took off his sunglasses. 'I am Gandar,' he intoned, staring straight into Rex's eyes. 'And you - will - obey - me!'

'Yes,' said Rex, suddenly feeling the happiest he had ever felt.

'Groovy,' giggled the girl. 'Now come on, let's get you some food. You've got a lot of work ahead of you, Rex.'

* * *

The Brigadier placed the plastic cup of coffee in front of Bedser. The airman had a Caesar cut of dark hair, and an unshaven, thick-jawed face that looked as if it had been injured by rugby. He was sitting at a tiny table in a brightly lit grey room. A guard stood by the door.

'So,' Lethbridge-Stewart began, aware of the irony that, only a couple of hours ago, he'd been in a very similar situation. 'What did you do with our nuclear weapon?'

'I didn't do anything with the nuclear weapon, sir.' Bedser looked tired, his eyes imploring as he watched Lethbridge-Stewart sit down opposite him. 'Can I ask who you work for, sir?'

That standard dislike for the spookiness the UN badge brought with it on English soil. In continental Europe it meant peacekeeping. Here it meant Black Ops, and whispered canteen rumours of terrible things. Monsters. He hoped against hope that this was an old-fashioned UNIT matter. There hadn't been a large-scale flap for the organisation since the Ice Warriors, and some elements within the UN bureaucracy were now openly wondering about the expenditure of keeping the Taskforce active. Hence the call-ups for high security, but terrestrial, matters like this missing bomb, where it was all hands to the pumps and the Brigadier's combination of experience and new found vigour was particularly valued. The monsters from space, those shiny, scaly, obsessed things from other worlds, that had so delighted the Brigadier in his first youth, and given him the pleasure of risking his life for the whole planet – they didn't come any more. He looked through the official files sometimes to picture them again, because in his mind's eye they had become frail things, like something out of a dream. Lethbridge-Stewart got the feeling that one day, when he was old again, he would be left in the corner of an old folk's home, the only one left who believed in monsters. He missed them. These days, his conflicts were bitter, prosaic ones, and all the dragons were dead.

He realised that Bedser was waiting for an answer. 'I'm something to do with the UN. I'm just here to ask you a few questions.' He flipped open an empty file and studied a blank piece of paper for a moment. 'Now, I gather your aircraft went missing from the radar of the two other aircraft in your flight over Oldbury Castle. You were gone for twenty-six seconds. In that time, the tactical nuclear bomb that you had slung under your wing went missing.' The Brigadier watched the man's face as he delivered the verdict. 'The obvious conclusion is that, either through incompetence or deliberately, you dropped an armed weapon on to the Downs.'

Bedser was shaking his head. 'Sir, I did neither. The flight recorder will –'

'The flight recorder malfunctioned for exactly those twenty-six seconds.'

Bedser stared at him. 'What are you setting me up for?'

The Brigadier let out a long breath. Then he reached down and unbuttoned his holster. 'Let's cut to the point, shall we?' He produced his Webley revolver, checked the chambers, and flicked off the safety catch.

He stood up and pointed the weapon at Bedser's head.

The guard at the door, to his credit, didn't react in the slightest.

'There are teams out all over the Downs,' said the Brigadier. 'And yet nobody has called anything in. It's broad daylight, but nobody's seen anything. This is a nuclear bomb we're talking about, not a lost balloon. So who picked it up? Who are you working for?'

'You can't kill me,' whispered the airman, looking at the barrel of the weapon in terror.

'Oh, you'll find that in practice I can. An accident with ordnance. Nobody misses a traitor here and there. Who are you working for?'

That had been an unfortunate choice of words, back there, not that anybody else in the room would have realised it. Cronin would have been delighted with that slip about the balloon. Why couldn't they come back, the monsters? Give him something honourable to shoot at, a good way to die?

The words, when they came, from the terrified man, were not those he expected.

'All right! I gave it to someone... but only in a dream!'

'What are you talking about, man?'

'I think I might have fallen asleep. In the cockpit. I remembered this in a dream last night, after I landed. There was this huge bird in front of me. It flew at my cockpit. Not a bird, a dragon. A dragon!' Bedser was babbling now, staring up at the Brigadier, pleading to him with his eyes.

The Brigadier raised an eyebrow and considered the matter. Then he flicked on the safety catch of his revolver and replaced it in his holster. 'I passed a rather charming tearoom on the way through the village. Do you fancy a spot of lunch?'

Bedser stared at him.

'So. Tell me about the dream.'

The other customers in the little tearoom were staring at the man in the dirty flightsuit and his uniformed companion, but Bedser didn't seem aware of their attention. He put his palms on the table, as if to ground himself, obviously still getting over the idea that the madman who'd pointed a gun at him was now listening to him quite cordially. 'I'm in my cockpit. Suddenly, there's this huge black shape against the window. A bird strike, I think. So I try to turn. But the aircraft isn't moving. It's like I'm on the ground. But I'm not. There's an... acceptance on my part. I dreamed something else about filling in forms, but I know that bit's not as real as this bit... I feel like I signed away the bomb. But I know I didn't. I mean... it feels like it went to someone official.'

'Tell me about your control surfaces. Before and after. Do you remember anything noteworthy?'

Bedser closed his eyes. Then opened them again, smiling at having managed to recall something. 'The fuel level was down.' Then he frowned. 'My God, we must have lost about two hours' worth of fuel in that twenty-six seconds.'

Lethbridge-Stewart looked at Bedser for a long, hard moment. Then he turned and signalled to a wary-looking waitress. 'Could we have the bill, please?'

'So you think he's telling the truth?' Wing Commander Wilson, Bedser's CO, looked steadily at Lethbridge-Stewart over his desk.

'Indeed. His story isn't worth a damn. If he was working for someone, they'd have provided him with something better than that.' The Brigadier felt uncomfortable in the plush chair.

'He can't have been got at, can he? By a foreign power, or… something from your field?'

'I don't know. It's possible. The navigator, Hodges, says that he was out for those twenty-six seconds, too. Their stories are identical.'

'Weird thing from the ground staff.' Wilson threw a file in the Brigadier's direction. 'The Tornado's chronometer came back two hours fast.'

The Brigadier glanced at the file. 'Still no sign of the bomb?'

Wilson grimly shook his head.

As his car climbed the long hill out of Devizes, the Brigadier contemplated what the evening would be like for him at home, now that his duty today was done. They'd just wanted him for his knowledge of the military mind, his decades of experience with men like Bedser, men who'd experienced pressure beyond the norm. Now he could go home. To cooking for one, and the approximation of a life he'd made for himself in the house that still echoed with her voice.

She used to rub his back with liniment at the end of the day. Part of their bedtime ritual. He'd cleared her things out of the place, sent them off to her mother. He'd kept only some old letters and some photos, and had put them in a drawer that he was terrified of opening.

One week ago, he had managed to get it open to retrieve one photo, which he'd put on his desk, and which hurt him every morning and supported him every night.

He and Bedser had both become victims of their dreams.

Suddenly, with a jerk of anger, he spun the wheel. He turned off the road at the signs that said Cherhill, and headed across the Downs towards Oldbury Castle.

Compassion sat on two packing cases at the westernmost point of the Iron Age hill fort. She had parked the van on the road and lifted the first packing case up the chalk footpath that ascended one side of the Downs. Then she had walked back down the hill and brought the other up. She'd left the van unlocked for whoever wanted it, with the key in the ignition.

The green, flat landscape of Wiltshire stretched in all directions under the glare of the afternoon sun. At intervals bodies of water reflected the light, and the patterns of roads and settlements and the distant lines of an airbase were all visible from the downlands. She'd walked past a large picture of a horse cut in the chalk, its eye glittering. The eye seemed to be made of some sort of quartz rock. The wind had buffeted her ears on the way up, and she'd sought shelter from that, opting to carry the cases along the deep ditches that once had formed the boundary of the hill fort. Past the gateway, she'd found a point where the messages in her skull told her that the TARDIS would materialise, and so she had settled there, mostly out of the wind, but from time to time having to hold her wide-brimmed floppy hat on her head.

She'd been here five hours now. She had five more to wait, by which time it would be night. But the night would be warm, certainly not cold enough to harm her by the time the TARDIS arrived.

On several occasions now, men with strong shoulders carrying packs or rucksacks had walked past her, carefully examining the ground as they walked. One had gone past with his eyes fixed on the packing cases, then had come back twenty minutes later. Then two more had come from the other direction. One of them had artificially attempted to strike up a conversation with her. He had an accent that was right for the area, but that was the only thing that was right about him.

'There's a lot of history up here,' he'd said.

'Obviously, there's a lot of history everywhere.'

For some reason, he'd laughed. 'People have seen ghosts.'

'They must be mistaken. I don't believe in ghosts.'

'A local vicar saw a whole phantom army, Celtic warriors, marching over the hills.'

'Yes.'

'What are you writing?'

'A poem. It's the first one I've ever written, and I have to finish it within the next five hours.'

'Why?'

'The answer to that is very complicated.'

The men had exchanged looks, almost certain now that she wasn't the enemy that they were looking for, and that whatever radioactive item they sought wasn't in the packing cases.

'Are you from around here?' the other one asked.

'I'm from the city of Bristol.'

'What's in the cases?'

'Everything I own. I'm meeting someone.'

They made their goodbyes and left, but they looked over their shoulders at her as they did, and several others had returned in her direction in the next few hours.

She tried to get on with her poem. She was writing it with a biro on the bottom of the parchment that the Doctor had left her with. His own scrawly handwriting, in quill ink, covered less than half of it.

Things to Do

Live among humans.
Make friends.
Get a job.
Eat chips.
Write poetry.
Kiss someone (properly).
Get a cat.
Fall in love.

At the bottom, he'd sealed it with a wax sigil in High Gallifreyan. Compassion translated his chosen name: 'Foolish Wanderer'.

She had carefully ticked each point out as she'd done it. She had hesitated before ticking point eight, but she was fairly sure that Allan was in love with her by now. So she'd got halfway to that.

The poetry was proving problematic. In preparation, she had read several books of poetry, and several on the art of it. She had decided on a haiku verse, the shortest actual form.

Compassion concentrated once more on her work as the sun swung overhead, changing the angle of the shadow her pen made on the paper.

The Brigadier had taken a room at the Black Horse Inn in the small village of Cherhill, and changed into his civilian clothes. From the beer garden by the road, he contemplated the smooth green slope of the Downs looming over the rim of his whisky glass. The white horse didn't look Celtic: it was too smooth and rounded, built to be seen from the road. His host, a happy little man called Frank, had explained that, back in the Victorian era, a local dignitary, standing near here, had shouted the instructions for the horse to a gang of men who stood on the hillside, armed with wooden stakes.

He had five straight whiskies, and avoided all human contact. He heard the distant mutter of the test match from inside the pub, with people reacting every now and then to a good ball or the fall of a wicket. He watched the cars go by, sometimes with caravans on the way to holidays. Sometimes boats on trailers. There were lorries, too, some from carefully anonymous companies. He was grateful nobody from the search popped down the side of the hill for a jar.

They must be getting worried by now. There was so little cover up there, nowhere for a bomb to hide.

They would search all day. But he was waiting for night. He didn't know why. It was as if something was speaking to him from deep inside, but he couldn't hear it properly yet. Something awaited him on those hills in the mystery time, in the twilight. Among the rough shapes of the hill fort's walls, the man-made lumps against the smooth flanks. Among the dips and angles of the barrows. Something final was waiting for him, and he longed to meet it.

He finished his latest glass, watching the shadows of clouds slowly swing across the hillside.

* * *

Compassion watched the bulk of the full moon rising over the opposite wall of the hill fort. The sun had set an hour ago, but the sky was still full of light. The moon was red with the dust of the cornfields. The last birds of the day were darting above the downlands, snatching and weaving for insects. And now, all over the Downs, she saw the lights of groups of men, still searching.

Her poem was not going well.

Lethbridge-Stewart had returned to his room as the light faded, and took his Webley from his luggage. He sat down at the dressing table in front of the mirror, ejected the rounds from the chambers, checked the barrel, disassembled and reassembled the weapon. His hands shook a little as he did it. Probably the drink.

He reloaded the gun, and slipped it into a shoulder holster. He checked the look of it under his jacket, and decided that it wouldn't attract undue attention.

He considered calling his ex-wife, Fiona. He hadn't done that for such a long time, though. She had a life of her own. Or perhaps Kate – he could have a chat with young Gordy. Well, not so young now. With a jolt, he realised that he was planning on saying his goodbyes. He was anticipating the walk up the hill, but had no thought in his head of returning.

'Well, that's all right, isn't it?' she said. 'You just see what happens.'

'You sound like you want me to finish it tonight.'

'Of course not. I just don't want you to be unhappy.'

He coughed a curt laugh. 'You should have thought of that before you died.'

He left the room neat and tidy and locked the door behind him.

He made his way slowly up the rough chalk track, his brogues kicking aside flints. It was a lovely summer night, with the red moon sailing high above the dark bulk of the downland. False-looking hikers passed him on the way down, their conversations carefully ceasing before he could hear them. He kept his cap down over his eyeline, in case any of them should recognise him.

He checked his palmtop. The Ordnance Survey map was

overlaid by a tactical display he'd downloaded. It showed in detail the area where Bedser's aircraft had vanished, and the search areas that by now must have been combed a dozen times.

Bedser had only a matter of hours, he realised. Sometime in the small hours, they would drag him from his cell and give him to another interrogator, one who would be authorised to do whatever he or she had to. And the man had nothing he could tell them, Lethbridge-Stewart was certain of that. He was sure of his ability to know when a military man was telling the truth. The poor devil. But still, that was how the world turned. There were terrible injustices everywhere, and he couldn't be responsible for them all. That was another odd thing: his temper these days seemed to want him to try. He'd seen a small boy being bullied by his peers as he walked one morning near his house, and had run after them, yelling, scaring not just the bullies but their victim, too. When they'd gone, he'd rounded on the boy and asked him why he had let himself be a victim of such cruelty, why he couldn't be stronger.

His mother had come to save him from the madman.

He wondered what Cronin would think about his folly this evening. Incomprehension, probably. That someone so troubled by dreams would seek a dream out.

The top of the path levelled out and he was walking along the upper ridge of the Downs, heading for the hill fort, the moon casting crimson shadows on the ground in front of him.

He walked the banks of the hill fort anticlockwise, taking his palmtop out occasionally to check his location by GPS. He marvelled at the efforts of the Iron Age builders of this place, the Celtic tribe who had anticipated the Roman invasion and prepared for it with these bastions that still stood. In its time, this place would have had fences and sentry posts. There was an atmosphere about the ditches where he walked, where in the shadows the grass was already wet with dew. The gentle bluster of the wind was muted here into whispers, and all you could see overhead were the ancient stars.

'I wish you could see this.'

'Silly thing, I can.'

'But you're not real, dear. You're a symptom of grief. A very lovely symptom, but a phantom all the same.'

'Stop being so damned rational. You're here to experience, not to analyse.'

'I might come and see you tonight.' He felt the weight of the gun swinging under his arm. 'It's lovely here, and you're so close, and the dawn will bring... well, merely another day without you.'

'We'll see.'

He laughed. 'That's typical of you! You never could make up your –'

He stopped walking and stopped the conversation at the same time. His palmtop was delicately cheeping. He took it out of his pocket and sighed. He'd set it to go off when he entered the area beneath the point where Bedser had had his experience. He was at the perimeter now. The centre was around the curve of the hill-fort ditch.

Regretting losing Doris in midstream, he marched around the curve, and stopped dead.

Right at ground zero, exactly at the point where Bedser's aircraft had winked out of existence, a young woman was sitting on two packing cases, writing on a sheet of parchment.

Giddily, he approached her. It looked as if she was waiting for somebody.

She looked up, and looked surprised at him.

'Hullo!' he called. 'Good evening. Hope I didn't scare you.'

'Brigadier Lethbridge-Stewart,' she said. 'What are you doing here? Oh, I see. You're probably helping to find the nuclear device.'

Then she returned to her writing.

The Brigadier put a hand to his brow, wondering for a moment if he'd already entered the land of the pixies. 'Do I know you, Miss...?'

'Compassion. No, you don't. I've just heard of you, that's all.'

He stepped forward. 'May I ask why you're sitting in that exact place?'

'I'm waiting for someone. And they'll be here in about a minute, so –' She stopped. Frowned. Put her pen down. 'Wait. Something's wrong.'

Lethbridge-Stewart felt it, too, a prickling up the back of his neck, an ancient, primal sensation that made him spin and look for snipers, his hand straying towards his jacket. He felt suddenly nauseous and fearful. It was as if a great, unseen shadow was sweeping down over the hills and they were at the centre of it. A predator was diving down at them, the pressure building and building.

He realised that he could feel the gap between his shirtsleeves and his skin. Every hair on his body was standing on end. He could hear the air crackling, and his nostrils filled with the smell of stripping ozone.

Compassion's red hair stood around her shoulders, her dress billowing as though she was a puppet, being slowly raised on strings. She stood on the cases, looking quickly to the left and right, needing desperately to know what was going on, even as her expression remained composed.

They were going to be hit by lightning, he thought. Out of a clear sky. He should throw himself to the ground, but the ground was swelling with an awesome potential, too.

The mystery was going to rear up out of the Downs. It felt as if it would kill him.

But behind the singing of the mystery in his ears there was a sound that he recognised. Aircraft engines. An apt sound, because now he was somehow pulling g, his vision tunnelling into darkness.

He looked up into the sky and saw it. A low familiar shape, its running lights against the moon. Wilson must have sent up a test flight, operating under exactly the same conditions.

It was going to run into this... whatever it was.

Compassion raised her hands to her face, clearly wondering about what was happening to her eyes. The air around the two of them was actually starting to spark and flash, and Lethbridge-Stewart's vision was full of blazing golden trails.

The aircraft, roaring, bore down towards them. It seemed to be slowing, as if time itself were turning into a nightmare.

The Brigadier made a decision. He hurled himself towards Compassion, his arms gathering around her as he reached the packing cases. 'Come on!' he yelled.

The impact surprised her, pushed her along, made her take the first few faltering steps of an off-balance run that was slowing and slowing as the great heavy thing in the sky drew down towards them.

Its engines were roaring above the clear note that was echoing up from the Downs. The resonance between the two was buckling the air into great, dancing waves that went beyond heat haze, making the stars bloom and vanish.

But between these sounds there came another sound, one so familiar that Lethbridge-Stewart was now certain he was dreaming.

A wheezing, groaning sound.

The sound of time and space parting.

But this time the wheezing and groaning were those of a dying man, the sound warped and painful, as if its source was being torturously dragged into a point it could not, would not, fit.

Compassion started screaming.

The Brigadier swung round his head and looked at the spot where the packing cases stood. The familiar blue police box was heaving into existence, the light on its roof pulsing insanely, the exterior stretching and warping into shapes that his mind couldn't grasp.

The pressure built.

The sound reached a pitch of screaming nothingness.

The police box could not hold.

The Brigadier slowly flung himself over Compassion, without thought, putting his body between her and the blast.

Which came.

The TARDIS exploded into a ball of flame and matter.

And the sky swept down and crushed them between it and the land.

Chapter Three
Into the Fire

The Brigadier was dreaming.

To his horror, it was the other familiar dream. The one that described events as they'd actually happened, that terrible night.

The little yacht was caught in a storm, and Doris was holding on at one end of the deck, her expression stressed but sure, certain that her Alistair was going to get them out of this, get them home. Water smashed against the side of the boat and rolled away again, time after time.

It had been his idea to take the boat out today. They hadn't listened to the weather forecast. They were so close to shore, they were on holiday. It shouldn't have mattered. She'd said earlier, let's head in, but he'd said he fancied handling a bit of choppy sea.

He was at the tiller, trying to keep them facing into the waves. Failing. He'd been very scared, but hadn't shown that to Doris, keeping up a smiling eye contact, and the occasional wink or laugh when an especially big one had broken over the side.

'This can't keep going for much longer!' he'd shouted through the streaming rain. 'They must be running out of waves!'

'I'm sure that –' she'd said. She was reaching to attach the hook on her lifeline to a new ring, to get more comfortable. He hadn't bothered himself, of course, having to handle the tiller and the sail.

And then the big wave had rolled across the surface of the ocean and folded the boat into it.

He didn't recall the moment of impact. He just suddenly realised they were underwater, with the deck of the boat a deadly lid above them.

He'd slammed his way along that surface, fighting the buoyancy of his life jacket, his arm stretched out for her. She'd reached out for him, too, but then the surface had bucked under an impact –

That last expression in her eyes.

Her hand had been whipped out of his grasp.

Her flailing form shot away into the darkness under the sea.

I will come and find you, he had thought. I will save you.

And then there was black for an endless time as he thrashed around, caught in lines, his lungs desperate for air.

He'd smashed out to the surface and seen the lifeboat bouncing across the waves towards them, the RNLI crew holding on bravely in the face of the storm, calling out to him.

He'd looked round in all directions for her, even tried to dive back under as they pulled him out.

They saw her floating a hundred yards away.

And then she was on the deck of the lifeboat as a lifeboatman tried endless artificial respiration, refusing to give up as they headed back, as they were thrown back and forth, showing offhand, tremendous bravery.

He'd just looked at the white slab of her arm, and could see no life in it. Her hair was a wet mass on the deck. Her socks were stuck to her feet.

When the RNLI man had knelt up from her, his face a livid mixture of anger and pain, held inside by his professionalism, the Brigadier had gone to her and held her. Kissed her. But it was just holding an empty piece of meat.

In that moment, he'd felt a sharp, awful pain that had told him it was just the tiniest part of a larger, increasing pain that he had been given over to for the rest of his days. He looked into her empty eyes. Pain was to be his life, now.

And then he was underwater again, as he always was, and she had that look on her face as she always did, as she spiralled away into the darkness and was lost.

But this time he didn't wake up. He was still there, underwater. Good show, he thought. Just get on with it. I'll try to stay under, my dear, only this dratted body wants me to stay alive.

He thought about the moment the TARDIS had exploded. Was he dreaming it, or had a cloud of butterflies erupted into the air a moment later? Had there been screams, as if of dying men? Something terrible about those screams, as if they were being sucked away into nothing, consumed rather than killed. Taken by the machine.

He realised that he was remembering now, not dreaming.

He was enclosed in a small place, with water all around him. That wasn't like the dream, either. And he was fully clothed. And now strong arms had grabbed his, and he was being pulled out of the small space –

He fell against the man who had pulled him out into the bright sunlight. They were in some sort of room. He found himself staring straight into his face.

It was a lean, angular face, with curls of brown hair that fell over intelligent temples, the look of a composer or painter. The man had deep blue eyes that seemed to be continuously mocking until you looked deeper and saw that he was laughing with you and not at you. The cheekbones were high and chiselled. The lips were pursed in a startled expression of joy, which as the Brigadier watched burst into a smile. The man, the Brigadier noted, was wearing a collarless shirt with the top button undone, under a long frock coat.

'Alistair!' he cried. 'Excellent to see you! What are you doing here?'

The Brigadier looked down at his sopping jacket and trousers, and turned around to see a large cauldron, water still lapping from it, lolling about on a stone floor covered with rugs. He turned back to the man, and said, 'Do you know, Doctor, I was rather hoping you'd tell me.'

The Doctor looked round, obviously taking in the look of the place himself for the first time. 'I don't know any more than you do.' He pointed to a metal chest on the other side of the room. 'I stepped out of that box a moment ago.'

The Brigadier carefully put aside the whole matter of how he and the Doctor had got here, wherever here was, and followed his training, getting a feel for his surroundings. They were in some sort of banqueting hall. A huge place, with a great wooden table and many seats. A great fireplace. Furs on the floor and weapons on the wall. An odd clash between ancient fittings and relatively modern comforts. The room might have been chilly, since it was built of great stone blocks, but the windows let in shafts of brilliant summer sunshine. Daylight. Which came as a shock in itself. He must have been out for a long time. But he felt more jet-lagged than knocked for six. His body was saying it should still be night.

He glanced back to the Doctor, who was turning on the spot like a weather vane, soaking up the decor, doubtless drawing a thousand conclusions. The Brigadier was trying to hold down the relief he felt at seeing his old friend again. He was ashamed that the first thing at the top of his mind was to take him aside and tell him about Doris. In clipped, restrained tones, of course. So that they could be the Brigadier and the Doctor again, and the Doctor could say something profound and healing to him, the sort of thing the Brigadier would never say.

Or he could just offer to go back in time and –

The Brigadier made himself hold that sudden vast and exciting thought in. He would ask about that later. Not now. That wouldn't be seemly. He settled on, 'How's your new body working out?'

'Beautifully! What about yours?'

The Brigadier found his cap on the floor and wrung it out. 'It has its ups and downs. It prefers being dry. Have you come to any conclusions about our surroundings?'

'Some.' The Doctor's eyes were flashing all over the room. 'The decor says pre-medieval to me. Celtic. This is a banqueting hall, where the tribe gathers. See the swords and the shields on the wall? Their edges are chipped, they've been used. The furs on the floor haven't been chemically treated.'

'But they have a chimney. Some sort of theme park?'

'Possibly. That's Sol, your sun, outside the leaded windows, and it's at exactly the same point at it's solar cycle as the year you're from, which would be about, oh, 2012? Isn't that strange?' He ran with great, easy strides to the wall, and slapped his palms on it. 'And worrying, because that's one of the years that prophecy has always suggested for the end of the world. Terence McKenna's Timewave graph. The Mayan calendar. I hate landing in those years. I always end up having to save everybody.' He cast an eager look back at the Brigadier. 'But this wall is better constructed than anything your time period should be able to make.' His eye caught something on the opposite wall of the great chamber, past the great wooden table and huge wooden seats, past the banners and the shields and the vast fireplace. 'And of course,' he whispered, 'there's that.'

The Brigadier followed his gaze. Set high on the wall, above what could only be a throne, at the other end of the room, was a tactical nuclear bomb.

He wandered up to the Doctor's side and put his hands on his hips. 'Jolly good,' he said. 'I was wondering where that had got to. So how do we get it home?'

The Doctor looked at him, smiling with pleasure at their familiarity. 'Alistair, I have no idea where "home" is. One moment I was in my TARDIS...' He suddenly put a hand to his temple. 'My TARDIS! That must be... Oh no. All the toings and froings, the way she kept being difficult, misbehaving, as if – as if she was afraid of something. This must have been what she was anticipating, what she was trying to avoid, the moment of her own death!'

'Oh.' The Brigadier remembered, and felt his hopes fade again. 'Is what I saw correct, Doctor? Did it really...?'

'Yes. I have a sense of its existence in my head, usually, but now...' He sagged against the wall, putting out one long arm to support himself, his eyes frantically scanning the empty distance ahead of him. 'No, I mustn't think that. She shouldn't have come apart just like that. Perhaps she's been weakened by how close she's come to death recently. Perhaps she was prepared. Perhaps she's healing herself somewhere... There's always hope, there has to be. Without the TARDIS... Without her I'd be trapped here. Wherever here is.'

The Brigadier found that he couldn't quite sympathise with his old friend's loss, the loss of a vehicle. 'Any other crew?' he asked.

'One other. My companion, Fitz Kreiner. If we got here... however we got here...' He let go of the wall and ran a hand through his hair, sounding urgent again. 'We have to find out who's in charge here.'

'Get arrested, break out of jail, meet the powers that be...'

That made him smile. 'Of all the people I might have found myself stranded with, Alistair, you're the one I'd have picked. But there's something different about you...' His inquisitive face fixed on the Brigadier, as if this was as important a matter as the destruction of his Ship, and Lethbridge-Stewart suddenly felt very awkward indeed.

'Doctor,' he began, 'perhaps there is something you –'

There was a sudden yelling from outside, voices raised in anger from behind every one of half a dozen doors, running footsteps all heading in their direction.

The Brigadier felt relieved and angry at the same time.

There was a crash as the first of the enemy burst into the room.

It was a huge warrior of some ancient tribe, his face streaked with blue dye, his muscular arms tattooed, his red hair ringed into great strands. He was screaming, and swirling a great sword above his head.

More like him burst from every door.

'Of course!' the Doctor gasped. 'The Catuvelauni! The Kingdom of the sleeping King Constantine! I've always wanted to pay them a visit.' He leapt to one side as the warrior swung his sword down, cleaving the air. 'Just stay alive for the next –' He grabbed a chair, swung it to parry another sword swing, and threw it and the warrior aside – 'oh, ninety seconds or so, and everything will be fine.'

Another warrior was running at the Brigadier, swirling an axe over his head.

Good, he thought, as his hand automatically went to his jacket. Perhaps it's now. But with the Doctor here... The thought ended on an awkward negative as the training took over.

The Brigadier calmly drew his pistol, aimed at the warrior's abdomen, and fired.

The bullet bounced off a small round shield the man carried. The Brigadier aimed again, no part of his body admitting fear.

And found his weapon sailing across the room on the wrong end of a candlestick holder. He saw a flash of a surprised, dark frown from the Doctor, who was pirouetting with furniture, his feet swishing at rugs as yelling men tripped and fell around him, at the centre of a blizzard of flesh and metal as a dozen warriors tried to get near him and found themselves falling into the walls, the floor and each other.

A screaming blow swished by the Brigadier's ear as the warrior he'd fired at arrived. He caught the arm with the sword in it, found the centre of the man's body weight, and threw him, breaking the arm as he went. The man's scream mixed with that of the next upon him, who impacted him in the chest, with his full weight on a small, round shield. The Brigadier rolled right over, going with the force of the blow, then heaved his legs up to throw the man over backwards. He rolled back on to his own feet, and kicked the sprawling man across the jaw. Another grabbed him across the shoulders, and he slammed his elbow backwards into the warrior's abdomen, then spun as his grip released and cuffed him about both ears, breaking his eardrums.

Yes. Some part of him exulted as he felt the blood rushing round his limbs anew. Yes. 'Come on!' he heard a voice that seemed to be his, bellowing at them. 'Come on!'

Suddenly, he heard another voice, and everything went silent.

'Cease!' the voice had said. And it was soft and powerful at the same time, and it made him want to turn and scream that he was just getting started, that he was just starting to lose himself in the fight. He swung round with that thought and stopped at what he saw. The warriors had stopped their frenzied attack. Even the ones he'd injured were lying where they fell, regarding the figure that had just entered with awe and dismay.

It was a woman in her early thirties. She was tall, nearly as tall as he was, and she had a mass of dark hair that fell freely over her shoulders, mixed with braids and knotted gems. She had high cheekbones and odd, wry blue eyes that were looking straight at him. She wore a red shirt with matching men's trousers, and a slim sword at her belt. He noticed that she had tattoos on the back of her neck and down her bare left arm, where she wore only a series of golden rings. Around her neck she wore a tiny item of jewellery which... the Brigadier unconsciously coughed. He'd never seen the male genitalia presented as an amulet before.

She was beautiful, probably, a long-deserted part of him was saying. Her mouth had a joke about it, and her face was that of someone who had never had a painful notion. A lush, countryside beauty.

He killed the unfaithful thought.

They were looking at each other, he realised, he and this woman, as if this moment were somehow important.

Her glance broke from him quickly, and swept around the men, her men, he was certain.

'Knotheads!' she shouted. 'Hop-addled fools! What d'you think you're doing?'

The Brigadier felt his anger fall from him, and was surprised that he was smiling.

'Queen Regent…' This came from one of the men who'd surrounded the Doctor. 'A serving girl heard voices and saw these two through a keyhole. They'd just appeared. We sent for you as soon as –'

'Queen Regent?' The Doctor's head popped up between two of the warriors. He stepped through them and their weapons as if he was making his way through a hedge, and peered at the woman for a second, smiling like a child facing Father Christmas. Then he fell theatrically to his knees in front of her, his forehead pressed to the stone floor, his arms spread behind him like a swan. 'Queen Regent Mab, I'm the Doctor. I offer my life and allegiance to you, with all reverence due to the great trust you hold.'

'Oh, you know the words. Good for you!' Mab suddenly smiled, like the sun coming out. 'We're honoured to welcome you as our guest, the Doctor.'

The Doctor glanced over his shoulder at Lethbridge-Stewart. 'You as well. Quickly.'

The Brigadier got as far as lowering himself to one knee, then found himself hesitating, and awkwardly got back to his feet again. He cleared his throat, wondering what he could say that would be diplomatic and yet true to himself. 'My name is General Alistair Lethbridge-Stewart, Your Majesty.'

'But everybody calls him the Brigadier,' the Doctor added.

'I come in peace. My thanks to you for bringing this regrettable conflict to a halt. However, I'm afraid my life and allegiance are already taken, by another monarch.'

'Oh, terrific!' The Doctor leapt to his feet and ran to the Brigadier, spreading his hands in a pleading gesture. 'Alistair, this is bigger than your tiny loyalties. You're still in your own country. But your monarch doesn't rule it in this dimension. Mab does. Some of it. In a way.'

Mab was nodding, clearly entertained. 'Go on,' she called. 'Talk about it. We're ready with our swords here.'

'It's very complicated, but for now... My Ship may have been destroyed, I've lost my companions, I have no idea how we got here and I'd appreciate it if you didn't get us both offhandedly killed before I can find out.'

The Brigadier stepped up to Mab, and, as some sort of compromise, saluted.

She returned it, though it was obviously the first time she'd seen the gesture, fixing her face into a stony frown as she did it. He saw the look in her eyes, trying to get through to him. She was trying to communicate that she was a happy person caught up in a deadly serious situation. That she would have no option in front of her men. 'Go on, then,' she whispered, almost pleading. 'The words. The allegiance. Or death it has to be.'

He sucked in a long, regretful breath. 'Whatever the situation, Your Majesty, my allegiance isn't up for debate. I'm a professional soldier.'

Mab swiftly and expertly snatched her sword from its scabbard. 'Curse you for making me do this!' she roared. Her warriors jumped into fighting postures once more.

The Brigadier looked calmly back at her, his heart filling with a beautiful feeling of completion, of closure, as he saw in her eye her clear intent and the conscience that went with it. 'Go on, then,' he said. 'Do it. I'd thank you for it.'

'No no no!' The Doctor walked between them, shaking his head, sighing as if at squalling children, his hands outstretched. 'I claim the right of hospitality on behalf of my friend. We are your guests. You can't hurt us inside your castle.'

The warriors all relaxed at once. Mab herself swung away from the Brigadier, walked towards the far wall, cuffed over a chair, and almost threw her sword back into its scabbard, dealing with the rush of anger that she'd summoned to slay the Brigadier.

'Thank you for that, Doctor!' she called. 'At least one of you is wise enough to stay alive!'

The Brigadier made an effort to stop himself shaking. He had wanted that so much, wanted to meet death as a certainty, with no option. And now that thought felt obscene, wretched. 'Sometimes...' he muttered, then made his voice solidify into its usual certainty. 'Sometimes a wise man may choose to die.' He was aware, without looking, of the Doctor watching him.

'Dung!' Mab spat back. 'Save that for a war. I tell you what, though.' She walked back and pressed her fist into the Brigadier's arm. 'You're a warrior and a half, to face the death in my eyes like that.' She turned to her men, and bellowed, 'What a soldier is this, to bait Mab ab Mab Pendragon, Queen Regent of the Catuvelauni, Protector of Avalon, in her own castle!'

The Brigadier pursed his lips, having still not managed to look at the Doctor. 'Just doing my job,' he said.

Mab turned to one of the guards. 'Take the wounded to the mages. Quickly now. I can look after our guests.' The guards obeyed, and ushered a gang of nervous servants into the room, all of whom looked at the Doctor and the Brigadier with awe.

Lethbridge-Stewart, trying to hide his feelings, wandered over to where the bomb hung on the wall. And of course, the Doctor followed him, those blasted instincts of his seeing straight through him, probably. He fixed his expression, and made himself look the Time Lord in the eye. 'So, Doctor. King Constantine? The Catuvelauni? Avalon?'

'Later, Alistair. I have to find Fitz and –'

'That bomb isn't in danger of going off, is it? There's a firing tag still showing.'

The Doctor's concerned expression froze, and he jumped up on to the table to check the bomb. 'Maybe they're after a bigger one and a smaller one, like the Avalonian version of flying ducks.'

'You know what that thing is?' Mab wandered over, intrigued, all her anger vanished. 'My adviser, Margwyn, found it on the Downs the other day. It looked a bit martial, like a battering ram, so we put it on the wall.'

The Doctor glanced nervously down at her as his fingers expertly unfastened the weapon's casing. 'Well, perhaps that's the great magical change that we bring with us, taking this terrible thing back where it came from...' He flicked his attention to the Brigadier. 'Guests who appear out of thin air here are messengers of prophecy, beings of magical power.'

'That's why I didn't want to have to kill you,' Mab told the Brigadier. 'Bulgingly huge bad luck.'

'And here I was, feeling quite flattered,' the Brigadier countered.

Mab smiled a little girl smile at him. 'When he's finished doing what he's doing, let me show you the whole palace, and then we'll figure out why you've been sent to us.'

'Unfortunately –' the Doctor leapt down from the table, wiping his hands on his handkerchief – 'the bomb is still armed. There's not a lot I can do without specialist tools, but I can get those from the –' He stopped, and let his hand remain in midair as he closed his eyes for a moment. The eyes flicked open again, and the hand dropped. 'I think I need something to keep my mind off things. Queen Regent, you said something about a tour?'

Mab led them from the Great Hall through corridors illuminated by flaming torches, which seemed to be connected to some sort of gas supply. The castle, as Mab referred to it, was teeming with life: warriors and servants and courtiers and merchants, all recognisably Celtic, with their tattoos and braided hair, but with a strange modernity about their clothes and possessions. The Brigadier was by no means a style expert, but it looked to him as if these people had progressed to the extent of perhaps the sixteenth or seventeenth century, but independently from the Western culture to which they were still heir.

Everywhere they went, as Mab showed them around, through a

central courtyard crammed with market stalls, to an armoury filled with long spears and delicate, intricate armour, people's heads turned, and whispers grew into great shouts of pleasure. Crowds jostled to see them, only to part at Mab's command.

'Nice to be wanted,' the Brigadier murmured.

The Doctor still seemed utterly preoccupied. He'd been looking around in every room they'd passed through, obviously expecting to see his companions at any moment. 'How do you feel?' he muttered to the Brigadier. 'About this place, I mean?'

'Well...' The Brigadier watched as a gang of pageboys in long tabards leaned down over the balconies above the carpeted hallway through which they were being shown and pointed and whispered excitedly. 'It feels... strangely disconnected. I'd put the feeling down to some form of jet lag.'

'As if, old friend. You see, this is the land of dreams. Constantine's dream connects to the sleeping group mind of all humanity. In a very real way, we, and all the people who live here, are walking through somebody's nightmares.'

The Brigadier raised an eyebrow. 'So I gather we're not in Cromer any more?'

'I'll explain –'

'No!' Mab grabbed a bunch of keys from a startled official. 'The poor thing! The warrior's always led a merry dance by the mage! Why don't you explain right now?'

Mab used the keys to open a series of solid wooden doors, and led them down a dark, curling staircase that went so far underground that the Brigadier felt his ears pop.

'Ah,' said the Doctor. 'We're heading for the catacombs. Where the King is sleeping.'

'Bloody Brigida up a tree, you know a lot about us,' laughed Mab. 'Where are you from?'

The Doctor was still looking worried. 'I'm a foolish traveller. And I was actually travelling with friends when I ended up here. I was hoping to find them upstairs, but there's been no sign of them. Are there reports of any other visitors like us in the court today?'

'Not so far. But I'll have a word with the guards, make sure that if any have appeared they're treated well and brought to join us.'

The Doctor inclined his head. 'My thanks, Queen Regent. I'm very concerned for their safety.'

Mab acknowledged him with a wave of the hand and glanced back to the Brigadier. 'So what's your story? Your title's very apt. The Brigadier. A warrior for Brigida, goddess of dreams and poetry and war. I hope that's a sign of future good fortune.'

'I wouldn't know anything about that, Your Majesty. I'm from Earth, since you ask, which I gather has something to do with this place.'

'We call your world the Homelands. We only meet people from there every few centuries or so. This is the first time it's happened during my regency. Which obviously means big and meaningful changes for Avalon. And you must stop calling me Your Majesty, because I'm not.'

'Queen Regent, is it? I'll do my best. So, if we're such honoured guests, why did your men attack us?'

Mab made a tired little sigh. 'The Unseelie Court in the North, the Fair Folk, are acting up again. They've raided some of our villages. The warriors thought you were some of them, magically appeared.'

'Do we look like fairies?' murmured the Doctor.

The Brigadier raised an eyebrow. 'Don't tempt me, Doctor. So am I to take it that Avalon is actually... fairyland?'

'Sort of,' replied the Doctor. 'Save your questions. We're going to see the King.'

'And he'll explain, will he?'

Mab laughed again. 'If he does, brave one, we're all in bloody trouble.'

Fitz Kreiner woke up in his clothes and stretched, wondering what the new day would bring and longing for his first cigarette. His dreams had been the usual stately progress of sorted information, and it was always strange now to wake up into the relative chaos of waking life. There was light against his eyelids, so he didn't bother to open them yet. What had he got up to last night? His head didn't feel too bad, though there was an odd sensation about his temples. He felt as if he'd been put through a mixer, jumbled up and poured back into the shape of himself again. Though, actually, that also was a feeling that was there every time he woke up these days. But the other stuff meant, on the basis of previous experience...

He slowly reached a hand sideways across the bed. Sure enough, it encountered a warm flank. She seemed fully clothed, too. Which was odd. But at least this was an overwhelmingly familiar situation. 'Crazy!' he whispered. He rolled over and snuggled with her, rolling her curves to his, and she pleasingly complied.

Now, where had they been last night? Some club or –

A line of awful dominoes fell from one side of Fitz's brain to the other.

The Doctor and his TARDIS. Adventures in time and space.

Last night he'd been playing chess with the Doctor, who was terrible at it. The Doctor had decided they should spend some time together after their experiences on Skale. Indeed, it was in the ruins, as he was leading a party of survivors to try and locate a water supply, that the Time Lord had first mentioned taking Compassion to Earth. Her attitude to the suffering all around her was frankly pissing the locals off, and was getting in the way of the Doctor's efforts to bring all the factions together and kick start a new economy. Perhaps it was getting to the Doctor, too. It was unlike him to want to stay put, to deal with the consequences. He'd spent ages talking to the people he'd rescued from Mechta, sitting cross-legged in the meadow room, with butterflies settling on his shoulders. These days, he seemed to be concerned with everything, pondering the consequences of every action he took, involved with the people whose lives he'd crossed.

It was understandable really. The Doctor was trying so hard to be involved, to not treat the timesteam as a playground, the way the Faction Paradox did.

And of course Fitz himself had also become involved. His

thoughts murmured and toyed with the distant joy of remembering. Filippa. They had had a lifetime of togetherness during the reconstruction, weeks where he was certain he'd stay behind and live a life there with her. While the Doctor was gone, dropping Compassion off, they had lived together, doing their best with the recovering resources at hand.

It had come down to a moment as they all stood outside the TARDIS, the Doctor having made the decision to depart because it was becoming obvious that these people would survive now, that the sort of thing the Doctor did was no longer needed. So his conscience was clear and he looked happy. He accepted a little wooden figure, carved by a child. People cheered. Tattered flags were waved. It had been the exact opposite of slipping off. The Doctor had run about hugging everyone, telling them he'd come back and see them.

Fitz and Filippa had looked at each other. And before he'd even started to deal with how he felt, the love and the potential pain, she'd said: 'And will *you* come back and see me?'

He'd opened his mouth in surprise. Then he'd closed it again, realising that she knew him better than he knew himself. 'Yes,' he'd said. And he'd meant it. And they'd kissed at length like people on a promise.

The Doctor had looked absolutely surprised when Fitz walked to his side at the TARDIS door and started waving to the crowd too. As they went inside, he'd looked as if he might have asked Fitz a question, but then obviously decided against it and closed the doors.

Fitz's last look at Filippa had been on the scanner screen.

He'd been surprised that she was smiling. He'd been surprised that, for once, he'd done absolutely the right thing. Without quite knowing why.

One day he would be with her again. But not now. Perhaps the universe knew that some things were meant to happen. Despite all the latest evidence to the contrary.

They'd spent those days on the way to Compassion visiting strange dimensions. Worlds at an angle to reality. Dreamlike places.

Always shorter and shorter stops. And for some reason the corridors and the console room had started to become broody, in retrospect, full of shadows and an odd sort of sorrow, as if the TARDIS was a fond building full of memories. A house where there had been love, that one was about to move out of. The Doctor had felt it, too - he knew. He'd caught him talking to the craft late at night, his hands touching the roundels of the wall, his head leaning on the console.

So Fitz had been looking forward to their picking up Compassion, just so there would be someone else to inhabit what was starting to feel like a haunted house.

That was where they had been going on that last night. To pick up Compassion. That metal canary had been twittering and chirruping from its perch.

But: an alarm. A lurch. White light flooding the console room. The Doctor diving for the -

Boom.

Fitz's eyes flew open. He looked around.

He was in a medieval bedroom, in a vast bed, under a great mass of itchy furs. The air was full of spangly things that shone and floated.

He looked to his left.

There lay Compassion, snuggled up to him, asleep, a sort of sullen half-smile on her face.

He looked towards the door as it opened. A man with a black beard, dressed in black robes, had entered, and turned to close the door again without having seemingly noticed who was in his bed.

Wait a jiffy -

He looked back at the spangly things floating in midair. He'd made out the details of the nearest one, but his consciousness had been so surprised by it that it had told him to just move on past and get back to it whenever.

It was a tiny, sleeping fairy, its wings humming, its arms clutching its knees. It wore a little tunic and had a tiny sword.

It blinked. Opened its eyes. Looked at him.

The fairy screamed.

Fitz screamed.

Compassion woke up, looked at Fitz, and screamed.

The man by the door spun round and screamed.

Fitz and Compassion leapt out of bed on opposite sides.

All the fairies leapt, like a cartoon blob, into a jar in the furthest corner of the room.

The man by the door leapt to his desk and grabbed a sword, which he pointed waveringly in their direction.

Everybody stared at each other for a second.

'OK...' said Fitz, finally. 'We're all scared of each other, and that's very good, because I really need to know one thing.'

'Yes?' said the man carefully, keeping his sword aimed at him.

'Could you please tell me where your bathroom is?'

Mab and her party had reached a huge wooden door at the base of the stairwell. She took a key from a loop on her belt, and unlocked it. Then she put her palm on to the wood, which deformed round it for a moment. The Brigadier glanced at the Doctor as the door swung open.

'Magic,' the Doctor whispered to him.

They stepped into a vast chamber, lit only by the torches that were set into the domed stone roof at intervals in alcoves. Metal discs were set into the walls all around, shining the light back to produce a powerful glow, and the Brigadier had the sensation that he was standing in some sort of shrine. The air tasted of a church, chilly and peaceful. The torches flickered gently with the gusts of some impossible breeze that, had there been any dust, would have sent it rustling across the flagstone floor. At the centre of the room stood its dominating feature.

A simple ring of wood, on four supports, fenced off a pool of water from the narrow walkway around it, in which stood a series of lecterns carrying books, quills and parchment. A guard stood rigidly to attention at one of these lecterns, his eyes bulging at the sight of his Regent and the strangers with her.

But it was the pool itself that caught the eye. It was absolutely black, and yet ripples rebounded across its surface, catching the light of the room. It drew the eye in the way of something grand you meet in a dream. The Brigadier fought down a sudden urge to run and just dive in.

The Doctor obviously read it in his face. 'No bombing or petting in the deep end,' he whispered.

'All right, Doctor, Your Maj- Queen Regent...' The Brigadier corrected himself. 'What is this place?'

The Doctor shrugged off his coat, rolled up his sleeve, wandered up to the pool and dipped his bare elbow into it. 'Just right,' he said. 'Good to see that it's all still going so swimmingly. Swimmingly?' He looked interrogatively at them both, then shrugged his big shoulders. 'Oh well, please yourselves. At the bottom of this pool lies King Constantine, the ruler of this Celtic tribe, the Catuvelauni. Mab is the latest in a long line of his Regents, ruling for him while he sleeps, which he's been doing for over two thousand years. He's fine, or should be. This liquid is an oxygenated solution, replenished from an artificially created spring beneath the castle. He's connected to some very sophisticated temporal tracking equipment, and, moment by moment, his dreams maintain the existence of this pocket dimension, this other reality.'

The words seemed to connect to something for him, as he stood up from the pool once more, and he put a horrified hand to his mouth, deforming his expression with his fingers. 'Of course. Avalon was always her ultimate destination. Why she was taking four-dimensional telemetry from Earth. She got a sense of where the maze would lead her, what was lying at the centre of her pentagram program. This place. All those strange realities were her trying to escape her fate, trying to convince herself that... That she might find some sort of transcendence. That she wasn't going to die when she hit the gap between worlds.' His hand slowly dropped from his chin, and for a moment he was staring into space once more. 'If she's dead... If she's really dead...'

'I remember something similar to this sleeping king from Lewis Carroll,' the Brigadier said quickly, glancing between the Doctor and Mab.

'Yes, well...' The Doctor snapped out of his fugue and waved his arm to dry it. 'I may have let something slip on one of my visits. Constantine decided on this course of action during the first Roman police actions along the south coast of Britain in the first century. The Romans were invited in by one of the other tribes to settle a border dispute. They didn't realise that, when you invite a superpower over for tea, they'll be outstaying their welcome by supper and take over your spare room for the rest of the week. But the Catuvelauni were fortunate in that they'd been chanced across by a roaming unit of Gallifreyan Interventionists...'

The Brigadier glanced at Mab. She had an expression on her face as if she was fast coming towards a conclusion. He found himself tensing again.

'They,' the Doctor continued, putting his jacket back on, 'provided Constantine with the technology to dream everybody in his kingdom off into another reality, away from Roman aggression, using the collective power of the human unconscious to do it. Other tribes quickly took over the forts they'd left behind, and the location of the lost tribe became the basis for the Celtic legend of Avalon.' He looked up. 'Was there anything else?'

Before the Brigadier could ask anything, Mab interrupted.

'You're a bloody Time Lord!' she yelled. 'Why didn't you tell me, Your Lordship? We'd have sacrificed the herd and given you the pick of the youth! My adviser, Margwyn, will want to meet you! Brigida, but I've treated you roughly!' She ran to the Doctor and tried to kiss his boots, making the Doctor leap about as if his feet were on fire.

'The culture here is very influenced by Gallifrey's,' he explained, testily. 'The Time Lords, for all their professed disinterest, have interfered in the lives of billions of beings, all over the universe. The Catuvelauni are a rare example of a successful intervention on the part of my people.'

'And the weight of prophecy that you bring!' Mab continued, almost babbling. 'Something bloody huge is going to happen! The Fair Folk are probably going to invade in their thousands tomorrow!'

The Doctor, looking as angry as the Brigadier had ever seen him, finally reached down, grabbed Mab's hand and positively wrenched her to her feet. He glared at her, obviously wondering how he was going to deal with this adulation, then glanced across at the Brigadier. 'Once they were here, the Catuvelauni discovered that Constantine could manipulate this blank new reality at the vacuum level of quantum particle fluctuation.'

'Sorry, Doctor, I've lost you there.'

'As well as an exact copy of the land they'd lost, he gave his people magic, Alistair. The ability to do, build and think impossible things. Those that choose to study those arts, at least.' He turned back to Mab, his expression serious. 'But, of course, that's all over now.'

'What?' whispered Mab.

'Didn't I say? That's what I'm here to do.' He reached into the pocket of his jacket, and pulled out a tiny device. 'The deal's off, Mab. I was just playing for time until we got to this room. On behalf of the Time Lords, I'm only here to switch off Constantine's supply.'

For a moment she looked at him with dismay.

Then the Doctor was on his back, his device splintered into fragments against the far wall. Mab had her sword to his throat and her knee in his chest. 'Die for your masters, Time Lord!'

The Brigadier had started forward, but then he stopped himself, certain he understood what the Doctor was up to. The guard had reacted, too, but had stayed back, waiting for orders from his Regent.

The Doctor slumped back, letting his arms sprawl on the floor behind his head, then met Mab's gaze with laughing eyes. 'Oh, no, all my plans are foiled. Mab, Mab! Have I finally found what it takes to get you to treat a Time Lord like you treat everybody else?'

'What?' Mab looked suspiciously at him.

'Fitz will be very upset that you've broken the remote control for his telly. And we're hardly in the right place to get a new one.'

Mab got to her feet, sheathed her sword and pushed her hair back, slighted. She looked down at the Doctor. 'I could have killed you, oxhead.'

The Doctor gave her his hand and she pulled him to his feet. 'That's better.' He smiled at the Brigadier. 'So. Everything clear?'

'As crystal, Doctor. As always.' The Brigadier marvelled, once more, at this man's ability to do whatever it took to make everybody underestimate him. 'But you still haven't explained what we're actually doing here.'

'Oh. Well.' The Doctor looked sheepish. 'I haven't quite worked that one out yet.'

Mab clapped her hands together at a sudden idea. 'Oh! Come on! Let me show you some magic!' She ran to the door, then glanced back to the Doctor. 'A Time Lord. Gods. We're in for trouble now.'

'Strangely enough,' said the Brigadier, 'that's often my reaction, too.'

Margwyn gently fed the strange girl some healing potion from a beaker. 'This will ease the passage between dimensions for you,' he said. 'It also cures several common ailments, clears the skin, and can be used to strip polish from furniture.'

He watched as she sipped from the cup, aware that there were now three or four different things he had to take care of urgently, his mind swiftly balancing them against each other. The gods had placed the strangers in his chamber, so they brought a message for him personally, but already the castle was alive with rumours of other strangers. So many at once. It meant that a great change was coming. Margwyn had the terrible feeling that he knew just what that change was. It was up to him to make a balance.

He was aware of the boy stepping back inside his chamber before he spoke. 'So where are we? Who are you? Have you got any aspirin?'

Margwyn laughed, and turned to address the young whelp. 'My name is Margwyn. I'm sorry about the sword, but it's been a long time since anybody arrived in my bed unannounced, as you might imagine. I am chamber adviser to Regent Queen Mab, in whose court you, arrivals from the Homelands, have found yourself. And I don't know what aspirin is, but you should try some of this instead.' He poured Fitz a draught of the potion and handed it to him.

Fitz sniffed the cup suspiciously. 'Chamber adviser? What does that mean?'

'You choose the smallest possible question, how interesting! That means I do and say those things that have to be done and said, but that nobody wants to admit to doing or saying.' He stood up, and went to put the lid on his jar of fairies. 'Here's the situation in detail...'

Margwyn went on to explain the geographical and spatial location of the court, and how the two strangers must have got there. During his explanation, the lad had to sit down, but the girl just looked at him with patience, absorbing all he had to say. Then he asked them for their stories in turn, and grabbed a quill and parchment to record them.

He managed not to drop the quill when they first used the word 'TARDIS'.

A gentle breeze ruffled the Brigadier's hair, drying his clothes.

High up, where they were, the air was cooler, even on this shimmering summer day.

He found that he kept looking between the building behind him and the countryside all around, and feared that, if he kept on looking, some part of his mind would go beyond boggling and never return to reality from this land of dreams. He closed his eyes for a moment and just let his face appreciate the sunlight, but then had to open them to remind his senses yet again about the impossibility of where he was.

The three of them stood on a balcony on the highest tiny turret of the treelike castle that grew like a great silver oak beneath them. Its great bulk made the sun shine back at the sky. They were at least seven hundred feet off the ground. Beneath them, the castle blossomed into hundreds of turrets and spires. Inside, visible through a window at the rear of this highest observation deck, a ring of fortifications stood around the bustling tents of the central courtyard, far below. Outside, they stood above the great gates, where a bridge that looked too massive to raise lay across a great moat of shining water. Carts and horses and individuals came and went across the bridge, and off along a roughly paved road that vanished over the Downs. The countryside beyond was a bright, clear vision of green slopes, with luxuriously verdant valleys in the distance. The Brigadier saw little trails of smoke from tiny hamlets, and thin, dotted roads, but no industry, no motorways, no vehicles bigger than the tiny specks of more distant carts.

He realised that he was enjoying the act of breathing, and consciously sucked in a breath. The air was as pure and clear as the hour after a thunderstorm.

He noticed that the Doctor was looking at him again, but this time with a tiny, sad smile on his face. 'Isn't the air delicious?' he said. 'If one has to be marooned –' He shook his head as if to shy away the thought, and bounced one elegant finger along the slope of the Downs. 'Look. You can see that the shape of the downlands is the same as in your dimension.'

'Good gracious. So it is.' A sudden dark thought struck him. 'So is this the other dimension that Morgaine came from? Should we be on the lookout?'

The Doctor shook his head. 'Same idea, different dimension. The concept of Avalon recurs and reflects across the multiverse. Probably something to do with Constantine's creation of this place. I got caught up in one such recurrence myself, recently. This place really is a well at the centre of time, a space where great changes happen.' He put a hand to his temple and groaned, seeming to realise some further detail. 'My TARDIS felt this place in her future. Feared her own destruction approaching. Sensed the nature of that death. So she must have started searching for it, circling it. The dimensional disturbance on Drebnar, the gestalt dream on Skale – and finally the two together in Avalon. Why didn't I see?'

'Gods,' muttered Mab, 'death comes soon enough. Why seek it out?'

'She must have felt it was more important to face her fear,' whispered the Doctor, his eyes staring into the distance, 'than to go on living.'

The Brigadier couldn't trust his expression not to betray him. He turned aside and took his palmtop from his pocket. He hit a couple of buttons, and the device bleeped and fizzed.

Mab looked up from comforting the Doctor. 'If that's a communication device, and you're trying to get through to the Homelands, don't bother. There's no straightforward way back there. Visitors such as yourself come by accident and go by accident, as the King turns in his sleep.' She looked sadly between her two visitors. 'Forgive me, there's no easy path home for you.'

'And for me,' the Doctor added, still staring, 'there's no path anywhere.'

The Brigadier squared his shoulders. 'So if your TARDIS is gone, how did we come to be here in the first place? This magic business?'

'I think that must have something to do with it. The TARDIS was returning to this place...' The Doctor gestured to the countryside in front of him. 'This geographical location, but in your world. The TARDIS and Compassion chose the place together, of course. Tragic fate. There are no accidents.'

'Compassion? Is that the young lady I encountered on the Downs?'

'You saw her?' The Doctor leapt up from his introspective posture and clapped both hands around the Brigadier's shoulders. 'Tell me!'

'Well, I'd just met her, sitting on her packing cases, waiting for you. Then a jet went overhead, your box of tricks started to appear, everything became... strained, somehow. And your vehicle exploded.'

The Doctor turned quickly back to the battlements and gazed out over the fields once more, leaning heavily on the stonework. 'She hit the... call it a wall... between this other dimension and yours, Alistair. Constantine may have unconsciously tried to save us, by pulling us into the quantum field created by his dreams.' His voice turned dark again, as if he'd started to contemplate once more the subject that he was trying to avoid thinking of. 'Is there still no word of them?'

Servants had been reporting to Mab every few minutes, with awed little glances at the two strangers. 'No, nobody's seen anything. But there's no reason they should be in the castle. This world's as big as the whole Isle of Greater Pryddein.'

'Sorry?' asked the Brigadier.

'Britain,' translated the Doctor.

'They could be a few towns away, or even to the north, at the Unseelie Court.'

'That's comforting, thank you.'

Mab glanced at a sundial on a lower part of the tower wall, and slipped an arm round the Doctor's shoulder. 'Take yourself away from pain for a moment. You asked to see magic. It's here.'

The Brigadier and the Doctor looked up at the same moment, as something rushed between them and the sun. A dark mass had billowed out overhead, and it took the Brigadier a moment to realise what it was. A living creature. A vast pair of scaly, reptilian wings, beating the air slowly, unaerodynamically, held together by impossible sinew, tautly stretched muscles. A thin green body that tapered to a tail with a perfect, arrowlike point.

A dragon.

'Good Lord,' said the Brigadier.

The Doctor was smiling sadly up at it. 'It's beautiful.'

'Well, I say magic...' Mab put her chin on her fist, leaning on the balcony, gazing girlishly up into the sky. 'The dragons are bred and created through magic, but live as real creatures.'

There was some sort of harness fitted to the back of the beast, and, as it passed into the distance, Lethbridge-Stewart saw that it carried a rider and, behind him, a pack of secured goods the size of a lorry. 'Practical, too. You run these dragons to a timetable?'

'Right,' Mab nodded. 'They take supplies between the big farms and the communities that are far from farmland. Before you ask, yes, we could just leap them there through magic, but the power of mages is limited and needs to be conserved, used like golden leaf on the page of a book.'

'Because Constantine's management of his unconscious is also limited,' agreed the Doctor. 'He couldn't handle massive changes all the time. Every time a mage uses magic, they draw on some of the psychic energy of the King himself. I must watch that in action.'

'Oh, you will. You can become my court mage, if you like.' Mab threw her other arm around the Brigadier, then reacted to what she saw in his eyes and quickly withdrew it again. 'And you can train my warriors. Because, sorry as I am to say it, I think you'll both be staying here.'

The Brigadier and the Doctor looked at each other uneasily.

Two servants, one female, one male, stepped quickly into adjoining alcoves and watched as Mab and the Brigadier marched through the door from the battlements and off down the stairs.

'Where's Margwyn?' the woman whispered.

The man pulled a dial from his pocket. 'Going to meet Mab and the rest of the High Council. Right on time.'

'I'll get after him. You check on the weapon.'

'Why not the other way round?'

'Margwyn's a magician. He might see through your make-up.' She gestured at the man's red hair and Celtic, freckled face.

'Your call, sweetheart. The way I see it, after that nice rumpus you caused – Faerie invaders in the Great Hall! Call out the guard! – you're in charge on this one.'

'You say the sweetest things.' She placed a kiss on his cheek, but then they both started at the sound of footsteps, and leapt back into their alcoves.

The Doctor trotted past, his features grim, intent on nothing but what was in front of him.

The two servants watched him make his way down the stony stairwell.

'So... That's him,' whispered the man.

'Phwooarr!' said the woman.

'Fitz...' It was the first time, during their discussions with Margwyn, that Compassion had spoken directly to him. She was fingering her earlobe. The guy in the black robes had taken a moment to pop outside and 'take care of something', and she'd moved closer to him and, her voice level, had let out something she'd obviously been waiting to reveal. 'My link with the TARDIS has been destroyed. That means the TARDIS has been destroyed. And that means... That means something wrong is going to start happening. I don't know what. I don't know how this can have happened.'

'But...' Fitz opened his mouth in protest.

'But more than that. The last thing I know from the link – the thing that, with the last of its consciousness, the TARDIS told me – was that the Doctor was still there at the moment of its death.' She stared at Fitz blankly, as he struggled to find the feelings he needed to find at that moment in her face. 'He's dead, Fitz. He's really dead.'

'You can't be sure.'

'I am sure.'

Fitz swore, and leapt to his feet, not wanting to believe a word of this. 'We're just dreaming. This is just another dream world, another Mechta. Never mind what that guy said. We'll wake up soon and it'll just have been a trippy dream.'

She was shaking her head. He went to the door and tried to open it. It was locked. 'Yeah,' he nodded. 'I've had dreams like this.'

'Fitz... It's not a dream. Not in that way.'

He looked at her for a long moment, then went back to the door and tried it again.

Chapter Four
Woad Rage

There was something about this particular servant girl.

Margwyn stopped, as he hurried back through the carpeted halls towards his chambers, and turned to look at her, without her having uttered a word.

She was going along the skirting boards with a strange sort of duster that resembled a pink ball of feathers on a twig.

'Tell me,' he said, taking a step towards her.

'Why, sir,' she purred, looking up at him. 'I don't know what you –'

'I can see the magical aura around you, girl.' Margwyn dropped his eyes and his voice as a courtier hurried past. 'You've been near magic. Now tell me what it was or I'll break your neck.'

She appraised him for a moment, the smile staying on her face, as if daring him. 'Sir,' she said. 'I was with some of my fellows over by the dewpond on the Downs, and we saw a metal bird. Loud and high up it was. It appeared and then it vanished, with a glow about it like a rainbow. Maybe that's the magic you see on me.'

Margwyn looked hard at her, wondering if she was telling him everything, wondering if he was missing something.

She looked back, innocent.

He had no time left. He couldn't afford to ignore this, and he had to know the truth before the High Council meeting. 'Tell no one of this,' he said, and marched off down the corridor, trying not to run.

When he glanced back over his shoulder, the servant girl was gone.

The manservant was setting wine in place, alone in the great banqueting room, as the Doctor entered. He had to move aside as the Time Lord marched up to the wall and gazed at the bomb, his fingers absently twiddling.

The manservant just managed to overhear what he muttered to himself. 'What's wrong with all this? What am I being set up for now?'

When the Doctor left the room, the manservant hung on for another few moments, then burst out laughing.

Margwyn wrapped a cloak about himself and strode off across the Downs, following his senses. He'd cast a small glamour on his body so that he wouldn't be noticed. He followed the road for a while, stalking past the traders as they headed to and from market, and then struck off the road at an angle, running up and down slopes, searching desperately for the dread thing his researches had been predicting for the last year. The thing that the servant girl's story seemed to confirm.

He'd been looking into it on that fateful evening two nights ago, seeking out the place where the dreamfield was weakest, wondering if he could do anything to heal it and support the power of the sleeping King. His measuring instruments then had taken him to the same location his senses were now leading him, to his growing fear.

That night, as he stood at one corner of the castle's flattened approaches, the darkness of the castle eclipsing the full red moon behind him, he'd been aware of the approach of something huge and terrible through the sky. He'd felt the dreamfield vibrating, and wondered if everything was about to collapse, there and then, if all his plans to support the King's dreams were about to come to nothing. He'd summoned a small dragon, by speaking dragon tongue into the air and sledding it through space to him from its nest deep under the castle. He had been aware that every use of magic put more pressure on the dream, but he needed to be in the air at that moment, to meet this threat head on. And he needed nobody to know. He'd taken on this problem as his personal responsibility.

He'd hung in the air on the back of the dragon, whispering little commands to it, drumming his fingers against the nodes on its back, licking its third eye, set far back and looking upward by the saddle, to keep it calm.

The dreamfield had chimed, oscillated to a frightening pitch, then burst, for a tiny moment. Margwyn had waited for the collapse, but it hadn't come. The air was rainbowing all around them, burning away, bright like the sun.

He cast a glamour to shield them from the castle, hoping that none of the other mages were watching.

The atmosphere gave a final heave of exchange between dimensions. A wave of stinking air washed over him.

And in front of him the metal bird had appeared.

The very look of it filled Margwyn with disgust. The way the thing was designed to slam through the air, with no respect for the weave of reality that its curt wings were made to push away.

Without a moment's thought for his own safety, knowing the dreamfield would fall at any further magic taken from the King, he'd taken a decade of his lifetime and turned it into power. In agony, he made the complicated gesture and spat out the words to halt time.

He lanced the dragon through the air, and jumped on to the wing of the giant arrow. The wing had wobbled once at his impact, and he'd staggered, until the tail of the dragon had whipped round and steadied him. Far below, the timeless downlands waited for him to fall.

He tripped forward, and landed with his palms against the glass of the bird. Inside, he could see two men, their helmeted heads locked in their last gesture. Black visors made them look like terrible insects. The one in front was looking straight at him.

What could he do with this thing? He could send it back, but the dreamfield had been fundamentally weakened, as his studies had shown that it was weakening all the time. Was there some intelligence he could gain here for the war he was certain now must come?

He felt around the edges of the craft with his mind, and found it painful. The principles of impersonal weapons, designed to kill those whose faces these insect people had never seen.

When he came to the devices that hung under the wings, he had nearly fainted.

He'd put his forehead to the glass and made eye contact with the lead warrior. 'You are giving your weapon to me,' he told him. 'And that is good, you feel. That is necessary. And believe me, it is.'

He'd got back on to the dragon's back, and swung the beast under the wings. With magical digits, he'd negotiated the release of the metal tube that contained such vast, city-destroying evil. Then he had made the dragon take him and the device away, and, reaching delicately into the dreamfield, had nudged reality. The field sprang back to where it had been, and the metal bird had vanished back into its own world.

But looking over his shoulder, as the dragon had flown him back to the castle, Margwyn had understood that the weave of the dream had been for ever weakened. It was thinnest at that very point where he'd met the terrifying war craft from another dimension.

He'd given the tubular device to Mab, claiming that he'd found it on the Downs, as objects from the Homelands often appeared. The power of the thing was too obvious for him to hide it: the mages of the court would have been at his door in moments.

As Mab had delighted over the find, wondering about the best place to display it on the banqueting-hall walls, Margwyn had watched her, sadly, feeling every bit of the love and loyalty he'd ever borne her. Knowing that he was going to have to lie and lie again, and finally, if it came to that, betray this innocent and delightful woman, in order to save what she stood for.

He had gone to her as the servants had hoisted the weapon into position on the wall, and embraced her, kissing her forehead.

Now he stood at that same point on the Downs as he had been before, and looked in sadness at what stood in the air before him.

A rippling curtain of air, a vortex that was growing ever stronger as the atmosphere had begun to rush from one dimension to another. He heard a distant call, and saw a farmer with his horse and his child, ploughing a far hillside. They were pointing towards the effect.

He couldn't hide this now. It was too big. He must take his courage in his hands and do the terrible things he needed to do.

'I am a leaf in the wind, Mab,' he whispered. 'I am powerless to prevent this. May all the gods forgive me.'

Then he turned and marched, then started to run, back towards the castle.

Mab settled herself into her throne in the High Council Chamber and waited. She was the first to arrive under the hexagonal ceiling, as always. She seemed to be the only one of the Council who actively enjoyed these weekly discussions. And today she had so much to tell them, if they hadn't already heard the rumours rippling around the Court. The first Appearance of her Regency, and it was an actual Time Lord! There was darkness in that, of course, the worry about the size of the change to Avalon that his arrival indicated, but still! Her mother, the previous Queen Regent, had paid host to a group of people called Muslims, fifty years ago, and declared a holiday. She must think of something grand besides tonight's banquet.

And with the Time Lord had come the warrior of Brigida. That was so apt. He bore some private pain, and bore it well, but it was eating him inside. He was waiting for the breaking wave of chaos which those who followed Brigida embraced, the feeling of being swept downstream. He needed that, anyone could see, because he was keeping a fortress inside, and supplies and guards were down to a minimum.

He would need help, also, with that pain. Someone to talk to at length. She wanted to hear about where he came from, the wonders of the Homelands. And the wonder and purpose that brought him here. He had a face that would smile well, she thought. She would like to see that more.

She realised that she'd got so deep in thought, a little smile on her face, that she hadn't acknowledged Gwyn, the troubled Captain of the Guard, and Castellan McKewon as they took their seats. She did so now, a little inclination of the head. The Keeper of the Memory bustled in also, chuckling to himself.

Dear Margwyn was the last in, sauntering through the door as always, with the easy confidence of someone who knew everybody's business. She hoped she could surprise him with the news. He took his seat and cast a plain smile in her direction. Perhaps he hadn't heard, because he looked almost bored. Wonderful!

She clapped her hands. 'In Constantine's name, let us begin. The first point, as always –'

'The raids by the Fair Folk in the North!' Gwyn leapt to his feet, as he always did these days. 'They took loot and children, children to be their changelings, from three villages last month! The Northern folk call on us every day to do something! Fairy dragons have been seen as far south as Gallowmyr! When are we going to take action?'

Mab sighed. On today of all days. But Gwyn was right, at heart. 'That's been your only bloody point for the last six months, good Gwyn. Our Northern villagers have been guilty of raiding their sets, too.' She looked to Margwyn. 'And I suppose your counterargument is the same as always, dear Margwyn?'

'That we should send another ambassador, arrange an exchange of visitors, deal with the Unseelie Court.' Her chamber adviser had closed his eyes, his head resting on the back of his chair, looking tired of these arguments. And who could blame him? 'We are in their land. They are the original inhabitants of this world, the originators of magic before Constantine brought us here, the stock from which even our dragons are bred.' He opened his eyes again, and spread his palms on the table. 'By Brigida, why can we not talk to them?'

'The mages do have an ambassador in training. It takes time to prepare for the Unseelie Court.'

Gwyn was yelling now. 'One swift, dragon-borne strike, one great magical blow to wipe them all –'

'One great magical blow?' Margwyn looked aghast. 'Against the progenitors of magic? What sort of soldier are you, to put forward such disaster in the name of tactics?'

Gwyn snarled. 'You always were half-fairy, Margwyn! Your loyalties aren't to your own kind!'

'My loyalties?' Margwyn stood himself, and for a moment Mab thought she saw a flutter in his composure. 'My only loyalty is to my Queen Regent and to the safety of Avalon!'

'You are both loyal subjects!' Mab bellowed, tired of this. 'Sit down! And now, yes, today, I know that I vowed that we would come to some decision between your two desires.'

'Between –' began Gwyn.

'However,' she interrupted. 'There's a new factor arrived. Which is why there's the feast tonight – you'll have seen the preparations. Dear friends, can't you just shut up for a bit? We have guests from the Homelands!'

'What?' Gwyn burst into a smile. 'I've waited my whole life for this!'

The Castellan stroked his long white beard and smiled toothily. 'I had heard rumours of strangers, but I had not dared to dream…'

'The last time this happened was during your mother's time,' noted the Keeper of the Memory, who was bald, and wore a little white cap above his ceremonial collar.

Margwyn met Mab's merry glance, and gave in with a happy chuckle. 'Yes,' he said. 'I'd heard, because it's my job to hear. But I thought I'd let you make the announcement.'

Mab thumped the table in friendly frustration. 'I knew it. I suppose it was sending those guards around asking after strangers. Have you heard anything about any other new arrivals?'

Margwyn spread his hands before her. 'If we had any more guests, I'm sure they would have come to my attention by now.'

The Brigadier had been wandering the castle, trying to make his senses fully understand where he was. Everywhere he went, he was surrounded by groups of people, who wanted him to sit down and answer questions. Initially, he'd done so, holding particular court on a wet step outside a storeroom doorway in the market, with the crowd around him growing bigger all the time. 'Are you a sign that we'll go to war with the Fair Folk?' one man wanted to know. The Brigadier had simply said that he was here by accident, that this seemed like a dream to him. He had wondered why that had elicited laughter until he remembered what he'd been told about this place.

He'd stood up, patted down his trousers, and tried to get away, which had proved impossible, the crowd pushing after him this way and that, until a guard who'd been watching from inside the storehouse had unlocked the door and let him escape to the cooler air inside.

From there, he'd returned to the battlements for a while to stare out at the placid expanse of the downland. It was like when he'd first arrived in Africa, that sense of physical surprise, which so much fades with repeated travel, that there are people here, in a place you never knew existed, who have agendas and goings on of their own. The land of dreams. He watched the watercolours of rain clouds on the horizon. He wondered if this was in some way heaven, if she, or the dream she lived in, was out there somewhere. He'd been so busy since he got here, and now he was so tired.

Mab had said something, before she left him, about a banquet tonight. He didn't want that. She'd also said that she meant to talk to him at length later. He wanted that, but not the way she did. She had the same thought in her mind as Cronin, he could see it in her eyes. She wanted to split him open so that everybody would feel better about how he was feeling now. Except him. His own thoughts of talking at length with Mab would be about asking her about this place, hearing about the peoples here, and their history, and getting some gen on these Fair Folk and what sort of a threat they posed. She would be entertaining company.

He closed his eyes and gently stubbed his toe on the battlement he was leaning against, the smallest possible kick. Bad thought. Couldn't think like that. He found himself on the far shores of sleep with his eyes closed like that, and saw bubbles coming up from deep water, and felt the coldness around him again, her flailing away through the foam.

Never see her again.

It was a long way down from here. He could feel the warmth and the late-afternoon wind on his face, and the thought of death made him feel close to her again.

I will come to you, I promise. Soon. These distractions only hurt.

'Alistair.' The gentle breath of a voice made him open his eyes.

He turned and smiled at the Doctor.'Good Lord, Doctor, I nearly fell asleep. Occupational hazard of hopping between dimensions, this time-lag business, what?'

He wasn't going to be deflected, standing there with his arms by his side, silhouetted against the low sun, still full of his own pain.'Alistair, what's wrong?'

'Wrong?' The Brigadier made an expression as though he was considering a menu.'Nothing in particular. Tired, as I said.'

'You might never get home again. You're separated from everybody you care about. But you're just tired?'

He gave a little laugh, which he choked on, and had to turn his back, pretending to look out at the Downs again.'You know me,' he managed to say.'A bit set in my ways, but always ready to -' Suddenly he felt really angry with himself. He was being a coward. He turned back to the Doctor and squared his shoulders.'Actually, Doctor, there is one thing you ought to know. Change in my life. Probably won't mean much to you, but -'

The door to the balcony burst open and Mab barrelled in, now clad in a green gown that displayed a vast cleavage, flowers garlanded in her hair. She still wore the amulet that had made the Brigadier harrumph to himself the first time he'd seen it. 'There you both are! Didn't you hear the trumpets? Everybody's waiting for you! Now come on!'

She grabbed them by the hands and led them off at a sprint down the stairwell.

The Doctor managed to turn back to the Brigadier as they were dragged along.'What is it? You must tell me.'

The Brigadier was holding the muscles of his face tight as his stomach cramped. He was holding so much inside, and, being a bloody fool, he had nearly let it all out. He managed something that was in some way like a merry look.

'I'll explain later,' he said.

Fitz and Compassion jumped as the key turned in the lock of the door. They dived from where they had been examining Margwyn's books and instruments, and back to the same position they had occupied when he had left them, sitting on his bed.

Margwyn came through the doorway carrying a bundle of cloth under his arm, a frightened expression on his face. 'Do you trust me?' he asked. 'No, you haven't yet had time to, but you have to make a decision.'

'What?' Fitz could hear the tone of near panic in the mage's voice.

Margwyn uncovered his bundle quickly and set it down upon the bed.

'Now that...' Fitz waved a finger in the air. 'That's a bomb, isn't it? And that's a radiation symbol. You know, I was really hoping never to be in the same room as one of those.'

Compassion reached out to touch the bomb and nodded to him. 'It's a real nuclear device.'

Margwyn wrapped it up again. 'A gateway has opened between this dimension and your own –'

'Great! Sod this for a game of soldiers, let's get back to our own planet.'

'If only it were that simple. The gateway is guarded. My tribe, the primitive fools, have made a bargain with those that rule the land of Britain in your dimension in your year of –' he made a quick calculation – '2012. Those rulers are weak and mean of heart.'

Fitz looked to Compassion again. 'You were there. Is that true?'

Compassion thought for a moment. 'Everybody seemed to think they were. But it wasn't a military state or a dictatorship.'

'Doesn't have to be for big stuff to be going down.'

Margwyn grabbed his arm. 'We have no time for debate. Those rulers have given my tribe this bomb and will give them many others. They are savages, not ready for such knowledge. I intend to take the bomb to the Faerie Folk, a more civilised race.'

Fitz felt his brain gurgling with the strain again. 'Fine. Arm the fairies. Good luck with that. Now about that gateway home –'

'You do not understand! My people know you're here. They are coming to kill you! Here –' he tossed them two robes from the bundle – 'put these on. We will flee North. I think I can get you down one of the side stairwells that only I know about, but we have only minutes.'

'Why do they want to kill us?' asked Compassion.

'Because you are visitors!' he started hauling her arms into the grey robe. 'The tribe fears visitors. They are often ritually sacrificed in the wicker gods. I was hoping I might use my influence to have you treated as honoured guests, like the invaders from 2012, but Gwyn, the other mage, detected your presence. Please, my life is at stake, too! I sheltered you!'

Fitz looked desperately between the hawklike mage and the calm visage of Compassion. 'What do you think?'

'We have no way of knowing.'

'Then how...?' Fitz paused. From down the corridor he could hear a great shouting approaching. He swore and dived for the robe. 'Fine! I hear them! Let's get out of here!'

Margwyn opened the door, looked right and left, and shouted for them to follow. Just about in their robes, which turned out to be grey cowls with long hoods, Fitz and Compassion raced after him out of the doorway, and into a side door opposite.

After a moment, in the room they had left behind, the lid of the jar that contained the fairies sprang open. In a blur of energy and light, the tiny creatures swirled about the room, making selected items of furniture and equipment glow with magic. The mass of fairies then leapt to the window, and became a thin beam of light, which, bathing the room in a golden haze as it went, focused at a point on the northern horizon, blazed for a moment, and then vanished.

And when it vanished, the items in the room that had been glowing vanished with it.

Outside in the corridor, the noise of a great crowd roared up a flight of stairs, round a corner, and swirled outside Margwyn's room, rising to a crescendo before it too started to fade away.

Soon, the light and the sound had gone, and the corner of the castle where Margwyn had lived was quiet again, and far emptier than it had been before.

And in the sky towards the North, framed in the window of his rooms that looked out in that direction, a dragon flew as fast as it could go, bearing three figures on its back.

Mab led the Brigadier and the Doctor down a curving marble staircase that led to the doors of the banqueting hall. The doors were ceremonially closed, with a huge wooden bar laid across them, and four burly servants standing ready to lift it aside. The whole lobby outside the doors, the Brigadier noted with a little lurch of his stomach, was full of people: courtiers in elaborate robes, ladies in the most beautiful gowns and hats, minstrels with bagpipes and stringed instruments. Everywhere was fur and silver and a liquid style of golden ornament where legendary creatures with bulging eyes stared back from buckles and brooches that clasped cloaks over the shoulder. The folk, bearded, long-haired, fair-skinned and freckled, had started to shout and stamp their feet in welcome. Among them were already moving servants with gleaming shields upon which sat beakers and metal flagons and skins of wine and beer. All the gleaming surfaces reflected light from a huge wooden chandelier, a wheel of torches, which was suspended overhead from several taut ropes.

Mab waved her arms in the air for silence. Then when that didn't work she hollered, 'Oh by Cernac's Cauldron shut up!' The noise died down to merry chuckles, people craning their necks to see the two strangers better. 'These are our guests, the Time Lord called the Doctor –' a great roar again – 'and Alistair Lethbridge-Stewart, the *Brigidier*, who's one of us!' The *Brigidier* was oddly gratified that his roar seemed just as loud. 'Now let them into the hall and let the feast begin!'

The servants lifted the great bar away from the doors, and the crowd rushed back to allow Mab and the strangers through. Mab stood aside, and indicated to the Doctor that he should open the doors.

With a little self-mocking smile, he put one palm to each door and pushed forward.

The doors swung back. Inside the hall, vast tables were laid with generous helpings of food, with whole animals roasting on spits.

Minstrels struck up a blaze of piping from both inside the hall on galleries and outside in the crowd. But, among the colour and the noise and the food smells that flooded his senses, the Brigadier could see only one thing about the room in front of him.

There was still a pair of brackets on the wall above the great fireplace. But now they were empty.

The nuclear bomb had gone.

As the crowd flooded into the room behind him, he turned and tried to make his voice heard above the noise. They didn't understand – most of them wouldn't have known that the bomb had been there in the first place. He struggled through the crowd towards the Doctor, who was similarly working his way through to Mab.

They both got to her at once.

'Queen Regent,' began the Doctor. 'Your people are in terrible danger. We must –'

The noise was so huge that it took the Brigadier a second to register that it had arrived.

All the windows exploded at once.

Shields flew from the wall.

The great crowd all fell in the same direction, swept off their feet. Mab grabbed at the Brigadier and they fell together, hitting the surface of a table that had pitched up at an angle, throwing its contents to the floor.

He took her head and buried it in his shoulder, thinking, in that animal second, that it was the bomb going off. That in a glorious moment they would all be dust and he would be free.

The Doctor had remained on his feet. He sprinted across the room, leaping over people, hurdled his way up on to a table and made it to a window where he could look out over the land.

'What is it?' called the Brigadier, as he and Mab clambered to their feet. 'What's happened?'

The Doctor was staring out at something on the downlands, his eyes full of terrible thoughts. 'The sky's falling,' he whispered.

The swiftly assembled cavalry unit galloped across the Downs,

Mab and the warrior called Gwyn at its head, the Doctor and the Brigadier somewhere near the back, struggling to keep up with the Celts. The Brigadier had worried, for a moment, in the light of Mab's threat, about stepping outside the castle, but the Doctor had assured him that now all ceremony had been forgotten, as it was by the Celts when it suited them.

Their target loomed ahead, the terrible thing that the Doctor had seen through the castle window. It was a rainbowing circle hovering just above ground level, a steady vortex of peacock colours that spun and shimmered in the twilight. Through it could be seen a clear circle of bluer sky. A patch of daylight against the dark.

Mab and Gwyn dismounted with a leap. By the time their two guests had caught up, they were already gazing through the circle in horror. It was an astonishing sight, a wheel like a galaxy spinning in the air, its nethermost tip dipping beneath the level of the ground and making that spot look almost translucent where it touched. It made no sound as it spun, and smelled of ozone, of molecules being ripped apart. Through its centre a patch of downland was visible that was the perfect jigsaw match for the Downs that lay all around them. Except here it was evening and there it was daylight, and in that blue sky the Brigadier could see a distant aircraft passing.

'Is it stable?' Mab was asking an elderly man with a beard and a high collar.

The Doctor ran up to the vortex and held a palm out, like a mime artist describing a wall. 'Oh yes, it's stable all right,' he called out. 'It's sustaining itself, drawing energy from both worlds. I have no idea how, but...' He put a hand to his chin, forming his mouth into a thoughtful oval. 'This is going to be a regular fixture of your land, Queen Regent.'

'Jolly good.' The Brigadier glanced at the horrified faces around him. 'That means we can get home, doesn't it, Doctor?'

'Yes, Alistair, yes!' The Doctor sounded like an adult admonishing a backward child. 'But it also means a lot more than that. For everyone in this world and everyone in yours.'

But the Brigadier had seen something through the vortex. He stepped forward, despite Mab's sudden grab at his sleeve, a protective gesture, and approached the circle of daylight. A figure was slowly, carefully, making its way across the glimpsed patch of downland in the other dimension, heading for the circle. It was a man, and from the look on his face he could obviously see the effect from his side as well. The Brigadier thought he understood now. 'I take it you mean that, after so many years of separation, a gateway between dimensions like this could cause havoc.' He glanced back to the others.

Mab nodded desperately. She looked utterly lost. 'It's the prophecy you brought with you. It's the end of everything.'

'Not necessarily. I may not be a mage like the Doctor, but I am good at certain things, you know.' He took a step closer to the vortex, clasped his hands behind his back, and cleared his throat. The figure on the other side of the vortex was close enough to make out now. It was a hiker with a huge rucksack on his back. 'Corporal Chambers, isn't it?' the Brigadier called out.

The man didn't answer. He just approached the vortex until he was a few feet away, staring at it with his mouth open.

'I asked you a question, Corporal!' called the Brigadier. 'Come on, man, we haven't got all day.'

The man snapped to salute. 'Sir, yes sir, Corporal Chambers, sir!'

'Good man. Glad we found a UNIT chap up here. You'll be able to take this on board, get the job done and not ask a lot of fool questions, won't you, Corporal?'

'Yes, sir.' The man's gaze had gone past his superior officer to rest on the Celts now.

The Brigadier was aware, with his old battlefield senses, of the warriors getting scared, probably putting their hands on their swords. 'I want you to round up everybody patrolling the Downs, Corporal. Top priority. Get them to erect an emergency perimeter around this site. Put a tent over this thing. Then get on the blower to Colonel Munro at HQ. We'll need an exclusion perimeter around the entire Downs. Nobody is to see this effect unless they're military. Our military. Do you understand?'

'Sir.'

'What time is it over there?'

'Six hundred hours, sir.'

'Then you've got a bit of time to get this done, haven't you? Move!'

The man, all uncertainty banished, ran off back across the Downs. The Brigadier turned back to the others. 'Damage limitation, at least, Queen Regent,' he said. 'You won't get tourists wandering in.'

Mab and her warrior chief were still looking superstitiously awed and afraid. But it was the look on the Doctor's face that worried the Brigadier most. He was staring straight at him, looking as if he had already weighed up all the possibilities and come to a horrifying conclusion.

He was looking at the Brigadier as if he, suddenly, had become the enemy.

'Well,' said the Brigadier. 'Don't thank me all at once, will you?'

Mab ran up the stairs, wishing she could be without the sick fear that made every step feel nightmarish. It was just change. A warrior rode change like an unruly horse, and laughed when it threw her. She'd been afraid during every skirmish she'd fought, as she was certain all good warriors were, and the feeling wasn't a stranger. She'd always stayed on top of it, always laughed with it, even when a brigand in Savernake had cut her off from the cavalry and put a sword through her side. She'd known in that moment that she might die, but had used the rage that had given her to lop the man's head from his shoulders. And the next, and the next, until her own troops had found her and she'd let herself collapse, bellowing with laughter at her own foolishness.

This fear was different, a fear of impotence, where a warrior or ruler needed to lay her hands on the reins, to do something. This was the sort of fear she'd never got the hang of.

She'd left a troop of cavalry, and the Keeper, at the gateway to watch developments on the other side, as well as to keep back the awed crowd of those who'd arrived for the banquet, and then she'd immediately called a High Council meeting. She'd added the Doctor and the Brigadier to the Council for the time being. However, after a few minutes, it had become clear that Margwyn wasn't going to arrive, that the tolling of the great bell had failed to summon him.

She shouldn't have come in person, she chided herself as she reached his door. As they rode this crisis, that was an impulse she was going to be able to follow less and less, to do everything on her own. Why hadn't Mother survived for this?

She thumped on the door urgently. 'Margwyn! Are you there? We need you.' No response.

She tried the lock and found the door was open.

The emptiness of the room shocked her. Made her fearful. And then, as she threw aside the quilts and pulled over the empty bookcases, and kicked open the chests, that fear was replaced by a more overwhelming horror, something that made her stop in the middle of the room, panting.

She knew now what had happened. It took her a moment to make herself take it on board, to try to ride it.

If Margwyn had been taken, then those who had taken him had also taken his every useful chattel, even large items of furniture.

She ran to the window and spat curses to the North, hoping that some magical sense of his would let the man who had been her oldest friend, who had been beside her since childhood, hear them. 'I'll take your head myself, you traitor!' she screamed. 'I will take your head with my own sword!'

And then she sat down on the bed for a second, just a second, and clenched her teeth against weeping.

She found the rage and kept it. It let her go on.

She stood up straight, squared her shoulders, and put on her Queen Regent expression. The rage she fixed on to her face as determination.

She waited until the servants had opened the doors of the High Council chamber for her, and strode inside, unhurriedly.

Gwyn was pacing by one window, and the Doctor stood by

another, his hands curled behind his back. The Brigadier and the Castellan were sitting at the great table, waiting.

'Well?' asked Gwyn. 'Where is he?'

'Be silent,' Mab said. 'Sit down.'

Gwyn looked at her, shocked, then smiled as he went to sit, as if pleased by this change. The Doctor turned from the window and wandered to his seat, his eyes elsewhere.

'So,' the Brigadier began. 'What's become of your chap?'

Mab waited until she had seated herself, and regarded them all coolly. 'Margwyn has betrayed us,' she said.

High in the sky above the land of dreams, the dragon bearing Margwyn, Compassion, Fitz and the nuclear bomb powered its way north. The mage's eyes were fixed on the horizon, his hands taut on the reins that kept the great beast set on course. The air, even this high, was warm, and Fitz had succumbed to the shock, asleep in his harness.

Compassion looked down at the landscape beneath her, the tiny villages and the long, winding roads, the lakes and streams shining in the moonlight, and found herself thinking about change.

There was a feeling to change, she decided. The future arriving, with all its surprise, could feel like swallowing something too cold to keep down.

And the change that was coming was going to be bigger than this, she knew somewhere inside her. This was only the beginning.

She turned on to her side, pulled the harness more tightly about her and made herself sleep.

Mab found the Brigadier waiting in her chambers, standing stiffly by the window, looking out as the full darkness of night fell. Among all the chaos of calling in the warriors and dispersing the banquet guests and the planning meetings with the High Council that had gone on for hours, she had taken a moment aside to order him to come here alone. There was bad business, secret business, to be done.

'You can smell the change in the air,' he said, his hands clasped behind his back in that odd, knotted way of his. 'It's coming through the gateway. The pollution.'

She went to him, now deliberately avoiding putting her hand on his shoulder. 'You know why I called you here.'

He turned to her, and she saw that his eyes were red from the strain of the day. 'You want to know the situation with my people. Who's in charge. What their attitude is. How we can help if you have to confront your enemies. And you will have to. Because now they have that bomb.'

They both sounded as if they already knew where this was going, she thought. As if they were being thrown by a wave, swept along by history, not quite managing to ride it. Their voices sounded dead. 'So your people can help?'

'Of course we can. I know what my people will say.'

Mab nodded. 'Because we're a strategic resource to you. A great shelter. A place to hide things from a storm. A place to come out from in unexpected directions.'

He looked her in the eye. 'You have magic. We have science. We can help you win any war you choose to fight. You can help us win any that we do.'

'So we benefit each other.'

'Indeed.'

She folded her fingers to her lips, surprised at the feel of human skin again. 'Gods, this will be so terrible. Everything will just unfold and it will be beyond our power to stop it. Can we do this?'

The Brigadier looked terribly sad and serious. He was, she realised, just as lost as she was. 'Can we not?' he said.

The Keeper of the Memory was meditating when he felt the shadow fall across him. His examination of the contents of his own mind, and of recent events, halted. His senses prickled with the presence that now swept over him.

The shadow was a cold thing, a path where something without comfort, without hearth, had trodden. The chill it brought with it was that of the first breeze of autumn at the end of summer. It was a cold that said everything could change, and that those things one held on to were impermanent.

The Keeper opened his eyes, not knowing what he was going to see standing at the threshold of his chamber.

'Doctor,' he said. 'I am honoured.'

The Doctor stepped into the manuscript-strewn room, barely acknowledging the Keeper, and his shadow moved with him, away from the old man, to be thrown instead on to the far wall of the chamber, where it loomed like a demon. 'I hear you can tell me what I need to know,' he said.

'That is my function.' The Keeper got to his feet, scared by the presence of the Time Lord. 'I record the past and observe the present.'

'Then tell me this...' The Time Lord flexed his fingers behind his neck, aching with the weight of the burden of whatever question he'd brought here. 'Are they alive?'

'Who do you –'

'My TARDIS. And my friends who were passengers in it at the site of its destruction. Can you find what happened to them?'

The Keeper inclined his head slightly, and went to fetch his small cauldron from his shelves. Into it he poured a quantity of blessed water from the castle spring. Then he added the correct herbs, and ran his finger round the rim, humming the words of power out of his diaphragm, the words that made the cauldron glow and the water turn into star stuff.

The Doctor strode to his side and looked boldly into the vessel as the water became a vortex. A grid. A map.

A circle swept at the centre of the map, the centre of a pentagram. And towards the centre was swirled a tiny star. The star hit the circle, and was dispersed into a sweep of colour, then vanished with a whisper.

The Doctor made a little dying noise, deep in his throat.

The Keeper, more scared than ever, dipped the tip of his finger into the liquid, closed his eyes, and let the memories flood into him. He was more thankful for their message. 'As for your friends,' he said, 'I have no knowledge of them. They may be shielded from me. But there is no information concerning their deaths.'

He opened his eyes to offer words of comfort to the Time Lord. But the man had gone, taking his shadow with him.

The Keeper let out a long, low breath of relief, and sent a prayer to his gods to protect the Doctor on whatever path he had now set himself.

They took an honour guard to welcome Colonel Munro through the gateway. Lethbridge-Stewart had sent ahead for a dress uniform. It was a relief to be back in it, out of those wet clothes.

UNIT through and through, he thought as he watched the stern-looking elderly man step on to the furs that had been thrown down in front of him, looking around with no more interest than if he'd just got off the shuttle to Edinburgh. It was completely dark on this side of the gate now, and the other side was a sickly green, sunlight filtered through a camouflage tent. The scene on this side was lit by an avenue of blazing torches carried by servants. Lethbridge-Stewart looked at one of them. The young boy was staring at the man who'd just stepped through from another dimension, openly terrified of him.

'Queen Regent, sir, Doctor.' Munro nodded in all the right directions. The Brigadier had been briefing him from just the other side of the gateway via his palmtop. Things over there had been happening with frightening speed since he'd put Mab's offer to the Prime Minister. The PM had already heard intelligence reports from soldiers on the Downs, so there was no credibility problem. The Brigadier had specifically mentioned the pilot who lost the bomb, the man Bedser, and made certain that now, in the face of developments, he'd face no more questioning of his loyalty or sanity and would be returned to duty. Such preliminaries over with, the PM had asked him why he was bringing this to her, rather than to Geneva, and, when he had no good answer, had then ordered him not to take the information to anyone else.

That had been a relief. He hadn't questioned the PM's ability to give him that order, he'd just said 'Yes, ma'am'. He had no idea why his instincts had led him that way, other than the rather disturbing thought that his immediate impulse these days was to take care of his own and damn the rest of them. That this was the first strategic advantage Britain could claim for her own in years. That it was a vast one, and that it was theirs, and shouldn't be shared.

He hadn't even thought about why he was doing it that way at the time. Jolly good thing, too, some part of him whispered. There was a time when you would have fought for your independence and fair shares all round. But now you know life isn't fair, that everyone has to look out for their own – in this world or Avalon.

This isn't you, part of him whispered. This is what they fished up out of the ocean. It looks like you, and it's kept going in your place, but it isn't you.

He shoved the thought back down inside him.

Behind Munro came a squad of Royal Marines in full camouflage gear with yomping packs and slung weapons, their faces not quite as stony as Munro's had been. 'I bring greetings from His Majesty and the Prime Minister,' said the colonel.

Mab stepped forward, carrying some sort of ceremonial mace. Servants held the train of her robe behind her. 'And I offer the hospitality of the Court of King Constantine of the Catuvelauni.'

Munro looked behind him, and the Marines stepped aside to allow the new arrival through. A slim, dapper man in a suit and tie stepped through the gateway, carrying a briefcase. 'Allow me to introduce Sir Charles Finningley, Ambassador to the Court of St James.'

Finningley bowed. 'My job, Queen Regent, is to establish full diplomatic relations between the United Kingdom and the Kingdom of the Catuvelauni.'

The Brigadier became aware of a tall presence behind his shoulder. He didn't need to look. 'Doctor,' he murmured. 'Thought you'd be pleased. No danger of discord between dimensions.'

'Don't patronise me, Alistair,' the soft voice murmured back. The tone was mild, but there was no denying the force behind the words. 'Why isn't this a UN delegation?'

'Simpler to begin with –'

'Because an extradimensional bolt hole is a strategic advantage.' The Brigadier looked up, and saw that the Doctor was hugging himself, as if he was cold in the warm evening. 'You haven't told the UN, have you?'

'It's for the good of Avalon, also, Doctor. The Unseelie Court apparently have the ability to duplicate our nuclear bomb with great speed. With that, they could come south in strength, perhaps conquer the entire dimension. Our presence –'

'What's happened to you? What's changed you to make you capable of this?'

He carefully finished the sentence that he'd started. 'Our presence here will see to it that doesn't happen.'

The Doctor's gaze settled on him, and the Brigadier almost flinched at the wildness that was now in those passionate eyes. They seemed to glitter slightly in the twilight, two mad stars. Lethbridge-Stewart made himself gaze steadily back, although the look made something tremble in the pit of his stomach. He wondered briefly if all the monsters this man had faced had also known they were wrong, and if they also, like him, knew they had no alternative. 'So you dare to do this in the Land of Dreams?' the Doctor whispered. 'Such arrogance. Such interference. There's bound to be war here now. You know that, don't you?'

The Brigadier composed himself. 'I know nothing of the sort.'

The eyes held him for a moment more. Then their owner was gone, without another word.

Lethbridge-Stewart turned back to where Finningley was kissing Mab's knuckle.

He realised with a jolt that he was full of rage again. That he just wanted to throw down his cap and stamp on it.

He squared his shoulders and folded his shaking hands behind his back. From now on, there wasn't a damn thing he was going to be able to do about that.

The manservant and the maid met outside a particularly large store cupboard at the back of the pantry. They smacked palms and wrapped their forearms together.

'What fools these mortals be,' said the manservant.

'Every single detail went as planned!' giggled the maid. 'They all acted just how we thought they would! Are we time meddlers or what?'

'We make Faction Paradox look like Melkurs! So, are we out of here?'

The maid kissed the manservant deeply, and licked off a thin streak of his make-up. 'Mmm, vanilla. Exit Cavis and Gandar, stage left.'

'And when next the curtain rises...' He took a key from his pocket, opened the cupboard, and beckoned her to go in.

'We rejoin them in the Unseelie Court. For Act Two. War in the land of human dreams. And the dreams of our mistress will all come true.'

They stepped inside the cupboard, and closed the door behind them.

After a moment, with a wheezing, groaning sound, the cupboard faded away.

The Doctor stood on the highest balcony of the castle, his arms straight rods, his hands clasping the parapet. He watched the tiny parade of torches below grow bigger and bigger, and then washes of brilliant, artificial light arrive as the mechanical cough of a generator truck started up, and destroyed the peace of Avalon.

He let go of the masonry, disgusted, and straightened up. He made as if to go for a moment, but then turned back to the night, and addressed the northern horizon. 'Compassion, Fitz, wherever you are...' he murmured. And wherever that was suddenly felt like a vast distance, further than he could even imagine, a distance that made an irony of his words. 'Hold on. I will find you. I will save you. I promise.'

And, looking as if he didn't quite believe himself any more, he opened a door and slipped back into the castle.

Part Two
War in Avalon

Chapter Five
And You May Find Yourself

Look at the Kingdom of Avalon down there, that small group of islands, nestling in its own little dimension. To the south there is downland and the great forests. To the west stretch vast marshes and mines and island communities. To the east is fenland, flat stretches of farmland reclaimed from the sea. How the Catuvelauni have prospered here, over the centuries, filling the whole space with their kin! Celts trade and fish and mend and build, and in the bigger communities they speculate and insure and mortgage and invest.

But to the north, past the lakeland fishing communities, we find the grey area beginning. Here, isolated villages of the Fair Folk nestle along the curves of the rivers beside villages of human kind. There is trade, some exchange of ideas, visitors come and go. But there has never been trust: these transactions are always noted, always careful. For each community fears what lies beyond: the dark, swirling, magical lands of the Unseelie Court to the north; the insectlike breeding and building of the base humans to the south. And each fears that the other will expand. Indeed, we have reached the point where one or the other will have to. The humans think the Faeries steal their babies, perhaps a gut reaction to the terrible knowledge that the humans have stolen the Faeries' land and their magic. But the humans would say that Constantine the Great brought them all here. He took the humans from their Earthly home, and with them he must have brought some spark of belief or knowledge about the Fair Folk, or perhaps some individuals that everyone thought to be only legends, from caves beneath the Downs. However he brought them, they fed on magic and prospered, and somehow acquired a history here, an origin far back in time, before this dimension existed.

Perhaps they are here because this is where Constantine's unconscious thoughts, unruly as they always were, put them.

Perhaps the Celts needed something to be guilty of, so they would not think this place to be a heaven.

Or perhaps there was a darker impulse at work, determining the possibility of war.

But now there is conflict in Constantine's dreamlands. Along that river border walk two thieves, clothed so he cannot properly see them. Where they walk, villages explode in flame, babies cry and are silenced, ships are holed on rocks that were not previously there. They make him tremble in his dream, at the thought of such an infection. He can sense a purpose in the dreamlands that, for the first time, is not his.

If this is not heaven for the Celts, why, then this must be an Earthly paradise. A paradise that will fall.

Unless someone can redeem it.

The Brigadier woke suddenly, thrashing his arms out to find her in bed next to him, to find the female voice that had been talking in his ear.

Alone. Of course he was alone.

Mab had made a number of the castle's dungeons and chambers available as extra accommodation for the troops as they arrived at the base, and he'd stuck his head inside what might once have been a child's bedroom and nodded. The ornate plaster ceiling and the golden decorations on the walls had escaped his notice completely until now, when he was noticing them only because, his eyes blinking and full of water, he was searching the place for her.

He looked at his watch. He'd been asleep only five minutes.

Suddenly, he was filled with a desire to end the frustration that had been plaguing him for weeks now. Following the setting up of official links between Mab's Regency and the British government, a detachment of British armed forces had entered Avalon through the gateway as peacekeepers, the aim being to let the now atomically capable Unseelie Court know that Mab had similarly powerful allies. The Brigadier had been put in charge of organising and co-ordinating the movement of this detachment through the gateway that had now stabilised atop Oldbury Down. To achieve that aim, he'd had an area of the Downs forcibly bought from the National Trust, and, among huge protests that were probably going to get as far as an Early Day Motion in the House of Commons, had arranged construction of a small MOD testing station there, behind a high-security fence. Inside one of the prefab buildings there stood the gateway. The Royal Corps of Engineers had laid metal trackways down the chalk path he'd walked it seemed an eternity before, and, to the amazement of the locals, main battle tanks and other pieces of hardware regularly trundled up to the station in the early hours, the drivers as baffled as anybody else as to what they were going to do at such a small facility.

He'd taken a squad of young Welsh Guards, still not briefed, into the building that contained the gateway, and nothing else, for what else was needed? He'd watched their faces as he explained that no harm would come to them, and ordered them to walk into the glowing gap in front of them, through which they could see hillsides and bright blue sky. They'd looked at each other, astonished, obviously thinking that they were being ordered to butt their heads against some sort of projector screen. But then they realised they were hesitating to obey an order, and their sergeant stepped forward without a glance behind him and marched straight at the gateway.

They'd audibly gasped when he'd gone right through it. He'd turned and raised a thumb from the other side, and then there had been a barely orderly scramble to follow.

That had made Lethbridge-Stewart smile a little. These soldiers were getting a small glimpse of the sort of action he'd seen all his life.

He knew that people in the villages of Calstone and Heddington were already saying that the vehicles that went up the Downs didn't always come back, but he also knew from his years in UNIT that just saying that would content most of them, that the British constitution rebelled against considering the impossible. Twin-engined transport helicopters had delivered the huge crates that contained Harrier strike aircraft, their wings folded alongside them. And one night, with special guards and as swiftly as the helicopter pilots dared, the three crates that contained the vast, rocketlike bulk of the Aurora spyplane, the one on loan from the USAF to the security-cleared UNIT UK, had been delivered. Colonel Munro had kept the bureaucracy off his back, sealing off the channels of information that led from the British branch of UNIT to HQ in Geneva and the other sections. As far as they were concerned, it was business as usual. Once, Lethbridge-Stewart was aware, such a conflict of loyalties would have bothered him.

He knew that lay at the heart of his conflict with the Doctor.

Which was why he had to tell him. Tonight. Tell him about Doris, to show him that he was still the same man underneath.

He got to his feet and headed for the door. Then he stopped, his hand on the door handle, and realised that he was still in his pyjamas.

Sighing, he went to put his uniform on.

A little flight of stone steps led down from a solid-looking wooden door into the vaulted space of the cellar. The room had been recently cleaned, and a number of long tables installed. On them sat cauldrons, braziers, pestles and mortars, racks of ingredients and instruments. Over the back of a chair hung a long green frock coat.

And in one corner of the room stood the solid, familiar shape of a mid-twentieth-century London police box. There was the smell of fresh paint and woodchip in the air, and a number of empty tins of 'Metropolitan Livery Blue' lay discarded in a corner. From inside the police box came the noise of sawing, and a singsong voice that fluttered over the highlights of Carmen at slightly too fast a tempo. Two booted feet stuck out of the box as their owner reached round some difficult low corner inside.

The Brigadier had knocked, but there'd been no response, so he'd entered anyway, and made his way downstairs, looking around the room with a little smile of recognition. He always felt, on entering the Doctor's domain, that something magical was about to leap out at him. He noticed the feet and proceeded over to talk to them. 'Ah, there you are, Doctor. Still can't get it to work, I see.'

The legs stiffened. The body seemed to consider for a moment, then the Doctor, in his shirtsleeves, straightened up to a kneeling position and regarded the Brigadier. There were wood shavings in his hair, which he angrily brushed out with a hand. 'Don't do that,' he said.

'Do what?'

'This isn't UNIT HQ, and I'm not your scientific adviser.'

'Indeed.' The Brigadier looked round the room again. 'A very smart deal you struck with Queen Regent Mab, to become her Magical Adviser. I particularly enjoyed your resignation letter. Chaps in Geneva have never had to deal with one written in Old High Gallifreyan before.'

'I think the sentence in English got my point across. The rest is for history. If there's going to be any of that, now.' He slid to his feet and clapped his hands together to rid himself of the wood dust. 'You all really have no thought between you of what the consequences of this are going to be. You're such an idiot, Alistair.'

The Brigadier raised both eyebrows for a moment, then lowered them. It took him a moment to frame a suitably nonchalant response. 'I daresay in your terms I am, Doctor. But the agreement between Avalon and the United Kingdom makes strategic sense for both parties.'

'And what if this confrontation escalates into warfare? This is the land of dreams, directly connected to the human unconscious.'

'I'm aware of that, Doctor.' He was trying to find a moment in this conversation where he could raise the subject of what had happened to him. This difficulty between them had cramped and made awkward every opportunity they'd had. Every time they'd met in the last month the Doctor had been angry towards him. He just couldn't see that, militarily, there had been no alternative for any of them, ever since Margwyn had taken the bomb.

The Time Lord stalked over to a bench, bent to check a scrawled list of ingredients and angrily crossed one out. 'Why are you here, anyway? Hoping for a quick nostalgia buzz? I could arrange for some giant maggots if you'd like.'

The Brigadier cleared his throat and adopted a chatty tone. 'Just came to see how the new TARDIS was getting on.' He didn't want the Doctor to realise how important the thought that one day his old friend might be able to travel in time again was to him.

The Doctor, still glowering at him, pointed at the police box. 'That's not a new TARDIS. That's a wooden box inside which I'm going to try to grow a new TARDIS using the magic of Avalon. Which may take centuries, if I can get my head round it at all. Right now, if you gave me a hat and asked for a rabbit I couldn't oblige.'

'I see.'

'You see?' The Doctor's eyes fixed on the Brigadier's, and once more he had the uncomfortable sensation of being the enemy. 'You've had the privilege of seeing more than anybody else on this planet has seen. But, no, Alistair, I don't think you see. If you saw this whole nightmare as I'm seeing it, you'd get your forces out of Avalon and let me find a way to seal that gateway.'

The Brigadier found himself replying, anger rising in his throat, before he could stop himself. 'I'm sorry for saying so, Doctor, but I think that's a very naive point of view. We've sent Sir Charles Finningley North, to point out that Avalon now has its own deterrent. That should create diplomatic opportunities, not stifle them. Besides, what's the alternative? These Northern fellas replicate the bomb and hold Avalon to ransom, take their country back. We can't have that.'

The Doctor was suddenly in his face, his hands on the Brigadier's lapels, bellowing at him. 'You have no proof they're going to do that! Just because that's what you'd do with a nuclear deterrent! Your tiny government wants this place for its own ends, and if this opportunity hadn't presented itself so neatly, you'd probably have invaded!'

The Brigadier looked at him coldly. After a moment, the Doctor let his hands drop. He wandered off towards the benches again, his shoulders hunched.

'There have been incidents all along the border, reports of

human settlements being razed to the ground. We're not talking about pale thin chaps with chiffon wings, Doctor. Do you know what these beasties look like?'

'You never used to be a hypocrite, Alistair,' the Doctor murmured, running a hand through his hair. 'Whatever's happened to you, this regeneration doesn't suit you.'

That should have been the moment. The Brigadier could have brought the subject up then. He could have told his old friend what happened, and tried to regain the trust between them.

He tried to frame a reply to do that.

But he found that, once again, he was too angry to speak.

The Doctor turned around at the sound of his workshop door slamming. He put a hand to his brow, regretting what had happened, what always happened these days. Alistair was only human. That was the joy and the horror of him. There had been so many moments when his simple goodness had been an inspiration. But his small viewpoint led him into such things as this. The obvious solution. The consensus of opinion. Common sense. The Doctor had spent all his life battling against consensus and common sense.

He went to the blue shape of the police box and hugged it, feeling the newly painted wood against his cheek. This ridiculous shape was all he had, now. Sometimes the urge towards community was so strong. He remembered feeling it in those last years with Alistair on Earth, when he'd had the whole of time and space gifted to him once more, but had chosen to stay with his new-found family.

He'd been dwelling on one terrible thought, these past few weeks, now that he was trapped. Without his Ship, his home, his companions, he'd had no option but to dwell on it. He could get angry with Alistair all he liked, but the reality remained.

While Faction Paradox existed, there was no reason for him to do anything. Everything was negotiable. The child from their ranks had told him as much. His birthright, his culture, the things he'd defined himself against, were all variables now. He remembered his father, but he also remembered the loom, being twice born. He didn't know which he remembered from life and which from dreams.

He was sure they'd done something to him, to his past, an alteration to who he was, to the very weave of his biodata. But he didn't know what, or how he could even start to put things right again.

The Faction undermined him, and the interferences he made in history. They could rewrite every better outcome he accomplished. They rendered him impotent and meaningless. This was the thought that brought people to them, he knew. It was almost as if they had him already. He raged at Alistair every time they met because it was so tempting to throw his lot in with him and just decide that his viewpoint was right and that his side was the right side, in order to have his last friend back. In order to be part of something! To create some moral certainty for himself, when at the core of his being he knew now that no moral certainty was possible.

He raged at Alistair to stop himself from giving in to that. And he raged against him because, nevertheless, he couldn't find it in himself to do anything to stop the horror that his old friend was creating in Avalon. It was going to be like Skale all over again. Millions of people were going to die and he was going to watch.

He gently thumped his head against the wood.

Mab woke with a start and gazed at the figure at the end of her bed. Her hand was already on the dagger that lay under her pillow. She lowered it as she made out the silhouette of the Doctor, carrying a candle, a finger to his lips.

'Doctor,' she whispered. 'My guards... How did you get into my chambers?'

'I just did,' the figure replied, sitting down on the edge of the bed. 'We have to talk.'

Mab rubbed her eyes to get the sleep out of them. The last few days had been draining. But, when she saw what had happened to the man, she found herself laughing. 'Blessed be, why have you painted half your body blue?'

'Have I? Oh. Right. I see...' A smile fluttered across the Doctor's face for a moment. He produced a vast handkerchief, thought about which side of his face to wipe and then started to do so.

Mab tried to stifle her laughter. She hadn't done that for days, either. 'What do you want to talk about?'

'I feel impotent. I need your help to do something about that.'

Mab laughed even harder, and put a hand over her mouth to avoid disturbing her guards. 'That's a new one! But, y'know, whatever I can do...'

'What? Oh, no, don't be... not that you... anyhow...' He stood again, a nervous smile pursing his lips, and reached out a hand to her. 'Come on, this'll be easier outside.'

He led her out on to the balcony, from where the whole of Avalon at night was visible, stretched out before them. A new feature scarred the downlands below. Two long lines of light stretched off into the distance, the first stage of a rough landing strip. Canvas battlefield hangars stood to one side, under which lights illuminated the black shapes of two Harrier aircraft. A series of prefabricated huts had been built down one side of the runway, and from them, borne on the warm summer air, a distant repetitive drumbeat wafted.

The Doctor winced. 'It's being spoiled, Mab. I haven't been witness to many golden ages, but this is one, and it's coming to an end.' He laid a hand on her shoulder. 'You said you respected my authority as a Time Lord. I couldn't just order you to stop this, could I?'

'Ah, well, if you did that, I'd be in a quandary, with who you are and what this world needs and...' She stopped herself, made herself look him in the eye. 'What I mean is: no. No, you could not. I know this is wrong, but it's also for the best. I've learned, you see. That's what being a ruler means, being able to think things like that.'

'But that's not –' The Doctor saw the look on her face and visibly changed tack. 'Look, I'm Merlin, if that helps.'

'Who?'

'After your time.' The Doctor folded his arms behind his head in a posture of pure suffering, and marched back and forth across the balcony. 'If I stay in this castle, knocking around like a marble inside a jar, I'll just keep getting more and more angry. Alistair and I will keep colliding with each other. I have to take action, but I don't know what action to take. I dress like a pop star, and I think I should act like one.'

'What are you talking about?' Mab found herself reacting to the Time Lord as though he was a lost little boy. She wanted to give him a hug. But proper Queen Regents couldn't do that sort of thing.

He spun, pointing at her. 'I'm talking about the fallen land, the kingdom destroyed by the betrayal of a dolorous stroke! I'm talking about the Fall, re-enacted in every single player here, myself included! And I'm talking about myself: sick at heart, incapable, letting it all go on without...' He threw down his hands, obviously unable to finish even his sentence. 'I won't be distant from myself, Mab. I need to get out of here, to go and find those things that need to be found...' He swung his arms to include the entire view of the night. 'Those things that could save your kingdom. And yourself. And Alistair. And my companions, and the human dreaming. And me. I don't know what those things are, but they aren't to be found here.'

'You want me to grant you leave to go? But you're my token of prophecy. You're a sign that I might be doing the right thing.'

'Then it's right for me to go. Because you're not doing the right thing. But not to break faith with you, and for the sake of the -' his teeth hissed around the word - 'pettifogging forms they'll make you sign, give me a job. A task to accomplish.'

'You'll not go over to the North as well?'

He grabbed her hand and enclosed it with the two of his, his eyes burning with determination. He was holding it a bit too hard. 'I gave you my allegiance. I'm the Doctor. That still stands for something, I hope.'

'Then... There is one small matter. Which I can't talk to the Brigadier about.' She lowered her voice. 'Some of our people are going missing. Above and beyond the ones the Fair Folk are said to have been taking. I know there are patrols and units and whatever the Homeland soldiers call them abroad in our lands now. I can't keep track of all of them. I fear they may not tell me of all of them.' She saw the Doctor react with grand rage at that. 'I fear that they may be taking some of our people, for what purpose I know not. Perhaps to learn. If you could discover the truth of that for me... A personal mission for your Queen Regent...'

The Doctor fell to one knee and kissed her gathered hands. 'I am your servant, Queen Regent!' Then he leapt to his feet and darted back into the castle. He stopped on the threshold for a moment and looked back at her, his hair and the tails of his coat billowing in the wind. 'And I'm also the Doctor. Let me see if I can save us all.'

Then, at a run, he was gone.

'Make sure you come back!' she called after him. She leaned back on the balcony rail, enjoying the summer breeze through her nightgown. Then she smiled at a thought she'd had. 'Blue,' she whispered to herself. 'Brigida's colour. Blessed be. He may save us all at that.'

Sir Charles Finningley, Ambassador to the Court of St James, was having a wonderful time. He and his staff of three diplomats, plus his six-man UNIT UK bodyguard, had been flown by dragon to a place he regarded as Carlisle, a thriving town of cobbled streets. This being a Northern stronghold of Queen Regent Mab's tribe, he felt able to leave his people to settle in at the inn and go exploring himself. He found an old-fashioned market where a trader sold him that morning's shellfish. Everybody noticed the differences about his clothes, and everywhere he went he was surrounded by crowds of Celts who asked him - some scared, a few angry, most just astonished - what the situation was. So, he did what he liked best. He upended a crate and sat down, and explained the whole picture and took questions. By the end of those sessions, most of the people present would be nodding, relieved, on solid ground again. The talk in the taverns that night would be of the good works of the government, and how they had come to deal sternly but fairly with the threat of the Fair Folk. Certainly, there had been a few awkward moments, such as the rude farmer who'd asked what the Homelanders had been up to bringing a weapon here and then losing it, and the children who'd just yelled what he presumed were obscenities at him.

But, overall, he felt he was winning. Tomorrow, his party would head further north, and make contact with some of the more moderate Fair Folk villages. There was no solid border, apparently, and a lot of the townships shared farmland and fishing rights with this other species. There he would find local dignitaries capable of making representation for him further up the chain of command, so his arrival at the Unseelie Court a few weeks later would be with the understanding and perhaps even backing of factions of the Faeries themselves. So much easier that way.

Tonight, at the end of his day of exploring, he was sitting at a table in the corner of an inn, nursing a very rough pint of ale. He had already greeted several of the locals who'd come over to talk to him, had some engaging conversations, but now there seemed to be a general feeling that he ought to be left alone to enjoy his beer. Good people, these, to do that.

Someone sat down beside him before he quite realised they were there.

'Oh.' He looked sideways, startled. 'Hello. What can I do for you?'

She was blonde and robust and had an all-consuming smile that was directed straight at him. She really ought to have done her buttons up. 'You're the one from the Homelanders. Bless Constantine for that. You'll help me get my children back.'

Ah. Awkward. He'd heard these stories, about how the Faeries took youngsters. He hadn't found any such direct evidence for it before, though. 'We'll do our best, madam. Tell me more.'

She looked around her, obviously not wanting to talk of private pain in such a public place. 'Perhaps we could go back to my home. I have a brew there which might suit you.'

'Well, if your husband doesn't –'

'Sir, I have had no husband for five years now.' She paused, looking deeply into his eyes. 'You'll have heard of our hospitality. Of how we prize visitors for the luck they bring.'

A slow smile spread across Finningley's face. He drank up, got to his feet, and took her arm. This was the part of foreign diplomacy that he enjoyed most of all. 'Lead on, dear lady,' he whispered. 'You can tell me all about it.'

Fitz took two steps backwards, feeling as if he was on the rocking deck of a ship at sea. He and Compassion stood in the middle of an opulent throne room, where light shone in rainbows from every polished surface. Outside the green glass of the windows, dark-purple clouds swirled in liquid patterns. The light stone of the floor was set in intricate mosaics of complex... what had the Doctor called those? Yeah: fractals. In the centre of the huge, round room stood the circular dais of a throne, where two stone seats stood, back to back. Margwyn was prostrating himself in front of one of them, his forehead to the floor, his cloak stretched like wings behind him.

And on the thrones, and standing in a circle around the room, were the most outrageous beings Fitz had ever seen.

They were like a nebula glimpsed through a telescope, in that they changed depending on which part of your eye you used to look at them. Take the two on the thrones: Brona and Arwen, Margwyn had called them, the Queen and King of the Faeries. He got to see them from all angles as their throne slowly rotated, as it seemed to do all the time. Straight on, with the everyday cones and rods of your retinas, they were handsome, gleaming humans, with perfect brows and still, unmoving faces, who looked like they supped honey and ambrosia and had the cheekbones of Charlotte Rampling and Terrance Stamp. They wore golden armour and carried slim, pointed, silver swords. But at another angle, an angle he was trying to get now, actually, as he contemplated Brona's mane of red hair, billowing and filled with a floating cloud of tiny fairies, they were utterly naked, furred along the arms and calves. It was the third sort of glimpse that was the most disturbing, though. Every now and then, depending on the light and the angle of sight, you saw straight through those versions to a different aspect, one your brain kind of told you was the real thing. From that point of view, Brona and Arwen had hard, reptilian skin, set with jewels, complicated, wet carapaces, and circular mouths for that ambrosia, and, blimey, a third eye in the back of their heads.

The circle of warriors that stood around the wall went through those changes too, as the light reflected from the throne on to them. But it was the fashion for them to wear their extra eyes above their other two.

'Cosmic!' Fitz whispered.

Compassion moved close enough to him to whisper. 'They're quantum creatures,' she said. 'They keep reinventing themselves unconsciously. Visualising themselves into existence using random Higgs fields at the vacuum level of quantum particle decay.'

'Whatever you say.'

'They belong here. This is their world. They're part of it. Part of the dream state of human beings. Fairies, devils and angels. How does your mind feel?'

'Psychedelic.'

Compassion shook her head and turned back to what was happening by the throne. Fitz, finding that he was smiling all over his face, turned back, too.

'Rise, Margwyn,' Arwen was saying in his hooting, singsong voice. 'The weapon you brought to us has been examined, and it is what you claim it to be. You are a good servant to the Unseelie Court.'

Margwyn, shivering, got to his feet, but kept his eyes to the ground. 'Forgive me, King of the Fair Folk, but I am not your servant. I serve the interests of Queen Regent Mab, against the disaster that has tainted this land. The Unseelie Court is now the best protector of all Avalon against the invaders. Mab has taken false counsel and allowed herself to be misled in allowing these newcomers to build their bases, but my allegiance remains to her.'

A great hissing rose from the warriors gathered around the

room, but Brona raised her beautiful clawed hand and they hushed. 'Your words do you honour, brave Margwyn. The arrival of the new outsiders is indeed a time of great peril for this land. When Constantine created this world, he did so out of dream stock. He inherited us from the weave of his mindland. And for centuries the humans he brought here have respected our primacy, as we have respected their presence, and we have lived in peace. Now the gateway has been opened, there will come more and more humans. They will take more and more space. They will foul our lands with their machines –' she pronounced it like a curse – 'and with weapons like the one you brought us.'

Taking up the thought from exactly the point Brona had finished, Arwen began to speak as his throne moved into view. 'We could make many copies of that weapon. It would not take very long.' Margwyn started to protest, but Arwen raised a golden talon. 'But we have decided that someone must take responsibility for the good of all this land. Much as you did, Margwyn. We will not betray the peace you have attempted to create by bringing us this weapon.'

Margwyn bowed once more.

The mage led Fitz and Compassion down one of the low, organic-looking stone tunnels the Fair Folk seemed to favour. 'I've always dreamed of coming here,' he told them. 'I've read many manuscripts, been in communication with the Court here, but to actually tread these corridors...'

Fitz rubbed his brow. If only he could get his eyes to see straight. 'You're really sold on these guys, aren't you?'

'The Fair Folk are surprising,' said Compassion. 'They're Earth Reptiles.'

Margwyn looked puzzled at her. 'I've never heard them called that before. Where does the term originate?'

Compassion frowned, biting her lip in concentration. 'I don't know,' she said. 'I don't remember knowing that before.'

They came to a door, which Margwyn positively skipped up to, and flung open theatrically. 'Here's what they're doing with the bomb,' he said.

The small chamber was awash with green light. At its centre was a plinth, upon which the bomb was mounted, like an object of veneration. Around it stood various aged Fair Folk, their appearances rippling, contemplating it and taking notes.

Fitz winced, remembering a movie he'd seen in the TARDIS. 'Planet of the Apes,' he whispered.

'Yes, at the moment,' agreed Margwyn. 'But hopefully this will even things up. Below the plinth is a magical launcher. Not that they'll ever use it, of course. But they have to be ready.'

Fitz gave him the longest frown he had ever given anybody.

There was a banquet in their honour that night. Brona and Arwen sat at opposite ends of a long table, about which tiny fairies fluttered, bringing food in a blink. Fitz concentrated on his suspicious-looking soup, trying not to look at the eye-boggling stuff that was happening in his peripheral vision.

Margwyn had been encouraged, by Brona, to make a speech. He was on his feet now, a golden goblet of some honeyed stuff that Fitz had rather taken a liking to, actually, in his hand.

'It was not magic that brought me here,' he began. 'But politics. The moment the gateway between Avalon and the Homelands became permanent, I could see there was no way my people could prevent, even if they wished to, the encroachment of the inhabitants of Earth into Avalon. Indeed –' he glanced at Fitz and Compassion – 'my tribe had already established good relations with some of those folk. I acted on my best impulse, to bring you both the weapon that the Earth people would try to use to claim superiority here, and –' he gestured towards them again – 'two prophetic visitors, with their power to bring lucky changes.'

Fitz frowned at that, too. He hadn't realised they were valuable. He'd thought Margwyn was just saving their lives. Now everything had slowed down he was starting to feel a long way from home. He missed Filippa. Why had he kept on going when he could have stayed there? And the Doctor was dead. When was he going to be able to start dealing with that?

Compassion nudged him, and forced him to look up. Twin Fair Folk messengers had arrived by the seats of the King and Queen, as Margwyn continued. 'With this new equality of power, I hope my people will pause before they embrace the new folk, and will give some thought to the quality of life in Avalon, how we all rely on the magic that your people have mastered, and how the new folk will try to replace that magic with their machines. I hope my people will now reach out to yours and reach a lasting peace. Then I may return home, submit myself to my Queen Regent's justice - and die having done my duty to her.'

He sat down again, to hooted applause. But Brona had now raised a claw, and the table fell silent. Bad news, Fitz thought, glancing at how far it was to the door. Right now we're the guests, but in a mo we might be on the menu.

'The villages of Hyskar and Patros have been attacked,' announced Brona.

'Their inhabitants slaughtered, the buildings set on fire,' chimed in Arwen.

'This was done with -' Brona's tongue slipped around the word awkwardly - 'technology... Things of science were found by our dragon scouts. The outsiders are trying to drive our people north.'

Fitz looked at Margwyn. He seemed astonished. Amazed that his instincts had failed him. 'But... so soon?' He whispered. 'No, there should be peace now. Why would they?'

Arwen stood, turning pages on a manuscript that the messenger had handed him. 'Not only that, but we have reports of their metal birds flying over our hatcheries under the lochs. We hear from the human towns where our people come and go that the locals are hostile now. They accuse us of stealing their children.'

An angry mutter went round the table. The slithering of shape and form seemed to increase, making Fitz's head ache once more. 'The old slander,' hissed a dragonlike woman across the table from him. 'We have not bred changelings in centuries.'

'We should do so again,' hooted a bulky man-thing in silks, his eyes blazing red.

'Revenge the villages!' screeched a courtier from further up the table, his teeth snapping in Fitz's direction. 'Use their foul weapon against them. Destroy the gateway!'

Margwyn was getting to his feet again, but a gesture from Brona stopped him. She had risen at the same time Arwen had. 'There is another way, a more peaceful way!' she said, animatedly, as if she had been seized by a sudden idea. 'Our War Mages conceived it three bloodswings ago. But we had not the means to accomplish it until now.' She gestured at the humans. 'Arwen, do you not think this is the reason our magical bounty is here? The War Mages prophesied that some way to complete the plan would arrive! This is the good luck the strangers bring us!'

Arwen considered for a moment, then slowly nodded.

Fitz lowered his spoon and glanced at Compassion. 'Oh dear,' he whispered. 'They mean us, don't they?'

The Brigadier had been intercepted on the way back to his room by a running subaltern, who urgently enquired whether his palmtop pager had been damaged. Cursing himself for leaving it behind when he'd gone to visit the Doctor, Lethbridge-Stewart had followed the man out to the command and control point, a lorry standing a hundred metres from the rough runway. He swatted away the insects that had gathered in the beams of the lighting rigs, and stamped his way up the steps, feeling ready to declare war on anyone and anything.

He was surprised to see Mab standing between the banks of instruments, being shown a display on a screen by a bemused young corporal. The royal wore only a simple white shirt, maybe even a nightshirt, tucked into her britches, and her hair was a mess. 'Queen Regent,' he began. 'To what do we owe –'

'They've killed your Ambassador,' Mab cut in sharply. 'The threefold death. Drowned him in a cauldron, nailed him to a tree, pierced his liver with a spear. It's a mockery of one of our legends. A deliberate blasphemy. Look, there are pictures.'

The Brigadier looked over her shoulder. This was footage being sent from the palmtop of one of Finningley's aides. His mouth set in a line. 'Damn them. They must know what this means. Can we be sure who did this?'

Mab pointed at the screen. 'You see the mark carved in his chest? That's two letters in their language: Ab Weo. "We will take, or kill, or harvest, your children." It's been used in the past as a declaration of war. But it's a very strange thing for –'

An urgent shout came from further down the vehicle, where the radar monitors kept track of the readings from the nets that spun outside. 'Sir! I don't know... It could be...'

'Well? Spit it out, Symcox!'

'It is!' The woman's voice switched from astonishment to a businesslike speed as her training took over. 'We have incoming! Incoming confirmed! I am hitting the alert siren and informing Delta Com for a possible intercept –' The words were repeated and added to in a blur of efficiency by workers up and down the centre.

A blaring, repetitive noise began to echo across the downlands and the castle precincts. Lethbridge-Stewart saw these youngsters who had never faced combat looking across to him, expectantly, fearfully.

He shouldered past Mab to put a hand on the radar operator's shoulder. 'Good work. Steady now. Where, what and when?'

'Coming straight down from the north. Mach... Mach eight! A missile. Big one. Vector... zero! Straight at us! And...' The young woman looked straight up into the Brigadier's face. 'Sir – duck and cover!'

The Brigadier just had time to turn round. Mab was already moving, grabbing his arm, wrenching him towards the door.

They fell in a mass into the night air, tripping on the steps as something huge like a comet coloured the sky, washing the shadows red, a great sound rising from across the Downs.

The shadows swept round in a flash.

The sound peaked.

She fell on top of him and held him down in the mud, shouting at him to stay there, fighting his desire to give himself up to –

It hit.

The flash made everything white, their shadows streaking

brown across the grass as light intruded into them.

The explosion ripped across the night and echoed back again, the boom resounding right round the cavern of the sky.

Mab let him up, as she herself struggled to her feet. The highest tower of the castle was gone, the stump where it had stood a mass of flame. Secondary detonations were thumping all across that wing, the blaze making great shadows that swayed and flickered across the Downs.

An RAF fire truck sped off uselessly in that direction, alarms adding to the blare of the sirens and the concussion still resounding inside the Brigadier's head.

Mab looked at him, her face full of blame and anger. 'The High Council,' she said. 'Their chambers.' And then she was off, sprinting towards her castle, shouting for her mages.

The Brigadier turned back to the C&C van, but his legs gave way, and he fell.

He lay there in the mud, staring up at the burning castle, the light washing over his tired eyes.

And, for some reason that alluded him, he started to laugh.

Ten miles away, the Doctor's horse whinnied and bucked and nearly threw him as the blazing missile flashed across the sky. He hauled on the reins and steadied it, turning to gaze in horror at the blaze which flashed and then engulfed the southern horizon.

He hesitated for a moment. But he knew there was nothing he could do that others couldn't. The blue box that he'd made in his foolishness would have gone now. And that was for the best.

He had to go on. For the sake of everyone.

He turned the horse north again, and with a sudden cry spurred it forward.

There was much consultation between the King and Queen and a series of scampering reptilians after that, and at the end of the meal the royals left their guests to disperse and took their visitors aside. Fitz found himself and the others ushered into a room with a large circular table in the middle of it, with maps and manuscripts laid out. Some sort of royal operations room.

'Our War Mages,' said Brona, 'have prepared an excellent plan.' She raised a green wand towards a screen that had swung open like an eyelid along one curving wall of the chamber. She wiggled the wand and the screen glowed. A picture appeared, a map of Britain, contained within a swirl that connected to the head of a profile of a grim, bearded man, taken, it looked, from a coin. From what Margwyn had told them, Fitz took this to be Constantine.

'The entirety of the world we live in,' said Arwen, 'is imagined into existence every moment by King Constantine, who sleeps under the waters in the great castle of Avalon. If the King were to be woken, then the contents of this world would reappear in the original Homelands of the humans, the place they call Earth.'

'Therefore,' continued Brona, 'we must not wake him. That would make matters worse for us. But we need to influence his sleep. To try to make him close the gateway between Avalon and Earth. Our War Mages think they have found a way.' The picture changed to show a tiny figure, ringed among more tiny figures, on the surface of a curving planet or dimension or something. Fitz thought he was getting about half of this, but Margwyn and Compassion were nodding along. He wondered if the Fair Folk had developed tobacco at any point.

Arwen took up the briefing in that seamless way that the Faerie royals had. 'There is a legend that, while Constantine sleeps here, his consciousness walks his Homelands in physical form. If we could find this individual, it might be possible to influence him directly, through magic. We would have Avalon –' he slapped his hand shut – 'once more in our palm. We could expel the intruders back to their own world, and shut the gate.'

Margwyn looked slowly between the two rulers. He seemed surprised that their plans were so advanced. 'Yes, that would make good sense. If that could be done, Avalon would be safe from outside interference. But how are we to accomplish this? We would need a gateway of our own to send an agent to the Homelands.'

'We have the means,' said Brona. 'Our War Mages have seen to that.'

'Who are these War Mages?' asked Margwyn, looking puzzled. 'In all my studies of your folk, I have never heard –'

The doors to the chamber burst open. Through them came a tiny fairy, a glowing spark of light that whizzed into the room. Though its body was small, its voice was loud enough to make Fitz wince. Behind it ran a group of reptilian warriors. 'Your Majesties!' it shouted. 'You must come with us! Quickly! There is –'

And then there was a noise louder than any Fitz had heard before. He heard it in retrospect, realising only afterwards what it was, because the concussion took him in the pit of his stomach, and he'd fallen awkwardly to the floor before he was aware that he was hearing anything. His ears popped again and he heard screams from all around. The roof overhead had a jagged crack down its centre. A pile of rubble had engulfed the messenger and some of the warriors. Claws poked from it at horrible angles. Margwyn was kneeling down, gazing upward, as if he'd seen what had hit them and was astonished by it.

Arwen stumbled to his feet, helping his Queen up. 'What just occurred?'

Brona swept her claw at the screen again, and images scrolled across it, faster than Fitz could follow. 'A small object, coming in at high speed, dipping over the face of the land,' she muttered, as if in a trance. She seemed to be getting the information directly from some outside source. 'What the humans call a cruise missile. Our magical defences stopped it in the air just above the dome.'

Fitz suddenly realised the presence at his side that he was missing, and looked around for Compassion, but she wasn't where she should have been. He found her on the other side of the room, struggling to her feet under the heavy cover of a great stone ledge, upon which books stood. How had she got over there in time? He shook his head to clear it. His senses were messed up.

Arwen was gazing at the screen himself now, as his warriors tried to heave the mass of stones from off one of their still-moving comrades. The King was hissing hot breath in great clouds of steam. His voice was that of a dragon. He was reading something that had suddenly appeared in front of him. 'The governments of the Catuvelauni and the United Kingdom declare that, following the murder of their ambassador and the unprovoked attack on their forces, a state of war exists between them and the Unseelie Court. We demand that you surrender your forces, withdraw from –'

There came a high reptilian scream from one of the guards beneath the rubble as a block was heaved aside. With a flex of his claws, Arwen swung from the screen. 'War?' he bellowed. 'By my claws! By the blood of our children! We should destroy their castle, raze the Southern lands and erase the gateway with the fire the humans have brought!' He turned to his warriors as they got to their feet, and directed his fury to them. Fitz felt himself shaking like a mouse at the sounds the dragon king was emitting. 'We could use our magic to send our armies against the Celts, fight a land war in response to their aggression.'

The warriors hissed and growled in response. One of them looked at Fitz and pulled a serrated dagger from his belt.

Brona put a hand on Arwen's shoulder as he paced, and took over the royal voice in a more gentle tone. 'But we will not do this, because we are the Fair Folk, and we are stronger than they are. We elect to hold their terrible weapons at bay with our magic. We elect to shun the grand retaliation of which we are capable. We will not enter into a war in the land of human dreams. To do that would harm this world for all. For are we not the keepers of what makes this land what it is?'

Fitz let out a breath. The warriors were nodding. He saw that Margwyn was on his knees before the Queen, tears coming from his eyes. This was the sort of compassion that he'd always associated with the Fair Folk, Fitz thought. All the man's utopian dreams were coming true.

'So we shall give them war!' Arwen concluded. 'But our way. The way of the Fair Folk. We shall war on them through our wit and cunning!'

The warriors cheered above the weepings and shouts of the wounded. Brona took Arwen's hand in hers. 'Let it be so!' she cried. She pointed to Fitz and Compassion. 'They will be our agents in the land of the humans!'

'Oh,' said Fitz, turning worriedly to Compassion. 'That's what they meant.'

The War Mages watched from an alcove across the corridor as Margwyn led the strangers away. Then they checked on the health of the King and Queen, offered their joy that neither had been harmed, and stalked off towards their own chambers.

They turned two corners in silence, then stepped into another quiet alcove. They looked left and right.

Then they smacked their clawed palms together, and wrapped their forearms around each other. 'It's so easy!' exclaimed the reptilian female. 'They're just going along with everything we want them to do!'

'A cruise missile!' the male laughed. 'Straightaway! They are so into it! These guys deserve to have their time meddled with.'

They made glittering eye contact, then as one they stepped back into the corridor. Suddenly they both snapped into a victorious dance posture, one claw pointed to the ceiling, the other to the floor.

'Stayin' alive!' they warbled.

Then a fairy page appeared at the end of the corridor and they whacked back into the sober, square-shouldered posture of the Fair Folk.

The War Mages continued on the way to their chambers.

Chapter Six
Potence Postponed

The Brigadier walked with Colonel Munro along the side of the runway. An A-10 tankbuster in RAF livery was warming up, the engines of the stubby aircraft rippling the morning air and disturbing the peace with a whine that went higher and higher in pitch. Under its wings were slung two scarlet-and-white cruise missiles, their warheads painted with sharks' teeth.

Above the two officers rose the blackened bulk of the castle, the remains of the highest tower now supported with scaffolding, work crews dealing with the rubble on the ground. The hit had bored a hole right down into the foundations, destroying what had been the Doctor's laboratory, killing hundreds, as well as wrecking the tower.

'The policy of bombardment seems to be working so far,' Munro said, calling up strategic maps on his palmtop as they walked. 'We've destroyed a number of castles, and several other fortifications. The drones show no large-scale concentrations of Faerie forces building up. It's as if they don't want a confrontation. They're getting quite good at zapping the drones, though. They use some sort of heavy crossbow bolt, propelled by magic.'

The Brigadier made a note on his own palmtop. 'I'll have a word with the court mages about that. See if they can arrange some sort of protection. Pity we can't fly a satellite, but...'

'No space, sir, I know. There are stars at night, but they're ice crystals on the vault.'

'You should have been at the briefing for the stealth-bomber pilots, Munro. I felt something of a fool, telling them they shouldn't go too high or they'd hit the ceiling.'

They shared a UNIT smile for a moment. That professional irony that came with soldiering in places other soldiers had never dreamed of. Or, actually, in this case, a place other soldiers dreamed of every night. 'I can imagine, sir,' said Munro. 'We've had a large number of freakouts. The regular regiments who come through are holding intensive battlefield training sessions on the plains to the south of here, trying to let their men get their heads around it. The only ones who are into it are the Royal Engineers. They're out with maps of ley lines to run their cables along. Apparently they've always done that.'

'Indeed. At least there haven't been any more strikes like that missile attack to put the wind up them. We'll need them ready and able if the worse comes to the worst and the Unseelie Court decides to fight a ground war. We have the numbers in the enlisted forces to do that for a couple of years at least, but everybody in the high command is hoping that the air strikes will batter the enemy into submission.'

Munro paused, looking at his shoes for a moment. 'There is one thing, sir. A morale issue. The UNIT troops...'

'What about them?'

'Well, sir, they don't expect to have to fight a ground war. They're anticipating someone pulling a rabbit out of a hat and saving their arses. The Doctor, sir –'

'Is no longer one of us, Colonel. You're to tell that to anybody that asks, understood?'

'Yes sir, but in that case where is he, sir?'

The Brigadier looked stormily at the blackened spires of the castle. 'I believe,' he said, 'that he's got rather too close to the enemy.'

The Doctor sprinted for the ditch at the side of the road, holding the bundle close to his chest.

He leapt into the air.

The wooden stockade behind him exploded into an expanding ball of flame and debris.

He crashed on to the edge of the ditch, shards of wood zipping through the folds of his coat-tails, and rolled into a gasping mass of Fair Folk, their possessions and loved ones gathered round them. They were packed into the low space body to body.

He gulped down air for a moment, panting, then he unfolded his arms and handed the huddled civilians a tiny three-eyed baby, its hide still glistening with albumen. It was coughing, too, and whooping a long, mournful cry.

The reptile folk lowered their heads in a silent bow of gratitude as the baby's mother took him.

There was another long, low rumble coming from above. The ugly shape of the A-10 had slowly swung in the sky, and was heading back towards the village again.

'Why are they doing this?' cried the mother. 'We live in peace with the human folk on the other side of the river!'

Her mate shook his head. 'That was a mistake. We should have driven them from this land, before they brought this terrible magic.'

The Doctor looked anguished at them. 'You didn't make the mistake. They did. They've gone –' The screech rose to a pitch and he flung his arms over his head. Another explosion showered them with debris. He lowered his arms again and pinched his brow between his hands, trying to rub some feeling back into his temples. His eyes kept drifting back to the ruins of the village, where in the main square lay blackened forms, big and small. Someone had obviously thought this place contained soldiers of the Unseelie Court. Perhaps the humans across the river were telling tales, or felt threatened. He glanced over the hedge behind them, through which a great, scaly hide could be seen, heaving breaths.

The riderless dragon had spun into a rough landing there when its reptilian rider had been killed by the aircraft's machine-gun fire and had fallen from his mount. The beasts were obviously controlled through some kind of mental link, and the poor thing was scared and timid without a rider. The British pilots, thank the Other, must have been aware of that, because, having killed the rider, they hadn't gone on to attack the dragon.

Perhaps that was what had brought death to this place. The presence of one such animal on a reconnaissance mission close to the border with the humans. Or perhaps the Brigadier and his fellow generals were now making no distinction between Fair Folk military and civilians. 'Mad,' he whispered. 'They've gone mad.'

His gaze alighted on the door to a small hut. There was movement there. Two small faces peering out straight at him, too frightened to move.

'And now,' he whispered, getting to his feet again, 'so have I.'

He'd made his way north on foot, catching lifts with merchants, soaking up all the news and gossip he could, getting a feel for this world. Fear was everywhere. Nobody wanted war, because everybody was afraid of the two great and unknown powers – the Faeries and the Homelanders – and of what their terrible weapons might do to Avalon. He'd stayed at an inn where the windows were being boarded up, where everybody had charms to ward off Faerie magic. And everywhere there were stories of people vanishing, of missing children. The fairies took these and did something to them, it was said, and they came back changed. The Doctor had smuggled a woman and her returned baby out of a village by river, lying low with her in a shallow boat as the mob that wanted to kill the baby ran with torches along the banks, trying to keep up with them. The Doctor, when they reached safety, had examined the baby, and found nothing amiss. He suspected that what the woman had told him was true, that the child had just wandered off. She'd found him not far from where she'd left him while she picked berries. But that explanation was too ordinary for the villagers, who'd had their lives changed under such pressure. War made mad folk of them all.

Now he hushed the reptilians who were pulling at the cuffs of his boots, trying to make him come back into cover, and considered his options. The aircraft were wheeling around to make another pass at the village. The children were screaming now at the increasing noise level. He found what he was looking for in the sky overhead. A remote-controlled drone. He glared at it, hoping Alistair would see his anger.

Then he put one foot up on to the lowest bar of the wooden fence, and vaulted over it, tearing his clothes as he scrambled over the hedge beyond.

He landed, his boots in the mud, by the vast, breathing flank of the dragon.

It was green, its skin a mass of scales of varying sizes, each one reflecting the light from a different angle. Its wings were curled above it in an expression that spoke of fear and hiding. Its skull, twice as long as the Doctor was tall, lay flat on the ground, its catlike jaw shut in misery. One great eye, a pupil of rainbow inks in water, slid to contemplate the Doctor.

The magical creature smelled of burnt wood and cinnamon.

The Doctor ran to its jaw and slapped his hands against a nodule that spurred out near the back of the eye. He closed his own eyes and concentrated, locking out the start of the long attack screams from the planes above. He saw, as he sometimes did when he encountered a mind, the future fate of this dragon, and his mouth set in his own line of hurt.

But he would not seal himself away from this. He had come here to see what he could do, and he would keep on doing it until - if - he could make some sort of difference to the result.

He asked the dragon if it would support him, and when it saw what he was planning it said yes. So he patted it stoutly and clambered up on to the back of its neck, feeling his way desperately up the smooth scales, holding on by fingertips and the shape of his hands, until it rippled its muscles and swept him up into the seat.

The sound in the sky had now reached the point where the aircraft would be starting to dive.

The dragon fluttered its vast green sheets of wing into a blur, and suddenly they were airborne, the clawed ruts of the field falling away into nothing below. The hedge he'd scrambled through was now the line on the edge of a box.

He slapped his palms against the nodules on the dragon's neck, noticing the charring on the scales and the green blood where machine-gun fire had raked the creature's rider away. He put his forehead to the third eye and opened his own, metaphorical, one to it.

They were level in the sky now with the diving plane and the reconnaissance drone. Those metal things stood like falling objects, kept in the sky through brute force. They were always going to return to earth. The Doctor flexed his and the dragon's arms, and they were swiftly beside these alien shapes, because they belonged here in the sky.

The blue spun around the Doctor's head as the great breathing beast beneath him turned over in a smooth arc. It reared up suddenly at an angle to the two aircraft, and they split into two emergency pullouts, climbing chest to chest with the animal, then looping over themselves as the reptile swam through the air away again.

The Doctor concentrated on the drone now, a little black sphere with two whirring rotor blades and a tail fin. The dragon asked if it could burn it. The Doctor said no. They shot towards it.

The Doctor felt the two aircraft turn, and by all the rules of aerial combat fall in behind the dragon's exposed back.

With a reflexive jerk of his limbs he jumped to his feet, and spread his arms wide, his head thrown back, his eyes closed, maintaining the connection to the dragon through mind alone.

He heard the pitch of the aircraft engines increase, felt the tiny heat of the targeting lasers as they locked on to the base of his spine.

He hoped that the image would get through to someone in the high command. To the Brigadier himself, perhaps.

He felt the hard wind on the palms of his hands and heard, through dragon ears, the click of machine canon arming.

The Brigadier shoved the remote operator aside from the screen he was staring into, ripped aside the darkness hood, and swore curtly five times at what he saw.

The Doctor felt the lasers vanish from his back, and tensed his muscles, waiting for the bullets. Maybe next time he'd be someone who could control his destiny, and not have to make these gestures.

Then he felt the warplanes break off and sail away, in separate directions, before turning south for home.

He opened his eyes, and looked over the dragon's head at the drone that still fluttered above the village. Then he looked down. The reptilians had run to the remaining hut, and were grabbing their children and holding them.

He gave Alistair a moment to see. Then he let the dragon do it.

A curt bolt of fire spurted from the beast's muzzle. The drone exploded.

The Doctor let the dragon circle the village for a moment, and waved, grinning, down at the reptilians who were cheering him. They would be joining the long, slow processions of refugees heading north.

But he would not be going with them.

He sat back down in the seat on the dragon's neck, put his palms to the nodules again, and sent it heading back across the border into the human lands.

Fitz clenched his eyes, nose and mouth against the water and let the cold sink into his scalp. Then he flung his head back out of the bowl and let everything open, taking a deep breath. 'Ohh...' he groaned. 'This place is getting to my brain.'

Compassion and Margwyn were sitting in two plush chairs that had obviously been designed for bodies that were subtly different from those of human beings. The whole chamber spoke of that, despite some magical efforts on the part of their hosts. Everything was still green, and everything still didn't quite sit still where it should, shifting in the corners of his eyes. 'It's like the planet of tie-dye,' he grumbled, going to join them.

'Indeed,' said Margwyn. 'The lands of the Fair Folk are not hospitable to such as we. I have my magical protections, but you will both be experiencing negative effects.'

Compassion shook her head. 'It's bearable. I can deal with all sorts of environments.'

'Well I want out of this madhouse, as soon as possible.' Fitz used a finger to blow water from one nostril into his handkerchief.

'They said we were going to be their agents, Margwyn. If it gets us back to Earth, man, I'm all for that. Provided it doesn't involve anything like fighting, getting shot at, hiding in craters, that sort of rubbish.'

Margwyn stood, and walked slowly to the window, through which Fitz could see the oily green sky still boiling away. It was, he was sure, never just a nice sunny day in fairyland. 'That's why Brona and Arwen's plan seems so useful,' he said. 'All it involves is you going home.'

'Too right it seems useful!' Fitz slapped the dressing table. 'We can get back to London. If it's gonna be 2012 we can go visit Sam, get our lives sorted out.' He did his best to smile jokily as he settled back into one of the chairs. Neither of these two would get just how much he needed familiarity right now. 'I just hope it's better than Sweden.'

The Doctor had sailed on the back of the dragon to an area where great lakes split the forested countryside into small fishing communities. They were a few miles inside human territory now, as could be seen by the numbers of aircraft passing far below and high above them. Perhaps they had been given a corridor, allowed by Alistair's grace to fly where they wished. Entirely because the Brigadier still regarded the Doctor as a friend, even if not an ally.

That made him feel worse about this conflict, that he was being deliberately absented from it.

He had crossed the roughly defined border to the Faerie side two nights ago when he'd seen rockets bombarding towns and villages. Now he had decided that he hadn't spent enough time on the human side of this fence, particularly if he was sparing any thought to the mission Mab had given him.

But now he couldn't let the dragon come any further.

He put his forehead to the dragon's eye once more, and told it to go home, gave it a rough flight path that should get it back to its eyrie in the islands without encountering too much air power. It would take the story of what the Doctor had done with it. Then he told it what it should do next.

After a slight hesitation, the great beast obeyed him. It shifted its mass slowly to one side. The Doctor swung both his legs together on one edge of the seat, grabbed his bag in one hand and pinched his nose. He took one look down at the shining surfaces that lay a thousand feet below.

Then he slid off the back of the dragon, shouting, 'Geronimo!'

As the water shot up towards him, it occurred to him that dear old Geronimo would have been puzzled to hear that he was now remembered mainly by people who were about to fall from a great height.

Gwyllm was working on his boat when the explosion happened, painting pitch over new hullwork to cover the breach where they'd been driven on to rocks by the wind. The carpentry of the last day had been long, hard work, and his back was aching from all the bending down and carrying and sawing. It was good luck that Huw from the next stand up the beach had some cured hull braces that just about fitted his own boat. But even with those the labour had been awkward, and his head hurt from the noise of all the metal birds going over. The Queen Regent had sent heralds from town to town, announcing the arrival of their allies from the Homelands and asking the people of the Catuvelauni to give them help if they needed it.

Gwyllm didn't care one way or the other. They'd all been aware of the existence of the Homelands, distantly, a tale that everybody was told as they grew up, but it had always felt, when he heard it, like the story of something waiting to catch up with them all. When he saw things in the sky that should not be flying, he'd just thought, ho hum, now we're all going to finally get caught by the Romans. As long as he could keep his business going until that happened, he wasn't concerned.

Not that the war had come anywhere near the village of Llandach. The metal birds were striking at the Fair Folk a week's walk north of here, which he supposed was a moment to them, but it was far enough for the village to feel safe. He didn't know what the Fair Folk had done to them, apart from belying their name and often looking ugly enough to curdle the milk they sometimes used to walk into the village to buy. Old women said they stole children, but Gwyllm had never met anyone who'd had their children stolen. And now they had all gone from around here, heading north. Perhaps that was a good thing. He just hoped everything would work itself out, one way or another, and that he wouldn't have to do anything about it.

The explosion made him think for a moment that the war had come to him.

He spun round from his boat, and saw that a great plume of water had burst up into the brilliant sky. A moment later, the wave from the impact hit the shore, and raced high up the shingle to cover his boots and the struts he'd hauled his boat on to.

He continued to watch the waters, warily, hearing cries from the village now.

He watched for ninety breaths, then ninety breaths more.

And then a figure broke the surface of the lake, and started to swim towards him with powerful strokes.

Gwyllm took an awl from inside the boat, and held it ready.

The man reached the shingle, gained a footing and got to his feet. He was tall, fully clothed, and carried a grey cloth bag. He smiled at Gwyllm and gave him a cheery wave before loping towards him through the surf.

When he got to the fisherman, all he did was extend his hand. 'I'm the Doctor,' he said. 'I'm here to help.'

That night found the Doctor sitting by a bonfire on a patch of common land just across from the inn where he had taken a room, a jar of ale in his hand. He wore a borrowed shirt and breeches, and thought that he made a passable Celt. 'Parallel technological evolution,' he was saying. 'Coaching inns for cartways. It's all very interesting.'

His new friends from the village of Llandach stared at him across the bonfire, some of them nodding politely, some of them exchanging laughing glances.

He laughed himself, and took a quick swig of the ale, then wiped his lips on the back of his hand.'You think I'm some sort of nutter who fell out of the sky on to his head.'

'No, we think you're a mage.' Gwyllm the fisherman looked dour as always. 'Mages are always... what did you call them? Nutters.'

'Oh, I agree. Can I have some more of that beer?' A farmer passed him a skin and he poured himself another cupful of the brown, bitter, liquid. 'I'd pay you in kind but the water messed up my scones and I used my gold to get the room. I'll give any of you a day's work for this.'

The villagers muttered as if insulted. 'You'll take our hospitality and like it!' growled the farmer. 'What would Bran think of us if we denied anything to a stranger? Sleep with my wife if you want to! I'll have your head when you leave the village, mind –'

The Doctor grinned and held up a declining hand. 'Thanks, but I'll stick with the beer.'

'What we want to know,' said Gwyllm, carefully, 'is what brought you here from out of the sky. You're a magical visitor: that means changes. Now you're a mild man, so we'd be glad if you stayed. But what does your coming here mean?'

The Doctor took a deep breath, and, over a few more cupfuls, described to them his mission from Mab, and, in more general terms, his dislike of the war. 'It's no good to anyone,' he finished. 'It's not as if the Fair Folk can all be lumped together as one community. We don't know if their leaders were responsible for the death of the ambassador. The Homelanders are using this conflict for their own ends.' A sudden thought struck him, as he saw the villagers nodding, doubtless remembering the 'invitation' made to the Romans that was at the root of their own founding tradition. 'And perhaps there's someone else – someone who's encouraging these nations to fight, not for fun, but for...' His beery gaze had swept up to take in the curious constellations glittering above, a perfect replica of the stars seen from Earth. The thought, and his occasional gift of prophecy, finally eluded him. 'Some other purpose,' he finished lamely. 'I think we're all missing a lot.'

A shepherd who the Doctor remembered had been called Arun

raised his hand. 'A friend of mine went missing,' he said. 'I left him down by the river, fetching water he was, to pass round the lads in the high field on a bright afternoon. He was a bit of a –' he smiled at the new word – 'nutter, like you say, a dreamer, too much into the business of the gods in his head. So he might have wandered off, like. But he didn't come home to my master's house that night, and nothing was heard from him again. His room's still full of his things.'

The Doctor put a finger to his lips, pondering. 'You say he was very religious. What sort of things did he do?'

'He was devoted to Brigida, the mad fool. Always writing poetry and sealing it up into little twists of paper and leaving it in trees for her. For some people that's all right. For me, if the gods don't bother me, I don't bother them.' He made a sudden reflexive horn sign with his hand. 'Blessed be all of us.'

The others did it, too. The Doctor did his best to join in, but got his fingers mixed up, and finally sat on his hands in embarrassment. 'You don't think the Fair Folk got him?'

'No... Well, I dunno. But if they did they did it without a struggle, and why they'd want a mad young shepherd boy...'

Gwyllm had been silent. Now he picked up his own skin and went to refill the Doctor's cup again. 'I follow Brigida as well. It helps with the fish. Practical, like. Whatever Arun says, we aren't passionate fools who wander off and drown.' He sat down beside the Doctor. 'The wonderful thing about Brigida –'

'Is that Brigida's a wonderful thing?' returned the Doctor, a bit tipsy. 'She's bouncy bouncy bouncy bouncy, fun fun fun fun fun?'

'No,' said Gwyllm, perplexed. 'If you follow Brigida, she'll answer your prayers. Here and now. None of this metaphor rubbish the druids tell you. It's a practical belief for a practical man like me. Gets results.'

There was laughter and a few choice remarks about Gwyllm's 'practicality'.

'But doesn't Constantine look after everything?' asked the Doctor. 'If his dreaming mind runs this dimension, then why don't you pray to him?'

'Because the old fool's asleep!' said Arun. 'He just keeps the whole thing ticking over, and every now and then you might see something sweet and you think, Oh aye, Constantine's perked up a bit and he's taking notice. But no, he's got the right idea. He doesn't look after every sparrow and think every little thing needs his attention or is his fault.'

The Doctor rubbed his brow and smiled gently, wondering how he was ever going to get to grips with all the details of this vast new world. Arun's version sounded more likely. He wasn't sure he believed the fisherman and his tales of an interventionist deity, but didn't want to hurt his feelings. 'That's... a great thing, Gwyllm,' he said. 'To have a faith so strong it feels practical.' The others laughed again, and he frowned. He didn't want anybody to be laughed at. 'So...' he asked, 'do any of you know any good songs?'

The gathering around the bonfire broke up around midnight, and the Doctor told his new friends that he was going to take a walk around the village before going to bed. Gwyllm tried to persuade him to wait until morning, or at least to let him accompany him, but the Doctor gently dissuaded him. He wanted, he said, a constitutional to walk off the effects of the ale, and knew the others all had work to do tomorrow.

In truth, he'd wanted to see what the defences of the village were like, to meet the watchkeepers who sat in huts by the gate, and check for gaps in the stockade, and, indeed, meet anything strange that might be abroad in the place at night. He knew he was missing something now, because, even with all the obvious political reasons for this conflict, there was still a weird flavour to it. It was all too perfect. It should have the messy knotting of history about it, but instead it looked like a narrative. It was as if... He shook his head again as he strolled away across the common towards the sighing shapes of the trees by the river. He still couldn't see it.

And, when he couldn't see what the enemy was doing, it had been his way in the past to tempt the enemy into coming to get him.

When he reached the river, he started to whistle the tune he'd taught the villagers. The theme from The Great Escape.

He followed the river around the village, hopping over it from time to time to inspect a rotten timber in the stockade, or leaving it entirely to follow something moving among the huts in the moonlight. Possibly an animal, and on one occasion definitely a scavenging badger, but often something that darted away from his gaze and moved with and about him.

He started to walk more cautiously now, aware of what was behind him, and of the noise his footsteps made. Come on, he thought. Here I am. Take the bait. Arrest me. Lock me up, take me in chains to whoever's really in charge of this game.

He remembered a time when that would have been enough, when from that point on he would have been utterly confident of winning. A time when he could be certain of what 'winning' meant. He was doing this almost out of habit, but what else could he do?

He knew it was going to happen a moment before it did, on the edge of a small, tangled copse of trees.

There was one splash from the river behind him.

Something was thrown over his head. He shouted. He was in darkness.

A cord was pulled just tightly enough about his throat. He stopped shouting.

He relaxed immediately. They could have killed him then. They didn't want to.

His hands were swiftly tied behind his back. They hit his wrists against a tree when he attempted to flex against the knot.

Experts. Plastic line, so not the Celts. British military.

They walked him swiftly towards the fence. Pushed him to his knees. A rifle barrel at the back of his neck. He crawled through a gap that he had failed to notice earlier. Another rifle met him on the other side.

At least two of them. He heard the other one follow him through the gap, and replace the wood behind them.

He was dragged to his feet, and pushed off at a run, two rifles nudging him to and fro.

They ran him about a mile through bracken and then through branches, grabbing him by the arms, obviously to navigate him through trees. Then they stopped and threw him to the ground.

A moment's silence. The bag was ripped from his head. The cord about his throat was released from some sort of lock at the back of his neck.

The Doctor eased himself into a sitting position, his arms still bound behind him, and looked at the man standing over him. He had a shaven head, wore camouflage fatigues, and held a knife on the end of which was a piece of freshly cooked meat. The insignia on his uniform indicated he was a captain. He was regarding the Doctor with a chillingly professional disinterest that was slightly more disturbing than rage and hatred would have been. Behind him stood the two men who had taken the Doctor, similarly dressed, both corporals. From the smell of it, they were near a campfire, deep in the woods. Around the rough camp, large packs of equipment had been opened out to create sleeping areas and a central billycan stove. From the number of positions, it looked like there were seven men in the group, but there were packs for eight.

'OK,' the Doctor murmured. 'You won that time. Now you go and hide.'

The soldiers looked at each other, laughing expressions on their faces. They thought he was being foolishly brave. The captain squatted down to his level, sucked the gobbet of meat off the knife and idly pointed it towards his throat. 'OK, Taff boy. You're going to tell us everything you know about Faerie movements in this area, and about British prisoners in Taff villages. You do that, we let you go.'

'No you won't.'

'Now why do you say that?'

'Because you've let me see your faces and uniforms. You're an eight-man patrol from D Squadron of the Special Air Service, out of Hereford. You've lost a man, which is why you're asking about prisoners. And you recently abducted and killed a shepherd with religious inclinations.'

The man's face showed no response. But the knife didn't move. 'Where did you get all that?'

'If I tell you, will you stop calling me "Taff"?'

The captain leaned closer, and stuck the knife exactly into the Doctor's neck, the pressure just insufficient to break the skin. 'No, Taff, I'll just let you live a bit longer.'

The Doctor held the man's gaze for a moment, then let his lips curl into the words: 'I'm Zachary.'

The captain sized him up for a second, then swept the knife into a pocket. He reached out and thumped his palms against both sides of the Doctor's chest. Then he swore and stood up. 'Steve, untie his hands. I've always wanted to meet this guy.'

They offered him some of their rabbit, but the Doctor turned it down. Within a few minutes, the other four remaining team members returned. They'd been on a yomp up a small hill nearby with the radio transmitter.

'We've been out of touch with base for two days now,' explained the captain. 'There's something about this place that causes radio interference. That, and we need to get a line of sight, because there's no ionosphere up there.' He shook his head and swore again. 'I will never laugh at a UNIT trooper again.'

The Doctor found a handful of nuts in the ashes of the fire, and started to split them open. 'So who exactly are you? What's your mission?'

Some of the soldiers exchanged glances, but the captain shook his head to them. 'The Doctor's cleared more than we are. He knows all about... What do you call them? Ogrons?' The Doctor nodded. 'I killed one of those, once. In single combat. Strangled the brute. Kicked like a horse.' The others joined in the chuckle. 'And you take on things like those on a regular basis.' He held out his hand to the Doctor. 'Captain Mark Caldera. We are Delta One Five patrol, His Majesty's green-eyed boys in fairyland.'

'Green-eyed boys in fairyland!' the soldiers bellowed.

The Doctor gingerly shook the man's hand. 'And your mission?'

'We're heading north to paint lasers on targets as they present themselves for precision bombing. On the way we're being dropped off at intervals for general recon, noting security issues and mapping the territory.'

'And you've lost a man?'

'Yeah, my second in command, Joe Boyce. Two nights ago he left camp to take a slash, and that's all we saw of him. No noise, no sign of a struggle. Nothing. We searched twenty-five square kilometres and reconned every nearby village. You were our last shout. It's like he just walked off.'

'That's what they say happened to the shepherd, too.'

'Could have done. Could be the Faeries. We didn't kill him. We haven't had to kill any Taffs yet.'

The Doctor put a hand over his eyes. 'I don't know why I always end up with military men. What's your final destination?'

'Aurora photographs suggest there's some sort of palace just north of what we'd call Inverness. One cruise missile managed to target it using overland mapping. Then they changed the geography, messed everything up in the sky as well, so they can't target it again. Until we get there and set up beacons. Then: wham. That one strike might end the war.'

The Doctor's mouth had dropped open. 'That sounds to me like suicide.'

'About fifty-fifty, we reckon. We've got a rendezvous with a stealth chopper at midnight that'll take us within fifteen kilometres. If Joe doesn't get a move on, we're going to have to leave him.'

A slow smile played about the corners of the Doctor's mouth. He'd just had a very silly idea. 'Can I come with you?'

The soldiers erupted in laughter. Caldera put a hand to his blackened brow. 'Erm, we don't really have room for passengers.'

The Doctor leaned forward and looked him in the eye. 'I can walk you through any security system that building has, scientific or magical. I'd say that without me, your chances are more like ninety-ten. And that isn't a good ninety.'

Caldera weighed him up for a moment. Then he nodded. 'All right. Your reputation precedes you. But why do you want in on this mission?'

The Doctor folded his arms around his knees, satisfied. 'Let's just say that my aims are much the same as yours. But I'm going to employ different means.'

Chapter Seven
Nothing Can Stop Us Now

The Brigadier slumped on to his canvas bed and stared up at the ornate plasterwork on the ceiling above. He'd been up all night co-ordinating strikes on the Northern enemy. Strikes they'd largely turned aside. Their magical advisers were countering the offensives as swiftly as the Celt magical advisers could devise them. It didn't feel like a real battle, although the screens had lit his face with images of bombs falling into cross-hairs and of model-railway boxes of buildings exploding.

One of the MOs had taken him aside and ordered him to sleep.

He couldn't obey that order. He felt so utterly numb. He wondered whether anybody would notice if he left his post and wandered off into those green fields out there, bought up some land and made a garden. The war would go on, because it had to. Avalon was too strategically significant for the British forces to stop now. Even if the enemy agreed to the terms of ceasefire, they'd find some reason to stay put and offer Mab protection. He didn't feel hypocritical about that. It was just the way of the world. Terrible things happened. One had to watch out for one's own interests.

'I'm sleeping in the spare room tonight,' Doris said, marching off towards the door, in a huff.

'Don't be so –' he started to reply. But she was gone, out of his tired mind. She'd swum in and out of his life over the last few days. It was frustrating, seeing her for five minutes here and there. He hoped that he might get into actual combat soon. He'd let that settle the matter.

The thought made him smile. He closed his eyes, and might have been able to get some sleep then. 'Soon,' he said to her. 'Hang on, my dear.'

There was a knock on the door. He sat upright, thinking something terrible must have happened. 'Yes?'

It was Mab. She was dressed in a long grey cloak, with a hood over her head, her familiar obscene amulet sparkling in the torchlight. She looked, thought the Brigadier, as though she'd been weeping.

'Are you alone?' she said. 'I heard voices.'

'What the hell –' He was on his feet in a moment, grabbing his dressing gown to cover his pyjamas. 'Do you mean to imply by –' He stopped himself, and closed his eyes, holding in the anger. 'You'll really have to excuse me, Queen Regent,' he finally managed. 'I'm extremely tired. What can I do for you?' He walked to the door and ushered her in, closing it behind her. 'I was just about to make a spot of tea, actually. You're welcome to join me.'

She sat down on a canvas stool by the bed. She drew back her hood and shook out her hair. 'It's been a long time since anyone shouted at me,' she said. 'I think Margwyn was the last. When I was much younger.' She'd definitely been weeping.

The Brigadier ignited his stove, and poured some water from the jug by his bed into the kettle. 'As I said, my apologies. It's been a hard day. The voice you heard was me. Talking to myself. A habit of old soldiers, I'm afraid.'

'You sounded gentle. As if you were talking to a woman.'

He opened the drawer in his bureau that contained his can of tea. 'Indeed?'

She waited for a moment, as if needing to be certain about her intuition, and then said, 'Who is she?'

'Who?'

'This woman you were talking to.'

He found the teapot, the same carefully absent lack of thought in his head as when he'd been under fire. 'Do you take sugar?'

There was a moment's silence from behind him. Then, in a voice full of heat: 'Of course I don't bloody take sugar. We don't have sugar. I don't know what that drink you're making is, and I didn't come here to talk about it!'

He turned back to her, teapot in hand, and this time he kept his voice clipped. 'I'm not used to being shouted at either, Queen Regent. And I'd appreciate it if you didn't seek to interfere in my personal affairs. Now on what business did you come here?'

She looked at him for a long moment, her eyes blazing, then obviously, mercifully, decided not to pursue the question of his talking to himself. 'I feel...' she began, more gently. 'I feel we've made a mistake. All four of us.'

'Four? Who do you mean?'

'That traitor Margwyn, the Doctor – who knows it, he's gone out there trying to put it right – me and you. I feel this on the basis of my religion, of the feeling of Brigida I get when I look to the green slopes out there.'

The Brigadier, finding himself unable to manufacture any sort of coherent reply, put the kettle on the stove and began to fill the teapot. 'I see,' he finally said. 'You think that we're all missing something.'

'You see?' She bounced on the stool. 'That thought wouldn't have come to you if Brigida wasn't with you, too, *Brigidier*! That's why I asked who the voice was. I thought she was here in your room. I thought you were communing with the goddess!'

'Not my sort of thing, I'm afraid.'

'Oh, so you'd like to think! Stop fighting it!'

He watched as the kettle boiled. 'It's immaterial,' he said. 'The things that cross one's mind. So much nonsense. I have to do my duty.'

She stood, and put a hand on his shoulder, quite deliberately. He turned his head and looked at it. 'I had a dream tonight,' she said. 'In which Brigida came to me, and told me that you wanted to die in battle for her. For me.'

He coughed a laugh. 'No, ma'am. Not for either of you.' He took the kettle off the stove and poured the boiling water into the pot, concentrating to make sure his hand didn't shake. 'Perhaps we could save this debate on comparative religion for another occasion?'

'You must know... I don't know how it is in your tradition, but for ours the sacrifice of a warrior is meaningless if he does it for the wrong reason.'

He placed the pot on the side table, and found that he had

nothing left to do. He sat down in his chair and saw his slippers under the bed. He reached out and put them on.

'For the sake of all the gods, you stupid man!' she exploded in frustration.'I woke up crying about you tonight! About you, and Gwyn, and McKewon and the Keeper! Now, them, I can be joyful for them: they'll be back on the wheel of life soon enough and I know I'm only weeping for my lack of them. But you! I'm weeping for you because you're dead inside, but you're still walking about! Who was she? Who was this woman who's half killed you?'

He stared at his feet, aware of the thousandth thing that had reminded him of his wife. Doris had bought him these slippers when his old pair had developed obvious holes in the toes. 'Obvious holes in the toes.' He could hear her saying it. He looked up at Mab again, his eyes sparkling with the memory. 'She was very dear to me,' he said.'I see her in dreams. Still. It's been over a year.'

Mab let out a deep breath, pleased.'If you give your life for her, then you'll be giving it for the wrong reason. And that will be an insult to your goddess.'

The Brigadier found that he was already uncomfortable at the thought of having told her so much. This blasted woman had succeeded in doing what she'd wanted to do all along: crack him open and get at the flesh inside.'And you wouldn't give your life for your fallen loved ones, I suppose?'

'Bloody Gwyn Mab Nud and his flying horses! I hope not! For my living folk, yes, but...' She trailed off.'We're thinking the wrong thoughts, and doing the wrong things, you and I,' she said.'And we still can't see another way to go. But our goddess, *Brigidier*, wants something more from all four of us. Something different from what we've been doing.'

'And what would that be, exactly? Surrender? Give up? Let the world just do what it wants with us?' The Brigadier slapped his palm on his knee. 'I'm just a soldier, Mab. I'm not the Doctor. I don't get to ride on the backs of dragons and offer myself up for death like some foolish –' He suddenly found that he was quite choked by something, and didn't understand why it had come now. He got to his feet, leaving his sentence, and the anger, hanging, and put his hands to the pot, pretending that he needed to feel how warm it was in order to produce good tea. The thought of the Doctor. Of how terrible it would have been to see him shot up there. To have him die, too. Stupid, just one person... The thought that he might lose another...

Something needed to escape him then and he finally let it.

'Her name was Doris, since you ask,' he said quickly, not looking at Mab. 'My wife. Tragic accident. Nothing to be done. All over in a –' He stopped, and grimaced, and found that he was foolishly unable to stop cupping the warmth of the teapot in his hands. He shook his head, his lips pursed, as he felt Mab approaching him. She laid her arms around his chest, and pressed her breasts to his back and her cheek against his shoulders. Utterly naturally, as if she was gathering a child to her for comfort.

He did, and most certainly did not, want to be a child.

He could not move or speak. He fought not to start shaking, because if he started, he knew he wouldn't stop.

'Tell me it all,' she whispered gently. 'You have to start this somewhere. It's been a year, but you haven't let it take you. Come to my chamber, bring your tea, we'll talk of –'

'No. I'm sorry. Please... Leave me.'

She didn't move.

He suddenly found that it was too much to bear. 'Get out, damn you!' he bellowed.

She hung on for a moment, and then let go.

Defeated, as if everything now was lost, she walked back to the door. She paused on the threshold and looked at him with infinite sadness. 'We can't leave it all to the Doctor,' she said. 'All of us are going to have to find a way to be him, if anything at all is to be saved.'

And then she was gone.

The Brigadier slowly put the teapot down.

He made his way back to his bed and sat carefully down on it. He was shaking. He took a deep breath and held it. He stopped.

After a long moment, he reached for his palmtop, and tapped in a few commands: a request to be sent into combat as soon as the opportunity arose.

'Very good,' he whispered to himself. Then he put down his palmtop, lowered his head slowly on to the pillow and resumed his staring at the ceiling.

'A time vortex, of course. It had to be something like that.' Compassion walked towards the swirling butterfly tunnel and stared into its violet depths. She reached out a hand and paused, then reached further, a questioning expression on her face, as if she wanted to touch the surface of the rainbowing apparition on the wall.

Margwyn snatched her hand away. 'If you touch the portal,' he said, 'you'll be whisked off to some random time and place.'

'No,' she said. 'Not random.' Then, with a frown: 'Yes, that's right, what am I thinking of?'

Fitz was leaning on a workbench at the back of the room, picking his teeth in bemusement. Compassion had begun to have funny five minutes, during which she briefly seemed to become a real, emotional, complicated person. He was all for that, obviously, but it made him as uneasy as everything else here did. It was not good, he thought, to have a time vortex mounted like a picture on the wall of your laboratory. You might trip over and end up on Pluto. At least this room being a laboratory made it more familiar. The Fair Folk War Mages were experimenting with science, so they had been told, a programme that had been going on for years, but that had become a subject of much interest now they were at war with a scientific enemy.

Fitz snorted at the name: Fair Folk! Maybe they were just very even-handed. Which, he supposed, made the Celts and their British allies from the far future world of 2012 the Unfair Folk. Margwyn had asked the War Mages if he could show Compassion and Fitz the portal through which they would be travelling tomorrow morning, when it seemed the phase of the moon or something would be exactly right. Not that they had a proper moon here. That thing up in the sky was apparently some sort of cosmic light show, projected by the mind-boggling King Constantine to make his Celts feel more at home. Fitz felt his brow again, wondering once more if this whole adventure was the product of too much cheese before bedtime. Constantine probably shone that moon out of his –

'Pay attention!' snapped Margwyn, and Fitz jumped. The black-clad mage was holding a device shaped like a divining rod. Two slim silver limbs stretched from a knobbled centre, upon which were set switches and dials. It looked like exactly the sort of scientific gizmo that people used to magic would produce. He pointed to the wall. 'That's the one-way dimensional portal that the War Mages have managed to create. I must say this business of science surpasses my own knowledge. I know not how this is done, but my magical senses tell me it is so.' He held up the device. 'And this is the sensor device that the War Mages have created to help you find the wandering form of the King –'

'Why can't they come and explain all this to us themselves?' Compassion asked.

'They're a little shy of us,' Margwyn frowned. It looked as if he was in the uncomfortable position of explaining something that he wasn't quite sure of himself. He was using his zeal for the cause, Fitz thought, to carry himself along. He was like the Red Army soldiers Fitz had marched with, forever reaching for their little red books. 'That's their natural inclination,' finished Margwyn, 'and, with our peoples now at war, I think the very sight of us disturbs them.'

'No kidding,' muttered Fitz.

'That's the situation we seek to correct, in the most peaceful way possible,' Margwyn insisted. 'If we can make Constantine close the gateway and expel the forces from Earth, then these folk can make peace with my people, and everything will be settled.' His voice took on a wistful quality. 'We will return to the state of tangnefedd, the great peace of grace and gentle rule.'

Fitz snapped his fingers and pointed to Compassion. 'Hey! I've just thought! Tangnefedd! That's Welsh or whatever! The first thing he's said that I didn't understand, like what sometimes happens to us on another planet if the language is complicated! Don't you get it? If the TARDIS has been destroyed and the Doctor's dead, why can we still understand what this lot are saying?'

But Margwyn was shaking his head. 'In Constantine's dream all peoples can speak to each other.'

Compassion nodded. 'I don't think the Doctor will save the day this time, Fitz. If the TARDIS still existed, then I'd feel it, feel it...' She frowned again. 'Holding me back. Saving me.' She raised a hand to stop Fitz asking what she meant. 'I think all we can do is decide what the Doctor would do, and pursue that aim.'

'So do you think he'd go along with Margwyn's plan?' Fitz watched the mage's face.

'I don't know...' Compassion replied. 'I think Margwyn's an ethical man, but...' She reached out her finger to hover just over the surface of the vortex once more. 'I just think there's something that we're all missing.'

The sleek black helicopter sped north, dipping and bobbing over the terrain below. The air around it was getting thicker and thicker, full of drops of green fluid that splattered against the fuselage and were flung aside in great sweeps by the blades.

At the back of the aircraft's cabin sat the Doctor, half asleep, his head nodding to the beat of the rotors. In his mind, a woman was touching his brow with a cool hand and telling him all was not lost.

He jerked awake and looked around wildly when Caldera touched him on the shoulder. 'Two minutes to go,' he murmured. The Doctor noted that the men all around him were tensed, all looking towards the side door beside which one of their number sat, his hand on the release lever.

They had split up for a while before midnight – the soldiers to make one last pass through the woods for their missing man, the Doctor to return to the village for his normal clothes. The soldiers hadn't understood that, and had been amazed by what he'd returned in.

On his way out of the village, he'd noticed something strange. From the hut by the pebble beach that he knew belonged to Gwyllm, he'd heard the sounds of a woman wailing. He'd gone to the window, in the darkness, and looked in. A handsome woman, he presumed Gwyllm's wife, was holding his clothes to her chest, sobbing. The Doctor knew the instant he saw her that the fisherman had vanished, gone into the night like the others, and that the only comfort he could offer would be to solve this as part of the greater mystery of Avalon.

For that he had to travel north, to follow in the footsteps of this man Margwyn and speak directly to the Unseelie Court. He could try to persuade them to communicate with Mab once more, offer his services as an intermediary. Perhaps they might also have news of Compassion and Fitz. Perhaps Constantine had given the courts of this world one set of strangers each.

The thought had come to him, as he found the soldiers huddled around a clearing in the woods, that if they knew what he was planning they wouldn't be offering him a lift.

The black helicopter had come out of the night sky almost silently, showing only the blink of its navigation lights. As he stepped inside the cabin, the Doctor had looked back. The helicopter was already rising into the air, and he'd seen the village by the lake, a few lights here and there, a dog barking. It looked utterly unprepared for war to fall upon it.

Perhaps he could make sure that it never would. Or, perhaps, the damning thought struck him again, he could never be sure of that no matter what he did.

Now, he took his place at the back of the two lines of men that formed along the walls of the cabin. The floor swayed beneath them, the pitch of the engines changed, and there was a gentle bump as the skids just touched the ground.

'Clear?' asked Caldera into an intercom. Then he replaced the receiver and swept his arm across his chest. 'Go go go!'

The soldier by the door slammed the lever up, and the door hissed open. The first two SAS men leapt out into the green fog and hit the ground running, night-vision goggles wrapped around their balaclavas. The others sprinted out after them, the Doctor and Caldera last. They dived into loose shrubs at the base of a forest, and stayed perfectly still as the blizzard of twigs and leaves from the helicopter raged, died, and then stopped, and the soft noise fluttered away into the sounds of night animals and birds. The Doctor looked up. Above the canopy of trees, two tiny lights were heading south again. Then they vanished into the mist.

There came a sound from the bushes ahead of them. One of the men was retching. Caldera made a complex whistle, and a moment later a muted hoot came back. The captain smiled at the Doctor and nodded. The Doctor could feel why the man had reacted like that. Apart from the tension of rushing into danger, the atmosphere of this wood was like nothing he'd ever experienced before. The canopy of trees overhead, and the bracken they lay in, looked perfectly familiar, and all the little noises of birdcalls and rummaging night creatures that one might expect from Britain in summer could be heard. The smells too were ordinary, the delicious mixture of summer loam and the cold dew that suppressed the carpet of pollen and kept the flowers fresh for the morning. But above and beyond this was an all-devouring sensation of... presence. It was like being in a spotlight on a stage, going into the most important meeting of your life, wondering if a girl would accept your proposal of marriage... well, probably. If it made him feel vulnerable, he could imagine what it was doing to these soldiers, trained to hide. This was what differentiated Faerie from the lands available to the humans: the quality of the dream.

He made a sudden unilateral decision, and got to his feet. The captain leapt up and tried to bring him down, but he hopped quickly sideways out of his clutches and wandered off, his hands in his pockets, towards a forest track he could see through the green mist. 'It's this way!' he called over his shoulder. 'You can come out, there's nobody around!'

After a moment, and a lot of hooting, the soldiers rose from their cover and trotted warily after him.

The Doctor allowed himself a little smile at Captain Caldera.

* * *

They strode and marched, respectively, down the track through several miles of the shifting, shimmering forest. The Doctor could feel the men getting restless, looking left and right as they went, their weapons held unslung and at the ready. He was starting, on the other hand, to feel almost at home. This place was like the Matrix on Gallifrey, and, with his senses pitched at just the right angle, he was certain that he would feel any oncoming –

He stopped suddenly, and the men all stopped with him. 'Someone's coming,' he said. 'Lots of them.'

Captain Caldera swung a finger in the air. There was an explosion of movement, and the soldiers suddenly all vanished. A head popped up from the plant life by the side of the path, a hand frantically beckoning to the Doctor. He knocked his brain into gear and vaulted into the ditch beside the captain.

They lay still, hardly breathing, as tramping feet, Faerie and animal, passed by. The animals were bipeds as well as the people, and the Doctor guessed that some of the Fair Folk were riding small dragons. With the footsteps came the clatter of ordnance, the whir of things flying by. Caldera had his eyes closed, listening to every detail.

They waited for ten minutes once the last noise had passed. Then Caldera put his head out of cover, looked slowly around and whistled. The soldiers leapt back on to the path.

'A small patrol,' whispered Caldera. 'They still don't seem to be forming up for action anywhere. It's as if they're saving their forces. Doctor, you saved our arses: lead on.'

The Doctor stopped for a moment to psychically sniff the air, then motioned for the soldiers to follow. 'We're getting near to the fortress now,' he told them. 'Try to think happy thoughts.'

They managed to cross the forest without encountering any further Faerie forces, but at the edge of the trees the party stopped, gazing in astonishment at what lay ahead.

They were on the edge of a cliff, the roots of the trees making the cliff edge crumbly and treacherous. Great gaps in the stone indicated that the forest was continually undermining the edge of its grounds, that every month a tree or a line of trees would plunge off the side and fall the hundreds, possibly thousands, of feet to whatever was obscured by the darkness below. The cliff face stretched round, curving out of sight in both directions, forming a great circular crater.

But it wasn't the plunge that was the most extraordinary feature of what stood before them. In this great chasm in the earth, far below sea level, there stood a huge shape, what the Doctor at first took to be the opposite cliff face. But then he realised that it was an object standing in the centre of a vast quarry, a giant omphalos about which the earth had been cut. It grew up from far below them, and continued high into the air above. It was illuminated in the darkness by thousands of lights inside it, where Faeries worked and lived in the night.

It was a vast, knotted tree, perhaps a mighty oak, alive and turning at the centre of the world. For moving it certainly was - too slowly for human eyes to see. It was spinning on its axis, the centre of the world Constantine had created.

'Behold,' whispered the Doctor. 'The Unseelie Court!'

He fell full length on to the grass, and squirmed on his elbows to the edge of the cliff. From there, he cautiously poked his head over, and gazed down into the abyss. He could see nothing but swirling green fog, but he could smell... brimstone. Sulphur! The Court tree was standing in, drawing its nourishment from, an active volcano!

He moved gently back from the edge, and returned to squat beside Caldera. 'What do you think?' he asked. 'Aren't you moved to tears? Stimulated? Turned on? In a creative sense, I mean.'

'Big target,' said the soldier. 'No way of getting across.'

The Doctor looked at him for a moment. 'Sometimes I think I made a mistake giving you guys fire.' He waved a hand in front of Caldera's face. 'Hello? Where do you think that reptilian patrol came from?'

'Don't patronise me, Doctor. I assumed they flew over somehow, by magic.'

'No, magic takes energy, even here. You don't use it when you don't have to. There must be something... Tell your men to search the ground around this side of the crater.'

Caldera issued the order, and within half an hour a series of whistles took them to a small clearing, a few hundred metres back from the edge of the cliff, where a simple golden disc, about the size of a manhole cover, gleamed dully on the ground. A soldier was squatting beside it.

'Well done.' The Doctor slapped the soldier on the back. He strode on to the disc, and put a finger to his lips, pondering. 'Now, how would this activate? I've got to start thinking backwards, get rid of all the science and try to get my head round Constantine's version of magic. Erm... abracadabra? Open sesame? Izzy whizzy, let's get busy?'

Nothing happened.

He tried placing his forehead to the plate and concentrating, yelling a variety of variations on simple commands to open, meditating over the plate in a yogic posture.

Nothing continued to happen.

He stamped his foot on the plate.

There came a whirr of power from underground, and, round the plate, a circular section of ground about twenty feet across separated itself from its surrounding and began to revolve. Some of the soldiers on the edge were caught unawares, but Caldera motioned for them to get inside the circle. They had to jump a couple of feet as the circular section, still spinning, lowered itself at high speed. Swiftly they were below ground level, inside a polished green shaft, the walls of which gleamed like jade. A circle of night sky grew quickly smaller above them.

The Doctor slapped his forehead. 'It was just a door. No security system involved. They've never needed one. Oh, Doctor, sometimes you don't see the galaxy for the solar systems.'

'If they didn't need one there –' began Caldera.

'Yes. We may be lucky.' The Doctor ran a hand back through his hair. He hoped this wasn't going to be difficult. 'Listen, Captain, if we do make it inside the castle, I'm going to go my own way. I have a mission of my own here. I don't want you to wait for me.'

'What?' He'd only just started to react when the timbre of the noise all around them changed and the descent slowed. Light burst in in a ring around their feet, then spread upward, and as their eyes adjusted to the glare they could see they were coming to rest at the centre of a round, silver room. Dark arches led off in several directions, and lines were painted on the floor. A staging area. Or rather a room recently converted into one. The ring elevator must be on top of some sort of piston, thought the Doctor, as they came to a sudden halt, level with the floor.

There was silence. 'Ready,' said Caldera. There was a sudden clatter of slipped safety catches. 'Which door, Doctor?'

The Doctor put a finger to his lips. 'I think –'

There was a light in one of the tunnels. The Doctor looked up and flinched.

A noise –

One of the soldiers collided with him and fell away, his fingers plucking reflexively at a thin metal shaft sticking from his chest. He was screaming as he hit the ground.

Then the air was a blizzard of the shafts and their ears were full of the rattle of weapons. The soldiers had started moving at the first shot, sprinting for one of the other tunnels as two of their number returned fire, their automatic rifles blazing down the tunnel ahead of the platform.

The noise filled the chamber.

The Doctor found that he was crawling towards the screaming soldier. He glanced back, and saw one of the men who were firing caught by more shafts. In the stomach, the shoulder, the head, the impacts twisting him in three sudden directions, his gun continuing to fire for a moment before it spasmed out of his hands and clattered across the floor. He hit the ground at such an angle that the shafts sliced back through him and he was still.

The Doctor turned back. He was nearly at the screaming man.

A hand caught him by the collar and pulled.

'Leave him!' Caldera was screaming. He seized the Doctor in one arm, and spun him back across the room in an arc, firing back down the corridor almost casually as they went.

The soldier who was still firing was ducking in and out of the archway opposite. The remaining three were waiting there, and now one of them swapped positions with the firing man and started blazing away from a different height and angle. Caldera shoved the Doctor through the archway and put him up against the wall in cover, his thumb on his carotid artery. 'We are going to do this now, right? We've come too far to pull out. No time for heroics. Show us the way.'

There was a further hissing of metal through the air from the arch of light around the corner. The firing soldier ducked back. The screaming cut suddenly into a shout, a cough, then stopped.

'All right!' the Doctor shouted, feeling sick to his stomach. There were sounds coming down the corridor they were in. Running footsteps. Screeches. 'That way.' He pointed straight up.

On the ceiling above them was set a metal grille.

The six of them crawled swiftly through the darkness on their elbows. From all around them, they could hear alarms and shouts and hisses and roars, as the castle came to life in the night, angered by their presence inside its system.

'Why can't you just get out and run for it?' the Doctor yelled.

'Because nobody else is going to get this far!' snapped Caldera. 'If we place our radio beacons correctly, this lot won't find them all, and the bombers will be able to get a target fix.'

'Then can't you place them now?'

'No. We want the centre of power. The one big room. You kill the right ten people and you end the war. Always.'

The Doctor felt for a moment like using one of the soldier's own curt swearwords. He'd thought that he would navigate them through a security system, that these men would hide, do their job, and leave, after which he would have the bargaining chip of the location and removal of their homing beacons to offer the Unseelie Court. Instead of which, there had been no security system, just, he guessed, alert guards, and he had offhandedly led these people into what was turning into a massacre.

From ahead there came a light. 'We're heading for some sort of storage area,' the Doctor shouted. 'Follow me. Try not to kill anybody.'

Cavis lay in the crook of Gandar's shoulder in their bed of furs, her palm against his scaly chest. 'I like you as an Earth Reptile,' she decided. 'I want to have your eggs.'

'I swear,' he rumbled, 'that is the only reason you do this stuff. For the clothes.'

Cavis leaned back and stretched, luxuriating in the knowledge that everything was going right, as it always did for them. Truly, they were the zenith of what the Other had intended when he founded the Interventionists, all those millennia ago. 'And the travel. And the extreme violence. Murder, sex and adventure in exotic frocks. Who could ask for anything more?'

A beeping came from somewhere off the bed, among the clothes and chests and apparatus that filled the untidy little bedchamber.

They both sat up at the same instant.

'Othering Omega!' said Gandar. 'That's –'

'The Time Lord proximity alarm,' whispered Cavis. 'Which means –'

They said it together. 'He's here!'

They looked at each other with something approaching awe. 'The ultimate test,' said Cavis. 'We have to take him out.' Then she giggled.

He started to laugh, too. 'So let's get it on!' He kissed her quickly, then leapt up to grab his clothes.

She reached under the bed and pulled out a shell-like communicator. 'Security,' she said into the horn. 'This is a priority order: seal off the ventilation ducts.'

The Doctor swung out of the ventilation duct and let go just as a metal panel slammed across the gap where his fingers had been. 'They know me too well,' he muttered.

He and the five soldiers he'd shepherded out in front of him were standing in a stone passageway that led at an angle downward. The Doctor closed his eyes, turning on the spot, his hands jumbling in front of him as his boots danced over each other, trying to orientate himself. Then he suddenly pointed up the passage. 'That way!' he exclaimed. 'I've been mapping this place in my head, and if I'm right that'll lead to the kitchens under the central chambers. You should find what you're looking for somewhere there.'

'And where are you going?' asked Caldera.

The Doctor pointed down the slope. 'That way,' he said. He'd got the directions exactly the wrong way round, of course, as far as he could tell. He'd led the soldiers as well as their pursuers a merry dance, up and down the ventilation ducts, the equivalent of putting a bag over their heads and spinning them round. The upward slope should lead them to a side gate, from which they might feel obliged to make their way back to safety. Short of arranging for them to be spirited home, that was the best he could do. They were already probably far too associated with him for his diplomacy to succeed. But he had to try.

Caldera marched up to him, and swung the muzzle of his gun to cover his chest. 'And if I told you to stay with us?'

'I'd still go that way.' He took a pace forward and looked the soldier in the eye. The sudden awareness of what was to happen to this man came to him, as it often did. This time, it was very reassuring, and the Doctor was filled with an absolute certainty about the future, the like of which he hadn't felt for a long time now. He knew that, for this man at least, there was the possibility of a happy ending. The thought of it gave him a moment of pure joy. 'When you get back home to Cheltenham,' he said. 'Avoid the sushi. Bye.'

Then he turned, holding Caldera's gaze for a moment, and ran off down the slope.

When he turned the corner, he slumped against the wall, astonished. 'They actually didn't shoot me!' He laughed. 'Woo.'

After a few moments to get his breath back, he grabbed a blazing torch from its holder on the wall, and headed cautiously on into the darkness.

* * *

He walked past the open door without thinking, then stopped, realised what he'd just seen, and, astonished, retraced his steps.

He peered through the arched doorway, his mouth falling open in wonder. He was looking into a laboratory, a scientific laboratory, which was extraordinary in itself. But it was what was on the wall that amazed him most.

In a metal frame, an activated time vortex was silently spinning away.

That familiar sight from his childhood was what had caught his notice as he trotted by. The Fair Folk must be attempting, and quite successfully at that, to find a means to escape this dimension. Were they really advanced enough to do that?

He entered the room, still gazing at the vortex, and noticed what had been written on the blackboard beside it, in big, chunky capitals: CHANGE CONSTANTINE'S DREAM AT SOURCE, EXPEL INTRUDERS, CLOSE THE GATEWAY.

'Good idea,' he whispered.

He spun round at the sound of the door slamming behind him.

Two figures emerged from the shadows. They were dressed as Fair Folk mages.

Both were pointing guns at him.

'We really should have erased those notes,' said the female figure.

'It doesn't matter,' said her male companion. He stepped into the light. 'Good evening, Doctor. What a pleasant surprise that you could join us.'

'He does this so well,' said the woman.

The man indicated his gun. 'This is a Gallifreyan Patrol Staser. One of the few hand weapons in the universe that can kill you outright. As I'm sure you're aware.'

'Oh, I'm aware,' the Doctor muttered, looking between them. He recognised them even through their quantum disguises. 'Suddenly I'm very aware. You're Cavisadoratrelundar and Gandarotethetledrax, two Interventionists recruited out of the Patrexes. I've heard stories about you. About what you did to the Vardans.' The two agents stole a pleased glance at each other. Proud, he thought, racking his memories for details. Involved with each other. But still two of the most cruel and sadistic individuals you could ever hope to avoid. He took a couple of steps towards them. 'I knew your father, Cavis. He visited my family at Lungbarrow, once. Perhaps I bounced you on my knee.'

Cavis looked skyward for a nanosecond. 'Oh, please. Does that matter?'

'He was a staunch anti-Interventionist all his life.'

'Absolutely. Which was why we had to kill him.'

Gandar nodded. 'I did it. I thought it was best to spare her that.'

The Doctor hugged himself, and glanced over his shoulder at the time vortex behind him. 'So the Fair Folk have developed temporal technology, and you're here to stamp it out.'

'As if!' Gandar shook his head at him as if he was an idiot. 'We're here because –'

'Hey!' Cavis yelled at him. 'No!'

Gandar's jaw dropped open. 'Oh, man.' He smiled at the Doctor. 'I really have to congratulate you, sir. You're the consummate professional.'

'A gifted amateur.' The Doctor allowed himself a smile in return. 'So were you two responsible for the missile attack on Mab's castle?' They looked uncertain about how much they should reveal. 'Oh, come on,' he prompted. 'That's an easy one. This is the point where you're allowed to boast before you kill me.'

Cavis started giggling. The Doctor got the feeling that both she and Gandar were a little in awe of him. Perhaps he could use that.

'We put our TARDIS in the path of a small asteroid that was due to burn up in Earth's atmosphere,' she said. 'It whizzed in through the doors, and kept going, because we'd configured the entrance into endless-tunnel mode.' She looked meaningfully at her partner, encouraging him to finish the story.

'Then we rematerialised in Avalon, opened the doors, and let the thing carry right on through,' he concluded proudly.

The Doctor applauded, which seemed to please them. 'Oh, I'd heard you were good. You've got a wonderful reputation for mayhem. I suppose you arranged for the gateway to open up between Earth and Avalon.'

Cavis frowned like a baby. 'Uh-uh. That's kind of why we're here. Gallifrey Central knew it was going to happen. A happy accident.'

'You young fools,' muttered the Doctor. 'Don't you know by now? There are no accidents.' His thoughts were racing. He was just starting to see the bigger picture, and what a worrying picture it was. But he forced himself to continue playing this game. He had to find out as much as he could. 'Central, eh? So what's Goth been telling you about me?'

'President Roma–' Cavis started to correct him, then put a hand to her mouth. 'Now I'm doing it.'

'Romana?' The Doctor stared at her, aghast. 'You're here on her orders?' He suddenly found he couldn't be flippant any longer. 'Just what is your game here? What are you planning?'

The agents exchanged an edgy, awkward look. 'Enough of this stuff,' said Gandar. He aimed his weapon straight between the Doctor's hearts. 'No more chitchat. Let's just kill the Otherf–'

The Doctor leapt forward, on to a lab bench, and kicked backwards.

He somersaulted in the air, two staser blasts dissolving the tabletop where his feet had been a second before, and spun straight into the time vortex.

As he sped off down the butterfly corridor, feeling his mind and body start to fragment in the turbulence, he held his consciousness together with just one tiny hope.

The writing on that blackboard had been terribly familiar.

'He did it to us! That stuff he always does! He did it to us!' Cavis leapt forward and aimed her staser at the speck that had vanished off into the depths of the vortex. But he'd gone. With a little gasp of annoyance she snatched it back to her side again. 'This is all your fault, you and your hero worship!'

'On the contrary, my dear. We now have the Doctor exactly where we want him.' Gandar sauntered up to the control panel, and spun the dial. 'Which is... a random location in time and space. With all of infinity to choose from, I doubt he'll end up anywhere he can harm us.'

Cavis looked uncertain for a moment, then reached out to give the dial an extra spin herself. 'Just to make sure,' she said.

Fitz woke up to the sound of a great thumping. He was lying across two of the vastly uncomfortable alien chairs. His head had been hanging at an awkward angle, and an instant after he'd got the being-awake bit, and the now familiar sense of not-quite-being-himself bit, he got the being-mightily-ticked-off bit. Outside the window, it was still... green. Dark green. So it was still probably the middle of the night. He looked over to where Compassion was looking up, eyes wide, from her rugs on the floor, and hauled himself to his feet. He went to the door and opened it.

Margwyn nearly fell into the room. 'Quickly!' he yelled. 'The castle is under attack! There are enemy soldiers here. I come from the throne room. The King and Queen want you to depart on your mission, before it's too late!'

Fitz reached around the back of his head and scratched his neck. 'So... OK...'

The hand of one of the guards reached past Margwyn, grabbed Fitz's collar, and ushered him forcefully out of the door.

They ran down a series of sloping corridors, two Fair Folk warriors behind and in front. Margwyn pressed the divining rod device into Compassion's hand. 'This will lead you to the Earthly form of Constantine.' Then he handed her a second device, a stubby black wand with a button on it. 'The War Mages have also given me this. When you find your target, point this at him and press the button, and he will be put in enforced communication with the mages here, a sudden and confining trance. They will do the rest.'

'And... why us... again?' wheezed Fitz, trying to keep up.

'Because none of the Fair Folk, and not even I, could pass without note among the humans of 2012. You are the Unseelie Court's only hope.'

'I hate it when that happens,' gasped Fitz.

Suddenly, there came a great commotion from behind them. Cries, and the sounds of running feet. Fitz recognised the unmistakable sound of machine-gun fire.

The rear Fair Folk turned, and swung their weapons up. The front two dropped back to let the humans pass.

Fitz grabbed Compassion's hand and glanced back over his shoulder. Five black-clad figures had rounded the corner behind them. Weapons swung in their direction.

The Fair Folk jumped into the middle of the corridor, deliberately putting their bodies between the soldiers and Margwyn's party. Both sides opened fire at the same time and the corridor exploded with noise that echoed back and forth along it.

Compassion pulled the other two humans to the ground as the brickwork around them started to explode. Helplessly, Fitz watched as a reptilian's body clattered backwards, green blood exploding from dozens of wounds. He bit his lip hard, agonised at the sight. A soldier, down the corridor, cried out as a metal shaft sliced through his thigh, and, staggering into the centre of the corridor, he was jerked about by a handful more that turned him into a pin cushion. The stubby guns the reptilians held were whooshing with sustained fire.

One of the Fair Folk threw down his weapon, and stepped courageously forward into the centre of the corridor, his whole body starting to vibrate. A light flashed down the corridor from something in his head, and two more of the soldiers glowed and screamed, their bodies thrashing as they died.

Margwyn, huddled beside them, suddenly shouted out, 'No!'

Fitz glanced up. A black cylinder was bouncing down the corridor towards the three remaining Fair Folk warriors. He leapt up, unconscious of what was brave and what was cowardly, and threw his body over those of Compassion and Margwyn.

There was a concussion. His ears popped. Something heavy and dead collapsed on to his back.

Yelling incoherently, he heaved it aside, and yelled at it some more when he saw that it was the torso of one of the warriors, looking like something from a doll now, with so little blood. He was standing, and the others were sitting, among pieces of the Faerie warriors. Silence rolled across them, and a wave of smoke that made Fitz cough and start to retch.

Compassion tried to get to her feet, slipped and stumbled. Margwyn helped her.

Through the smoke, the last two soldiers were walking towards them, intent.

'We are like you!' Fitz shouted at them.

No response. The leader was a captain. He looked too angry to do anything now but kill. They had their weapons ready.

'Hey,' said a voice from behind Fitz. 'Duck.'

The War Mages stood there, incongruously holding silver pistols, which were pointed towards the soldiers.

Fitz and his friends fell to the ground again.

Two white bolts blasted off the soldiers' chests. The captain staggered for a moment, trying to stay on his feet. Another bolt hit him. He jerked backwards and crumpled into a heap.

Silence finally, and fully, fell.

'Come on, then,' said the male War Mage. 'Move it. Time to go.'

Fitz took his clawed hand, staring incoherently up into the shifting face, unable to think or speak. 'Thanks,' he whispered finally, not meaning it.

The woman was walking down the corridor towards the soldiers.

That was the last thing Fitz saw there before they ushered him into the laboratory.

It was only when they were standing in front of the time vortex that Fitz started to wonder if he really did want to go through with this. OK, so it would get him back to Earth, but if Earth in 2012 was going to be some sort of fascist utopia, the sort of place that created soldiers like that... He turned to Margwyn, who was holding both of Compassion's hands, looking at her as though she was his daughter. A moment ago, Compassion had sadly wiped her description of their mission off the blackboard. 'Erm, don't we need to wear spacesuits or anything?'

Margwyn looked up, and let go of her hands, almost guiltily.

Behind him, the male War Mage was busily programming the control panel. 'I don't know what those are, but no: the War Mages tell me that, if the direction of travel is controlled, you rush straight down the centre of a tunnel, as if you've been picked up by a whirlwind, and pop out on the other side.'

'As if you've been picked up by a whirlwind.' Fitz nodded to himself. 'Reassuring.'

The War Mage straightened up from his work. 'All is ready,' he said.

Fitz frowned at that, but it was Compassion who spoke up, going straight over to him and reaching out to touch his face, an expression of intense interest suddenly on her features. 'You change the way you talk,' she said. 'All the time. I hear you do it in my head. What you are is complicated.'

The War Mage looked at her for a long moment. Then he bowed. 'Thank you, my lady,' he said. Then he straightened again. 'Now if you please…' He waved a claw towards the vortex.

After a moment's thought, Compassion went to stand in front of it.

'No, I'll go first,' said Fitz. It wasn't normally like him to be gallant, he thought, but he kept expecting people to burst into the room and shoot them all.

But Compassion raised her hand. 'No,' she said. 'I want to go. I'm going home.' And she stepped into the vortex. There was a sudden blur of movement as she was jerked inside, and Fitz saw her spin away down the tunnel at high speed, vanishing to a point.

No sound. How weird.

He took a step forward himself. Looked at Margwyn. Margwyn nodded back. He shrugged and leapt.

It was only as he watched the tiny window to the Land of Faerie vanish into the swirling purple distance behind him that he realised he'd completely forgotten to say goodbye.

When Gandar returned to the War Mages' chamber, he found that Cavis had made a real mess of the place. She'd been torturing the human captain, the one called Caldera, that they'd stunned in the corridor. What was left of him was spread out across their bed, a tightly stretched mass of barely recognisable flesh. He'd been dead for a few minutes now.

She was lying back in a chair, toying with one of the human's eyes, replete. He went to her, took the eye from her by the optic nerve, and kissed her passionately. He could taste the blood in her mouth. 'How was he?' he asked.

'Noisy,' she said. 'Almost as noisy as that ambassador.'

'You left almost all of it.'

'All those babies,' she sighed. 'I swear I couldn't eat another one.' She patted her stomach. 'I'm getting fat.'

'Never. Learn anything interesting?'

'When his team realised they were going the wrong way, they started to place their radio beacons. I don't know how many, but we can find them all using our trackers. I sent the other soldier home with the right stories in his head. Did the pawns get off all right?'

He pulled her into his arms, and they fell on to the floor and rolled in a loving embrace. 'The pawns are on their way. The trap is set. We defeated the Doctor.' He threw his head back and allowed himself a villainous chuckle. 'We Faraqued the Ka Faraq Gatri!'

She knew him so well that they chorused it together then. 'Nothing in the world can stop us now!'

But in the darkness of a watercourse deep in the Unseelie Court, just above the level where the tides washed back and forth, a tiny black sphere was fixed to the wall. A red light blinked at intervals on its casing.

When the Gallifreyan Interventionists came to search the castle for the radio beacons, this one would not be found.

Part Three
The Taking of Avalon

Chapter Eight
Call it an Exorcism if you Want

Lethbridge-Stewart sucked in a breath as the ground fire once more blew the gravel away from the ridge just above his head. His men reflexively ducked once more as small stones and clods of earth pattered down on their heads, the concussion ringing in their ears. They had swarmed up the side of this hill during the night, winding their bodies from side to side through the long grass, roaming from cover to cover at high speed. It had looked then, as it had looked on the tactical maps back at C&C, as if they could reach the Faerie installations along the top of this line of hills before the dawn.

Mab's mages considered these green domelike structures, newly appeared on the Aurora's digital scans a few miles into what was considered Faerie territory, to be where the various magical fields that were halting the air bombardment were emanating from. The Brigadier had chosen two companies from the UNIT regiment, supplemented by two companies of Welsh Guards, to take the installations and bring down the barriers. The men had chalk dust rubbed into their hair, and streaks of woad across their faces, and specifically designed and personalised tattoos rubbed into their skin with henna. The troopers had laughed at that, the Welsh Guards more than the UNIT men, of course. But he suspected that they all secretly appreciated the decorations.

The Brigadier himself had turned down all such defences, even though Mab had tried to force him to take one of the charms from her hair. He said these things just weren't him, and she'd spat in front of his boots and said that Brigida would never accept his sacrifice.

They'd landed under the range of the magical auras, which had knocked helicopters out of the sky before now, and had made their way up the hillsides without incident. Until there had come a shout from the right flank and the sudden bloom of an explosion - and then the night air was full of blistering random fire, the metal spikes coming at them, mixed in with blazing phosphorescent bolts that set men on fire and reduced them to ashes in an instant.

The advance had collapsed, fallen into little patches of cover all across the hillsides. They'd thought that the bombardment would lessen as the Faerie defenders sought to conserve their ammunition, but it had just kept on going, for six hours now. The long grass was full of the spent shafts. The sun had risen, and was now high in the sky. They were dangerously exposed on this hillside, vulnerable to dragon attack. And they were getting low on water. The Brigadier's little group were sheltering in the lee of what might have been a primitive chalk quarry, a crumbling ridge cut in the ground. Thankfully, there were quite a few of these across the fields.

The Brigadier saw the faces of the men crouched around him. Professional, afraid, hopeless. They'd calculated the position they were in. They were getting pent up, needing to do something to ease the cramps in their calf muscles and get them away from the distant cries of the wounded, many of them still out there in the exposed grass.

He activated his palmtop. 'Hawkins, any sign of that air support?'

'Windmill keeps trying, sir. But the enemy know we're coming now. They keep directing these rays at the choppers, the aircraft, even the supergun shells from the lakes. Everything's being forced down.'

'All right. Put me on to the general channel, won't you?' He turned to look at his own men as he spoke to the soldiers all across the hillside. 'Now listen, men. You're all aware of what the situation is. If it were up to me, I'd call in evac and get us all out, because this is all getting a bit tiresome.'

Liar, he thought to himself as he said it. He wanted to stay.

'But the choppers can't get through. Our situation isn't going to get any better. Unless we make it better ourselves. Unless we take those domes. Right here, right now. Now, you see me over here…'

He stood up, out of cover, and turned to look uphill at where the green gloss surfaces blazed like tortoiseshell in the sunlight.

Two bolts slicked past his shoulder. He ignored them.

He reached for the holster at his hip, unbuttoned it, and took out his revolver.

More bolts. He didn't see them, just felt their passing on the skin of his wrist and cheek.

'I don't know about you...' He glanced over his shoulder at his men and raised an eyebrow at them. 'But I'm going to do something about this.' He raised his voice to a controlled bellow, and put the palmtop to his mouth. 'Charge!'

Then he threw it aside and started to run uphill, aware that there was only a kilometre or so between him and the domes. He heard the yells begin behind him, the chorus of over a hundred men, letting their fear out in a single breath as they scrambled to their feet.

The air became grey with metal.

He sprinted into it.

Had he the right to make them come with him? Had he the right to do this to anyone but himself?

He heard cries from all around him, under the collective yell, as the missiles brought down men to the left and right.

But still they missed him.

One tagged his epaulette and bruised his shoulder with the drag, but he spun on his feet and ran on.

Come on, he screamed through his teeth at himself. Don't make me wait for this.

The domes were getting larger. He could see ditches, with individual reptilians standing to aim at him. He couldn't help but take running aim and shoot one down. He couldn't make this body yield to death.

Come on, one of you. I'm afraid of the waiting. I'm afraid I might start wanting to live just before death comes.

The screaming all around him rolled into one great wave of a shout, and suddenly he and a row of a dozen men were falling under their own momentum into the trenches, falling into the reptilians as flying corpses carried along by the rest fell beside them.

He shot to his left, brought one down, turned right to blow the face off a reptile that was running at him, a blade in the air.

No adrenaline, turning like an automaton, firing carefully as soldiers hacked and strangled and kicked and bit and bayoneted around him. A reptilian fell against his legs, and he kicked it aside, breaking a bone in its dead jaw.

He used his three last bullets, each on a different reptile. One that had just cut a man's throat with its claws, one that was staggering back, trying to aim its weapon along the trench, one that was up and running off towards the domes.

That last caught the Silurian in the back, sent it flying forward like a punch between the shoulder blades, a single blurt of green blood rocketing it into the grass.

He was out of bullets now.

A great screech resounded off the hills, a soaring roar that made everyone look up. A shadow had covered the sun, and was getting bigger every second.

Above them a dragon was bearing down, its mouth open, a glint of flame far back in its throat, beyond its polished teeth. Across the fields, men who'd got separated from the attack were running desperately, getting cut down as they broke from cover to sprint towards the trenches.

The Brigadier leapt on to a dying reptile. It was trying to speak to him, whispering something from its round lips. Its third eye was glowing weakly. He wrenched the long weapon from its claws. He found the trigger and the slippery growth that changed settings. He hoped that wasn't the safety.

He swung the weapon into the sky, looking through a fish-eye globe that made everything loom roundly at him. There was the eye of the dragon, accelerating towards him. He couldn't get an angle past the face of the beast to target the rider. He looked into the eye again. It shone with intelligence, shone like oils on a pond in the sunshine.

He felt suddenly, in the calm at the heart of the fear all around him, that he and this beast were connected in some way. That he'd seen it before.

A puff of flame appeared at the edge of his vision, making the globe sights flare. The jaws swung open. He found he was calmly aiming between them.

He made his hand into a claw and clenched the trigger.

A burst of the flaming bolts lanced into the sky.

The dragon exploded.

With a great cry and a flash of wings, every part of it became fire. Every scaly limb combusted into ashes, flame exploding along its length as if small charges were detonating inside it. It jerked in the air, gouts of it showering the ground below with burning shards, screaming at the top of its bellow.

Then the bones and the skin and the eyes exploded into a cloud of ashes.

There was silence across the battlefield as the rain of ashes and scraps of bone began to pelt down.

Then a great yell of victory started to come from the parched throats of the soldiers. Through it, the Brigadier could hear the shocked wails and cries of the reptiles.

He put down the weapon by its owner, who had ceased trying to talk to him and died.

He walked serenely along the length of the trenches, among the close-quarters fighting. The reptiles were dying in numbers now, as the last stragglers of the men – he noted that about a third of the force had got through – ran into the trenches. The fields were covered in bodies under the rain of ash, two or three of the camouflaged lumps every few metres. The men were opening up trapdoored holes and dropped grenades down them.

It occurred to him that he'd like to take a look at these domes they were supposed to be attacking.

He stepped up out of the trenches on the other side, metal darts zipping at his feet from a few fleeing reptiles who'd turned at the cover of the edge of the domes and were desperately trying to make a stand.

He waved his empty gun at them and started to walk towards them.

The oafs turned and ran.

Maybe they assumed he was protected by a blessing of some kind, when actually he seemed to be protected by a curse.

The screams of the fighting started to fade as he reached the domes and placed his hands on the gleaming surface of one. Perhaps that was just his ears.

It could have been any length of time before the young sergeant ran up to him, a vast, battle-bloodied survivor smile all over his stupid, obscene, face. 'Sir!' he gasped. 'We did it, sir! We won! And if I may say so, sir, what you did –'

'You may not, Sergeant.' The Brigadier took his hand away from the glossy, organic surface. 'Beautiful, aren't they?'

'Sir?'

'Find a sapper that's alive. Bring some explosives. Blow them up and then...' He tried to sound pleased. 'We can all go home.'

He was aware of another man running up to them. 'Sir! Sir!' he was shouting. 'I thought you'd want to see this, sir!'

He carried with him the Brigadier's palmtop. Very good work, sending someone back down the field to find it. Couldn't have one of these falling into enemy hands.

It was shoved into his grasp. On the screen was a man with a bandage over one eye. An SAS uniform. He was trying to tell a story bravely and was shaking as he did it. 'The Doctor...' he said. 'They killed him. Over and over. Until he was finally dead.'

Darkness closed around the edge of the Brigadier's vision.

He was never entirely sure of what happened next.

The next thing he knew he was lying on the ground, curled around his stomach as if he'd been hit. But he knew he wasn't. Because he desperately wanted to be.

With a drunkard's tiny focus, he saw something sticking out of the cuff of his uniform. Aware of shouted questions from all around him, of figures converging on him, he pulled at the cuff.

A tiny curl of paper came away in his hand. It had been sewn into the fabric with the big stitches of a woman who'd never sewn in her life. On it was a scrawl of Celtic script.

He started to laugh again, and kept on laughing until he choked on ashes.

Chapter Nine
If you Live a Lie, You Die a Liar

Mab used the spade to pat down the soil, then wondered if it ought to be ruffled up a bit. So she did that for a while, then straightened up and mopped her brow. She had planted the garden just out of the shadow of the castle, at the point where the flowering shrubs, and, in time - if there was to be time - trees, would get the most sunlight during the day.

In the ground here were buried the ashes of her High Council, the garden being their memorial. She'd said goodbye to their old selves as she did it, and murmured the songs about the joy she'd feel when their new selves appeared, in the future. She wasn't the most devout worshipper in Avalon, but she felt as if she needed those old songs now. She kept hearing the voice of the Keeper of the Memory, assuring her that what once was would be again, that there was permanence in impermanence, comfort in change, grace in all the seasons.

She had appointed a new officer to each Council position, but they were all so young and scared that she felt like a dictator now. It'd be years before they questioned anything she did.

She wished that, if the Doctor was really dead, as they were saying he was, he could have been here in this garden, to be part of Avalon again.

She wished for different reasons that Margwyn was here with his fellows.

At least the noise from the metal birds was less here now. The air bombardment of Faerie fortresses had resumed, now the domes had been destroyed, and a large number of the aircraft had been sent north to rough airfields that were being constructed in the field. Now all the pilots had to worry about were the individual magical defences of particular fortifications.

This seemed a sad and awkward way to fight a war, with everything at a distance. It felt cowardly to her. What Alistair had done at the domes was what war should be like. She wished she had been there with him. They might have had no option but to fight this war, but they could at least fight it directly. That would make it all seem cleaner, somehow.

A shadow fell across the soil. The man Cronin was standing there, the warrior whose job was to care for the other warriors. He was sweating in his uniform, his untidy hair a mess from being rubbed back from his brow.

He had arrived yesterday, when Alistair was brought back from the battle. Mab had gone straight to see him, but his attendants had told her to stay away. She had started to shout at them, to say that they asked her to stay away from everything, that this was her war, too, and she should fight it. But they'd said it was his wish, that he'd specifically said, in his delirium, that she was not to be admitted.

Cronin had managed, after ten minutes of looking around in wonder, to slip in and see his patient, and, as far as Mab knew, had spent the night with him. When she herself couldn't sleep, she'd gone to the door of his quarters, stepped past the guard they'd posted there, and listened. There were shouts and cries and the sounds of things being smashed.

'How is he?' she asked now.

Cronin stretched. He'd been up all night, by the look of him. 'He's a textbook case of post-traumatic stress syndrome.'

'Yes, but how is he?'

For some reason he smiled at her tone. 'You two even deal with me in the same way. OK: he's consumed with grief, blames himself for the deaths of not only his wife, but of this guy the Doctor, and of all the men who died in battle yesterday.'

'That's bloody ridiculous!'

'That's why they call it mental illness, Queen Regent. Whoever sent him into active service again is the one who's being bloody ridiculous if you ask me. But they're not asking me, because they still think he's some sort of talisman to the men, and they don't want him sent home to a nice quiet hospital, and of course neither does he...' He massaged the top of his nose, obviously aware that he was misdirecting his tired anger. 'Damn it. Do you mind if I sit in your garden?' He dropped into a sitting position, and then, with a groan, rolled on to his back.

Mab suddenly knew that she liked him. She put down her spade and went to lie down, too. They both looked up at the blue sky for a moment. 'Is he going to be all right?' she asked.

'Sure, if he ever lets himself start to heal. I don't think he's even grieved for Doris properly. He's still a control freak, still hanging on. He won't let grief do its work on him.'

'Would it help if another woman had fallen in love with him?'

Cronin paused for a long second, a grin flashing over his features. Then he coughed and resumed his learned tone of voice. 'Right now, absolutely not. That'd just give him an excuse to hide in that and not deal with anything. And of course, if this woman were to go into battle, to put herself in danger...'

'Which she will. This woman we're talking about needs to take heads.'

'Then he'd be devastated if she got hurt. He'd think that he should have saved her. That he'd lost another one.'

Mab was silent for a time, looking up at the clouds that flew high up in the sky, beyond the reach even of dragons. 'That would be bad,' she finally said.

Cronin propped himself up on his elbow and looked seriously at her. 'But of course, if this woman really loved him, she'd stay around and be his best friend, and make sure the idiot has someone around to look after him!' He'd allowed himself another shout. He rolled on to his back again. 'Sorry.'

'You care about him, too, don't you?'

'Yes, well, it's hard not to. He embodies things which... Boyish dreams, yes, but... When he's himself, he's...' He visibly found that he couldn't make any more sense. 'Yes.'

She laughed with him.

'The ironic thing is,' he continued, 'if there wasn't a war going on here, this'd be the ideal place for him.'

'What? We don't even have tea.'

'I mean that it's so obviously a dream. Heaven knows, I'd prefer to be in here, too, rather than back home at the moment, where the whole world's going gaga. I spend a lot of my time getting my patients to access archetypes from their unconscious – Jungian therapy we call it. Here they're just walking around. I mean, look at you. You're a matriarch, the big-chested mother to your people. Sorry.'

'Fah! I was starting to think they'd vanished, the amount of attention certain... people are paying.'

'And you live in an incredibly phallic castle, under which there's a King sleeping in a dark pool! And that thing round your neck! And you've all got your shadows living up North being the things you aren't!'

Mab started to laugh at the man's continuing astonishment. 'All this is just true. Why is it strange to you?'

Cronin just shook his head, unable to frame a coherent answer. 'You don't have much in the way of mental illness here, I'd guess. Apart from King Constantine himself, of course.'

'What?'

He blinked, and turned to her once again, serious. 'I thought it was obvious. Here we are in the man's dreams, and there's a war going on. Between the two parts of his psyche. Unless he can find some sort of mediation between the two, the poor guy's in trouble.'

Mab just stared at him. 'I'd never thought of it like that... Gods save us, we should never have started this war.'

'That's what they all say.' Cronin groaned and got to his feet. 'I'm going to get some sleep. Wake me if the traitor is redeemed or the hero returns.' He started to walk towards the castle.

'Is that likely?' Mab called after him.

'Likely?' he laughed. 'In this place, I'd say it's bloody inevitable.'

She smiled again. 'You've got something of the gods about you as well, d'you know that?'

'Whatever. It's a job.'

As he went on his way, Mab rolled back on to the ground and stared into the sky for a while.

Was that why Alistair wasn't seeing her, because some

unconscious part of him knew that he was vulnerable to her? She felt bad at that thought. It was half a hope and half a hope not. Maybe she was as divided against herself as Constantine was. Maybe they all were.

Mab got to her feet, and headed back to the castle.

On the way, she did up several of her buttons.

Compassion looked at the divining-rod device in her hands for the twenty-eighth time that day. Nothing. She and Fitz were trudging along under a motorway underpass, past anonymous square buildings. It was raining. None of this would have mattered to her in the past: they were just things that happened. But now they overlaid odd sensations on to her consciousness. It was very... something.

'It's very... something,' she said out loud, hoping that this might encourage Fitz's own comments.

'Oh yeah, right, very.' He nodded. 'We've been wandering aimlessly about London for two days, and that thing hasn't so much as pinged. And this is the future?' He gestured his arms around his head. 'This is the fascist state of Britain in 2012? The only big difference I can see is back there at the BBC: they made the bloody letters square!'

They had stepped out of a wall down a back alley in Soho, between two skips overflowing with builders' materials. 'Shh!' Fitz had said as the vortex glow faded from the wall. 'I'll go and take a look!' He'd tiptoed to the end of the alley, and looked left and right. Then he'd straightened up and walked back to her, looking disconcerted. 'A lot of people,' he'd said. 'Looking just about like we do.'

'I said that this didn't seem like a dictatorship to me.' They'd stepped into Dean Street, and watched people going back and forth, talking, filling the doorway of a delicatessen, eating sandwiches, couriers riding down the street on motorbikes, black cabs. There was sunshine, but nobody looked particularly happy.

'There've been a lot of dictatorships that treated their people well. It was just everybody else that hated them. Fascism's sometimes like that. For instance...' He rubbed the back of his neck. 'Oh forget it. D'you fancy a sandwich?'

They'd marched through the streets of the city centre at speed from that point, aware that the few valuables they had on them would purchase accommodation for a couple of nights at most. Everywhere they went, people seemed quiet and distracted. They saw an ice-cream seller crying openly in Hyde Park, just standing by his little cart and sobbing. It was a summer lunchtime, but the park was mostly empty, people sitting on benches, a few wandering among the shadows under the trees. Fitz had bought a paper at one point and leafed through it. 'Suicides, murders, people burning their own houses down. Riots in all the big cities. Curfews every night. This is not what I'd call the summer of love.'

'It's the war in Avalon. It's getting into their dreams.'

'Let's not sleep here,' he'd said. 'Let's just keep going.'

That had been fine by her. She'd taken the paper from him and read of bombings in city streets, and of how many different groups tried to claim responsibility for each. She read about seemingly random killings, with the killer walking away down the street, and never getting caught. When she'd last been here, a few weeks ago, something called the Silly Season had just been starting, with news that was frivolous or trite dominating the papers. Now that feeling of dizzy celebration – which, she'd been told, came over Britain every hot summer – had been replaced by a desperate carnival hangover. A party during earthquake weather. It was, she heard some people saying, like the millennium and the eclipse all over again.

She decided that she didn't want to sleep here, either.

Fitz had finally given in and slumped against her shoulder on an underground train, endlessly journeying round the Circle Line, at three o'clock on this rainy afternoon. He'd panted and yelled in his sleep, mentioned the name of a woman he'd known in Mechta, but the other occupants of the carriage had paid no attention. They knew the feeling from their own dreams, Compassion had thought, looking at their sleep-bruised white faces, their eyes all set at some point in the intermediate distance.

At the other end of the carriage as it rolled and bucked, a fight developed, there were shouts, a scuffle. It blew over, and the two men slumped back into their seats, glaring piteously at each other.

The punch-drunk city in the darkest summer. There was a regime of fear in this world now, Compassion thought, but it wasn't that of some dictator: it was the terror that came to these folk every night, in their dreams. She thought of the people she'd left behind in Bristol, and found herself... something, at the thought of what they might be doing now.

Fitz had woken, and had put a hand to his face, all his muscles drawn tight in shock. He wouldn't tell her what he had seen.

And so, having found nothing in the centre, not knowing if they should even stay in London, they'd had some thought about communication centres, and had taken the tube out to White City, to walk the detector past all the BBC buildings.

'Because, of course,' Fitz had said, 'a wandering dream in human form is going to want to be on the telly. That's what I'd do.'

She'd thought he was probably being humorous in some way.

Now they were heading for the last few buildings that had anything to do with this British Broadcasting Corporation, a cluster of units down a slight incline just past the underpass. Next, Compassion thought, they would try the scientific centres. They had to keep on going, there was no other hope. But how long Fitz would last with that sort of sleep... or without sleep at all...

She almost dropped the detector when it started to vibrate and chirp in her hands.

Fitz jerked alert as she did, looking desperately around. They were standing beside a row of vehicles stopped in front of a red traffic light. Compassion took an experimental step in the direction they were going, and the noise from the device increased in volume.

They broke into a trot along the pavement. 'Come on!' shouted Fitz. 'We can't lose it now!'

Both their gazes locked on the vehicle at the front of the queue. A vast limousine with black windows. They sprinted for it.

As they got there, as the detector started positively yelling at them, the lights turned to green.

The car accelerated away, leaving them hopelessly dashing down the pavement after it.

Fitz roared with frustration. He glanced over his shoulder, and yelled for Compassion to stop, waving his arms into the road.

The black cab with its sign illuminated chugged smoothly up to meet them. Fitz opened the back door and motioned Compassion quickly inside.

'I've always wanted to do this,' he said to her. Then he turned to the driver and pointed at the limousine, now just visible far up the road. 'Follow that car!'

The Doctor sped through the vortex, being tossed and thrown by the interstitial currents like a leaf in a hurricane. Inside, he maintained a solid calm, the only way to get through this experience. He was in a trance, his arms held aloft, fingers entwined in the Gesture of Warding, while his legs were furled beneath him in a high-degree lotus. His eyes were closed, and all his senses were devoted to holding his body and personality together.

He'd sensed, through the chakras of his Time Lord nervous system, an exit approaching, and, feeling the nuclear warmth of a star on the other side of it, had willed himself away, back into the vortex again. It was easy enough to do that, to pull oneself back when some contour in the void appeared. But that was nothing like positive navigation. He could not set himself on a course, even if he had any idea where his destination was. He may have to do this for centuries, for millennia... for ever!

He'd shut his body's needs down to the point where some cruising TARDIS, Dalek timecraft, anything, might find his desiccated husk in several hundred years and bring him back to life. This swirling, sucking void was infinite, and very few races tracked across it. The chances against his being found were infinitesimal. Unless it was by one of the predators. A Swimmer, a Polt, a Chronovore or its young. Even the tentacles of the Kraken might sweep him up and devour him into its invisible, eternal event horizon.

And yet he did not relax and let the time winds rip him apart. He persisted. Because now, whatever his situation, he had decided upon a purpose. Cavis and Gandar were, for whatever reason, ravaging the heartland of human dreams. Nobody else knew about that. Nobody else would stand a chance of recognising their threat. They posed a terrible danger to everyone he cared about.

He had to stay alive, because he had to stop them.

The taxi driver had been happy to take Fitz's watch in exchange for their trip across London to Docklands. Fitz got the feeling that the driver knew more about watches than he did.

He dropped them on a wide white pavement opposite a tall silver building. It was a great half-moon section of a tower, curling around a courtyard where a fountain was being blown back and forth in the rain. The tower, despite the gloom of an overcast summer's day, continued to shine. The building stood back from the road in a classical forum, with a shallow parade of steps leading up to the courtyard. Bushes and flowerbeds completed the picture of corporate elegance. The occasional businessperson made their way in and out. The limousine had entered at the rear, passing through a barriered security gate into an underground car park.

'Yeah, that's what I'd do, too,' said Fitz, nodding up at the tower. 'So he's in there, this dream guy, is he?'

Compassion turned through a hundred and eighty degrees, the divining rod in front of her. 'Yes,' she reported. She moved it up and down. 'He's heading upwards, at high speed.'

'In the lift, I guess. I wonder what he's doing here. I wonder what he's doing anywh-' He stopped, and slapped his own forehead, exasperated. 'You know, we could have just looked in the Yellow Pages.'

Compassion followed his pointing finger.

A sign by the revolving doors said 'KING CENTRE'.

'Where else would you find one?' Fitz smiled. 'Come on, let's go and knock on his door.'

* * *

'Yes?' asked the receptionist.

Fitz glanced at Compassion, and then smiled his most charming smile at the girl behind the big round silver table. A uniformed guard by the door had been glancing at them at intervals as they'd waited behind the last visitor, who'd been granted a bar-coded security badge before being shown towards a tubular silver lift. 'We're here to see someone.'

The receptionist flipped open a binder with a list of names. 'Name, please?'

'Erm, Constantine, King.'

The receptionist's smile notched a degree into uncertain. 'I don't think Mr King has any appointments scheduled for today.'

Fitz was so surprised that he couldn't help asking. 'Mr King?'

'Constantine King. That is who you wanted to see?'

Fitz turned to Compassion and gave her what he hoped was a very eloquent look that said, And I walked my arse off for two days! He swung back to the receptionist and took a deep breath. 'Indeed. This is rather strange – he's expecting me. Perhaps you could just check with his office? It's Mr Kreiner and Miss...' He thought wildly for a second. 'Galore.'

Compassion raised an eyebrow.

To his relief, indeed surprise, the receptionist picked up the phone. 'And what was it concerning?'

For a moment Fitz considered telling her in detail. But finally he settled on, 'The condition of a piece of Mr King's property.'

Fitz waited until the lift doors had closed on them before he let his mouth drop open into an expression of gaping astonishment. 'I didn't expect them to just let us go up and see him! I was just making it up as I went along! Perhaps he's really expecting a Mr Kreiner, eh?'

Compassion was frowning at him. 'Galore?'

Fitz switched on his Scottish slur. 'Shocking. Abgholutely shocking.'

'I have no idea what you're talking –' Suddenly Compassion gasped, and clutched her hands to her chest. 'Fitz. There's something... Oh. It's huge. A huge power. It's getting closer and closer as we go upwards. I can feel it.'

Fitz felt his stomach turn over. This whole mission had, previously, seemed a lot less dangerous than staying in Avalon. 'Are you getting it through your receiver?'

'I don't know. It's all new to me. It's part of... the change. The change which is coming. The change which is going to happen to me. It's going to be terrible and wonderful at the same time. Fitz, it's going to turn me inside out. I'm going to die. But –'

'You're going to what?'

A bell pinged. The lift doors opened.

Fitz tore his gaze away from Compassion's agonised expression and managed to take in what was waiting for them. He'd gone from brash confidence to absolute quaking terror in one lift journey. He hated it when that happened.

Standing right in front of the lift was a small, nervous-looking man in a white suit. He was extraordinarily thin, so much so that you could see the ribs beneath his white waistcoat. He had a stoop, which projected his head forward at an awkward angle, and while one eye was fixed on them the other flicked around the room, as if continually looking over his shoulder. He looked to be somewhere in his late fifties. 'Constantine King,' he said, his voice a high, reedy whisper. 'But call me Rex, I hate that name. Hate it.'

Fitz managed to get the words out. 'Fitz Kreiner, and this is my secretary, Miss Galore. Good of you to see us.' Fitz shook the man's hand, noting as he did so that Compassion was trembling, her eyes fixed on King as if he was some sort of predator who might attack her at any moment. The guy didn't look scary at all, though. Maybe, hopefully, this was more to do with the weird stuff she was going through. He took a look around, now that they'd stepped out of the lift. They were standing in the lobby of a penthouse suite that spoke of good taste, luxury and unbridled wealth. Everything was furnished in a sparse silver and black, but with enough designer tucks and eccentricities to suggest that no expense had been spared, and that every whim was catered for in some discreet corner or other. 'It's good of you to see us,' he said, regaining his composure somewhat at the normality of the place.

'You said property. I thought that sounded like...' King's words failed him. He visibly panicked for a moment, then seized on something he was certain of. 'Would you care for some champagne?' he asked, gesturing to an ice bucket with a bottle tucked in it. It sounded as if he'd learned the phrase from a book.

'Thanks.' Fitz nodded. As King headed for the ice bucket, Fitz glanced back to Compassion, and saw that she had produced the rod weapon from her bag, and was aiming it at King's back.

'Wait a moment!' he whispered.

'I don't want to wait! There's something about him. He could hurt me.' She registered Fitz's blank response and tried to clarify what she meant. 'He's capable of hurting me. He's... He's... scaring me!'

'But...' Fitz glanced back to the small man, his hands shaking with the champagne bottle, wondering how such a wimp was managing to do that. 'But, Compassion, think about this. He's just allowed us, two strangers off the street, to pop up and see him in his penthouse. Unless business practice has changed a hell of a lot in forty years, he must know why we're here. And he hasn't tried to imprison us or hurt us or anything. Look at him! He's the boss of a big company, but he looks like he needs someone to tie his shoelaces. Can't we at least –'

'No. I don't care.'

Fitz weighed his hands in the air, certain that his instincts were right. Just going along with anybody's plan wasn't how he worked, and King just wasn't the sort of target he'd imagined Compassion firing the device at. 'I just feel like we're being set up for something. Do you really think anybody's told us the whole truth?'

'No,' she said. 'I don't. All right.' She put the rod back in her bag. 'But make it quick. I want to shoot him.'

Fitz let out a relieved breath and turned smoothly to take his glass from the returning King the next moment, before the drink was all shaken out of it. 'So, Rex...' he began, nervously aware that

he was going to have to spin a number of plates at once here.
'Nice office.'

The sun was setting. The Brigadier sat on the ruined stump of the high tower, and watched the shadows across the airfield grow. There was no longer a balcony in front of him. He sat on a little ridge of exposed brickwork at the summit of the crumbling staircase. He'd stepped over a tape that said danger in order to get up here, and had made his way through the beginnings of the new construction work, where sappers were using big metal props to stabilise the tower before starting work on the structure itself.

This was the most isolated place to do it. They wouldn't find him here.

He was no longer of any use to his men. He had allowed over two hundred of them to be killed.

He winced, as the stomach cramps he'd been suffering from since the incident at the domes curled him up again. He made himself sit straight, sweat glistening on his face. That fool Cronin couldn't understand that what he was going through was entirely physical. Something had affected his stomach, returning at intervals, and sometimes his side, a paralysis of his right hand and shoulder. Some ray, some weapon... Though they said there was no such thing in the domes themselves. He'd argued with Cronin about it, and the arguments had become fraught, and the young fool had tried to give him a bloody injection, as if he needed calming down. So Lethbridge-Stewart had struck out at him, just a glancing blow, and the needle had broken against the wall.

They'd had to call in some men to hold him down, but the fact that they would not, that they hesitated and started to ask questions and tried to talk to their commander, had made Lethbridge-Stewart cramp all his anger back inside him and sit decorously back and let the needle go in.

He'd given Cronin a piece of his mind once the guards had gone, though. Oh, he'd given the laddie his best parade-ground bellow. For a long time, into the night.

Doris hadn't been to see him at all since he got back.

That damned Queen Regent had tried to, though. For some reason, nobody seemed to understand the anger he felt towards her for interfering with his uniform. Doris used to sew medal ribbons and the like on to it. For Mab to do what she had done was unforgivable. Somebody had said that the fools were going to give him a medal for yesterday, as they often gave medals to mad commanders who got their men killed. Perhaps the trollop thought she was going to sew that on, too, take Doris's place in all respects.

He put a hand to his forehead now and held it there.

They'd brought Cronin through the gateway in order to attempt to return Lethbridge-Stewart to some sort of combat readiness. Whitehall knew his value to the men. But instead, Cronin's arrival had crystallised the Brigadier's decision, during the long semi-sleep that had followed that shouting match.

He could not live like this.

Not with his body rebelling against him, not when he was unable to do anything but let his men down... The two hundred and three body bags that had been flown back to the gateway, all the slow, separate, secret excuses in many homes in many cities. The way the campaign might break down upon that secrecy, and its ultimate discovery.

All down to his failure.

He'd read the report on the Doctor's death at length. Killed in the line of duty, at the heart of the enemy's HQ. The soldier who'd come back had said that the Doctor hadn't been offering peace, but had been fighting the enemy, crawling through ducts, looking for a way to the heart of the palace. Doing those things he did that had made him such a fearsome enemy to the monsters he fought.

He'd had to go there on his own.

He should have said, when he'd made up his mind about who the enemy was. He should have called the Brigadier, and asked him to come along on whatever desperate plan he'd come up with. He would have been there like a shot. Like the old days. They could have gone together.

Her hand had slipped out of his, and she was pulled away into the darkness.

He had let them all down.

No more, then. It was time.

He took the revolver from his holster, and checked the bullet in the chamber. He had another in his top pocket, in case something went wrong. He was wearing his uniform. He'd sewn the cuff back himself. He'd left a letter in his room that cleared everybody else of this. Should have done it a long time ago. Got out of the way before he'd become a danger to those around him.

He slid the safety off, and, fighting his hand as it wanted to seize up, placed the hard rim of the gun barrel against his temple. He could feel it there, making a small circular indentation in his skin.

He felt the play of the trigger against his finger, and was pleased to find that he wasn't afraid, only anticipating.

He waited for a minute, appreciating the moment, and mentally ticking off those things he'd had to do, making sure he had left no loose ends.

Finally he nodded to himself. He was finished here. 'Sorry to keep you waiting, dear,' he said. His voice clipped and full again, all confidence regained in the certainty of his decision. 'I'm on my way now.'

He started to squeeze the trigger.

'This property to which we refer,' Fitz ventured, having fortified himself with a couple of glasses of the champagne. 'It's called Avalon.'

'Yes.' King nodded suddenly and intensely from the deep armchair where he'd positioned himself. 'I thought it was.'

To Fitz's surprise, Compassion spoke up. She'd been eyeing King nervously for the last half-hour. 'So you're aware of your connection to it?'

'It's where my real body is, isn't it?'

Fitz leaned forward in his seat. This was going to be easier than he'd thought. They could actually talk about this. 'I'm glad you're so up to speed with stuff. We expected to find a ghost, somebody who wandered around, not the boss of a big company.'

King giggled. 'They think it's a big company, the people who work here. They get paid, they feel happy. They don't do anything. Just a...' He spun his finger to indicate the building. 'A front. That's the word I was told it was called.'

Fitz kept the smile fixed on his lips. This guy must be a hoot at the annual general meeting. 'Why, though? What's it for?'

'People mustn't notice me. I read science, you see.' A sudden intensity gripped him, a bad memory. 'For centuries, I wandered the world. Nothing in my head. Not conscious. Homeless, a prisoner sometimes, a refugee. Didn't eat, didn't die, not aware...'

Fitz felt sorry for the little man. The pain on his features looked utterly genuine. They'd been right not to ambush him. 'That's terrible. So how did you get from that to... all this?'

A toothy smile. 'My friends helped me.'

'Your friends?'

King started to laugh. 'They showed me what I could do.' He clicked his fingers and a new bottle of champagne appeared in the bucket by Fitz's chair.

Compassion made a tiny squeaking sound.

And, then, to Fitz's amazement, she vanished.

'Hello, mate!' said a voice.

The Brigadier leapt up with a shout, and brandished the gun he'd had to his head wildly in the direction of the figure that was suddenly standing beside him. 'Who are you?' he yelled. 'Where did you come from?'

It was a man in the silver armour of a Celtic warrior. But his looks were those of an Anglo-Saxon. He stood stock still, where he hadn't been standing a moment before. He had a military haircut that had grown a little too long, a beaklike nose, and intense, searching eyes that were looking sadly at the Brigadier. He had a garland of faded wild flowers around his neck.

'My name is Joe Boyce,' he said. 'Formerly with the SAS.'

'What do you mean, formerly?' The Brigadier found himself hanging on to a tiny scrap of dignity. He'd been disturbed at the most private moment of his life and he felt absurdly vulnerable. 'If you're a bloody deserter –'

'No, no.' Boyce sat down calmly on what remained of the parapet, casting a glance at the sheer drop behind him. He was ignoring the gun the Brigadier was pointing at him. 'That's a different paradigm. My old world. If you want, you could say I transferred to another unit. Only we're not fighting the same war.'

The Brigadier lowered the gun. 'How did you get here?'

Boyce shrugged. 'Magic. Listen, my new unit, as you'd want me to call it… They're known as the Knights of Brigida. Our patron, the Goddess Brigida, she's interested in you.'

The Brigadier just stared at him.

'She saw you were about to take your own life,' Boyce prompted. 'So I was sent to interrupt. We look after our own.'

'Your own?' The Brigadier turned away, shaking his head forcefully. 'Oh no. That's this *Brigidier* nonsense that woman keeps spouting, I suppose. Well I don't know where you got your information from, but let me tell you, I was not about to –'

'The Goddess saw you from where she's being born.'

The Brigadier snorted. 'I don't believe in your "Goddess"!'

Boyce sighed. The Brigadier felt he was being patronised as if by the representative of a very powerful country, an ambassador who couldn't quite get him to believe the size of his country's arsenal. 'Whether you believe in her or not, she's real. She's being created by the dreaming King. As we speak. A new bit of his mind, splitting off and getting a consciousness of its own. Maybe that's what he needs to do to deal with this war.'

'Deal with it? Deal with it how?'

'By being a third power to take control of his fragmenting mind. Not his idea, mind you. Nor anyone else's. Constantine doesn't have ideas, being asleep and all that. Brigida formed by accident, around a concept that appeared in his dreams. She's his way of understanding something new that's going to arrive in Avalon.' Boyce smiled. 'I don't sound like a mad convert to some cult now, do I?'

'You're still not making much sense. You're a soldier in the

British Army, man. All this talk of a third power…' The Brigadier had started to pace the tower.

Boyce shook his head at him sadly. 'It's thinking like that that's got you where you are. Thinking that you're just this one thing. When that's a choice you made.' He turned to look out across the downlands. 'It's the best place, this, and Brigida's trying to save it. We all found her in our prayers. That comes naturally to the Celts, so there are more of them with us. Shepherds, fishermen… But, since we got here, quite a few of our lads have started to go native, too. We're what becomes of the vanished. We leave our normal lives and go into the forests to do Brigida's work. She wants us to be the opposite of what we are. Which is difficult for me, because I have to learn about art and write poetry and pick flowers. But that's the way it is. It's meant to be difficult. And that's what you have to be now. Because whatever you think, you're one of us.'

The Brigadier had felt all the anger drain out of him as he'd paced, listening to the gentle voice. Now all that was left was a bemused emptiness. 'I'm not one of you,' he said, forgetting that he was talking to a lower rank. He was aware that, from somewhere inside him, he was almost pleading with the man. 'I don't know what I am, so how could I possibly know what my opposite is?'

Boyce stood up. 'Alive, mate. The opposite of dead. That's what Brigida wants you to be.' He raised his palm in a simple salute, and smiled his sad and gentle smile again. 'And now that's what you are.'

There was a sound from the stairwell behind the Brigadier.

He turned to see what it was.

Something fluttered through his mind.

He jerked back to look.

And found that he was alone on the tower.

He had a moment to look wildly around him before a young corporal appeared at the top of the staircase and saluted. 'Been looking all over for you, sir. Colonel Munro was getting worried.'

'Indeed?' The Brigadier just about managed to return the salute. Suddenly aware of the gun in his hands, he fumbled a show of clicking open the chamber, as if for a final inspection, and then shoved it back into his holster. 'Well, you can tell him I'm all right, can't you, Corporal?'

He turned back to look out over the fields again.

The Brigadier felt the corporal pause for a moment. But then he evidently decided against saying anything more and headed back off down the stairwell.

The Brigadier let out a breath. He could start the whole thing again from square one, of course. He put a hand to his holster and felt the metal of the gun under the material.

For some reason it seemed ridiculous to continue now. He was certain the man Boyce had been caught up in some fancy of the magic of this place. He certainly didn't feel as if there was a goddess looking down on him.

But still it seemed that something in him had shifted a little.

To do it now did indeed seem foolish. And dishonest.

He would just have to find his fate on the battlefield.

From the mess, deep inside the castle, the Welsh Guards were singing 'Men of Harlech'.

'Damn it all,' he said to himself.

He buttoned his holster, and headed back inside.

Fitz blinked.

Compassion reappeared. Just for a moment, it had looked as if she was... not invisible, but as though she'd blended in with the silver and black of the sofa behind her, like a chameleon.

She didn't seem aware that she'd done that. She was still staring in alarm at the bottle of champagne that had materialised across the room from her. 'How did he do that?' she whispered.

King giggled at her reaction. 'I found out I can change things. Change everything. Take power from Constantine to do it.'

Fitz looked between them. OK, so neither of them seemed aware of the chameleon thing. Later for that, then. He saw that Compassion's hand had strayed to her bag again. 'Well, look, Rex,' he said desperately. 'Do you know about the war that's going on in Avalon right now?'

'Oh yes!' Rex nodded violently.

'So would your sleeping self know about it, too?'

'No! How could he? He's asleep.'

So an appeal to Constantine's sleeping self through this dream guy was out of the question. Just one more idea to try. He raised his hand a little to try to ask Compassion to wait a second. 'Well, the war might wake him up, mightn't it? And then I guess you'd blink out like the dot on a telly. So why don't you do us all a favour, and use these powers you've got in this world to close the gateway, maybe make the soldiers all come home?'

Rex swigged from his champagne and started to laugh, and Fitz saw his eyes twinkling over the brim of the glass. 'Why indeed?' he chuckled. And the laugh started to get higher and higher in pitch. And it didn't sound like it was going to stop.

Fitz joined in with a little chuckle, too. Then he looked quickly across to Compassion and nodded. 'OK. You win. Shoot him.'

In their chambers in the Castle of Faerie, Cavis and Gandar watched the scene on a Time/Space Visualiser that was fitted into the inside door of their ornate wardrobe. Cavis stood on the points of her clawed toes, still in her reptilian disguise, her gnarled fists bunched in anticipation.

'Go on!' she hissed. 'Go on! This is the bit everything's been leading up to! Checkmate! Game over! I love this bit!'

'It's got to happen any second now,' Gandar reassured her.

She could hear the tension in his voice. When this game of theirs was won, they had just one tiny final thing to do, and then they could take a long holiday. Somewhere where they could wear the lizard outfits.

'You've been saying that since they got out of the lift,' she teased her lover.

'It should have happened then. That guy Kreiner is just too laid back for his own good.'

Cavis looked at the screen again and screamed. 'She's going for it! She's reaching for the bag!'

'Yes!' cried Gandar.

Their hands knitted, ready for their victory celebration.

Compassion grabbed the weapon from her bag and pointed it at King.
  She pressed the single button.
  Nothing happened.

'Yes!' Cavis watched the sudden change in King's expression. His eyes flashed with childish, stormy, anger. 'Yes! Yes! Go on!'

Fitz felt a sudden sinking feeling as King walked towards them, his glittering eyes locked on Compassion as she tried time and time again to activate the device.
  'Oh no,' he said. And then again. 'Oh no.'

'Go on!' screamed Cavis again. 'You know what she's trying to do now!'
  'So attack her!' yelled Gandar. 'Take her out!'

King stopped before them, looking at them as if they'd betrayed him, contemplating them as if they were insects to be stamped on.
  'We are so screwed,' said Fitz.

'Now!' squealed Cavis. 'By the Eyes of Rassilon, now!'

King looked straight at Compassion, his eyes focused on some hateful point just between hers, and Fitz was sure for a second that her head was going to explode or something.
  But then he took a sudden step back, and his childlike anger turned into a frown of panic.
  'Excuse me,' he said. 'I have some things to do.'
  And then he ran past Fitz and Compassion, got into the lift, and was gone.

Cavis and Gandar looked at each other.

Their faces had drained of all colour, even through the disguises.

'He didn't attack her,' whispered Gandar.

'She didn't attack him,' whispered Cavis.

They looked at each other again.

'Let's run for it,' said Cavis.

'No... Wait...' Gandar held up his palm. He looked like he was thinking quickly. 'If –'

She understood what he was getting at. 'We go to...'

'And get them to...'

'Yeah.'

Another long pause. They bit their lips, feeling terrified for what, Cavis thought, was probably the first time in a millennium. Then, cursing in High Gallifreyan, they turned and sprinted from the room.

A moment after they had left, there was a movement from behind one of the tapestries that hung along the walls of their chamber.

The tall, thin frame of Margwyn stepped out into the light.

His face was set in a grim mask.

Fitz was staring at Compassion. 'Why didn't he –'

'I don't know. He has the power to. He has the power to do anything.'

'I think he was afraid.' He carefully watched her reaction. 'Afraid of you.'

The thought seemed to disturb her as much as it did him. 'Yes.'

There was an awkward pause for a moment. Fitz thought about asking if she was aware of the vanishing trick. No, he could do that later. He marched over to the lift. 'OK, the mission's scrubbed, the black box didn't work, so let's just get out of here before the little guy gets his courage back.' He hit the button, and the lift doors swished open.

Behind them stood a brick wall.

Swearing copiously under his breath, Fitz grabbed a metal-framed chair, ran to the window, and flung it at the cityscape below.

The chair went straight through the window, which disintegrated into a crashing curtain of glass shards.

And it bounced off the wall that was now revealed to be behind the illusion of London.

Fitz gazed at it, panting, his anger left with nowhere to go. 'What is this?' he shouted. 'What's he planning to do with us?'

Compassion was hugging herself. 'I think that, because he's afraid, he's decided not to hurt us. So instead he's just going to keep us locked up here.' Her eyes were wide with terror. 'For ever.'

Fitz didn't want to hear that. He ran to her and grabbed the weapon from her fingers. 'Damn it! Why didn't this work?' He used his fingernails to crack it open along a seam, and pulled the box apart.

He stared at the interior. Except for a tiny spring underneath the button, it was completely empty.

He threw it into a corner. 'We've been set up!' he whispered. 'We've been completely set up!' He felt sick in his stomach. It was all lost now. Why hadn't he stayed where there was a good life for him?

He turned back to Compassion, and saw that she had now curled up into a foetal ball on the sofa, her hands grasping her feet, her head buried in her chest.

She was muttering gibberish under her breath.

And that was the most frightening thing that Fitz had seen all day.

The Doctor fell through the vortex.

He felt the warp of the continuum vibrate around him again, and prepared himself once more to push away from a dangerous exit point. But then he felt a curious mental tendril brush into his mind, an incantation different from the ones that were howling around him begin to beat at the back of his temporal lobes.

There was something else alive in here!

His eyes snapped open.

He gasped at what he saw.

In the spiralling, flashing void in front of him, something huge was forming. Pseudomatter was vastly, slowly, accumulating. It looked like it had taken a timeless age for the process to get under way, but now it was happening as he watched. The white light at the heart of the spiral of matter burned so bright that even the Doctor's pupils fled from it. He put up a hand to shield his eyes. He couldn't make it out. Was that a figure? What was forming here, in the landscape that threaded through all space and time?

He concentrated on the mental tendril that had brushed across his mind, and found it again. An unconscious thing, something just being born. Here, outside of time, that meant that this object – no, this... being – was something that may or may not happen, according to the Doctor's own ever-collapsing wave of possibilities. He was watching the birth of somebody, or something – it was still open to debate – that lived here in the vortex, that was at home here, and yet was bound up with his own destiny. He latched on to the mental tendril again, and recognised the personality that was filling the vortex around him with its thoughts.

King Constantine. They had never met, but there was no mistaking him. His thoughts were of the rolling downlands of his kingdom, of the harvest and the business of bees. This area of the vortex must be where some of his thoughts drifted, in his powerful sleep, a kind of mental footnote to Avalon.

But Constantine had been around for centuries. This thing about to be born wasn't him. It was... forming inside him... Not in the dark way of a parasite, but like a pearl accumulating around a grain of sand in an oyster's shell. The King seemed to know, as much as he could know in his unconsciousness, and approve, because the emotional atmosphere as the Doctor orbited the twining mass of protoplasm was kind and nurturing. Constantine was either actively giving birth, which seemed unlikely, or he was interpreting, translating, some powerful event that was due to take place inside the dreamlands of Avalon, putting it into his own terms. The creation of a being here resulted from... the creation of what there?

Contemplating the possibilities, the Doctor found, was sapping his energy. He should shut down again. He was about to close his eyes, when he heard something on the edge of his senses. A distant call. He could hear it only because of how close he was to this thing being created in the vortex. The call was to it, an unconscious communication, a communion. There was someone, in some still more distant branch of reality, that related very directly to the being that was forming here.

Their voice, though there were no words, seemed very familiar.

Urgently, the Doctor reached out, grabbed hold of the voice like a lifeline, and began to follow it to its source.

Chapter Ten
War Fever

Margwyn ran as fast as he could across a balcony and down some back stairs to get to the Royal Planning Chamber.

He skidded to a halt on the threshold. Inside, the two so-called War Mages were already huddled in consultation with Brona and Arwen. Tiny fairy pages were whizzing in and out of the room. Margwyn spun his finger in the summoning gesture and one alighted there. 'What occurs?' he asked it.

The tiny being glimmered its response to him and buzzed off down the corridor.

He closed his eyes. It had told him the worst possible news. The catastrophe was upon them. The thing he had spent the last few years of his life anticipating and trying to avert was about to happen.

And his own folly had brought it about.

Suddenly, he could see his actions from the point of view of an outsider. And the thought of who he was now, from any position other than inside his own head, sent a shiver down his spine.

He had been the cuckoo in the nest of Mab's court. And all the while he had thought himself her most loyal servant.

He watched the body language of the four reptilians inside the chamber. The War Mages were known to Brona and Arwen of old, he had discovered from his readings since he came here. Arwen had introduced them to his court, the histories said, with a speech about holding them in the palms of his claws when they were newly hatched. As if they were old friends from the islands, brought to court.

But Margwyn had encountered no records of them, even in his deepest studies of Faerie lore, while back in Mab's court. He had a feeling the records here had changed. Perhaps time itself had changed. In any case, he could not take his tale to Brona and Arwen. They would never believe him.

He looked at the War Mages with contempt. The way they had reacted to the danger confronting Compassion! The way they had willed her destruction!

And yet they, too, would be serving some master.

And, unlike him, they were serving their master faithfully.

He felt his nails digging into his own palms.

He could still be happy here, the traitor part of him said. The part that had made every action practical, and had denied him the simple love that defies practicality and keeps families knitted against outside causes, no matter how fair or just. He could be happy here by choosing this lie, by staying in this blissful place and giving himself over to the side of Faerie in the long night that was about to descend.

That would be the practical thing, to forget what he knew, to live the lie.

He wondered for a moment how his definition of practicality had turned from one thing to another without his noticing.

He turned on his heel and marched away. And began to march faster and faster.

'With our agents captured, there is no alternative,' Brona hissed to her husband. 'But I wish there were.'

Cavis, in her guise as a War Mage, placed a caring claw on the Queen's forearm. 'In order for our last, desperate plan to work, we need this. There is no alternative.'

The Dragon King Arwen shook his head slowly, ponderously, like a continent shifting. 'The loss of life will be vast,' he said.

'Not necessarily.' Cavis was pleased that Gandar was finally backing her up. 'We know we can use the vortex tunnel to send a small force wherever we wish –'

'But to send that force right into the midst of the Castle of the Celts...' Arwen let out a long low jet of steam. 'They would be slaughtered.'

'But, Your Majesty!' Cavis forcefully made herself relax, unclenching her teeth. 'The Celts don't know we can do this. They think their magical defences protect the castle against materialisations. If there's only a small garrison there, we can rip straight through them, get to the pool where Constantine sleeps, enter it and affect his dreams directly. Close the gateway, expel the enemy, mercifully end this war.'

Or rather, she thought to herself, make Constantine's dream on Earth behave itself. On the way here she and Gandar had stopped for a moment and thought about just going straight in on their own. With both of them in new disguises, they could have got to the pool all right. But without some mayhem as a distraction, as soon as the alarms had sounded the pool would be full of Celtic warriors, ready to fight to the death. No, they needed a platoon of poor fools ready to die for the cause.

Besides, it was more fun this way.

Arwen slowly raised his head, his reptile eyes meeting hers, and suddenly shifting into beautiful, golden depths. 'If there's only a small garrison there.'

'Which is why we need you to launch a full-scale land war against the humans.'

A moment. Then Arwen inclined his great head. 'Very well,' he said. 'War it shall be.'

Group Captain Charlie Heineman stared up into the morning sky, his hand trying to block the glare from his eyes. 'What are they, Sergeant?' he asked. 'Are they ours, d'you reckon?'

He had stopped on his walk from the officers' tent to the morning briefing when he'd noticed a cluster of tiny dots, a circle of them, rotating at least thirty thousand feet above the forest clearing that formed this rough forward airbase. The sergeant had responded to his shout and run over a minute later.

'Dunno, sir. If they're ours they're something I –'

A sudden shadow slammed down from the sky, sending Heineman and his sergeant tumbling to the ground.

There'd been a sonic boom at the same moment, he realised, as he felt blood pouring from his ears.

It was dark. Why was it dark?

He looked up, into the mouth of a dragon.

Reflexes saved him. He dived sideways.

Behind him, his sergeant, the officers' tent and a large chunk of the runway dissolved into liquid flame. He lay in the ferns between the trees and watched flaming debris spiralling down around him in silence, the bracken nearby igniting as each piece hit.

He was too shocked to move.

He looked down, and saw his left leg had gone from the knee downwards. He laughed at it. It looked like a bad special effect. Blackened stump at the end. The heat.

He watched Michael Wheeler running for his aircraft, and started to cry at how brave that man was. Then another burst of fire billowed sideways through the trees, and Michael flew apart into a billowing mass of inky, liquid cinders, his helmet flying sideways like a rocket into the forest.

Somebody had got to one of the Harriers, and was taxiing it out from the camouflage-net hangars on to what remained of the runway.

Heineman watched the shadow fall over it, and nearly turned aside, but at the last moment made himself look.

One vast claw stamped into the cockpit, the force of the impact crunching the body of the jet into the ground like a mashed paper cup, the wings cracking upward.

A second later, the aircraft exploded into flames.

The claw whipped away into the air, faster than Heineman's eyes could follow.

And, with a billowing of air and a blur of movement, the dragons were dots again, high in the sky, heading south.

Heineman wrenched himself forward, and started to crawl back towards the camp. He had to reach a radio.

Colonel Munro was eating dinner in the Great Hall of the castle, trying to insulate his headache from the echoing laughs and shouts of some soldiers at a pool table. He was regretting avoiding the fish in the Officers' Mess. His palmtop bleeped.

He pulled it from his pocket, and stared at the line of green situation points that had appeared all at once across northwest England.

He leapt to his feet so fast that his chair went flying.

The hall went silent, all eyes upon him. They knew what that meant. So he composed himself, turned to them and said, 'The balloon's gone up. Briefing in tent six, twenty hundred hours. Everybody.'

He left swiftly, not wanting to linger in the urgent silence that had descended.

The animated map filled the entire northern end of tent six, a marquee-sized venue that was packed with chairs and standing soldiers. On the map, Munro used an animated pointer to indicate various situations.

'They're coming at us at full speed, hitting hard and fast and taking out everything we've got in a line from here to here. It's what we feared: they have the capacity to win almost any engagement they choose to initiate. So they must have been conserving their forces so far. Aurora says –' the map flicked into a photographic mosaic of northern England – 'and we have now lost the Aurora by the way –' a whisper of dismay went through the troops in the tent – 'that there are three large concentrations of Faerie troops, here, here and here.' He pointed to dark masses on the map. 'Heading south. At least two hundred dragons in an air-support role. We have no reason to think that their objectives now are anything short of taking the entire country.'

A major raised his hand. 'Are we keeping up the remote bombardment?'

'We would if we could. They started taking out our cruise missiles last night with nearly a hundred per cent efficiency. They must have made a breakthrough with their magic. We've got the mages in the castle working on that. Artillery shells are still having some effect, but we're running out of forward bases to support the guns. And spotters are now at great risk. No, I think this remote war of ours is at an end. We're going to engage their forces on the ground with main battle tanks, Apaches, the infantry. Everything we've got.'

From somewhere among the Welsh Guards, cries of applause

broke out. 'About time!' and 'Let's get on with it!' Munro managed not to smile at the brave idiots.

'Look at your palmtops,' he said. 'Now here's the order of battle...'

Lethbridge-Stewart sat at the back of the briefing. He saw several of the young soldiers turn to look to him, and he made reassuring eye contact with each one, a confident smile on his face, an eyebrow raised here and there.

They're all going to die, he thought.

He fought down the drowning sensation that he couldn't save them. He would be there with them, and he would have to try.

He hadn't told anyone of his encounter with Boyce on the tower. It felt like just another part of this nightmare he was now doomed to play out. A footnote. Another door closed.

He looked up at where Munro was going through tactical plans for the interception of the Faerie ground troops.

Another scared young man, a pilot this time, looked back at him.

The Brigadier realised that he recognised him. It was Matthew Bedser, called back to duty, the man who'd lost the bomb in the first place and started this whole terrible dream. He still wore his hair cropped short, still had the same haunted expression. Obviously, with all that had happened, he had been cleared of all charges and returned to duty.

They shared a look of resignation for a moment.

Then the Brigadier remembered where he was, and turned his grimace into a smile.

'I will lead my forces!' Mab bellowed, smashing her fist into the table. 'If we are to fight them face to face, I will lead!'

Munro went to the door of the throne room and closed it. Then he turned back to Mab. 'Queen Regent, why do you have a Chief Warrior, exactly?'

'My new Chief Warrior is a child! He has spots on his face! He hasn't had a woman! He's –'

'I've talked to Owen. He's got a good head for tactics. He's eager to lead the Catuvelauni regiment.'

Mab drew her sword in one fluid movement. 'Don't interrupt me, you thin-blooded Saxon oaf!'

Munro looked at the sharp edge of metal. He paused before he spoke. 'Forgive me, Queen Regent, but you have no children. We have no right here but for the treaty you have signed with us. If you're killed, then the Unseelie Court may start to be seen as the legitimate power in this land.' He saw that Mab was making herself listen. 'Stay here and keep an eye on things. General Lethbridge-Stewart and I will be at the forward HQ in Nottingham.'

The two warriors made eye contact. Finally, Mab curtly nodded, and Munro turned and left the room.

After he'd gone, Mab slammed her sword back into her scabbard, and spat on the ground. 'Caergonwy!' she bellowed at the door, correcting the too-thin man. 'Nottingham, my arse!'

She went to the window, and watched as the armies of Earth formed into rigid squares on the fields of Avalon, waiting for the horrible metal birds to take them away. By midnight, she had been told, the only troops left at the castle would be her Celtic auxiliaries and a handful of guards on the airbase.

'One day I'll be rid of all you lot,' she spat. 'Brigida save me, I hope I can be now.'

Cavis and Gandar marched past the room where the bomb sat on its plinth. Now it was slowly rotating, Fair Folk mages checking its readiness for launch.

'Aimed right at the castle of the Celts,' Gandar nodded. 'If the humans go nuclear, so will Arwen.'

Cavis kept walking at speed. They had scheduled a final briefing for the warriors who were coming with them in a few minutes. 'Rex will be pleased. But do we care?'

'Well, I've programmed the projectile carrying the bomb to get through the Celt defences. If we fail in our mission, then the shock of being nuked might just make Constantine's unconscious lash out.'

'If we fail, then we're dead, Gallifrey's dead, the whole Othering universe is –'

'So we won't fail.'

'I have a bad feeling about this one, Gandar. Ever since we misjudged what Rex would do. I feel like something terrible is going to come down on our heads.'

'Be cool. We can do this. Remember who we are.'

They came to the door of their quarters, and Gandar marched straight in.

'We have to get packed,' he said, heading for the bed. 'Reconfigure the TARDIS for –'

Cavis spun at the sound of the scream.

'Death to traitors!'

A man. Flying. A blade.

The blade impacted Gandar and went straight through his chest. Then it flashed out and struck again.

Her lover fell, screaming, as the flying, screeching figure whirled, its black cloak scattering things from a table, the blade spitting blood as it slipped from the wound.

The figure sped for her.

It was Margwyn, she realised as her reflexes made her reach for her staser.

'Die in the name of Mab!' he screamed.

'Die yourself,' she hissed.

She fired point-blank.

The white blast sent the blade flying.

He spun in the air under the impact.

The blade impacted and stuck point first into the wall.

The killer hit a wall panel, which flipped open and closed behind him.

And he was gone.

Cavis ran to the panel, kicked it open, and fired burst after burst down the long dark tunnel she found there, screaming oaths at the magician.

Then she heard a groan and spun to see Gandar crawling across the floor towards her. He held one hand to his chest, and one hand stretched out to her.

Light was gathering around him, starting to blaze from every pore, turning the shadows of the room into a compass of concentric lines circled on him.

She grabbed her lover's hand, and shielded her eyes as the light arched through the spectrum, vortex colours flashing against the panelled walls, turning them purple and red.

She knew he had no Watcher, that he was doing this on his own. She felt the flesh on her hand burning, but held on. She was going to be here for him.

The light faded. She bit her lip against the pain coming from her raw palm, and turned and looked to see how Gandar was.

He was lying among the bubbling, mewling remnants of his reptilian disguise, his new hair fair, his skin light and freckled across his shoulders.

She bent to touch his head.

He opened his eyes. 'That guy,' he murmured. 'Knew about us. He tried to put one through each heart. Missed the second one. Oh, he is going to die over a very long and pleasurable weekend. I really liked that regeneration.'

Cavis kissed him. 'So did I,' she whispered. 'Now sit up. Margwyn will be on his way to the Celts. We can't wait any longer. We have to end this now!'

The Brigadier and Colonel Munro stood by the ramp of a C-130 transport aircraft. Arc lights shone down on an empty airfield. The last contingent were on their way. Everybody was being sent into the fight in the North.

'So how are you, sir?' asked Munro, as the last of the men ran up the ramp. The big props were already turning over, rippling the air around them.

Lethbridge-Stewart had found, now that he had his kitbag slung over his shoulder, that he kept looking back to the castle, as if he was expecting something. The harsh tone of Munro's question snapped him back to where he was. 'I take it you disapprove of my being given command, Colonel?'

'I didn't say that, sir. I just think that...' He paused as the last soldier ran past them up the ramp.

'You have permission to speak, Munro. For God's sake, spit it out.'

'If I were your MO, sir, I would have declared you hors de combat.'

'He tried to. I told him that if he did that, I'd blow my brains out.' Before he could say anything more, the Brigadier leaned in closer and looked him in the eye. 'We both know the odds, Munro. We know what these lads are in for. I will not allow them to face that without me. Do you understand?'

'Sir, yes, sir!' He looked away.

'Good.' The Brigadier looked up at the castle again. A figure had emerged from the gatehouse. 'Now you can forget the formalities. Do we have the Rules of Engagement yet?'

'They just came in. If the enemy uses the nuclear warhead, we've been ordered to go for full retaliation.'

The Brigadier tried not to think about what the Doctor would have said. He focused on the small figure who was standing a long way off, on the bridge over the moat. He couldn't make out the details. But he knew who it was. She had come back. She was looking at him. Trying to communicate that care that stretched across time and death itself.

The Doctor was dead. The land of dreams was going to tear itself apart. But he was a soldier, and all he could do was play this game to the best of his ability, to the last possible instant.

His heart felt eased by seeing her again. Just eased enough to get him through what lay ahead.

'Carry on, Colonel,' he said. Then, with a final glance back at the distant figure, he shouldered his kitbag, and turned to walk up the ramp into the aircraft.

From the bridge over the moat, Mab watched the great cargo door close. The props became a blur, and the huge metal bird started to move down the runway, faster and faster, until it smoothly slid up into the sky.

After a moment, it had vanished into the darkness.

She watched the tiny lights blinking away, and listened to the sound fading, until both had vanished.

Then she turned and headed back into the castle.

Margwyn ran as fast as his legs would carry him, and hit the control for the lift that would take him to the surface an instant before he fell into it.

He watched the Unseelie Court fall away below him. He knew now that he had to get back to Mab's court, whatever that meant for him. He had to put right that which had gone so very wrong. 'A curse on both these courts,' he whispered. 'A flaw at the heart of Avalon. We are at war with ourselves! Brigida and all the gods, who can save us now?'

Chapter Eleven
The Return of the Hero

Compassion was rocking back and forth, breathing in tiny gasps, her eyes locked shut.

She'd been doing this for hours now. Fitz felt he should be doing something. Anything. 'Compassion! Come on! It's not as bad as all that!'

'It is!' she whispered. 'The change wants to come! It wants to get us out of here. But I won't let it! I can't! I'm... scared!'

'This isn't like you. Compassion, you're scaring me!'

'That dream man knows!' she insisted, seemingly oblivious to him. 'He saw what was going to happen to me! He's afraid of it, too! That's why he didn't attack us, why he locked us up for ever!'

A thought occurred to Fitz. A desperate little victim trick, but... 'It's all right,' he whispered, lying in as convincing a manner as he could. 'He doesn't know about our ace in the hole. About what he's missing back in Avalon.'

The far wall of the room warped and parted like water, and suddenly King was standing in front of them again.

Fitz didn't have to pretend to be scared at seeing him again. 'Mr King!' he stammered. 'When are you going to let us out of here?'

King strode up to them. Compassion started to shudder. Fitz felt the power rippling between them. Two huge sources of energy, regarding each other like sumo wrestlers, seeking any tiny weakness. But Compassion didn't want to play.

Reluctantly, Fitz stood up between them. 'I said –'

'What were you talking about?' King asked, his tone a touch on the shrill side.

'What do you mean? I don't understand.'

Fitz suddenly found himself flying across the room. He hit the wall with a force that knocked the breath from him.

He tried to inhale, but there were invisible hands at his throat, the air itself forming thumbs that held his windpipe expertly. He dangled three feet up the wall, his limbs flailing, his lungs feeling as if they were about to burst.

'Tell me!' screamed King. The hands eased the pressure for a moment.

Fitz realised with a sick feeling that he didn't have anything to tell. Typically good plan there, Kreiner.

Compassion's eyes were blazing with colours.

Air slammed Fitz's head back against the wall. The man spun to regard Compassion, fear on his face.

She was holding tightly on to the arms of the sofa, as if fighting the change that was about to overcome her. Her mouth was forming words faster than Fitz could follow.

King pulled a long blade from his sleeve. Or, rather, from out of thin air. He strode purposefully towards Compassion. He must think that she was vulnerable at this moment, Fitz realised, that she could do nothing but whatever she was doing, that now he could strike.

He tried to shout a warning, but his voice wouldn't come.

Compassion could see King moving towards her, through the torrent of information that was pouring into her brain. She was seeing him with senses other than sight. And that scared her. But what scared her more, more even than the long knife he was going to use to kill her, was the demand that was now raging into her brain.

Let me loose, it shouted. Become me! Let it happen!

'No!' she screamed.

She desperately called out into the darkness for help.

And, to her astonishment, from the darkness there came an answer.

She concentrated on it. Cried for it to come to her.

There was a flash from the ceiling.

Something fell into the room.

King raised his blade to strike.

Compassion opened her mouth in a great shout of horror.

And then a familiar hand tapped King on the shoulder.

He spun round.

A straight right hook sent him flying.

The Doctor pointed at where the man lay on the floor, staring up at him in astonishment. 'Hey,' he said softly. 'Leave my companion alone.'

'Doctor!' Compassion yelled, leaping to her feet. 'You're alive!'

She ran to him and hugged him.

The Doctor grabbed her head to his chest and breathed a deep sigh of relief. 'I thought it was you out there,' he murmured. 'But I didn't know how it could be. Wow.' He suddenly realised, and held her at arm's length. 'You're hugging me. You're happy to see me!'

He felt her freeze in his arms. 'It's to do with my changing,' she whispered. 'This big change that wants to happen to me. It expresses its feelings. It wants me to be like that. But it's so big –'

There came a croak of warning from the far wall.

The Doctor looked up in time to pluck the speeding knife out of the air between his thumb and forefinger.

He let go of Compassion and nodded to Fitz. 'Thanks.' Then he looked to where King was pulling another long blade from his sleeve. 'OK, enough of the knives.' He broke the one he had across his knee and pointed to Fitz again. 'And let him go.'

King glared at the Doctor for a moment, then clicked his fingers. The knife vanished. Fitz fell from the wall, gasping.

'That's better,' said the Doctor. He went to Fitz and quickly started to rub his neck, finding the pressure points and massaging them.

Fitz gazed back at him with new hope flooding through him. The Doctor was alive. That meant freedom, hope, maybe even a happy ending, somewhere down the line. 'Doctor,' he croaked. 'You don't know how glad I am to see you.'

The Doctor smiled at him. 'Everything's going to be all right,' he said. 'I'm back.'

And Fitz found that he was grinning too.

* * *

The Doctor glanced back to King. 'So, you are...?'

'Constantine's dream,' Compassion told him.

'Fantastic,' murmured the Doctor, looking the dream man up and down. 'And why is he trying to harm you?'

'They...' King looked uncertain for a moment. 'They want to close the gateway. And it isn't time, yet.'

'Ah!' The Doctor smiled across to Compassion. 'Change Constantine's dream at source, expel intruders, close the gateway. I thought that was your handwriting.'

'It's not our plan,' croaked Fitz. 'Those two War Mages set us up! We were told to nobble this guy here, to get at Constantine's dreams, but the gizmo they gave us was just an empty box.'

The Doctor looked angry for a moment. 'They're not War Mages: they're the source of all the suffering in Avalon. But, if they wanted you to fail, that can't be their plan...' He smoothed his chin with his fingers. 'I wonder if they care about what happens to the gateway at all.'

'They care!' King suddenly screeched. 'They're my friends! They wouldn't send these two to hurt me!' He advanced on the Doctor, pointing at his own chest. 'It was my plan to close the gateway! I hate Constantine! He's falling apart! That's how I got a mind. Just a bit of a push from my friends, and I got a mind!' He tapped his head.

'You're Constantine's shadow,' said the Doctor, nodding, beginning to understand. 'In psychological terms, I mean. His rampaging id, set free and unfettered. Cavis and Gandar made you self-aware...'

'And in the vortex, another bit of him! Brigida! My sister! I hate her, too!'

'We've met. One of you is formed around one idea, and one of you around another. She's his ego, trying to organise things, to regain control. The poor guy's in a bad way.'

'Yes.' King's voice dropped to a whisper. 'But he's my power source. I could use his power to make things happen here on Earth. But then I got a plan –'

'You mean Cavis and Gandar gave you a plan.'

'I got a plan so I could change things in Avalon, too.'

The Doctor's mouth drew sideways in an astonished, lopsided grin. 'You created the gateway, didn't you?'

Compassion suddenly yelled, as if something had burst up out of her. 'It's a wormhole!' she called, and to the Doctor's ears it sounded as if she was surprised by what she was saying. 'A wormhole between dimensions! Constantine acts as a perfect mirror, a source of negative matter, against his will, allowing the worlds to connect!' She closed her mouth again with a little snap of her jaw. 'Ow,' she said.

'So...' The Doctor looked back to King. 'How did you manage to set that up?'

King started to giggle again. 'By killing your TARDIS!'

Fitz groaned. 'So it's true.'

The Doctor's smile faded.

King leapt down on to the carpet, eager to explain, his hands drawing patterns on the ground. 'Matthew Bedser! My pilot! He kept flying over the place where the worlds were close! I affected him. Took control. He flew my flight path. Many times. Took my power with him. Made a geometry to fold space-time. Made a trap. Your TARDIS is coming. I saw it coming. It arrives –' He slapped his hands together. 'Bang! Space-time broken! Constantine has to make wormhole, or universe goes boom.'

The Doctor put a hand over his eyes as he slowly worked it out. 'So, Cavis and Gandar wanted me and my crew to be trapped in Avalon. You wanted to open the gateway so you could start to influence things there. So far your aims are the same. But now they've sabotaged their own plan to close the gateway, a plan which you say is too soon...' He took the hand away and looked around the room for help. 'No, I'm baffled.'

King smiled. 'I want the gateway closed only when my own plan is finished. When no one can live in Avalon any more.'

'And, erm,' Fitz said, raising a hand, 'why is that going to happen?'

'Because I kept a secret from my friends. Bedser is back in Avalon. He's still in my power. He's going to drop a bomb on the Faeries!'

* * *

Gandar had groggily recreated his disguise, Cavis had bound her injured hand, and now the two of them were watching as a column of Fair Folk warriors marched purposefully through the large arch in the throne room wall that was the new shape of their TARDIS doors. They had deactivated the time vortex: for this job they needed something that could get their forces out again at the end of it.

Well, something that could get the two of them out, anyway.

The last warrior entered.

Cavis and Gandar turned and bowed to Brona and Arwen, who made gestures of blessing and honour.

'Triumph in the name of your race and rulers!' called Brona.

Cavis followed Gandar into the travel capsule, and paused for a moment before she closed the doors. 'OK,' she told the King and Queen. 'We'll do just that.'

She pulled the double doors shut, and a moment later, with a wheezing, groaning sound, the arch faded away.

The Doctor, Fitz and Compassion all stared at the madman in horror.

'The Faeries will fire back,' he continued, still chuckling. 'They'll shoot Margwyn's bomb at Mab's castle. And then: boom! Nukes back and forth! Death on death! Nuclear winter! Constantine can't stop it, he's too weak from all that magic used in the war! Everybody leaves, except Constantine and Brigida! Then I'll seal the gateway. And my hated ones will rule over nothing, and they'll just be a power source for me. And I'll be complete, and whole, and real!'

The Doctor glared at the giggling man. 'Cavis and Gandar should have realised you'd have ideas above your station. Whatever your function was to them originally, this isn't what they've got planned.' He walked up to King and stared into the madman's eyes, shaking his head slightly in wonder. 'But, d'you know, you've sorted something out for me. Something important. Look at you. All you are is a distillation of the desires of others. A product of your environment. A result rather than a person. But even you...'

He started to smile as the liberating idea took hold in his mind.

'Even you discovered that you had choices, volition, a plan of your own, however warped that plan might be. No matter what interference there is, from Faction Paradox or whoever, there'll always be someone willing to interfere back, to come up with a stupid idea of their own.' He turned back to Fitz and Compassion and smiled at them, suddenly spreading his arms wide, delighted. 'Don't you see? Just because nothing's written in stone doesn't mean I can stop kicking over the statues!'

Fitz was looking over the Doctor's shoulder. 'Erm, Doctor...'

With a screech, King leapt forward.

His hands warped into blades.

The Doctor spun round and whipped his hand out into a fierce point that put his finger right between King's eyes. 'No,' he said.

The monster halted in midair, its eyes and maw still screaming hatred.

The Doctor held it there with his unblinking stare. 'Phew,' he said. 'I'm glad I was right about that.'

'What have you done to him?' asked Compassion.

'I'm just mentally suggesting that he stay right there. This is how Cavis and Gandar got to him, why Rom–' He didn't want to say the name until he was sure. 'Why whoever came up with this whole scheme chose him in the first place. He may have ideas when he's left to himself, but he's still completely susceptible to suggestion.'

'Which is why, even though he's magic and all that, he hides away from everybody,' added Fitz.

'Right.'

'Doctor,' muttered Compassion, glancing between the Time Lord and what he held at the end of his finger. 'How are we going to get out of here?'

'I have absolutely no idea.'

There was a sudden convulsion from the monster. It roared, trying to reach the Doctor, but the best it could do was to wrap itself into a muscular knot, blobs of protoplasm squirting out in all directions. The exertions and screeches continued, until the screaming thing was a mass of tentacles and limbs, spinning faster and faster.

And then, to the Doctor's horror, it started to grow.

'It's drawing on the power of Constantine,' he whispered, sweat breaking out on his brow as he tried to hold the expanding sphere back. 'I think that in its rage it's forgotten its human form.'

It was growing faster and faster.

He backed away from it, and Compassion and Fitz backed away behind him.

'It's outflanked my will!' he gasped. 'I'm still holding it back, but it's going critical! If this thing gets out of the building, people will be terrified of it. And they'll suggest that fear to it. And then the more terrifying it'll become! An infinite progression!'

Compassion stepped out from behind him. 'Let me,' she said.

She stared at the monster. Her fingers curled hard into her palms and her brow creased with effort. There was a rending and warping of the air as great forces surrounded them.

There was a sudden concussion, a pure note that echoed and reflected about the room as if a resonance had been struck.

'That's it!' Compassion stepped back and turned to them. 'I forced a spatial shape on to it.' She looked at their blank faces. 'A non-infinite curve. A maze.' She sighed. 'Look, it's stuck in that shape for now –' She pointed at the halted, frozen sphere of meat, which still seemed to ooze with pent-up violence. 'But it's only a matter of time before it works its way out of it.'

'And it's only a matter of time before this guy Bedser starts a nuclear war in Avalon!' added Fitz.

The Doctor grabbed both his companions around their shoulders, and grinned at them. 'So we're going to have to put things right, aren't we? Now, when I say run –'

He leapt free and sprinted to a fire-escape door that suddenly appeared in the far wall. With one kick, he made it fly open, then turned and slammed his palm on to a fire alarm on the wall. Alarms blared all over the building.

'Run!' he cried, and dashed off down the fire escape.

Fitz and Compassion looked wryly at each other, and then ran after him.

* * *

The sky over London was low and looming and overcast as they sprinted away from the King Centre, a crowd of workers flooding out into the courtyard amidst the sound of alarms.

The Doctor leapt up on to the rear platform of a double-decker sightseeing bus as it started to move off from the pavement, and hauled Compassion and Fitz up after him.

He ran forward, and plucked a hand-held radio from the hands of the astonished driver, reaching with his other hand into the cab to twirl the dial to a familiar frequency. 'Windmill Leader, this is Zachary. Repeat, this is Zachary. Requesting priority pick-up. Triangulate this radio source.'

An astonished voice buzzed a confirmation in return, and the Doctor tossed the radio back to the driver. 'Three for the tour, please,' he said grinning.

They threw themselves into the back seat of the near-empty top deck, open to the sky. The handful of other people there were all tourists, with bleak, sleep-ruined faces, who looked as though they were grimly going through the motions to hold off despair.

An old woman beside them looked across at the Doctor, as if puzzled by his look of determined joy, as if he was the only colourful thing in a monochrome world.

He smiled proudly back at her.

'So,' asked Fitz, 'Cavis and Gandar are...?'

Compassion grabbed the Doctor's arm, as if suddenly in the grip of a seizure. 'Cavisadoratrelundar and Gandarotethetledrax, Time Lord Interventionists,' she cried. Then she put her hands to her face. 'There's more data if you want it. I suddenly just knew it all.'

Fitz looked at her uncertainly. 'So they set us up to get a good kicking from King?'

'They wanted him to attack me, I'm certain,' Compassion added. 'He didn't want to, because he was...' She buried her face in her hands. 'Afraid of me. Of what I'm becoming.'

The Doctor reached out and gently took her hands away from her face. 'It's OK,' he said, looking into her eyes. 'I'm not going to let you come to any harm. Everything's going to be all right. All we have to do is get back to Avalon, stop a nuclear war, foil the villains, give these people back their dreams and prevent the destruction of all life on Earth. Then we can find out what's happening to you.'

For some reason, she smiled at him, and so he smiled back.

He noticed that the old woman was staring at them, her mouth hanging open in amazement.

Fitz pointed up. 'Look!' he called.

Over the Thames, coming in low and fast, heading straight for the bus, a UNIT helicopter was approaching. From it was unfurling a long rope ladder.

The Doctor leapt to his feet, and grabbed Compassion by the hand. The helicopter matched speeds with the bus, and swept over it, causing the tourists, who were now swarming up from the lower deck, to duck and hold on to their hats.

The Doctor jumped on to the seat, grabbed the bottom of the rope ladder and handed it to Fitz, who, with a little look that went beyond astonishment, started to climb it. Compassion followed.

There were gasps of amazement from the crowd.

The Doctor glanced up to see that his companions were nearly in the helicopter, and then stepped on to the bottom rung of the ladder himself.

'Young man!' cried the old woman, trying to stop her bonnet from flying off her head. 'Wait! Who are you? What are you doing here?'

The Doctor grinned at her. 'I'm the Doctor. And I'm here to save the world!'

He waved a hand to the helicopter, and the ladder ascended into the sky, the Doctor hanging on for a moment to smile back at the crowd diminishing into the sweep of London beneath him.

'Because I choose to,' he whispered triumphantly. 'Because I can!'

Chapter Twelve
And This Gives Life to Thee

The Brigadier looked out across the battlefield in the early hours of morning. Somewhere out there, a lone voice was screaming.

It had happened so quickly. The Allied forces had landed at what remained of the forward airfields in what, geographically, were Nottingham, Liverpool and Chester. From there, using the main battle tanks as a spearhead, they had pressed ahead, anxious to engage the enemy as far north as possible. Their fighter cover had met with a few dragons on reconnaissance missions, and generally come off better, which had encouraged the men. But they had all been aware that ahead of them, moving as fast as they were, came the main body of the Fair Folk's army.

The spearheads had met in open country north of the Pennines. Both sides had increased speed, hoping to gain the high ground, and the tanks had got there first, holding a forward ridge while mechanised howitzers were rushed up to support them. The Fair Folk had opened up with everything they had, balls of flame and clouds of illuminated darts pouring on to the ridge, as Celt mages danced between the tanks, trying to hold off the barrage.

Radio communications had faded into a blaze of white noise, and the entire army had fallen into one of Munro's prepared formations. The ground troops had been brought up, the Brigadier at their head, in choppers and APCs, and had held the ridge, sustaining severe losses.

Sustaining severe losses. Indeed.

He'd had to yell at soldiers to dash from one piece of rough cover to another. When a volley of fireballs had looked like opening a gap in the line, he'd sent five men forward, watched them cut down by volleys of darts, and then sent another five, wide-eyed, straight after them.

He'd tried to stay at the very front with every step. His uniform was now almost entirely coated in mud, and there was someone else's blood down his left leg, and some fleshy scraps on his shoulder, which he'd tried to scrape off with a branch. His sense of smell had cut out, which was familiar. He was partially deaf, and had some flash damage to his left cornea.

He was certain that he also had a confident smile fixed on his face.

The scream came again. A soldier was stuck out there between the lines, wounded. He'd been screaming for the last three hours.

The Brigadier was standing in a hastily constructed foxhole on the ridge that he had so expensively bought. The ridge itself, and the low slope in front of it, had been reduced to a muddy morass. The plain beyond, where the Fair Folk were, was a rugged landscape of mud and scorched grass. The only actual features one could have seen, had it been light, would have been trees along the far horizons. Both sides had dug in now, with only sporadic noises of fire from either direction. They were all waiting for dawn.

The Brigadier was alone, having encouraged the men on this part of the line to get some sleep in the holes dug into the walls of the foxhole. He could see the silhouettes of sentries in the distance to his left and right.

He gingerly reached up and removed his cap. He touched his hair, and was surprised at the civilised feel of it, under what had coated him.

'You haven't even been injured.'

He glanced sideways at where she sat on the edge of the foxhole, swinging her legs. 'I thought I left you back at the castle.'

'That wasn't me.'

'Of course it was. I know you when I see you, after all this time. You haven't been around for a while, anyway. What have you been up to?' She yawned and stretched. 'Getting bored being here on my own. I think you've stopped trying.'

'I assure you, dear, that a large number of my men have been in exactly the same situation as myself, and it's worked for them.'

She tutted. 'You don't even believe in an afterlife!'

He blinked at her, surprised. 'It's not the first time I've

entertained an idea just so we'd have something to talk about.'

'What I mean is, if you don't believe I'm anything more than a grief symptom, what's all this rubbish about joining me? In this place, where death is something these young men spend every moment trying to avoid, isn't this all a bit... well... selfish?'

He looked appalled at her. It took him a moment to choose his words, because for the first time he'd felt the urge to bellow at her. And, if he did that, he had a terrible feeling that she would vanish again. 'Do you know,' he began, 'when you first... left, the most painful thing were the thoughts which in the past would have ended with your name? That's a nice rose, I must get a cutting of that for... There's that song again, the one I danced to with... And so the most everyday things became matters of tremendous pain. A moment of joy, and then always that connection to pain at the end.' He walked up to her, and reached out to touch her hair, to remember how it had smelled. 'The world, which used to be informed by - about - our love for each other, became merely about that love ending. Even now, that condition persists. You and I still being able to talk, well... that's the only relief. And I know perfectly well that that's a fantasy. So don't deny me my last exit, will you, dear? Don't tell me my only thought for the future is a selfish one.'

She still looked uncertain. He wanted to kiss her, but for some reason he hadn't been able to do that since she'd died. 'You couldn't do it yourself.'

'Ah... Bit undignified, I thought. That indeed, would be selfish. I can be of help here, do it in a good cause.'

'And if you win, and you get to go home?'

'Absolutely not.' He shook his head. 'I have no intention of going home.'

'But what if there's someone else who loves you? What about them?'

He grabbed her by the shoulders, horrified by what she was saying. 'Don't talk rot. Even if there was, that'd be just someone else who... Someone else I couldn't... Besides, who else could there be? I can't love anyone apart from you.'

'But you can't keep on being in love with me.'

'Who says I can't?' He was aware of the pain at the back of his voice. 'If the Doctor had lived, I'd have got him to take me back and rescue you from the bloody yacht.'

'He wouldn't have let you.'

'Then I'd have held a gun to his head and made him!' He found that he was shouting into her face. 'Don't you understand, you stupid woman? I can't move on, I can't be free, because I'm never going to stop loving you!'

She looked into his eyes, her gaze searching his face sadly. She reached up to touch his cheek. 'Then, my love,' she said, 'I have to go.'

And suddenly the Brigadier found that he had been talking to a muddy slope.

He staggered back, his hands reaching into the air in front of him.

'Oh no,' he whispered. 'Oh please, no.'

He reached out to touch the mud and felt it curl in his hands.

And suddenly he was back under the water again, where he'd been for the last year.

He put a hand to his mouth and forced his eyes closed, yearning for his thought and existence to end. 'Please,' he said again. 'Please come back. Don't do this for my own good. Please.'

A terrible coldness spread through his limbs. The water. He couldn't keep on going through the motions any more. Without love, life was just a series of things that happened.

And there was to be no more love for him, now.

The scream rang across the battlefield again.

The Brigadier's face cracked open in a smile. So there it was. His chance to die well.

With a little grunt of effort, he slithered up on to the muddy bank where Doris had been sitting, and stood, looking around him.

They were shouting at him, the sentries. They were running desperately down the trenches towards him.

So he took two more steps out into no-man's-land, swinging his arms. Big, confident strides.

He looked back. They had stopped. They were pleading with him, reaching their arms out towards him. He couldn't hear the words, just saw their arms reaching, their mouths moving, fading away into the distance.

He turned back towards the wilderness, and started to walk, lightly and confidently, as if he was out on a stroll with Doris.

Because what was a battlefield, what was anything, without love? It was just a place, something to walk through.

And instead of acting as though it was sensible to stand there listening to the screams of the dying, did it really take an insane, shell-shocked, grief-stricken man to be sane enough to go for that walk?

'I'm coming,' he called lightly into the silence. 'Hold on.'

The scream came again, and he changed direction, heading faster towards it, looking into the night in front of him with interest, with imagination. This felt like the first purposeful thing he'd done in a year, the first thing that had been his.

The fire came now, blazing darts whipping past his right shoulder. They'd seen him on the other side.

So be it. He kept on walking.

'If I go first,' she had once said to him, when she had been real and could say real things, 'then you will go on, won't you? You won't –'

He had put his hand over hers and hushed her. Because the world then had been all about love, and he'd never imagined it being any other way.

She had loved the sun, but had needed to wear big hats to keep it from her skin.

She had loved her roses, and the old music that he had brought into her life and that she had learned to dance to.

She had loved her soap operas, The Archers and all that. And he remembered that she had once asked him why he couldn't get caught up in them as she did. He'd told her that he didn't think they were drama, really. That, although so-and-so might have enormous things happening to them this week, you knew that eventually they'd get past them, and that something equally enormous would start to happen to them again in a couple of weeks' time.

'Stories are about endings,' he'd said. 'They don't mean anything unless they come to an end.'

He had loved her so much. He had let his whole person slip into being someone who loved her. And though some part of him now protested at that, saying that he shouldn't have made himself so vulnerable, as he walked on through this night, he knew that it had been the right thing to do.

The brave thing to do, to love wholeheartedly and well. The thing that allowed him to do this, now. To know that somewhere inside you was a man who could love and had been loved.

That there were, despite all the melodrama and noise of war, some things that were stronger than death.

He knew now, as he felt the presence of that death right in front of him, that if he could have his time again, could meet her again, knowing about the ending and all the pain to come, that he wouldn't have turned away from her. He wouldn't have done this any other way.

The ending made the story what it was. Made him what he was. Time, death and pain existed so that tiny human beings like him could stand against them.

So that they could do the best they could.

The scream came again. It was about a hundred metres ahead of him, to the left, where the ground became a mass of shadows and ridges.

'Hold on,' he called again. 'It's the Brigadier here. You just keep on calling and I'll come to you.'

The yells increased, and another flurry of darts smacked the soil around his feet.

He stepped over them. They had no power over him now.

He made his way through craters and troughs where the ground had been ripped up by shellfire. He walked across a warren of shell holes, and tripped and fell on their ragged edges. He climbed over a final bank into the cutting of a small stream.

By it lay a UNIT soldier, a private, curled in a ball. His left arm was a mass of flesh, cut off near the shoulder. He'd managed to tie it up. There were anaesthetic needles lying everywhere. Around the private lay, in dangling, absurd positions, the bodies of his friends.

'Sir!' he gasped. 'What are you doing here? You'll get yourself killed!'

The Brigadier squatted beside him. 'Don't be ridiculous, Private. If I got killed –' And then the thought suddenly struck him that what he was about to say was true. That, incredibly, it must have been true when he started this walk.

He found himself smiling at how ridiculous it was that he had come all this way just to discover that.

'If I got killed,' he finished, 'then I couldn't get you home.'

They watched, the soldiers and their commanders, as the two figures appeared out of the darkness. They watched through light-sensitive goggles, for fear of putting light on them. They cheered them on inside, silently, for fear of letting the enemy know how close to home they'd come.

Through the darkness, the Brigadier had the private braced across his shoulder, and was half walking, half carrying him home.

The other soldiers were aware that they were investing too much in this one tiny thing. That they were risking themselves. Because if one of the darts that flashed across the field hit its mark, then their hopes would die, and they would feel something cramp inside of them, and this place would be given over to fear and rage completely.

They watched desperately then, unable not to care.

From the other side of the lines, others watched also.

Arwen looked into the green pool that rippled along one wall of the porcelain chamber in their castle from which he and Brona were controlling their forces.

In that pool, they could see and hear the two tiny humans struggling through the mud, the one urging the other on with proud, hopeful words in a place where there should be no hope.

Brona placed her palms flat on Arwen's scaly back, the gesture of greatest intimacy among their kind. 'You should stop them firing.'

He let out a long breath. 'Where is their triumph if I do that?'

'This is not a game,' Brona insisted, gently.

Arwen thought for a moment. Then he said, 'If I am to stop one weapon, I should have to stop them all.'

Brona looked at him enquiringly.

Cavis flung open the door of the new cabinet that had appeared in the Great Hall, and fired two precise staser bolts, cutting down the nightwatchmen who had run into the room at the noise of the landing.

Gandar sprinted out behind her, his gun held in front of him. Cavis didn't know if she'd ever get used to the fair skin, but her love's bright eyes and alert look hadn't deserted him.

'Omega's teeth!' he shouted. 'We were supposed to land near the pool!'

'Maybe Constantine's realised we've come for him.'

'Then this is going to be hard.'

'Right.' She checked the door, and grabbed his hands for a moment as they shared their look again. 'Come on, let's just do it.'

They kissed each other hard.

Cavis saw Gandar's eyes suddenly widen.

They leapt out of the embrace and spun to fire together at the dying guardsman –

Whose hand had already closed on the bell rope.

He fell in a blaze of white light, but as he did so, a huge rousing bell started to toll somewhere high in the palace towers.

Gandar pulled the lever that made the door of the cabinet fall open.

A horde of Fair Folk warriors sprinted out of the TARDIS, screeching their complex, high-pitched battle cries.

'Go!' Gandar yelled at them. 'Secure the stairwell! Kill the Celts! Kill everything!'

The lovers looked at each other as the warriors swarmed past.

Then they took a deep breath.

'So much for stealth,' said Cavis.

Then, yelling themselves, they followed their reptiles into the fray.

Mab ran out on to the landing outside her bedroom in her nightgown, and skidded to a halt looking left and right. The alarm bell was booming out across the castle. It had woken her and sent her yelling from her bed. She'd grabbed her sword from its scabbard on the bedpost.

Her eyes widened at what she saw in the corridor.

A Faerie warrior was sprinting straight at her.

It was bellowing steam from its mouth, its three eyes locked on her, glowing red. It held its blade in a stabbing posture.

Mab allowed herself a moment to smile.

Then she leapt straight for it, bellowing, too, swinging her sword around her head.

The warrior tried to stop. It had obviously timed its attack thinking she'd run away. Its claws skidded on the mat.

Mab flew past it, stopped her swing high on her left shoulder, and beheaded the reptile with a sidelong swipe across the back of its neck. She used the momentum to swing her body round, grab the jerkin of another as it emerged from round a corner, and pull its neck down on to her blade.

Ripping the sword away, she stumbled into a third that was just raising its sword, threw its comrade at it, making it spin, and when it swung to take her on again, hacked its arm off.

It screeched backwards, stumbling to reach for a handgun at its side, and she leapt forward and split its skull sideways, mowing the body into the wall.

She spun round, heaving her sword from the corpse, and found no more targets.

From all around the castle there came the sounds of screams and running feet and shots and swordplay.

'Finally!' she bellowed.

Then she ran for the stairs, yelling for the Captain of the Guard.

* * *

The Brigadier stumbled the last few steps.

And a great mass of the men rose out of the trench in front of him, oblivious to their own danger, and took the young man from him, and rushed him off to the medics, and pulled him, cheering and shouting and yelling, into safety.

He stared at them for a moment, as they wrapped their arms around him, offered him brandy, pulled him to their muddy chests, looking at him with the awe of children. The noise of their celebrations echoed along the trenches.

He threw his head back then, and started to laugh with pure, clear relief.

Chapter Thirteen
Reason

The UNIT helicopter containing the Doctor and his companions touched down at the experimental station on Oldbury Down, and the Doctor was out and running, his hands over his head, before the landing struts had fully come to rest. 'Come on!' he yelled to Fitz and Compassion, waving them towards the small cluster of buildings that had grown up on the tiny site.

The pilot had tried to link them by radio to the forward HQ of the Allied forces by way of the cable that had been strung between the testing station and the C&C van at RAF Avalon, through the gateway. But he'd been told that the Faeries were laying down a magical communications blackout right across the North country.

The Doctor reached the guard post by the door of the prefabricated block, and slapped his pockets, looking for his UNIT pass. Finally, he gave up, shouted, 'It's me, OK?' and ducked past the guard.

Thankfully, the man seemed to have been fully briefed by the pilot, or perhaps, the Doctor thought, there were standing orders about him that included his capacity for sudden and eccentric arrivals.

They ran down the corridor of the tiny building and skidded to a halt in front of the gateway, which stood incongruously in the middle of the room, its circle of approaching dawn oddly muted against the bright lighting.

'We have to stop Bedser taking off!' he yelled.

He ran at the gateway and leapt through, the others on his heels.

At a forward airbase near the front line, Matthew Bedser, his eyes hidden by his visor, made an affirmative sign to the ground crew. They pulled the restraints away from the wheels of his Tornado, and he started to taxi the aircraft out on to the long runway ahead of him, burnt out of farmland a day before. Behind him followed the rest of his flight, five aircraft in all.

They were scheduled to attack the enemy reserves as they were brought up over the hills, cut off their supply lines.

But, in the dreaming state of his mind inside his helmet, Bedser knew that he and his navigator would be going much further north than that.

'Tower, this is Tango One, we are ready to fly,' he said.

Clearance was given, the Tornado accelerated along the runway, and then sprang into the sky, the landing gear retracting as it raced up at the acute angle designed to get it quickly to combat height.

Bedser hit a switch on his control panel.

The light came on that said the nuclear weapon was armed and ready to go.

Mab and a band of her warriors sprinted along one of the landings and rushed out across the great stairwell that ran all the way down the castle in stages, like a river running from lock to lock.

Rushing down at them came the wave of Fair Folk warriors, their battle cries echoing off the marble.

Mab's warriors attempted to run up at them, but were met by a cloud of darts, flickering from their guns. Mab saw one of the men catch the blades in his throat and chest and fly back over the banister to his death.

'Fall back!' she shouted. 'Hold them at the bottom!'

The warriors dived back round the foot of the stairs, ducking out again in random order to fire their short bows up at the reptilian warriors. A clatter came from the other side of the stairwell, and Mab raised a hand to hold back a squad of British soldiers, the guards on the C&C post, who fell into firing positions on the other side of the landing and started blazing upward, too.

A couple of the Fair Folk fell. Not enough. They were using their life energy to sustain magical shields. A desperate mission, then. They were heading downward – they must be try to get to Constantine in the catacombs. Which was why she'd intercepted them here, rather than trying to run after them downstairs.

But equally that was why this couldn't last. The enemy had the height. She'd have to send a group of her warriors around to take them from above, conceal how small their numbers were.

A black cylinder came bouncing down the stairs.

'Get down!' she shouted, and flung herself aside.

The blast sent chips of marble flying to embed themselves in flesh. The British soldiers took most of the blast, flying in all directions under the impact.

Through the cloud of smoke, Mab saw the Fair Folk rushing at them now, coming at speed.

She leapt to her feet. 'For Constantine!' she yelled.

The Celts leapt into the smoke and threw their bodies and swords against the reptiles on the stairs themselves.

Mab slashed to her right and left, working her way up, step after step, hauling and chopping and punching, trying to find whoever the commander of this force was, glad of the smoke and the close combat.

She broke free of a pair of claws at her throat, and reached out for the next scaly body.

And suddenly found a gun jammed into her neck.

'Queen Regent!' murmured a male voice. 'I must protest about the quality of your servants' accommodation.'

The reptilian mage threw something to the floor, and, with a flash, the smoke vanished.

Warriors of both sides spun to see Mab standing coolly, her sword ready in midair as Gandar held his staser at her neck.

'Throw down your weapons and lead us to Constantine,' said the Time Lord agent. 'Or she gets a third eye, too.'

The Brigadier stumbled back into his rough, dug-out quarters, a plastic-lined hole with his kitbag and a bunk, and fell on to his bed, adrenaline suddenly making him feel faint.

For the first time in a year, he felt as if there might be something in the future for him, and he was giddy with the sudden vertigo of it.

He'd have to make choices again, now. He'd have to start thinking about living.

Somehow, he felt that he could.

'Alistair,' he whispered to himself, 'for you, the war is over.'

And then something happened all around his bed.

He sat up with a start.

Boyce was standing right next to the bunk, his armour shining. But this time on his face was a look of terrible determination. 'For us, it's beginning,' he said.

This time, there were others with him. Four of them in all, all dressed in the same way, all looking enraptured and deadly.

'What do you mean?' he asked.

'The battle for the soul of Avalon has begun,' another of the men said. This one looked like a Celt.

'Have you sorted yourself out?' asked Boyce.

'Yes, I suppose I have!' The Brigadier found himself smiling out of sheer exultation at the way he felt. 'I feel as though I've gone from one extreme to the other, at any rate.'

'Oh, not yet you haven't,' said Boyce, and his voice sounded as dark as a ghost's, his odd, angular face set in fearful contemplation. 'There's just one more thing. This is where we're heading. Look.'

He waved his hand in the air. And there appeared a vision, floating in front of the Brigadier.

Mab was being held by - the vision blurred then cleared once more - by a man disguised as one of the Fair Folk. He held a silver pistol at her neck.

The Brigadier stood up, his lungs suddenly contracting with fear.

He saw Mab drop her sword. The expression on her face was composed and courageous.

She was about to do something incredibly brave for her people.

'Enemy forces at the castle. I have to tell HQ…' he whispered, caught up in the nightmare again.

'Oh, is that what you have to do?' said Boyce.

The Brigadier looked at him.

* * *

Mab ignored the pistol at her neck and stretched out her arms, readying herself for the embrace of Brigida.

'What are you doing?' hissed the voice of her enemy. He sounded scared. 'You're a hostage, act like one!'

She chuckled, and said it loud so her men could hear it. 'Think again, coward. I'm only your hostage if I'm alive.'

The man reacted by tightening his grip. The warriors around her tensed. The Fair Folk reached for their weapons.

She made eye contact with Rhodri, the oldest of her warriors, at the base of the stairs. He had his hands on his bow. She knew he could snatch it up and fire in one movement.

'Brigida,' she whispered, suddenly scared of what she was about to do.

She opened her mouth to give the order to fire and give her life for her King.

There was a sudden flash from the ceiling.

The man holding her looked up, then shoved her aside as he tried to raise his gun.

Too late.

Something grabbed his wrist and twisted it. The blast from the gun went skywards.

He went staggering backwards into the mass of Fair Folk, staring at what had hit him.

The Brigadier's stern gaze flicked from him to Mab. 'Are you all right?' he asked.

'You saved me,' she whispered.

'Yes.' He raised an eyebrow. 'I suppose I did.'

She stopped herself from kissing him. Instead, she grabbed her sword from the ground.

The Brigadier drew his pistol.

She realised that a number of new warriors had appeared among them, clad in gleaming silver armour, their swords raised for battle.

And then –

'Kill them!' shouted Gandar.

And chaos erupted around them.

* * *

The Doctor, Fitz and Compassion dashed out of the gateway and on to the hillside as the sun was rising.

The Doctor noticed immediately that there were no guards on this side of the gateway. Then his gaze took in the deserted airbase, and his face froze in horror.

He looked to the castle. From inside there came the sounds of gunfire and explosions. And out of the main gates ran a continuing stream of screaming civilians, racing across the bridge with their horses and carts and belongings.

'So that's what they're planning!' he gasped. 'Come on!'

With Fitz and Compassion still trailing behind him, he set off for the castle at a sprint.

The reptilians battled the Celts and the British soldiers all the way down the stairs, pressing suicidally. The silver warriors, the Knights of Brigida, as Mab learned they were called, fought hard beside the humans, but the reptilians with their magical shields were stronger, and all around them warriors started to fall.

The clash of swords and the thunder of projectile weapons rolled all the way down into the main hall outside the banqueting room, the Celts stepping slowly down the stairs, their enemies on top of them, their slow retreat marshalled by the commands of the Brigadier.

Mab watched him as he fought, as he carefully chose his targets at speed. He looked confident again, as if he understood the gift of his life, and didn't want to die.

Every warrior in the castle and soldier from the airbase was with them now, having run in from all directions to join the fight. The merchants and the servants had either fled in panic or grabbed weapons from the walls and joined them. They fought until they were backed up against the doors that led to the cellars. The Brigadier called for items of furniture to be thrown over, and they formed a barricade there, making what was increasingly looking like a last stand.

The Brigadier ducked his head behind the wood, darts from the reptilians zipping over his head, and called out to the warriors as he reloaded his pistol. 'Hold on,' he cried confidently. 'Hold the line there!'

He looked at her then with something sad and proud in his eyes, and she knew he was certain this was the end for them. That, unless a miracle happened, they were probably going to die here today.

At the summit of the King Centre, the protoplasmic mass that had been the wandering dream of King Constantine started to shift, to move, to bulge and grow once more.

And high over the Cumbrian mountains, Matthew Bedser's aircraft broke from its formation and streaked off northwards, the pilot ignoring the rest of his flight's astonished signals.

'Ready to go, Steven,' Bedser's voice crackled over the intercom. 'We are cleared for bomb run.'

Chapter Fourteen
The Proper Use for Chandeliers

Arwen placed a beautiful finger on Brona's lips. 'Then I agree. Once our forces have done their work with Constantine, we will halt the battle at once.'

Brona inclined her head. 'There will be no more need of it. Let us see how close they are.' She touched a control and the picture on the screen changed. A small group of humans were holding back their brave warriors in the hall of the great castle, one of the War Mages at their head.

Brona hissed in puzzlement at the figure she saw on the other side of the barricade. 'Is that not the soldier we saw earlier?'

The Brigadier had decided this situation was apt. It was right that he should have chosen to live, and then found that he had no choice but to die. The soldier's life in one sentence, really. And if one was to fall in battle, then this was surely the way to do it, in the sort of hopeless last stand that the English so adored.

He'd found his opposite, then, had gone from being someone who had embraced death to someone who was fighting to his last breath for life.

He ducked from another volley of darts, and returned a careful shot back over the barricades. Around him, he was certain, were gathered all that remained of the castle's defenders, soldiers and warriors. They were all that stood between the enemy and the King.

They all ducked at once as a grenade burst in front of the heavy cabinet at the front of the barricade. It was shielding them so far, but it was slowly giving way under the weight of fire, and if the enemy could somehow ignite it... They were running out of ammunition anyway. He'd had them firing in short order on command for the last ten minutes. They could do this for perhaps twenty more minutes, then it would be time for close-quarter fighting again, and the superior strength and weapons of the enemy would overwhelm them.

He should say something to the men. They would have realised, now, that this was hopeless. He glanced at Mab again. She returned his look, fierce and certain.

'Listen to me, all of you,' he called over his shoulder. 'I do not intend to offer any form of surrender. What we're fighting for is too important. If any of you feel your conscience tells you different, off you go.'

There were proud and angry shouts back, and a single roar of defiance from the Celts.

'We're not here to give in!' shouted the man called Gwyllm on behalf of the Knights of Brigida.

He smiled again. 'Good lads. An honour to be here with you. Nowhere else I'd rather be. Perhaps this whole war was a mistake –' He stopped for a moment, realising what he'd just said. But it was true, and he wasn't about to die with a lie on his lips. He raised his voice to continue. 'And maybe the Doctor died for that mistake. But perhaps that was a good lesson for all of us, because let me tell you this: here and now, we are fighting for a just cause. For peace. For the ability of human beings to dream of being somewhere better. Someone better.' He took a breath. 'I think the Doctor would be proud of us, now.'

'Of course I am!'

The shout caused the Brigadier's head to snap violently round.

A figure was standing on a high balcony in the roof of the hall, behind the firing positions of the enemy forces.

As the Brigadier's mouth opened with a cry of astonishment and hope, the figure backed up, took a run, and leapt out into space.

His hands caught the wooden rim of the gigantic chandelier.

The ropes held his weight for a moment.

Then the chandelier swung down in a steep arc, its ropes screaming through their wheelhouses, as if paid out by some unseen helpers.

The Brigadier's lips managed to form the word. 'Doctor?'

All around him, the UNIT men had started to cheer.

'About time and all,' said Joe Boyce.

* * *

The Doctor swept down towards the ranks of the Fair Folk, their darts splintering the wood of the chandelier around him and zipping through the folds of his coat.

He grimly looked down on Gandar as the Gallifreyan agent leapt to his feet from the stairwell behind which he'd been firing at the Celts.

Gandar aimed wildly upward.

The white flash of a staser disintegrated the chandelier.

But the Doctor had already let go.

He landed right on top of Gandar in a rough tackle, knocking him from his feet.

The Fair Folk all around swung their weapons to cover him.

The Doctor focused all his rage, grabbed Gandar's collar, and with his other hand, despite everything existence was trying to tell him, snatched at the man's head.

His hand closed on something in the void between what was there and what should have been there.

And with a roar he wrenched the illusion away.

'Warriors of the Unseelie Court, you have been betrayed!' he shouted, holding Gandar's disintegrating reptile mask on high. 'What price your War Mage now?'

Arwen and Brona stared at the screen in horror.

Brona was the first to the message link. 'Cease fire!' she shouted. 'Cease fire on all fronts!'

Gandar looked desperately back and forth, his pale face trying to find support in any of the astonished gazes around him.

He found none.

With a desperate yell, he lashed out and sent the Doctor flying.

A shout came from across the hallway and the agent dived in that direction, firing his staser wildly, cutting down Fair Folk all around him. He threw himself headlong into a doorway which Cavis had opened for him.

It slammed after them.

The Doctor leapt to his feet.'Of course, standard Interventionist procedure. One looks out for the other.'

Down the stairs ran Fitz and Compassion, from where they'd been hauling on the chandelier ropes. 'Is it all over?' called Fitz hopefully. 'Did you get him?'

One of the Fair Folk's captains howled in rage. 'Who was that impostor?'

Another, of lesser rank, was staring at a device on his wrist. 'Commander, the communications blackout has ceased. The King and Queen order a ceasefire!'

'Good!' yelled the Doctor. 'Co-operate with this lot!'

With Compassion and Fitz on his heels he ran towards the barricades where the Celts and soldiers were hesitantly emerging, and started to clamber his way over them.

'Alistair!' he shouted.

Across the battlefields of Avalon there fell silence.

The forces of Britain and the Catuvelauni had continued firing for several minutes after the guns of Faerie halted. But then, on every front, something broke from the sky. A rain of magical white petals began to fall.

On every front, a glowing image of Brona and Arwen stood up out of the Fair Folk ranks and walked towards the Allied lines, their hands raised in gestures of peace.

The reptilian warriors, dull with noise and horror, hooted in peaceful, high tones at the sight.

The Allied soldiers, crouched and sodden and bleeding, began to dare to hope that this might soon be over.

One of the images, on one battlefield, met with Colonel Munro. It said, 'We offer a ceasefire. For we have all been deceived.'

Lethbridge-Stewart slowly stood as the Doctor leapt over the final charred piece of furniture and made his way to him.

There was a moment as they looked at each other. The Doctor spread his hands as if he was about to embrace him or some other such nonsense.

So the Brigadier straightened his back. 'Ah, Doctor,' he said.

'There you are at last. Spot of bother with these Faerie chappies. Good of you to help us out.'

The Doctor stared at him in utter astonishment.

Then he leapt forward and hugged the Brigadier anyway, laughing as he spun him round and round.

'Stop,' muttered the Brigadier, trying not to be hugged. 'Stop it at once, Doctor. The men are watching.'

The Doctor reluctantly dropped him, caught the reluctant twinkle in the Brigadier's eye and laughed again. 'Oh, all right. Business! Yes! Alistair, you have to call your air people. One of the aircraft on a bombing raid heading north will have broken from its flight plan. A pilot called Bedser. You have to stop it, or this whole world is doomed.'

'Fredericks!' yelled the Brigadier over his shoulder. 'Get on to Ops about that.'

In the air over Cumbria, a squadron of Harrier jets broke from their ground-attack mission and headed northwest, converging on a distant radar trace that was heading directly north.

It didn't look likely that they could catch it.

'Who was that human in the Fair Folk disguise?' asked Mab, who along with the rest of the soldiers and warriors was staring in consternation at the reptilians who were nervously approaching.

'That,' replied the Doctor grimly, 'was one of two Time Lord agents who for reasons I can only guess at have put your two communities at each other's throats. They're the ones who attacked your castles, killed the ambassador and murdered your children. I'm going after them.'

'Oh no.' Mab shook her head. 'We're going after them.'

They raced down the stairs that lay beyond the door they'd been defending, the Doctor leading Mab, the Brigadier, Compassion, Fitz and the Knights of Brigida. The Doctor had organised the combined forces of the Celts, soldiers and Fair Folk to comb the castle together in search of Cavis and Gandar. Meanwhile, they were heading down into the catacombs to make sure of the King.

'I suppose there's no other way down here?' called the Doctor.

'No,' replied Mab. 'This is the only stairway.'

They came at a run to the door that led to the King's chamber. 'So, no ventilation ducts, laundry chutes, that sort of thing?'

'Ah,' said Mab.

She gingerly reached out and touched the door. The wood deformed around her hand and the door sprang open.

And as she did so a vast chiming of thousands of bells broke out across the castle. 'The alarm on the King's pool!' yelled Mab.

Weapons drawn, she and the Brigadier leapt into the chamber.

The room containing the pool seemed still and silent as always.

The only change was the guard, who now lay beside his lectern in the awkward posture of death.

From the pool there came a burst of bubbles.

'They're down there!' The Doctor and his friends raced to the edge of the water. 'That's the air being forced out of their lungs!' He started to shed his coat. 'Brigadier –'

But the thought was interrupted by a sudden scream from behind them.

There was a blur of movement as they spun to look. Compassion was flailing up into the air, being hoisted aloft at speed.

The motion halted as the Brigadier and Mab swung their weapons and the Knights drew their swords. Cavis hung from the ventilation shaft in the centre of the ceiling on some sort of metallic line, clipped around her belt and shoulders. She'd discarded her reptilian disguise, and her blonde hair hung down.

She held Compassion tight against her, her staser pressed into her temples. 'Stay where you are!' she shouted. 'We've come too far to stop now!'

'Why?' yelled the Doctor. 'What is all this? What are you trying to do?'

'If you knew,' hissed the Gallifreyan agent, 'then you'd be helping us.'

'Then let go of Compassion and try me!'

'Sorry, Doctor. We can't take that chance. My partner's down in the pit with some equipment taken from our TARDIS. In a few moments, the dream of Constantine will be ours to do with as we wish. And then, trust me, everything will become clear. Meanwhile, I've got to take Compassion with me.' She nodded towards the pool. 'I wouldn't try to follow. Gandar has some nasty surprises arranged for you down there.' She suddenly giggled. 'Listen, that was nice going, getting out of the vortex like that. We are just so impressed. Perhaps next time we –'

'No,' said the Doctor, shaking his head. 'There isn't going to be a next time. Not for you.'

Cavis's expression grew stormy again. 'Then I'll see you in the Matrix, Doctor!' she cried.

And with a jerk on her line and an intake of breath from Compassion, she was gone into the vent.

The Doctor looked desperately between the pool and the ceiling.

The Brigadier ran to the door. 'Go on,' he called to the Doctor. 'Off you go and save the world. We'll look after the young lady.' Mab and Fitz joined him at a sprint.

'And we'll guard the pool,' said Boyce. 'If you're not out of there in two minutes we'll come in after you.'

The Doctor nodded to them all, relieved. 'Thank you.'

Then he shed his coat in one movement, took a few steps back and dived elegantly into the pool.

Chapter Fifteen
Victory is Empty

The Tornado aircraft flashed low over the mountains, heading north. Behind it, swooping down to intercept, came the flight of Harriers.

Matthew Bedser stared at the instruments in front of him, his eyes locked on to the beacon blinking away on the display. The beacon that led his aircraft north. He knew, somewhere in his droning head, that the light represented a tiny artefact, lost somewhere in the depths of the castle, an artefact that his master had used all his subtle power to place where it was, putting an idea in the head of an SAS man, and a bubble of stealth around the device itself.

The most the master could manage. He was, after all, merely a prince of this world, and not yet the King of all.

But it had been enough. And soon the moment of coronation would arrive.

Behind him, Bedser's navigator, Steven Hodges, was also frozen in his seat.

From time to time, Bedser's hands flashed to the controls, and he sent the aircraft into complex rolls and dips that shrugged off the aircraft that swung in to intercept him, his radio blaring with their warnings and threats. The air leapt and rolled around him, allowing him through.

Ahead, the target in his mind and on his instruments grew larger and larger.

On Earth, in Docklands, the stormy mass of protoplasm lashed out, and the walls of the room in which it had been confined gave way.

The thing burst out of the King Centre, its tentacles flailing, its vast, impossible potential attracting lightning down from the stormy skies.

It began to bloom, bigger and bigger, feeding on the fear of the people who ran and looked back over their shoulders and cried out, forced to believe that, here and now, their nightmares were coming true.

The Doctor swam powerfully down into the black depths, holding his breath, though he knew he didn't have to.

Suddenly, his hands met something in the water before him. A barrier of some kind. It flexed against him, then suddenly started to wrap around him.

He let it, for a moment, then at the last second, flexed his limbs straight out.

The sheet burst into thousands of tiny, flaring splinters.

As if summoned by the violence of the attack, tiny biomechanical fish rushed in from all directions, their eyes flashing bursts of heat that burnt the Doctor through his shirt.

He thrust under them, struggled to get his shirt off, then swung it in front of them like a lure.

They rushed at it, and he seized them in the garment, knotting it tight, then discarded it to dive deeper.

Behind him, the little bulb of movement disintegrated in a blast of heat.

Below him, he could see a light, the silhouette of something.

He powered down into the darkness towards it.

The Brigadier, Mab and Fitz rushed out on to the battlements, and saw running figures duck behind a distant turret.

'There they go!' shouted Mab, and rushed off in pursuit.

The Brigadier leapt after her, and impacted into her, knocking her from her feet, just as a staser bolt dissolved the parapet where her head had been.

She looked up at him, shocked. 'You saved me again,' she whispered.

The Brigadier's face was still for a moment. Then he smiled. 'Now I've started, I can't stop.'

'And now you've got your full weight on me.'

With a cough, he quickly sprang up on to his palms. He managed to do a passable impression of indignation. 'Do try to consider those projectile weapons of ours, eh?'

Fitz ducked into a crouch beside them. 'They're heading for the tower that's been blown up,' he said.

Mab and the Brigadier sprang to their feet, each trying to help the other, and ended up in an untidy totter.

They ran up the steps that led to the broken tower with the Brigadier in the lead, his revolver aimed at an angle up the stairs. He thought he had a good chance of one shot if Cavis decided to have a go.

But she didn't. He burst out into the sunshine to find the woman standing by the edge of the tower, holding Compassion in front of her as a shield, the futuristic gun still pressed into her face.

He snapped his own gun up into firing stance, hoping to make Cavis draw on him.

But she kept the gun where it was and just smiled the approving smile of a fellow professional.

The Brigadier acknowledged her and lowered his gun a notch. 'Give it up, madam,' he said. 'You've got nowhere to go.'

'You'd be surprised,' she replied, as Fitz and Mab ran out on to the tower. 'In a few moments, the travel options for all of us will have increased dramatically.'

Mab moved towards her, swirling her sword lightly by her side. 'I'm glad I've got the chance to have a few words with you,' she hissed. 'So you're the one who sent my people to war?'

'Well, Gandar and I did that together,' Cavis giggled. Then her voice took on the tone of a wicked schoolgirl. 'I'm the Time Lady who's been eating your children.'

'Oh, what?' muttered Fitz.

'Baby dumplings, baby pie, baby in a bun...'

The Brigadier glanced at Mab. 'She's trying to provoke you.'

'I know,' Mab replied, her eyes never leaving Cavis. 'She'll see where that gets her.'

Overhead, from out of the clear blue sky, there came a roar of thunder. Something huge was gathering, behind the Brigadier.

Cavis smiled. 'Right on time,' she said.

The Brigadier snatched a look over his shoulder. Clouds were rushing into existence out of nothingness. They were gathering and knotting at high speed to produce something that had the vault of heaven echoing with a deep, sonorous tone that sounded as if the world was coming to an end.

They were forming a human figure.

A vast face and hand had already appeared. They were those of a raging, bearded tyrant.

The hand was slowly reaching out towards the castle where they all stood.

The Brigadier glanced back to Cavis just as she twitched her gun.

He made certain of his aim once more. 'King Constantine, I presume?'

'That's him,' said Mab, unable to keep from staring at what was happening to the sky behind them. 'Gods and goddesses, we're in trouble now.'

The silhouette in the water resolved itself into a body. A large male form, floating naked in a foetal position, attached to the bottom of the pool by an intricate helmet that festooned his head with tubes and wires as if he'd been infested by sea creatures.

This was Constantine. His skin was deathly white, and his beard, hair and fingernails had all grown, if at an infinitesimal pace, until they waved around him like coral and seaweed.

Beside him stood Gandar, breathing easily of the oxygenated liquid, a monitoring device in his hand which displayed the lights that the Doctor had seen from far above. The device was attached to another, fixed into a slot in the helmet. A Gallifreyan back door, a means to broadcast information into Constantine's unconscious mind.

Even with his limited telepathic talent, the Doctor could hear the message that Gandar was feeding into that sleeping brain.

'Kill the girl!'

The Doctor locked his arms by his sides and kicked downward, heading straight for Gandar.

The agent looked up at the last second as the shadow swept over him, and snatched for his staser.

Compassion tried to keep calm as the spectre grew in the sky in front of her, blotting out the sun, becoming more solid with every moment.

That is, she would have tried to keep calm if, prior to recent events, she had known any other condition but calm. Now she was awash with what must be emotions, and they were terrifying. Even happiness was wild and unrestrained and worrying, but fear itself was… She had no words for what she was going through now. She wished she could have gone back to what she had been before. Then, she would have calculated the odds in this standoff, and been able to advise the others on the best course of action.

Emotions had reduced her to a screaming girl.

But, a part of her brain was telling her, was insisting every moment, you don't have to be this. You can give in and let the change come.

But that change would be enormous, and permanent, and it would be the most fearful thing of all.

Cavis brushed Compassion's hair back from her ear and whispered to her. 'I'm just going to hold you here while that enormously powerful being concentrates his entire destructive power on you. And there's nothing you can do about it. Scared yet?'

The change nearly reared up out of her spine then, nearly took her, but with a spasm of clenched teeth and a stifled cry she fought it down.

The giant in the sky, his eyes blazing, fixed his gaze on her.

And his vast fingers reached down through time and space intending to crush her.

The staser bolt missed him by inches. The Doctor impacted Gandar at high speed, knocking him away from Constantine, and darted back to pull the module from the King's skull.

He looked up just in time to catch Gandar's fist, holding a blade, as it sliced down towards his chest.

The two Time Lords struggled beside the sleeping King, their limbs flailing as they matched their strengths.

The Doctor realised he was running out of air.

A pair of cross-hairs on Matthew Bedser's instrument panel locked together around an image of a vast, treelike palace. Green lights flashed down his HUD display.

'One minute to target. Arming weapon.' He flicked open a series of toggles on his right-hand board and clicked along the buttons.

'Weapon armed,' the navigator confirmed.

On Earth, the protean mass of the dream-Constantine burst into a giant ball of energy, roaring down from the sky to threaten the city streets, sucking every dream and stray emotion from the masses who ran screaming before it.

Gandar was looking wildly across to where the King was stirring fitfully in his sleep.

The Doctor could still hear the beat of the thought: 'Kill the girl!'

In the Unseelie Court, the technicians overseeing the nuclear weapon stared at the picture of the humans' aircraft bearing down on them.

'It is cutting through our shields!' cried one of them. 'Are we to die without retaliating?'

'But the King and Queen!' shouted another.

The first technician sucked in a quick breath. Then he made his decision.

He threw himself towards the button that would launch the missile.

The hand of the giant in the sky rushed to grab Compassion.

She closed her eyes.

The Doctor grabbed the back of Gandar's skull and slammed the agent's lips to his.

He released all the air in his lungs into the interventionist's mouth.

Liquid burst from the man's nose and eardrums. He fell back, flailing, as the oxygenated solution of the pool rushed back into his system.

And the Doctor, with the last breath of air left in his respiratory-bypass system, desperately tore off the side of Constantine's mask, put his mouth to the King's ear and shouted:

'WAKE UP!'

The Brigadier blinked. He'd been preparing to leap between Compassion and the giant.

But then the image in the sky, just as its vast fingers were coming down around the head that Cavis had thrust forward to offer to it...

Vanished.

Cavis froze. 'What?' she said.

Compassion opened her eyes. And looked around as if she didn't quite believe that she was safe again.

'That'll be the Doctor, then,' said Fitz.

There came a vast, ear-splitting noise that sounded like icebergs screeching as they begin to separate.

They all tottered as a rolling earthquake shook the castle.

Mab grabbed hold of the Brigadier and pulled him to safety by the stairwell. 'He's woken Constantine!' she gasped. 'Gods save us! Avalon is slipping into the Homelands!'

Across the downlands, a group of farmers who had been watching what was happening at the castle from a safe distance turned at the sound of something rending.

They were astonished to see the gateway that they had grown used to begin to fade and flutter.

They moaned at something they'd been told as children. That one day the life of the Homelands would catch up with them.

Above their heads, the sky was getting darker by the second.

The night of another dimension was falling. And the day was screaming as it died.

The gateway flickered for a final time, and then – with a boom of imploding air –

It vanished.

The great sphere that was expanding and crackling above London brought itself to a peak of power and influence.

And then it, too, vanished like the dream it was.

Matthew Bedser jerked his head up from his instruments, and looked around.

He'd woken from a nightmare.

His finger had been about to launch a nuclear warhead.

He let go of the switch and swung his aircraft wildly off line.

In his ears he could hear the yells of trailing pilots, threats that they were about to shoot him down.

'Have we... aborted the target run?' he asked. 'Again?'

In the Unseelie Court, the other technicians hauled their younger colleague from the launch controls.

'Look!' one of them shouted at him. 'Look!'

On the screen above them, the aircraft was peeling away, heading south once again.

'Copy that,' said Bedser, acknowledging the threats and the pleas. 'We're heading home.'

And the aircraft swept in a long turn that would take them back into Celtic airspace.

Chapter Sixteen
What Matters is Who You Are

The Doctor burst into the air, sucking in a grateful breath. He hauled on the body under the surface, and a moment later Gandar appeared beside him, still wheezing and spluttering.

The Doctor made his way to the side of the pool, and was helped out by the Knights of Brigida. 'Take that man into custody,' he gasped to Boyce, pointing at Gandar. 'Keep an eye on him.'

The Knights closed in on the Gallifreyan just as a tremor hit the castle, sending everyone flying.

The Doctor struggled back on his hands and knees to look into the depths. There, a huge face had formed, the bearded, angry visage of King Constantine. His features were contorted in rage and pain.

'Who has woken me?' he boomed. 'Who disturbs the sleep of King Constantine of the Catuvelauni?'

The Knights screamed in agony, holding their hands to their heads. 'Brigida!' shouted Gwyllm. 'Our connection to her is being disturbed!'

Gandar grabbed his opportunity. He struggled out of Boyce's grasp, then lashed out with his foot, catching the Knight in the ribs. Before the Doctor could react, he had raced out of the room, heading for the stairs.

The Knights were rolling on the floor, now, the psychic link to their goddess shrieking with interference from the process of Constantine's waking. Even the Doctor could feel the psychic backlash.

He knew he should pursue Gandar, but this was more urgent.

He turned back to the black, liquid depths and yelled, 'Your Majesty! I am a Time Lord of Gallifrey! I had to wake you! Your dreams were being interfered with, they had gone insane! Return to sleep now! Take Avalon back into its own dimension!'

'No!' screamed the face of the King. 'I... cannot! The pull of the

Homelands... is too great! I have been weakened! I cannot return to sleep, and I cannot control Avalon in my waking state! I do not have... the power!'

The face contorted once more, and began to scream in earnest.

The Doctor got to his feet, and looked desperately around, wondering what to do.

Leaping over the comatose Knights, he dashed for the door.

The Brigadier, Mab and Fitz were hanging on to the architecture as the castle bucked and heaved like a ship at sea.

Overhead, the stars had started to appear in the warping, screaming sky.

Cavis was tottering about the battlements, still holding her gun to the head of the screaming Compassion.

'What happens if we land on Earth?' yelled the Brigadier.

'Our buildings and fortifications will overlie yours!' Mab yelled. 'Thousands of people will die! I have to talk to the King!'

She turned to run for the door.

But from it stepped Gandar, his staser in his hand.

'Get back,' he said.

'Darling!' shouted Cavis. 'Do I take it you messed up with the King-dream thing?'

Gandar stepped forward, covering them all with his gun. 'The Doctor intervened. We don't have any options left, Cavis.' He made eye contact with his partner. 'We're going to have to kill Compassion ourselves.'

Cavis looked for a moment as if she was going to argue. But then she flicked off a catch on her staser with her thumb and suddenly shoved Compassion away from her. She tottered off across the rolling tower, an easy target.

'Sorry,' she said, taking aim.

Then lots of things happened at once.

Mab screamed a battle cry and leapt for Cavis.

The Brigadier leapt at Gandar.

And something dark swept over them all.

The Brigadier knew, as he moved, that he wasn't going to make it. He could see the angled muzzle of the silver weapon pointing straight at his chest.

He was aware, even, that Gandar was squeezing the trigger.

But if it gave Mab a chance to save Compassion that didn't matter.

Cavis swung her staser from Compassion to fire at Mab.

The shot burnt cloth from Mab's shoulder.

She reached Cavis in one leap.

She let her instincts take her.

She moved faster than she could think. Her sword flashed out in a single swing.

She saw the sudden surprise on Cavis's face.

The blow connected. Cavis's head broke from her body.

It flew over the battlements.

Mab completed the sweep of her sword.

Cavis' body fell to its knees. Then collapsed on to its front.

Some sort of energy was streaming from the corpse's head, swirling about something that was quickly developing there, as if a new head was swiftly being formed where the old one had been.

Mab stepped forward and stabbed her sword down twice. Once for where there was a heart, and once for where one was about to be.

The outrush of energy ceased. Cavis lay still.

'Die in the name of my children, Time Lord!' whispered Mab.

Gandar had fired.

But then the dark thing had arrived in a blur of motion and air between the Brigadier and the Gallifreyan, and it had knocked Lethbridge-Stewart off his feet.

He groggily stared up at what had come between them.

A tall, dark figure, his hands clutching a long sword. It was that which had deflected the blast upward.

'Margwyn,' said Gandar. 'Of course.'

The mage merely inclined his head, waiting.

Gandar made as if to grab for a blade at his belt, and Margwyn leapt at him, his sword about to slash at the man's neck.

But Gandar used his gun instead, firing from under his arm before the Brigadier could even yell a warning.

Margwyn's body took the blast full on. He staggered back for a moment.

But then, his teeth clenched, howling, he threw himself forward again, the sword held before him with all his weight behind it.

It went straight through Gandar's chest and embedded itself in the stonework of the castle.

Gandar's hand dropped to his side and his eyes rolled skyward.

Margwyn held on to the blade for a moment. Then he fell, clutching at Gandar's writhing form, attempting to claw himself to his feet. His hands reached for the ragged burn on his own chest.

The Brigadier put his hands to the ground, still groggy, and tried to get to his feet, to see what had happened to Mab.

He had a terrible feeling that he knew what he would see. That he would have failed to save... someone else. He was tense inside, waiting for the pain that had become his life to return.

But all he saw when he stood was Mab swaying on her feet by the battlements, looking down at the body of Cavis. Fitz and Compassion were with her, Fitz making urgent enquiries about her condition.

Her shoulder was injured. The Brigadier could see from the angle of her shoulders that the warrior queen, no matter how bloodthirsty her actions had been, was looking down sadly at her fallen foe.

'Look lively,' he called. 'Man down over here.'

She turned with a look of horror on her face, and smiled when she saw that he was all right. But, when she saw who lay on the floor beside him, the horror returned.

All over the Britain of the real world, those people who were not getting their first undisturbed night's sleep for months were witness to strange portents and apparitions. Ancient buildings stood on corners in the corner of shift workers' eyes. Delivery drivers found themselves passing silent, celebrating armies on the motorways of the night. And those who woke from dreams of sudden happiness and hope stumbled to their windows, and looking up into the sky were unsure, for a moment, whether that was the moon or the sun.

The Doctor, naked to the waist, his hair still dripping, burst out of the doorway and stared at the little group gathered around the body of the fallen Margwyn.

He ran to the others and knelt beside them.

'Is there anything you can do?' asked Fitz.

'He was very good to us,' Compassion told the Doctor. 'He thought he was on the right side.'

The Doctor pulled aside the folds of Margwyn's black jerkin and looked at the wound. Then he pulled the cloth back together again and shook his head. 'I don't think there's anything I can do about anything,' he whispered.

Another tremor shook the castle.

'You mean we're –' asked Compassion.

'Heading for Earth, yes. I have no idea how to stop it.'

Margwyn groaned.

Mab smoothed a hair away from his brow. 'Hush,' she said. 'Don't try to talk.'

The mage opened his eyes. 'Queen Regent,' he croaked from dry lips. 'Mab. Forgive me.'

'Of course I do,' she said. 'You came back, Margwyn. You're here with me for the end.'

'Not the end.' He reached out a faltering hand towards her and grabbed the amulet that hung from her throat. 'In the pool.'

'What?' Her hand closed on his. 'This was passed down to me from my mother. Are you saying it does something to the King?'

'Emergency. Puts him to sleep again. Put it in the pool.'

'I didn't know.'

'My business to. I look after the –' He found something surprising that they couldn't see in his field of view. 'Queen

243

Regent,' he said. 'Your permission –'

'Go,' she said, her voice breaking. 'Loyal Margwyn.'

The muscles of his face relaxed and life left him.

The Doctor reached out for the amulet. 'I'll take –'

'No,' she said. Her face was rigid with holding back her tears. 'You stay with him.'

She fled towards the stairs.

The Brigadier stood up and dusted down his trousers with his cap. For a moment, apart from the rumble of the ground and the keening of the sky, there was silence. 'Terrible business,' he said. 'Should have listened to you from the start, Doctor.'

'I don't think it would have made a difference.' The Doctor got to his feet, too, and with Fitz's and Compassion's help, laid Margwyn's cape over the mage's body. 'Everything that's happened here seems to have been planned. A chain reaction of people and politics.'

'All to have me killed,' said Compassion, with a shiver.

'Yes. I wonder why.'

The Brigadier looked down at the figure under the cloth and seemed to steel himself for a moment. 'I never told you, Doctor. Doris, my wife. She... She passed away.'

The Doctor stared at him. He put his hands gently on the Brigadier's shoulders. 'Doris? So that's... Oh, no. And I once said I'd protect her.'

'I took that to mean in the event of my death, Doctor. I don't blame you for that.'

'But...' The Doctor looked lost, his arms dropping to his sides. 'Alistair, you should have told me!'

'Indeed. A long time ago.' The Brigadier looked aside with a sigh, and then, surprisingly, smiled. 'It's good that you haven't got your TARDIS, in a way. I was going to ask you to go back and help me get her.'

'Going to?'

'Well...' The Brigadier looked as if he was struggling to find the right words. 'It's recently come to me... About life. Well, it's only what it is because it isn't for ever. Good stories have endings. If we just tried to keep hold of everything we'd ever had... Well, I don't think that's living at all, quite, do you?'

'Cavis's TARDIS will be around here somewhere. Are you sure you wouldn't want me to intervene? To rewrite history for your own ends, to create a paradox to spare you from your grief?'

The Brigadier shook his head.'No, Doctor, I would not.'

A slow smile spread over the Doctor's face. 'Alistair, you continue to astonish me.'

'Do I?' The Brigadier looked startled for a moment. 'Can't say I ever noticed, Doctor. More the other way around, if you ask me.' He took the Doctor's hand and turned the grasp into a firm handshake. Then he disengaged himself. 'I'd better go and check on Mab. Make sure about the ending.'

'You do that.'

With a little salute to Fitz and Compassion, Lethbridge-Stewart strode off into the castle.

The Doctor drew his companions to him, one under each arm, and they wandered as close as they dared to the edge of the tower. The floor continued to warp and stretch beneath them.

'I still can't understand why they wanted to kill me,' said Compassion, wincing as she looked down at the headless body of Cavis.

'I have my suspicions,' said the Doctor, 'but no more than that. When we get back to the –' He stopped, and put his fingers to his brow. 'Sorry, force of habit.' He deflated slightly. 'Assuming that amulet works, we're going to have to go and find that other TARDIS. Either that or go out into Avalon and find somewhere to –'

There came a sound from behind them.

The Doctor turned, thinking that Margwyn was still alive.

Gandar, still hanging from the sword through his chest, was shakily aiming his staser in their direction.

'– live,' finished the Doctor, his eyes widening in shock.

'For Gallifrey,' said Gandar.

And he fired.

The bolt struck Compassion in the centre of her chest.

She was blasted backwards.

Over the edge of the parapet.

The gun fell from Gandar's hand and he slumped.

'Compassion!' bellowed the Doctor.

He and Fitz flung themselves to the battlements.

Compassion's body fell through the air as if in slow motion, her scream echoing on the wind. The Doctor and Fitz watched helplessly, their fingers gripping the wall, caught in this nightmare, as she spun towards the ground.

Compassion's head was filled with the scream.

But alongside it was a thought.

The staser bolt hadn't hurt at all.

She felt the change roaring up to take her.

She asked it if she would die.

It told her that the change would make her everything she wanted to be.

The bridge over the moat leapt up to kill her.

And she gave herself to the change.

The Doctor had told himself that he would not close his eyes.

His arrogance had killed her. He should have checked Gandar's body. Now he'd lost everything again.

He kept looking, helplessly, as Compassion neared the moment of her death.

But then a sound so familiar that it took a moment for him to realise what it was began to resound across the downlands.

The Doctor stared in astonishment. Was it his eyes failing him, or was Compassion –

Fading in and out of existence.

She was about to hit the bridge.

She vanished completely.

The Doctor restrained the urge to bellow a relieved laugh at the sky. The consequences of this were too huge. He made his fingers let go of the parapet and turned to meet Fitz's boggling gaze with a baffled smile of his own.

'What –' he began.

The Doctor put a finger to his lips.

From across the blackened turret, the sound came again. It started off distantly, something hard to distinguish from the background shudders and tremors that were still shaking the castle. But then it came more bravely and distinctly. The Doctor closed his eyes and luxuriated in it. Could it really be? To him that sound meant home, safety, freedom –

And adventures in time and space.

A wind started to whip up the ashes of the blackened tower. It increased with the volume of the noise until something started to form out of thin air at the centre of the vortex.

A human figure.

The Doctor opened his eyes again and stared.

With a wheezing, groaning sound, Compassion appeared.

Chapter Seventeen
The Return of the Villain

In the cellar of the King's pool, the Knights of Brigida suddenly all sat up.

The face of the King, seen in the pool beside them, was still screaming in pain, only now, they realised, they weren't connected to it.

They felt suddenly free, and scrambled to look into the pool.

Beside Constantine, for a moment, there stood a placid, female form, dressed in blue robes. She reached out to smooth the King's fevered brow.

'Brigida has been born,' whispered Gwyllm.

Then she gradually vanished. The King was still in pain, but the spasms that racked him seemed to have slowed somewhat.

The Knights put their hands to their heads. They could feel her with them, even now, in their faith. Avalon now had a goddess that was immanent and ever-present.

'The war is over,' said Boyce.

The Knights slowly nodded.

Through the door burst Mab and the Brigadier, who ran straight for the pool.

The room shook again and they all fell over.

Boyce and Gwyllm helped them to their feet.

Mab leapt to the side of the pool and started to pull the amulet from around her neck.

Compassion screamed.

She staggered, and would have fallen, except that the Doctor leapt forward and caught her. 'Are you... Have you...?'

He saw that her face was flickering through thousands of expressions, the muscles twisting into shapes that ranged from joy to terror. 'The change!' she gasped. 'My cells are being replaced by... by contours in space-time. I've become... I am... A TARDIS!'

The Doctor opened his mouth in horror at hearing that his fears had been confirmed. 'I'm sorry,' he said.

She coughed and jerked, her eyes imploring him, looking as if she was drowning. The Doctor felt that he could almost see the new paradigms invading her system, her biodata warping throughout the continuum. The pain in her face was terrible to see. He held on to her hands as her grasp tried to crush them, and made sure that he held her gaze steadily as her pupils shrank into the far distance of her eyes. Shrank... and vanished.

For a moment, he held in his arms what he could only take to be a dead body.

But then Compassion gave a jerk, and closed her eyes, and yelled again, and kept on yelling in a low, continuing scream that sounded like a birth.

The scream cut out, and she thrashed even more, and then was still. As if from a long way off, she started whispering, and the Doctor had to incline his head to hear what she was desperately trying to communicate to him. 'When you altered my receiver to pick up signals only from your TARDIS, you started this process. The Remote are built to absorb information. I was programmed with everything about the TARDIS: its culture, its personality. Finally, its abilities.'

'Like the chameleon thing, and teleporting across rooms when things are going to fall on you,' said Fitz, kneeling beside them.

Compassion jerked again. 'The block-transfer equations were solving themselves in my nervous system. That was the change that I could feel coming, the one I didn't want to embrace. You wanted me to be more human... But I've become something a long way from human.'

Then she opened her eyes again. They were spiralling with the colours of the vortex. 'I had no idea,' the Doctor whispered grimly. 'I would never have let this happen. Are you in pain?'

'Sometimes. And... I'm not sure it's pain, it's... Oh.' Her eyes flickered for a moment, faster than the Doctor could follow. 'I've just found out that I don't have to feel it like that. Just as... Ah!' With a jerk of her muscles, she sat up, suddenly in control.

'Information. That's better. Woo. That's... that's a relief!'

And to the Doctor's amazement, she actually started to laugh. He helped her to her feet, still horrified. 'Are you...?'

'I'm not who I was. And I can't go back.' Her head flicked back and forth between the two of them, as if taking on board the idea of seeing something. 'Everything I am has been replaced by something else, something other, but...' She took a step away from them, flexing her hands, as if her fingers were twirling through strands of information. 'I can find all the old pieces of me. Yes, there's me. There's what I was. Still got that. But... all this!' That was a sudden shout, of exclamation, of amazement. 'All this new... new...' She couldn't find the words, turning to stare at them exultantly.

'You're hysterical,' said the Doctor. 'All these new emotions...'

'Yes, yes! The big emotions of time and space. I'll have to learn how to handle them, but, Doctor, do you understand what I can see now? It's so astonishing. And complicated. And funny. There are all sorts of little built-in ironies and punchlines. It really adores itself, too, the poor thing.'

'Poor thing?' asked Fitz, still obviously a couple of steps behind.

'The cosmos,' she said, wonder still in her voice. 'You must let me show it to you. And you to it.'

The Doctor moulded his lips with his fingers into his familiar expression of pondering. 'So it wasn't my old Type 40 that those other TARDISes were talking to during the Fendahl affair, it was you! And this explains why the scanner blew up on Skale. And now I understand who I met in the vortex. Your future self, snuggled up in the dreams of Constantine. The only way his unconscious could make sense of you was as a goddess being born, so in his dreamscape he created Brigida, the power source for those who followed her. What a tangle of purposes.'

Compassion was about to reply with a laugh, a scream, another big statement.

But suddenly, from all around them, there came a blaze of noise. It was the same sound that Compassion had made on her arrival, the rending of space-time by powerful engines. But this time it was much faster, and it came from every corner of the castle.

The Doctor spun round.

The castle had developed hundreds of new towers, and from each one were emerging Chancellery Guards in their red and white uniforms, sprinting towards them with weapons drawn.

Then the noise was all around them.

And suddenly the top of their tower was indoors.

Compassion hiccuped. 'Oops. Sorry. TARDISes inside other TARDISes.'

They were inside a meticulously decorated drawing room in the style of an English country house in the 1920s.

Arranged across the marble floor from the Doctor and his companions was a chaise longue, with a Chancellery Guard standing to attention on either side of it.

And arranged on that chaise longue, in a long green gown with her pearls and an opal-jewelled headband across her brow, lay –

'Madam President,' said the Doctor. 'Romana.'

Chapter Eighteen
Interference Denied

'Doctor,' the Lady President nodded to him. 'Mr Kreiner.' And then she smiled broadly at the sight of Compassion. 'Type 102.'

The Doctor stepped between them. 'Her name is Compassion. And you've regenerated. You look like my mother. How worrying.'

Romana sighed in irritation and slid to her feet. 'And you, Doctor, look like a barbarian. Do put a shirt on. No, names are quite inappropriate for what your friend has become. She's –'

'The mother of your next generation of living TARDIS capsules,' the Doctor finished grimly. 'The type 103s. I've met one, and even she had a name. You think they'll give you the edge in the war that's coming.'

'We know they will. Your little jaunt into the Obverse, when Compassion's true potential began to be realised, tipped us off, Doctor. You set off such a disturbance there, set in train events that we really couldn't help but monitor. We saw so many shadows of the future forming in the blue, so many potentialities...'

'Iris tried to turn me away from there!' The Doctor clenched his fists, cursing his fate. 'She was too late.' He took a step towards Romana, his eyes interrogating her, unable to believe that this was what had become of his former friend. 'And that's why Cavis and Gandar were sent here,' he muttered through clenched teeth. He could still see the bodies arranged around the room, Gandar hanging obscenely from that sword among the coat hooks. 'To start this entire conflict, to convince the dream of Constantine that they were on his side, because he was one of the few entities in the universe powerful enough to trigger her final transformation, but weak enough for them to control!'

'The pieces did all fit together with a sense of historical inevitability, but we were wrong about the amount of encouragement your friend needed.' Romana smiled. 'I think the young lady rather wanted to be a TARDIS all along, though she didn't know it.' She turned to Compassion and cooed at her as if she was a kitten. 'Didn't you?'

The Chancellery Guards from the other TARDISes burst in through every doorway and surrounded them.

'So what happens to me now?' asked Compassion, stepping past the Doctor to face Romana.

The President reached out to touch her new prize, holding her fingers an inch away from Compassion's hair as if awed by her existence. 'You're our property, now. We'll take you back to Gallifrey, and mate you with another capsule. I'm sorry, I really am. I'm aware the process won't be pleasant, but none of us have any option. Don't think of dematerialising. This TARDIS is ready for you to try it. You'd only hurt yourself.'

'I won't let you do this!' shouted the Doctor.

The guards sprang forward and grabbed hold of him and Fitz, restraining them. He struggled to shout at his former friend once more. 'What is it about being President that does this to our people, Romana? There was a time when you cared desperately about slavery and injustice!'

'Please, Doctor, don't be so boring. I'm simply a servant of history.'

'Tell me! Tell me how much you knew! Did you know about the methods your agents would use? Have you really changed so much?'

Romana sighed and stepped up to him, reaching out to put a serious hand on his shoulder. 'I must do my best for the people of Gallifrey. That thought got me through this regeneration with my marbles intact. Perhaps that's the curse of the Presidency, you see, that you literally become someone for whom that office is everything. It's so beastly.' She lowered her head to avoid his gaze. 'No, I don't know all the details of what happened here in my name, in pursuit of my plan. But I'm not going to apologise for them, either.' She wandered over to the chaise longue and toyed with a cushion. 'When I say that I serve history, perhaps I should rather say that I am its slave. The development of the living time capsules in the future is a fact. It happens! We know it happens!'

She turned back to the Doctor, almost pleading with him. 'Even you wouldn't be so terribly foolish as to try to fight the destiny of the universe.'

'The destiny of Gallifrey, you mean!' muttered the Doctor. 'Has it occurred to you that perhaps the Time Lords aren't going to rule for ever? That perhaps your enemies will win?'

That seemed to sting Romana. 'Not,' she snapped, 'during my term of office.' She bobbed a glittering nail at Compassion. 'Take her! Let's finish this!'

Two guards approached, carrying a large piece of scientific apparatus which resembled nothing more than a pair of manacles.

Compassion looked desperately across to the Doctor. But all he could do was stare back at her helplessly.

The Brigadier joined Mab at the edge of the pool. In the depths, Constantine writhed in pain and torment. The castle was vibrating at a regular rate now as tremor after tremor raced through it.

Mab fumbled with the amulet. 'I suppose I just chuck it in there,' she said. 'And it sends the King back to sleep.'

'Wait!' Boyce squatted down beside her, looking alarmed. 'We're close to the Homelands now. You knock out Constantine again and everything gets dropped back where it belongs. Including you, General Lethbridge-Stewart, and me. And all the other Knights from Earth. And there'll be no going back, not with the gateway gone.'

The Brigadier looked between them, suddenly anguished for reasons he couldn't understand. 'What can we do?'

Boyce ran to one of the lecterns and wrapped himself around it. A number of the other Knights did the same. 'Hang on to something from this world,' he advised. 'If Constantine sees you want to stay, he might let you.'

The Brigadier went to crouch beside Mab again, looking at her interrogatively. 'Well, my duty is clear,' he said. 'I should get home.'

'Should?' She looked at him sadly.

He looked at her for a long moment, and couldn't say anything.

'It's your decision,' she said. '*Brigidier*, Alistair... Do you want to stay? Are you going to live in your past or in your future?'

From outside the castle came a final shriek of rending dimensions.

'All right!' shouted the Doctor. He turned to look into Romana's mocking green eyes. 'I may not like what you're doing, but we Time Lords have to look at the big picture. What's a single life, what are the thousands of lives given in this war, compared with the safety and security of the entire universe?'

'Doctor!' cried Fitz.

But Compassion was nodding. 'I agree. This is the sacrifice I was created to make. This is my destiny. I can see that now. Doctor, Fitz, you should be happy for me.'

'Just let us say goodbye,' said the Doctor quickly. 'Then you can be on your way and Fitz and I will find somewhere on Earth to settle down.'

Romana gestured to the guards to release them. 'Are you sure we can't take you anywhere else?'

The Doctor cradled his chin in his hand for a moment, thinking. 'Perhaps we could do with a lift. It is my favourite planet, but with Avalon landing there, it's going to be in a bit of a mess.'

'Well, I have plenty of TARDISes. I could lend you one to replace the Type 40 that got destroyed between dimensions.'

The Doctor beamed. 'Really? Great!' He grabbed both Romana's hands and shook them firmly. 'It's a deal! Can I have one of the Type 98s? With the holographic scanner? After all,' he gestured towards Compassion, who was speaking softly to Fitz, 'I can offer you a fantastic trade-in.'

Romana laughed.

The Doctor wandered over to Compassion and Fitz, and drew them to him in a hug.

As their three heads met, Compassion whispered, 'she doesn't know about the amulet, does she?'

'No!' cried the Doctor loudly, as if reassuring her that everything would be all right.

Then he pulled Fitz back from her and took a step back himself, taking a last look before he let her go.

He smiled at the assembled guards, who smiled back at this fine example of a Time Lord doing his duty to Gallifrey.

Then he reached out and fondly touched Compassion on the nose. 'Ding dong!' he said.

Compassion spread her arms wide.

And then, impossibly, her body folded open into a gaping doorway that was far bigger than Compassion herself.

A brilliantly lit tunnel lay beyond.

'Ow,' she said. 'I hope that gets easier.'

The Doctor grabbed Fitz by the collar and threw him through the doorway. Then he leapt for it himself.

The doors slammed behind him just in time to deflect a barrage of staser fire.

The Brigadier looked hard at Mab.

The screaming from outside reached its final intensity.

'Well. Perhaps I have done my bit.' He reached out and took her hand, formally, as though shaking it. And for a frightening moment she thought he was saying goodbye.

But he didn't let go. She looked into his eyes, and saw there, for perhaps the first time, a certainty of new hope.

He smiled with half his mouth in that way of his, and raised an eyebrow. 'Carry on, Queen Regent.'

Mab raised the amulet over her head, and threw it into the pool.

'You can't get away!' Romana shouted. 'You can't dematerialise!'

The guards were rushing towards Compassion with the manacles ready to snap on to her arms.

But then the room rocked with a sudden concussion.

The tired armies who had been celebrating the ceasefire had been frightened enough already, thrown off their feet by the earth tremors and the swift plunge into night. But then they had found themselves encamped among a landscape of phantom buildings that seemed to be gradually forming from mist, appearing with a screaming, rending sound. For the troops from Earth, it had been a vision of home, as a modern ringroad and shopping centre had started swimming into existence around them. For the Fair Folk it had been something alien and disturbing, and it had been all Brona and Arwen could do to stop them from taking up their weapons once more.

But now, with a sudden rush of clear air and a sun that sprang back into the sky, the phantoms vanished.

The battered countryside was soothed by a graceful breeze that flowed across it.

The noise ceased, and for the first time in months the only sounds that could be heard were those of recovering nature, distant birds and the lowing of cattle.

And, gradually, from the camps of both Celts and Fair Folk, the sounds of cheers and songs and cries of relief.

Avalon was itself once more.

Romana and the guards were flung to the right and then to the left by the concussion.

Sunlight rushed in through all the windows of the room.

And Compassion, who had drawn her hands together in an attitude of prayer, closed her eyes, concentrated –

And, with a roar of dematerialisation and a whirlwind of air, vanished into space and time.

With a despairing cry, Romana threw herself at the diminishing shadow, but her arms closed around nothing but a breeze that ruffled her hair.

'Madam President!' called one of the guards, gazing at a tracking device.'All our co-ordinates have changed! We've moved back into Avalon space!'

'He knew!' whispered Romana. And then the whisper became a shout.'He knew that was going to happen! He knew he could use that moment to get away!' For a moment, a smile almost crossed her features. But then she spun back to her guards.'Well, don't just stand there. Get back to your capsules and get after him!'

The guards sprinted from the room as Romana leapt for a bank of controls that rose from the surface of an elegant onyx table.

The new battlements and fortifications that had dotted the roof of the castle faded into the sunlight.

All that was left on top of the demolished tower were the bodies.

Colonel Munro landed on his feet, after a drop of about a metre.

He'd been dreaming, he thought.

Or was this the dream?

He was standing in the middle of a shopping-centre precinct, attracting odd glances from people who were interested in his uniform, and people who were obviously aware that he'd suddenly appeared out of thin air, and were probably about to demand some sort of explanation.

He straightened his uniform, saw a branch of W.H. Smith's ahead of him, and decided, until something better came along, to pop in and buy a paper and find out what day it was.

He was just at the entrance to the shop when he heard the first crash.

It sounded like... like a tank dropping from a height of about a metre.

He turned and saw that, in the middle of the pedestrian precinct, that was just what it was.

The driver poked his head out and looked straight at him, startled.

They both flinched at the sound of a rhythmic series of such crashes echoing all the way across the town centre, with tinkles of glass now, and angry yells and car alarms and police sirens...

Munro took a deep breath. He would figure this out at some point, probably, but right now...

'Corporal,' he bellowed, 'get that vehicle moving! Form a convoy! Jones, see if we can find someone to take those bollards down...'

He marched off to see if he could possibly keep a lid on all this.

And in some tiny place inside him he was desperately, horribly grateful that he was suddenly in the middle of a public-relations nightmare, and not a war.

The Brigadier opened his eyes.

Mab was holding on to him.

When she saw that he was looking at her again, she let go.

'You saved me,' he said.

'Yes,' she said. 'I suppose I did.'

The King's face faded from the pool, and the liquid grew calm and settled once more.

The Knights were cheering.

Across the room, Boyce took a careful look around and slowly let go of his pillar.

'Well,' said the Brigadier, not quite able to stop looking into Mab's eyes. 'Here we all are.'

Chapter Nineteen
Dust to Dust

The TARDIS called Compassion sped down the tunnel of the space-time vortex, a determined look in her eye. She held her arms crossed over her chest, her hands made into fists.

Right behind her came dozens of white, spinning capsules, gaining ground every moment.

The Doctor and Fitz raced along an ornately polished corridor of wood panels, past dignified oil portraits in styles ranging from classical to cubist of the Doctor's family, friends, and past selves.

'Very nice!' shouted the Doctor. 'But we need to find the console room!'

They skidded round a corner, and found that a banner hung across the hallway in front of them. It said, THIS WAY! in big happy letters, with an arrow pointing to the left. In brackets under the arrow, it added, EVENTUALLY.

They raced off again.

'You know,' Fitz panted, sounding utterly lost and boggled, 'in the past, whenever I thought about being where we are now, the whole experience was much more pleasurable.'

The Doctor gave him one of his hard stares before bolting off along another narrow corridor.

They raced past doors labelled AWFUL TRUTHS, HOPES FOR THE FUTURE and THAT DREAM ABOUT FITZ, from behind which they heard terrible screams in his voice.

'She's got a sense of humour now,' he said. 'That's going to take getting used to. Especially with her being a building.'

'More than a sense of humour: a sense of being human!' the Doctor called, leading the way over a narrow bridge that spanned a vast, dark chasm. He'd grabbed a shirt and a frock coat from an obliging clothes line that had been hanging across one of the corridors, and was tucking himself in as he ran. He suddenly halted, and put a palm up to stop Fitz as well. 'Which is even weirder in a building. Look down there,' he whispered.

In the depths below, nebulous forms swam and flickered with bursts of sudden illumination.

'I think that's her unconscious,' said the Doctor.

Beside him, he suddenly found there was a plaque upon which was engraved, DROP A PENNY, MAKE A WISH.

The Doctor fished in his trouser pockets, found a coin, and threw it into the depths. 'I wish to find the console room!' he called after it. 'Right now!'

He turned back to the bridge, and found that a series of plates had been riveted into the metal, each bearing the inscription CONSOLE ROOM HISTORIC WALK - THE PRETTY WAY.

They sighed and set off again. 'She's just showing off now,' Fitz muttered.

They burst open a pair of huge golden doors on the other side of the bridge and found themselves, to the Doctor's initial delight, in a forest.

But as the path turned into a track, and the light grew dim, he started to realise where they were. 'We're beyond the civilised self,' he whispered. 'In the places of nature and emotion.'

There came a cry from the distance that sounded like something human. The distant sounds of water, dripping from every branch, washing down through the soil and circulating the ship, were all around them.

The darkness only increased ahead. 'I'm never going to be in control of her,' he said. 'There's no certainty here. There'll always be something here to scare me, over on the dark side of her mind. And perhaps I deserve that, for letting this happen to her. Whatever brave face she puts on it, whatever joy she's accessed now, she must be absolutely terrified.'

Fitz kept his eyes on the path. 'Doctor,' he said. 'So am I.'

The Doctor just put a hand on his shoulder.

They came to a moss-clad flight of steps, and made their way down them.

At the bottom, there was a cave mouth.

They went inside.

It was dank in here, but there was something about the rock walls that was recognisably TARDIS-like. Pipes and valves led along the seams of the corridor, and every now and then there was the scarred hint of a roundel.

The floor became metal after a while, a grille, and the Doctor could see things moving under it, whispering past.

'Of course you put the console room here,' he murmured to the ceiling. 'To remind me of my responsibility. To let me know we're on the run, that your life's in my hands. I understand that. Perhaps now I can do what I couldn't when you were...' He made himself use the words. 'When you were human. Perhaps now I'll be able to look after you, and save you from those who want to hurt you.'

A door smoothly swung open before them.

They stepped inside.

It was a dark, forbidding space.

Above, the iris of a scanner swung through darkness, sweeping past stars that swam in the night.

In the centre, a steely, harsh-angled console stood on a circular platform, surrounded by a metal rail.

And below there was liquid darkness, the space into which the roots of the console plunged, drawing life and time up into the machine.

The Doctor and Fitz quietly stepped on to the platform and looked down.

'So who's sleeping down there?' said Fitz.

'Let's hope we never find out,' replied the Doctor, his eyes alighting on the big pair of front entrance doors with shadowy, changing sigils on them. Compassion, he realised, didn't know which side she was on, even now. Didn't know whose insignia to wear. 'You'll find something,' he said, talking with the gentleness he'd use to quiet a frightened horse. 'Let's hope it won't be the

Seal of Rassilon.'

Those two hopes echoed from the depths below to the iris above.

He could feel her presence in this space.

He reached out for the mesh of tiny gears that stood where the co-ordinate panel should have been, and put a finger on one.

When overhead there came a change in the quality of light.

They both looked up.

Romana's ghostly face filled the roof space.

'You can't fight history, Doctor,' she said, quite calmly. 'We'll catch up with you. We'll take back the Type 102 and we'll have our new race of time capsules. There's nowhere in the universe you can hide from us.'

The Doctor looked grimly up at her for a moment.

He reached for the power-boost control that Compassion had kept from his grasp until she'd been sure of him, until she'd reminded him of his responsibilities. 'Madam President...' he said. 'You can kiss my TARDIS!'

And he pressed the button.

Compassion opened her arms wide to embrace all time and space.

She blurred into motion, accelerating faster than the pursuing Gallifreyan capsules could follow.

And then, with a trailing echo that sounded like laughter, she was gone into the depths of the vortex.

Epilogue One

From the diaries of Lieutenant Anthony Cronin

I'm writing this for posterity though no one may ever read it. They have printing here in Avalon, but it's this strange method using wooden rollers, and the finished books look as if they're going to last about a week.

Once more, I'm led to wonder about what motivated me to instinctively hang on to the table in the farmhouse where I sheltered from the battle. I seemed to make a deliberate decision in that moment we shifted back into Avalon, but, not having been provided with any information on the subject, I have no idea how.

There are a number of us, soldiers and support staff, scattered across this version of Britain, who made the same instinctive decision. They present Mab with something of a problem, because they all have to be found positions in her new society. For myself, that's easy. The war caused enough pain to sustain my craft in perpetuity. Resentment between human and Fair Folk communities is a major obstacle to the peace, with the families of the dead petitioning the Peace Commission for all sorts of reparations that run parallel to, but nevertheless distract them from, their grief process. I hope neither community takes the easy option and blames us, those left behind, for their pain.

Lethbridge-Stewart may help to prevent that, along with my new patient, who I'll come to in a moment. All sides see the general as, at the very least, honourable and courageous, and the Queen Regent has set him up as a sort of symbol of the new diplomacy, an outsider who chose to stay, a warrior turned peacemaker.

How comfortable he is with that I can't say. But I do know that he seems to have found some peace within himself.

Brona and Arwen visited the castle here, much earlier than I would have expected. There are going to be regular exchanges from now on, a lot more cultural interaction. The races are going to stop taking each other for granted. That's one of the hallmarks of the era of Avalon's history that is already being called the Brigidian.

My most interesting patient here, and the one I intend to cover at length here, I discovered myself. I had returned to the castle with most of the other traders and locals, to hear the news and learn what sort of place the future Avalon was to be. I came across a great commotion, and followed a party of young warriors who had found Lethbridge-Stewart and were frantically asking for him to come with them.

I identified myself, and was allowed, as a medical man, to accompany them to the blasted tower. The bodies of the two agents provocateurs who had caused the war had been left there for some hours now, out of a general distaste and an unwillingness to grant them any kind of ceremonial. A wandering servant had noticed that one of them still seemed to be alive.

They gathered around the body, that of the man I later came to know as Gandar, like a group of vampire hunters around a coffin. The young warriors were afraid of the being that hung there on the sword, especially when he opened his eyes. They stepped back with a gasp and drew their weapons, ready to slay the beast.

But - and I think this is a very powerful sign of the journey he's taken, of how the rage has gone from him - Lethbridge-Stewart stepped forward and grabbed the sword from the hand of the Guard Captain. 'This man is a prisoner of war,' he said. 'And he is not to be maltreated. Is that clear?'

Nobody argued. But they looked angrily at Gandar and cursed him and spat on the ground as I attended to him.

He asked for Cavis. Lethbridge-Stewart told him she was dead, and he railed at the warriors and yelled at them to kill him if they had any courage. But the general told him that they would do no such thing, and made him tell us how to treat his wounds.

We pulled him off the sword, as he asked us to, and that's when I first saw the astonishing process that the Gallifreyans have come to call regeneration. I'm going to write a book about that alone, to go with the one recounting the dreams of my patients and the one about alien invasions.

I wonder if anyone from home will ever see them.

At any rate, in a few minutes, I had what amounted to a completely new patient. He had a mane of long red hair, and the pale skin of a Celt, and, to everyone's amazement, the third eye of one of the Fair Folk. He was quiet and mild from the moment he first spoke, and has remained so ever since.

He feels great grief over Cavis. His first action in his new body was to go to her and cry out for her head to be found, something which, thanks to Lethbridge-Stewart's efforts, was achieved within a few hours. It was found by dowsing, and had to be recovered from the moat. Gandar clasped it to his own head, and tried to absorb some trace of her personality. All the time, he lamented the lack of something he called the Matrix.

But it had been too long. He found he could not retrieve any single spark of her. So, finally, he made his own provisions for her body to be cremated. This caused fury among some of the Celts, who regarded Cavis as being unfit for decent funeral rites, but when Gandar went before them to plead his case, they were largely silenced. Everyone thought that the characteristics he shared with both combatant races were the mark of Brigida, a sign that Gandar had a part to play in bringing peace between the two races. The Knights of Brigida, who have been ordained as a genuine order of chivalry in Mab's court, and are seeking new members, see him as their natural leader, the personification of opposites in collision.

It is a role that, for the moment, he rejects utterly.

The other day, we went walking among the forest that has been established by magical means among the war graves. Gandar still feels guilt, abiding grief and a great rage concerning Cavis's death. He has been unable to bring himself to talk to the Queen Regent, nor she to him, and it's on her command that he wears cold iron manacles that are linked by sorcery to the castle dungeons. But he has never so much as raised his voice to a Celt, and regularly expresses his sadness to me over the loss of life caused by the war.

We stopped at the dolmen stone that marked the place where

Margwyn's body was burnt. It's covered with paint and flowers where all the children visit it. They already know him from stories of the war, and they write notes to him telling him how brave he was to realise that he was wrong.

Gandar read some of them to me, and said that one day he hoped he'd be remembered in the same way. He told me that he remembered times when Cavis had done the most beautiful things, had shown great mercy and kindness. That's when he first mentioned that he'd been dreaming about her, and that he'd like to tell me about some of those dreams.

I was pleased, obviously. We continued to walk through the stones and the trees, and we came to the edge of the forest, where rose bushes had been planted, the wild roses of Avalon.

A little distance away, in the meadow beyond the forest, Lethbridge-Stewart lay asleep on the grass. Beside him, the Queen Regent was still eating from the picnic they'd brought out on this summer day. Probably the first moment of solitude they'd had for some weeks.

I looked at Gandar. He had a complicated expression on his face. 'Not yet,' he said.

'Some other day, then?'

After a moment's thought, he nodded.

We turned back into the forest and went on our way before they saw us.

'So,' I said to Gandar. 'Tell me about the dream.'

Extract ends

Mab watched Alistair sleeping. It was good that they'd had this chance to sneak away from the million details of organising the peace. She'd given him a post on her High Council to help her deal with it all. She wished the Doctor could have stayed to advise them. Mab's mages had received a simple message in their scrying globes, a note from across time and space saying that he was safe, and was travelling again, and that one day he would come back to Avalon.

She hoped to live to see that. But she suspected that it would be someone else, down the well of deep time. Perhaps one of the young High Council members who were showing such promise now.

Or perhaps it would be the new Queen Regent, her daughter, if she ever got around to that.

She looked down at Alistair again, and wondered once more if she would ever be able to tell him how she felt. If he would ever be free from his lost love. Restraint wasn't in her nature. Well, perhaps like all the other changes to who she had been in the last few months, it was in her nature now.

As she watched, Alistair groaned, and rubbed his face, and woke up.

'Good Lord!' he said, touching his brow and finding it reddened by the sun. 'Why on Earth did you let me fall asleep like that?'

'I thought you deserved it,' she said, handing him a piece of bread and cheese so that she wouldn't be tempted to brush the grass from his hair.

He sat up, and took the bread. 'D'you know, I just had a recurring dream of mine.'

'Oh? Tell me.'

'Well, I remember that I used to be terribly afraid of this dream, and I have no idea why, because actually it's rather good. It's a memory, really, about a balloon I lost as a child.'

'I'm sure whatever a balloon is, you wouldn't want to lose one.' A sound came from Mab's belt. Annoyed, she took a tiny shell from a pouch and put it to her ear. 'What?' she asked.

The voice on the other end started telling her about the new chief mage setting too great a fire in the central boiler, and the kitchen staff evacuating for fear of an explosion, and that the servants had started to hear terrible rumblings in the outboilers, and –

She sighed. 'I'm coming. Tell the chief mage that he's got another explosion to worry about.'

Then, with that awkward little swing of her shoulders that was her stopping herself from touching Alistair, she rose to her feet. 'I have to take care of things. You will stay here, won't you? When I come back, I want to hear about your dream.'

She could see that he was about to argue and follow her. So she gave him a stern look, and he smiled. 'Your wish is my command,' he said, and lay back on the grass.

So Mab headed for the castle, still munching on her piece of bread.

If only, she thought.

The Brigadier watched her go, feeling troubled. As the small figure reached the chalk pathway that led from the brook at the bottom of the meadow up the side of the Downs to the castle, he got to his feet.

He would follow her. She knew he would, eventually.

But first, there was still something he had to do.

He walked into the shade of the forest, where the roses grew. The great shadow of the treeline stood stark on the ground against the sunlight, and walking into it left him blind for a moment.

He allowed the peace of the countryside to settle for a moment on his senses. He could hear only nature and the summer and the distance.

'Love?' he said. 'Dear?'

He felt foolish. He looked around him, and found only the creaking wood and the sway of branches.

But he had to continue. He took a deep breath and addressed the darkness, thinking of how she'd felt, and her scent, and the sound of her voice, trying to bring back to mind the ghost who'd walked with him for so long. He still couldn't help speaking to her as if she was just there, at his side. Perhaps he always would. He sat down by the roots of a tree and tried to think of where he should begin. 'You know,' he said, 'our love was the best thing in my life. I hope wherever you are now, if you're anywhere, you've got peace and love there for you. I wouldn't want you...' He bit his lip. 'I wouldn't want you to be alone. But... I have to continue with my life. No, I... want to continue. And I can't do that without -' He broke off, suddenly. He stood, walked a little distance into the wood, and stopped, with his eyes closed, listening to the sound of the forest about him.

He thought he could just about sense her now, in the distance. He was sure that she was listening. 'It didn't occur to me when I chose to stay here that I would be leaving your grave on the other side,' he continued. 'I know it's not you, I know you're not there, I saw you go, dear, after all, and I know I've been talking to you here, but... Please tell me that I've done the right thing. There'll always be something of you inside, when I want to find you, but I came here for... our parting. So I can carry on, now. Please, dear, won't you let me know if that's all right?'

There came a great, sudden sound. An explosion.

The Brigadier opened his eyes.

From a thicket beside him had burst two birds.

They leapt into the sky, leaves and pieces of grass falling from them as they climbed higher and higher.

The Brigadier watched them until they'd vanished into the distance of the sky.

'Yes,' he said. 'Goodbye, dear.'

He walked out of the shadows and into the light.

He stopped for a moment at the edge of the wood, and, on impulse, picked a single rose. His stray thought was that the red of the flower would go with Mab's hair.

It occurred to him only after he'd climbed the stile, as he stepped across the little stream, that that was an odd sort of thought for a soldier to have about a queen. The sort of thought that had been absent from him for so long that it felt as if it were brand new.

But, as he started upon the long path that led back to the castle, he kept careful hold of the rose.

The little boy wrenched his hand out of his mother's grasp. 'I'm going to get it!' he shouted.

The balloon was flying low over the path that led away from the caravan site. It looked just out of reach.

His mother and father sighed and nodded and made their way into the caravan, where their bickering would continue.

Alistair ran as fast as he could, his legs not going fast enough, like in a dream, his eyes fixed on the balloon as he clambered over the five-barred gate and shot off down the little gravel path.

He ran until he was panting with exertion. He wanted to shout out for the balloon to come back to him, but he was old enough to know that was stupid.

Beyond the next bush, at the side of the path, stood a tall tree, with sunlight slanting through its branches. Maybe the string would catch in them, and he could climb up and –

He stopped at the base of the tree, staring.

A man in a long coat was standing on the topmost branch of the tree. He was reaching out for the balloon.

With a little cry of triumph, he grabbed the string and hauled it in.

'Hey,' said Alistair. 'That's my balloon.'

The man noticed him, smiled and hopped down from the tree. He looked at Alistair seriously for a moment, and then carefully put the string in his hand. 'Look after it,' he said, in the most wonderful voice. 'Because nothing lasts for ever.'

Alistair said thank you, and paid careful attention to wrapping the string round his hand with several special knots.

And when he looked up from doing that, the man was gone.

So Alistair turned and started to march back home, smiling proudly at his balloon and at the sunshine.

Everything had gone from being scary to being all right.

Epilogue Two

The Doctor stood by the TARDIS console, both hands touching the controls, watching the ebb and flow of Compassion's feelings as they were reflected in every dial and display.

He doubted he would ever feel completely safe in this new vessel. But how safe would anybody feel inside the mind of someone they knew? He had explored parkland and wild spaces, interiors that felt like a hotel and interiors that felt like fearsome, terrified nightmares. All that the person called Compassion was, and had become, was in here. Emotion as architecture. Thought as action. Every chamber was haunted with her.

He looked down into the depths where her darkest thoughts shifted and whispered. Perhaps he could get used to this magical house being his home, but what about Fitz? The poor guy had already been chased down the corridor by a scream that wouldn't go away and had had shoes rain on his head. He was still obviously shaken, still searching for something that he could just call a place.

The worst thing had been that Compassion insisted they both live on the dark side, in rooms that adjoined the dank corridors close to the console room. The Doctor didn't know why she was so dogmatic about that, and it worried him terribly. Revenge again, perhaps. The insults and horrors that a woman giving birth hurls at the man she loves for bringing her to this pain. Out of that change, in the end, there came wonder and greater love. But would that also apply here?

Footsteps echoed along the corridor that led into the console room, and the Doctor turned to smile at Fitz, who entered carrying a card. He handed it to the Doctor, his eyes still full of fear and foreboding. 'I found this,' he said. 'I think it's from her.'

The Doctor examined the card. On one side was written the list of eight things that the Doctor had asked Compassion to do on Earth, each accompanied by a smart tick. Beside 'Write poetry' had been added a neat little 'PTO'.

The Doctor turned the card over. On the other side it read:

> The Doctor smiles now
> Understanding that pursuit
> Truly defines him.

The Doctor smiled.
Perhaps everything would work out after all.

'She's right,' he said. 'I may not feel at home here, but at least I know what being pursued is all about.'

'I've been wondering about that.' Fitz leaned heavily on the rail around the console. 'Do we really have to do this? They're your civilisation, the Time Lords. Can't you talk to them, sort it out?'

The Doctor saw something on the console, walked quickly past Fitz and hit a control to make a tiny course correction. 'I doubt it,' he said. 'Not unless they come to their senses.'

Fitz joined him at the console. 'But we can't live like this! It means that wherever we go, we're going to have to keep looking over our shoulders to see if the Time Lords have found us! Doctor, I have somewhere I want to get back to now. Somewhere I want to end my days. I don't want to be a fugitive.'

'I understand. But what choice do we have?' The Doctor spread his arms wide, taking in the horror and grandeur of the new TARDIS in one great sweep. 'President Romana seems set on securing what she calls the destiny of the universe. Until she changes her mind, or my people decide that they don't want victory at any price, we have to keep Compassion out of their clutches.'

'But,' Fitz insisted, 'she said it had already happened. That these living TARDIS things are part of Gallifrey's future.'

The Doctor pointed a steady finger at him. 'Nothing, nothing, is certain about the future! You and I know that, Fitz. It's going to be a terrible pursuit, but for Compassion's sake, we must keep one step ahead of them. Romana thinks of all this as something she can seize and use, a stolen TARDIS. But Compassion is still a person. We have to remember that.' He bent to adjust the controls once more.

'We just have to hope that there's an answer to our questions out there, somewhere in space and time.'

Fitz sighed, and rested all his weight on the console. 'Are you really telling me that you're prepared to go on the run from your own people in this "stolen TARDIS"?'

The Doctor looked up across the console at him, or rather past him, his eyes searching the future for possibilities. 'Why not?' he murmured, and he managed a cunning, hopeful smile. 'After all... it's worked before!'

The Eighth Doctor's adventures continue in THE FALL OF YQUATINE by Nick Walters, ISBN 0 563 55594 7, available March 2000.

PRESENTING

DOCTOR WHO

ALL-NEW AUDIO DRAMAS

Big Finish Productions is proud to present all-new *Doctor Who* adventures on audio!

Featuring original music and sound-effects, these full-cast plays are available on double cassette in high street stores, and on limited-edition double CD from all good specialist stores, or via mail order.

Available from February 2000
THE FEARMONGER

A four-part story by Jonathan Blum.
Starring **Sylvester McCoy** as the Doctor and **Sophie Aldred** as Ace.
With special guest stars Jacqueline Pearce and Hugh Walters.

It is England in the not-too-distant future. The Doctor and Ace find themselves at the sharp end of social and political turmoil. But as Sherilyn Harper, the charismatic leader of the extremist Britannia Party, moves inexorably towards power, the Doctor suspects the involvement of another force... a being embodying fear itself.

If you wish to order the CD version, please photocopy this form or provide all the details on paper. Delivery within 28 days of release. Send to: PO Box 1127, Maidenhead, Berkshire. SL6 3LN.
Big Finish Hotline 01628 828283.

Also available: THE SIRENS OF TIME starring Peter Davison, Colin Baker & Sylvester McCoy
PHANTASMAGORIA starring Peter Davison & Mark Strickson
WHISPERS OF TERROR starring Colin Baker & Nicola Bryant
THE LAND OF THE DEAD starring Peter Davison & Sarah Sutton

Please send me	[ ] copies of *The Fearmonger* @ £13.99 (£15.50 non-UK orders)
	[ ] copies of *The Land of the Dead* @ £13.99 (£15.50 non-UK orders)
	[ ] copies of *Whispers of Terror* @ £13.99 (£15.50 non-UK orders)
	[ ] copies of *Phantasmagoria* @ £13.99 (£15.50 non-UK orders)
	[ ] copies of *The Sirens of Time* @ £13.99 (£15.50 non-UK orders) - prices inclusive of postage and packing. Payment can be accepted by credit card or by personal cheques, payable to Big Finish Productions Ltd.

Name..

Address..

Postcode..

VISA/Mastercard number..

Expiry date..Signature..

For more details visit our website at **http://www.doctorwho.co.uk**

DOCTOR WHO: THE NOVEL OF THE FILM by Gary Russell
ISBN 0 563 38000 4
THE EIGHT DOCTORS by Terrance Dicks ISBN 0 563 40563 5
VAMPIRE SCIENCE by Jonathan Blum and Kate Orman
ISBN 0 563 40566 X
THE BODYSNATCHERS by Mark Morris ISBN 0 563 40568 6
GENOCIDE by Paul Leonard ISBN 0 563 40572 4
WAR OF THE DALEKS by John Peel ISBN 0 563 40573 2
ALIEN BODIES by Lawrence Miles ISBN 0 563 40577 5
KURSAAL by Peter Anghelides ISBN 0 563 40578 3
OPTION LOCK by Justin Richards ISBN 0 563 40583 X
LONGEST DAY by Michael Collier ISBN 0 563 40581 3
LEGACY OF THE DALEKS by John Peel ISBN 0 563 40574 0
DREAMSTONE MOON by Paul Leonard ISBN 0 563 40585 6
SEEING I by Jonathan Blum and Kate Orman ISBN 0 563 40586 4
PLACEBO EFFECT by Gary Russell ISBN 0 563 40587 2
VANDERDEKEN'S CHILDREN by Christopher Bulis
ISBN 0 563 40590 2
THE SCARLET EMPRESS by Paul Magrs ISBN 0 563 40595 3
THE JANUS CONJUNCTION by Trevor Baxendale
ISBN 0 563 40599 6
BELTEMPEST by Jim Mortimore ISBN 0 563 40593 7
THE FACE EATER by Simon Messingham ISBN 0 563 55569 6
THE TAINT by Michael Collier ISBN 0 563 55568 8
DEMONTAGE by Justin Richards ISBN 0 563 55572 6
REVOLUTION MAN by Paul Leonard ISBN 0 563 55570 X
DOMINION by Nick Walters ISBN 0 563 55574 2
UNNATURAL HISTORY by Jonathan Blum and Kate Orman
ISBN 0 563 55576 9
AUTUMN MIST by David A. McIntee ISBN 0 563 55583 1
INTERFERENCE: BOOK ONE by Lawrence Miles ISBN 0 563 55580 7
INTERFERENCE: BOOK TWO by Lawrence Miles ISBN 0 563 55582 3
THE BLUE ANGEL by Paul Magrs and Jeremy Hoad
ISBN 0 563 55581 5
THE TAKING OF PLANET 5 by Simon Bucher-Jones and Mark Clapham
ISBN 0 563 55585 8

FRONTIER WORLDS by Peter Anghelides ISBN 0 563 55589 0
PARALLEL 59 by Natalie Dallaire and Stephen Cole ISBN 0563 55590 4
THE DEVIL GOBLINS FROM NEPTUNE by Keith Topping and
Martin Day ISBN 0 563 40564 3
THE MURDER GAME by Steve Lyons ISBN 0 563 40565 1
THE ULTIMATE TREASURE by Christopher Bulis
ISBN 0 563 40571 6
BUSINESS UNUSUAL by Gary Russell ISBN 0 563 40575 9
ILLEGAL ALIEN by Mike Tucker and Robert Perry
ISBN 0 563 40570 8
THE ROUNDHEADS by Mark Gatiss ISBN 0 563 40576 7
THE FACE OF THE ENEMY by David A. McIntee
ISBN 0 563 40580 5
EYE OF HEAVEN by Jim Mortimore ISBN 0 563 40567 8
THE WITCH HUNTERS by Steve Lyons ISBN 0 563 40579 1
THE HOLLOW MEN by Keith Topping and Martin Day
ISBN 0 563 40582 1
CATASTROPHEA by Terrance Dicks ISBN 0 563 40584 8
MISSION: IMPRACTICAL by David A. McIntee
ISBN 0 563 40592 9
ZETA MAJOR by Simon Messingham ISBN 0 563 40597 X
DREAMS OF EMPIRE by Justin Richards ISBN 0 563 40598 8
LAST MAN RUNNING by Chris Boucher ISBN 0 563 40594 5
MATRIX by Robert Perry and Mike Tucker ISBN 0 563 40596 1
THE INFINITY DOCTORS by Lance Parkin ISBN 0 563 40591 0
SALVATION by Steve Lyons ISBN 0 563 55566 1
THE WAGES OF SIN by David A. McIntee ISBN 0 563 55567 X
DEEP BLUE by Mark Morris ISBN 0 563 55571 8
PLAYERS by Terrance Dicks ISBN 0 563 55573 4
MILLENNIUM SHOCK by Justin Richards ISBN 0 563 55586 6
STORM HARVEST by Robert Perry and Mike Tucker
ISBN 0 563 55577 7
THE FINAL SANCTION by Steve Lyons ISBN 0 563 55584 X
CITY AT WORLD'S END by Christopher Bulis ISBN 0 563 55579 3
DIVIDED LOYALTIES by Gary Russell ISBN 0 563 55578 5
CORPSE MARKER by Chris Boucher ISBN 55575 0

SHORT TRIPS ed. Stephen Cole ISBN 0 563 40560 0
MORE SHORT TRIPS ed. Stephen Cole ISBN 0 563 55565 3
THE BOOK OF LISTS by Justin Richards and Andrew Martin
ISBN 0 563 40569 4
A BOOK OF MONSTERS by David J. Howe ISBN 0 563 40562 7
THE TELEVISION COMPANION by David J. Howe and
Stephen James Walker ISBN 0 563 40588 0
FROM A TO Z by Gary Gillatt ISBN 0 563 40589 9

Printed by Libri Plureos GmbH in Hamburg, Germany